THE LAST
U-BOAT

JACK O'BRIEN

John — Hope you enjoy this from a perspective of a real submariner!

WHAT THEY'RE SAYING
ABOUT THE LAST U-BOAT

"Five Stars. The Last U-Boat is a fascinating read, particularly suited for those who enjoy historical fiction blended with modern-day adventure. It's an excellent choice for readers who appreciate a mix of history, mystery, and a touch of youthful adventure and those intrigued by the lasting echoes of the past in the present."

– Literary Titan Book Reviews

"What if you found a submarine in your own back yard? O'Brien carries that premise into a high-stakes adventure. Great story, memorable characters, well written."

– Doc Honour
Author of award-winning novel, Not Like Us
US Naval Academy, '68

"With adventure, history, science, and military-style action, this book has it all — told in a masterful way to keep you turning pages."

– Alexander Enders
Author and US Navy Veteran

"The Last U-Boat will take you on an unexpected adventure filled with danger, mystery, romance, and humor. An engaging story that will appeal to readers of all ages, much as Indiana Jones did. As a Marine veteran, I particularly enjoyed the mildly overblown character of GySgt Colt, who brings both humor and realism to the story."

– Carey Winters
Writer, editor, workshop leader, and
award-winning action/adventure author

Certain historical, and other notable facts, are referenced:

Operation Pastorius was a real Nazi sabotage operation and involved dispatching U-Boats and saboteurs to America.

There were German Bunds (German cultural societies) in western Pennsylvania during WWII.

U-22 was a real type 2 U-Boat, 142 feet long. It has not been found. It had two diesels and two e-motors. Karl-Heinrich Jenish was its captain.

Lake Erie is a small, shallow, lake, compared to the other Great Lakes. It was formed by glaciers during the last Ice Age and, in the story, its referenced dimensions are generally accurate.

Wolfpack is a real computer game that very accurately simulates a U-Boat's operation and can easily function with a crew of five or more. The Wolfpack name is used with permission (Wolfpackgame.com).

Copyright © 2024 by Coursaire, LLC

All rights reserved. No part of this book may be reproduced or in any manner without written permission of the copyright owner except for the use of quotations in a book review.

First paperback edition April, 2024

Cover design: Andy Bridge

Book interior design: Kelly Carter

ISBN 979-8-9901385-0-6 (paperback)

www.JackOBooks.com

Dedicated to
Jim Riccardi (1934-2009)

RICCARDI (RIGHT) WITH THE AUTHOR

I was Jim's partner briefly in a post-production house in Cleveland. Jim was my film and video production mentor and an Emmy Award winner. He was a quiet and decent man, a truly down-to-earth guy, and a tireless and talented professional. These were the days of 16 mm film, Movieolas, and editing with white cotton gloves, splicing machines, and glue.

We were shooting commercials for a regional bank near Presque Isle, Pennsylvania when I told Jim about my idea for a story about a bunch of kids who discover a pristine U-boat along the Lake Erie shore.

It was based on the idea that an enemy sub, loose in the Great Lakes, could have disrupted the critical wartime steel industry by disrupting the flow of raw materials. It could have devastated industry by destroying harbors, rail lines and docks from Chicago to Buffalo.

Jim thought enough of the idea that he bought me a book about U-boats. When he handed it to me, he said, "Get to work."

Thanks for believing in the power of a story, Jim.

ACKNOWLEDGMENTS

Thanks to Alex Enders and Carey Winters for beta-reading the manuscript and Susan Delay for patiently line editing.

Thanks to my workshop critiquers: Doc Honour, Barbara Rein, William Jansen, Shelley Jones, Keith Abbot, Susan DeLay, Linda Keenan, Rich Friedman and our group's founder, the late Phil Walker, who genuinely seemed to enjoy the presentation of each new chapter as the story unfolded.

I'm grateful for the advice and corrections regarding sailing scenes provided by Molly O'Brien, skipper of the SV Liebschen out of the Port of Los Angeles.

Thank you to my editor Amanda Sumner for her dank insights and for helping the manuscript glow up. Initially my kid characters sounded like they were from the 50s (go figure). Amanda caught contradictions, and a thousand little blips of one sort or another. She helped make the dialog real.

Thanks to Andy Bridge for his patience with my revisions and his amazing cover design and illustration, and for really working to interpret so effectively and beautifully the danger and adventure in the story.

Thanks, Kelly Carter for the stellar interior design. The more I read, the more I appreciated your contribution.

And Mrs. O'Brien, I thank God for you and I thank you for understanding what it takes, as only a writer could.

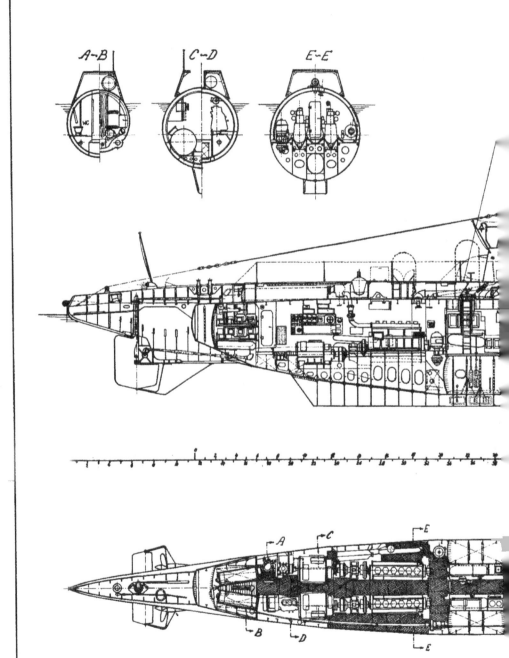

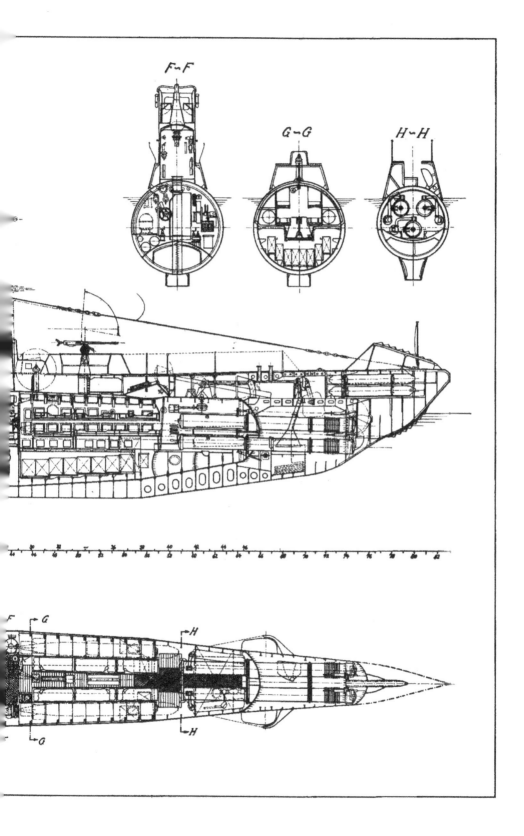

THE LAST U-BOAT

1943

The sliver of moon hung so low it looked to be resting on top of the spruce trees at the far end of the backyard. Its light revealed a black sedan, headlights off, speeding down the long driveway. The car screamed toward the house, barely missing the lamppost as it skidded to a stop. Gravel scattered over the front walk.

A young man in his mid-teens jumped out. He slipped and nearly fell on the loose stones as he bounded up the steps to the front door.

Gunther Kraus stuck his head into the living room, leaned against the doorway and shouted, *"Mutter!"*

He gasped, desperately out of breath. Seated in front of him, three women were listening to Heinz Wehner's *Das Fräulein Gerda* on the radio, as they sewed Kriegsmarine insignia on a stack of midnight blue uniforms.

"Wo ist meine Mutter? Kennen Sie?" he asked. The rules demanded everyone speak German whenever the *Bund* was gathered. The women looked at the boy and nodded toward the next room.

Gunther pushed himself off the door jamb and charged down the hall again, dodging scattered boxes on the floor. He slid through the doorway and into the downstairs bedroom.

"Mother!"

A small, attractive woman, with raven hair and an apron over her calf-length, flower-print dress, glowed when she saw her handsome young son. She stood before him gripping the barrels of two machine guns, one in each hand. Unfazed, she extended her arms, inviting a hug.

"Gunther. Hello, my boy," she said, as they embraced. "You were already gone when I woke this morning."

"After we were done down at the beach, I left to visit Uncle Karl. He's given us a mission. Operation Pastorius is underway." Gunther's cheeks were flush with excitement and his eyes sparkled as he spoke. "I must tell Hans. Is he home?"

Hanna Kraus laid the machine guns across the bed and smiled at her teenage son. His father, Wolf, had been briefed on Pastorius while visiting the Abwehr late in 1934. It was at that meeting that Admiral Canaris, head of German intelligence, chose the name Pastorius, a reference to Francis Daniel Pastorius, the first German-American settler in the fledgling United States. Canaris outlined a wide-ranging strategy of sabotage and terrorism designed to create emotional, economic, and material damage to the US war effort, which, the Nazis rightly presumed, would be forthcoming.

"Yes, of course, Hans is here somewhere. Your brother's always working. Go find him. Go on! *Schnell*!" Hanna Kraus's eyes lingered on the doorway where her son had been standing.

She spoke aloud to the empty room, "So it begins."

Gunther and Hans Kraus had spent the morning working together on several projects around the Bavarian-style country home, isolated and far from the city, perched near the edge of a cliff overlooking Lake Erie. Wolf Kraus, their father, built the house and then suddenly passed away following a heart attack, suffered shortly after its completion in 1939.

During the excavation of the basement, Wolf had ordered the steam shovel operator to dig well beyond the home's footprint. He had plans, he said, to install a giant swimming pool and terrace on the hillside overlooking a small stream. In truth, he never planned to build a pool. Instead, once the excavation was complete, trucks began to arrive nightly. The space soon filled with giant crates and raw materials like steel and lumber.

When the deliveries stopped, Kraus raised walls and a roof and covered it all with thick oil cloth, then blue clay and sandy soil. Grass and weeds soon grew, and the construction site became, once again, an ordinary shady hillside along the Lake Erie shoreline.

The hidden underground bunker provided the space needed to construct a weapon that could cripple America's war-making capability. To make it happen, the Wehrmacht had advanced Kraus' vision with money, material, and a support network that spanned halfway around the world.

Following his death, and owing to the tireless efforts of his wife, sons, and members of the Lake Erie German Cultural Bund, Wolf Kraus' mission was nearly complete.

Earlier in the day, Hans, Gunther, and their cronies had cut down two massive locust trees along the beach, leaving them to lie along the shoreline where the creek emptied into the lake. The week before, they'd used those very trees to anchor heavy pulleys. The pulleys helped the brothers build two retaining walls of mammoth grooved timbers that now flanked both sides of the gully. The ends of the timbers rose like a stairway in either direction, producing an earthwork with the appearance and scale of the monumental construction burgeoning in the Third Reich.

After felling the trees, Gunther had been gone for several hours. Now, he continued down the hallway searching for his brother. As he checked in each doorway, grim faces looked up from their work and then returned to their tasks.

Gunther respected these friends and workers, and he took great pride in the efficiency the group had achieved. In the living room, uniforms were being sewn together. In the den, machine gun magazines were being loaded with ammunition. In a bedroom, hand tools and notebooks were laid out and organized. In the kitchen, tins of food rations, water, and chocolate were being packed into boxes.

He wheeled into the kitchen, opened the basement door next to the kitchen table, and vaulted down the steps, into the darkness. At the back wall, he stopped in front of a shelf loaded with preserves, meat, and vegetables stored in canning jars. Gunther put his hand on a ceramic jug with a label that read, "*Gurken.*" As he tipped it, the entire shelf swung out, creating a broad opening in the wall where no one would have suspected a doorway.

He stepped into the secret chamber and descended a steep stair-case to the sandy floor of a cavernous sloping room. Overhead, a tidy hand-painted sign hung from an electrical conduit. It read *Der Tiefe*

Raum, The Deep Room.

There, Gunther stood many feet below the house and already several yards beyond it. His pulse quickened each time he stepped into its half-light. Just the thought of what they were about to achieve filled him with excitement.

Whenever Gunther entered The Deep Room, he changed. In his mind, he imagined himself a daredevil, a lionheart, or the mythical Siegfried.

A half-dozen men, hard at work in sleeveless T-shirts and blue pants, dotted the long, narrow space. Their skin and clothing reeked with a mixture of sweat, grease, ash, and grit. Gunther strutted past the workers imitating the way he had seen the Führer walking in newsreels.

The room was illuminated by sparks from grinders and the intermittent flash of welding torches. Gunther's wide eyes reflected all the sparks and flashes.

Nearby, a man pulled on chains to raise a heavy cylinder from a wooden crate with the words *Fait au Canada* branded into its side. Gunther called to him, "*Klaus, wo ist Hans?*"

"*Da drüben!*" he replied, as he pointed deeper into the darkness.

In the dim, flashing light beyond, metal parts gleamed as the men labored to assemble the pieces and moved them on to other team members. Gunther skittered past them all, his head turning left and right as he searched for Hans. The lack of adequate ventilation concentrated the heady vapors of oil paint and turpentine, and made Gunther's eyes water.

Beyond the welding, a single work light shone brightly against a plank wall holding back the earth. A long, dull gray metal tube formed the left side of the corridor, the far end of which was swallowed up by the darkness.

Hans was wiping steel castings to remove cosmoline packing grease. His new *Schmeisser MP 40 Maschinenpistole* leaned against the wall. He looked up when he heard Gunther coming toward him, breathing hard, and running flat-footed on the sandy floor.

"*Bruder, was ist los?*" Hans asked calmly.

"Hans, listen, Pastorius is a go. Onkel Karl has a mission for us tonight. I just came from his house."

Hans looked over his brother's shoulder at the men working in The Deep Room. Gunther turned to see what Hans was looking at. It was an impressive and inspiring scene. Here, in an underground bunker the size of a tennis court, these men were making history. They would not need Hans tonight. Their work was nearly complete.

Hans turned his brother toward him. "Are we to go now, Gunther?"

"Yes, immediately! Onkel Karl is sending us to the steel mill," said Gunther.

As Gunther drove toward the approaching city lights, he glanced in the rear-view mirror to see the face of his older brother. The worker, Klaus, was in the front passenger seat and Erich Dietrich, an electrician, sat next to Hans in the back. Hans happened to catch Gunther looking at him.

"Eyes on the road, Gunther. If you go off into a ditch, you know, it won't end well," said Hans.

Gunther didn't respond, except to focus on his driving.

His full-time commitment to the *Bund* meant he had no time for friends his age. What little happiness Gunther felt in his life of isolation came from being a part of something he believed to be important, and from having his big brother's respect. He was proud to carry on his father's vision and to be part of the restoration of Germany to its rightful place among nations.

Gunther watched the road, as tree-lined boulevards gave way to darkened city streets.

Hans spoke up as they entered the city. "Gunther."

"Yes?"

"Stay under the speed limit, and don't go through any stop signs or red lights. Be very careful." He used a soft and patient tone reserved for family.

The car crossed the Lake Central Railroad tracks and turned onto a dirt road alongside the rail line. The tracks climbed an elevated roadbed of crushed volcanic pumice, so the car could travel the final half mile hidden by the berm, unseen from the factories on the other side of the tracks.

The slight moon was now a bit higher in the sky, and just bright enough to allow Gunther to follow the road without using the headlights.

As they approached the Consolidated Steel plant, Hans began to give orders.

"Gunther, keep going forward slowly. Remember, we must stop as close to the electrical sub- station as we can. Ahead is the low spot, where no one can see the car from the factory.

"Men, listen. Watch each other for hand signals, because the noise near the plant will make it impossible for us to hear each other until we get into the maintenance building."

The overgrown weeds in the transformer yard would provide cover as the men headed for the small brick building on the perimeter, a guardhouse and break room for maintenance workers. Hans planned to hide there to arm their explosives. Then, they would plant them under the giant transformers in the yard.

The blast would cripple the plant for months, and perhaps much longer, if the molten steel could not be removed from the ovens before it cooled.

Hans reached over the front seat and massaged Gunther's shoulders.

"We are taking the war to the enemy, Gunther. Remember your training and we will be in our beds soon, resting well, content with a job well done."

Hans reached for the door handle. "Let's go," he said. "There's no time to waste." Gunther wondered if Hans's heart was pounding like his own.

They exited the car at once. Gunther opened the trunk, and the four men stared at two crates of dynamite, a canvas bag with leather handles, a motorcycle battery, and an alarm clock. When the trunk closed, Gunther replaced the keys in the ignition.

The most physically demanding part of the mission was climbing the hill of crushed pumice stone supporting the railroad tracks.

Over the lake, lightning had begun to fill the sky.

From the tracks, the men saw the silhouette of a guard, his back slouched against the brick maintenance building. Cigarette smoke drifted in the air around him, catching the factory lights. The guard tossed his cigarette butt into the weeds and put it out by relieving himself. He walked a few feet to the broad alleyway between the plant's two main buildings, leaned against the wall, and lit another cigarette.

Erich opened the zippered tool bag he had carried to the tracks. He withdrew a screwdriver and zipped the bag closed. He motioned with his hand open, palm toward the ground. "Stay here," was the clear intent. Hans nodded and Erich scrambled off into the darkness.

Less than two minutes later they saw him casually walking along the building's perimeter with the tool bag in hand, headed directly toward the guard.

The guard stepped forward and Erich kept strolling closer. At arm's length, Erich stopped and shrugged his shoulders, motioning in front of himself and behind as though lost

The guard tossed his cigarette to the dirt and twisted the toe of his right foot on its remains. He turned and began waving his hand, giving Erich directions.

In one swift motion, the point of a screwdriver in Erich's clenched fist slammed into the back of the man's head.

The guard's khaki cap fell backward as his chin jerked up toward the security light. Even from a distance, the confused look on the dying man's face was clear.

His arms convulsed and his legs buckled. Erich pushed his victim forward. The weight of the guard's body drew his skull off the screwdriver, and forward, falling hard onto the sidewalk.

Erich waved to his companions and bent down to wipe the bloody screwdriver on the dead man's shirt.

The men stood and collected their equipment, except for Gunther. He was still lying between the rails, propped up by his elbows, staring at the corpse a hundred feet away. Hans kicked the sole of his boot.

"Gunther, get up. This is a war. There will be casualties." Hans headed down the slope, not looking back. As Gunther realized everyone else had moved forward, he stood, grabbed the box he had been carrying, and sped down the hill toward the guard house.

Hans and Erich lifted the body and brought it into the building through an unlocked door. The approaching storm made it less likely other guards would come out looking for their missing companion.

They cautiously withdrew the dynamite from its excelsior nests, and bundled the sticks in groups of six, binding them with black friction tape. Then, they took blasting caps from the canvas bag and gently inserted them into two sticks in each bundle.

The last step was hooking up the battery.

Hans looked up at his brother. "Gunther, the small wrench is not in the bag."

"Maybe it fell out when I opened it," said Erich.

"*Ach*! I'll find it," said Gunther.

"Hurry," his brother said, and he gently pushed against his backside to hustle him out of the building.

Gunther climbed back up the steep mound of pumice. Stones spilled out from underfoot as he did, forcing him to use his hands and knees to stay upright. The volcanic stone sliced his trousers and hands like small razor blades.

As he reached the top of the mound, he cautiously stood to catch his breath. At first, he thought the sensation he felt was exhilaration, but then intense heat seared his back. He saw the scrub-grass field just beyond the car in front of him light up bright as day.

Suddenly, he was no longer on his feet, but airborne above the tracks, helpless to prevent himself from falling toward the car. A split second later, the sound of the blast shattered his eardrums. His body accelerated forward, into the side of the vehicle, arms helplessly flailing at his sides. His head whipped forward and smashed the heavy glass of the driver's side window. He fought to stay conscious, aware that if he lost his footing, his neck could be slashed by the crackling glass beneath his chin.

He reached through the shattered window and pushed down on the broken glass to gain enough leverage to plant his feet beneath him. Then he crawled back to the top of the rail bed to search for his brother.

His vision was blurry. One eye didn't seem to be able to focus at all. But, he saw enough to know that the building in which his brother and two others had been working, had been obliterated. The explosion threw the area into darkness, except for a strange, undulating light cast by small fires in the nearby weeds. Nothing was moving.

Hans, Klaus, and Erich could not have survived that immense explosion. The blast pressure had been concentrated within the tiny brick building. Investigators would not likely find any identifiable remains.

Gunther felt the emptiness of his soul being ripped from him.

The rumble of the factory continued. A light rain fell, and water began to roll down his face, mixing with his tears. Still, he knew he had to get out quickly. Ambulances and firetrucks would be coming soon, along with police.

The rain began to fall in earnest. Lightning and thunder filled the air. Gunther's hand shook uncontrollably with each flash, as he reached through the pain for the door handle. Much of the skin on his hand had been stripped away and his sleeve was shredded and blood-soaked.

The driver's seat was covered with chips of razor-sharp glass. He ripped the torn sleeve from his shoulder and wrapped it over his hand to sweep the mess onto the floor.

He removed what was left of his shirt and used it to soak up some of the blood streaming from the multitude of lacerations on his crushed face.

An explosion of thunder reverberated off the imposing metal walls of the steel plant and Gunther shuddered. It instantly made him feel sick in the pit of his stomach as he closed the car door, turned the key, and stepped on the starter.

He knew what this failure meant for their plans. The *Bund* was without a commanding officer. Hans had been a charismatic leader who kept everyone on task. Mother fulfilled her assignments but did not understand the enormity of the task the *Bund* had been given. Gunther knew he could not take on the leadership role. He was barely sixteen and terribly wounded. Though he would heal in a few weeks, perhaps, he feared he would forever carry the evidence of his complicity.

It meant he would have to hide, to disappear. Gunther could locate contacts in Canada, the underground that had provided so much in the way of parts and equipment, and the tools and materials they had received over many months.

Mother could shutter their project, Karl would alert the Abwehr. They had completed the construction of a great war machine, and there was a chance another crew could be brought in to take over. But the genius of his father's planning and engineering was as devious as a magic trick. No one could possibly figure it out. That's what made it so deadly.

As he steered the car back onto the highway, the rain fell in waves. Gunther extended his hand through the hole where the window used to be and let the rain wash over his bloody arm. He splashed his swollen face to cool it and ease the pain. Instead of comforting him, though, the water stung like a swarm of wasps.

Gunther reached up and turned the rear-view mirror toward himself. Flashes of lightning revealed the remnants of a face he no longer recognized, and the sight of it made him lightheaded. He struggled to keep the car on the road as he turned away and vomited through the broken window, again and again.

THE LAST U-BOAT

2023

Sharon LeClair put a hand to her forehead and peered down the hill-side looking for her boys. The LeClairs had moved into the Kraus home six months ago, and she was still checking out the neighborhood. The woods, the gully, and the creek remained a mystery to her.

It was 2023, and these were dangerous times. It wasn't like when she was a little girl and you could play outside all day in relative safety, without supervision. So, her momness would take over after a time and force her to check on the boys.

In the shade, sat little four-year-old Rocky, playing in his sandbox. His pudgy arms were gritty, and more than a handful of muddy sand had found its way into his ears and his curly blonde hair.

"Rocky, where's Charlie?"

"I dunno, Mommy." Sharon's felt her face heating up. She cupped her hands around her mouth. "Chaaaaarrrrllllieeeeee!"

Overhead, a chaotic rustling of leaves was followed by the sound of cracking tree branches, as a teenage boy fell hard several feet to the lawn. Sharon ran to him.

"Ow! Dammit!" said Charlie, putting both hands on his head.

"Charlie, language!"

"Well, it hurts, Mom…sorry." He straightened up and dusted off his vintage Cleveland Indians sweatshirt.

"You said you'd watch Rocky. But when I came out, you were gone."

"Dude, I was right *here*. I just fell asleep for a minute."

"Stop calling me that. I hate that."

"Yeah, okay. Sorry."

"And how can you possibly fall asleep lying on a tree branch?"

"I don't know. I was okay until you yelled."

No matter how much Charlie aggravated her, Sharon would always seem to soften when she looked at his big blue eyes "Are you alright? How far up there were you?"

Charlie tipped his head back and motioned with his hand. "Just the first branch. I'm okay, I think."

Sharon looked over at Rocky and blinked. He was shoveling sand into his socks. "Charlie, I want you to do something with Rocky, don't just—whatever it was you were doing. Play with him."

"He's four years old. What am I supposed to do with him?"

"You're smart. Think of something." She bent over and touched Charlie's back with her fingertips. "I have one more call to make, then you're free."

"Okay, Mom. We'll find something to do."

Sharon smiled, squeezed his shoulder, brushed back the curls that had fallen onto his forehead, and headed back to the house and her customer service job.

Charlie turned and tapped the top of Rocky's shoe. "Do you want to play trucks, Rocky?"

"No. I want to catch a frog."

"Cool."

"Then I want to eat it." Rocky made a face like he was just two seconds from throwing up.

"That gives me the ick, Rocky. You're a funny kid."

"Ick? Frogs give you ick?"

"Super ick." Charlie stood up and dusted himself off. "So, let's go down to the creek and look for frogs. You want to do that?"

"Yeah, Let's catch frogs."

"Okay. Mom can cook them for dinner."

Rocky giggled. "Ooooooh, ick."

Charlie took Rocky's hand and they walked across the lawn to the path down the hillside, leading to the creek below.

Halfway down the path, where it grew steep, Rocky stopped and asked Charlie to tie his shoes for him. There, in the shade, rose a squat circular steel platform, a manhole as big around as a truck tire, rising a little less than a foot out of the ground. It made a perfect seat, so Charlie lifted his little brother, set him on top, and took his shoes in his hands.

"They're already tied."

"No, they're loose, Charlie."

"Okay. Put your foot on my knee so I can tie it."

One shoe at a time, Charlie untied and re-tied Rocky's laces. When he finished, Charlie stood up, tousled Rocky's hair, and tried to lift him. But Rocky had a death grip on the big metal wheel recessed into the platform.

"I've got a steering wheel," he said.

"You've got the sewer, bruh. This thing is the door to the sewer. It's called a manhole."

As he held on, Rocky racked the wheel back and forth.

Charlie put his hands gently on top of Rocky's. "Let go, doofus. Stop messing with the sewer."

"What's a sewer?" Rocky asked, as he slid off the seat and stood.

"It's the big pipes that carry away everything you flush down the toilet."

Rocky immediately wrinkled his nose. He looked back at the manhole and then to Charlie without saying another word. Charlie took his hand and the boys continued their downhill trek.

Storms often brought great volumes of water raging down the creek bed, but today the water danced lightly through the cattails and over the rocks. Sunlight filtered through the trees, and spring flowers had sprouted along the bubbling creek. Charlie thought there was a good chance they'd see a frog.

But, instead of hunting for frogs, Rocky did what little boys often do when they see a creek. He started building a dam.

"That's a good spot, Rocky. I'll get you some more rocks, okay?"

Charlie gathered an armload and set them at Rocky's feet. Then he got down on one knee and began handing Rocky stone after stone. The two were so focused, they never noticed their neighbor, eighteen-year-old Stewart Swanson, come up behind them. Stewart had just traveled the well-worn path down along the creek from his backyard a block away, the sound of his approach hidden by the gurgling stream.

Stewart was a big-boned, fair-skinned, freckle-faced teenager. Despite his size, his restored '66 Mustang convertible, and his golden hair, he was a little too awkward to be considered cool by his schoolmates. Stewart responded to the role of reject by wearing a permanent scowl and acting irredeemably nasty to almost everyone.

While the two brothers concentrated on their work, Stewart lifted a large piece of slate from the creek bed.

"Here's a stone for you," he said, surprising the boys by dropping the rock flat into the puddle that had formed behind the dam.

The impact splashed a gallon of muddy water all over the kids' clean clothes and rosy faces. Rocky started to cry as Stewart laughed.

"You okay, Rocky?" Charlie asked.

Rocky rubbed his eyes with his forearm. "Stewart wrecked our dam."

Charlie glared stone-faced, standing toe-to-toe with Stewart, who had this weird open-mouth thing he did when he was being mean.

Two years, a foot in height, and a full octave separated Stewart and Charlie. Stewart walked around his two victims like a drill sergeant ridiculing recruits. He pointed and laughed at the mud on the back of Charlie's pants as he came around full circle.

"What happened here? Skid marks?" Stewart's eyes widened. "Oooh, that's a great name for you."

Charlie closed his eyes tightly in anger and frustration. *Don't give me a name.* He turned and glared at Swanson. "My name's Charlie."

Rocky spoke up. "Go away, Stewart. Leave my brother alone or he'll make you eat a frog."

Stewart laughed. He just shook his finger and smiled. "I like you, Rocky." He looked at Charlie. "Your little brother's cool, Skid Marks." Charlie reacted by shutting his eyes again.

He heard Danny Doubeck calling out from the hillside across the creek. Charlie and Doubeck were classmates who met soon after Charlie moved in and they quickly became fast friends. Danny could be unpredictable at times, but he was a kind person and a good listener. Doubeck, as his friends called him, had all the attributes of a great salesman.

Doubeck and three others were headed down the path from his backyard directly across the gully from the LeClairs. Charlie relaxed and sighed as he saw Stewart becoming distracted by the approaching group.

Doubeck walked alongside his neighbor, Marty Silver, who the group considered a certified genius. Joining Marty were their female friends, Amber Garcia and Michelle Murphy, also known as "Mish."

Seventeen-year-old Amber, among the prettiest girls at McCullough High School, was also sort of a nerd. She was the only child of Ana and Dr. Federico Garcia. Amber's completely natural beauty did not win her many true girlfriends. Most of the girls at McCullough were deeply envious of her dark complexion, curvy figure, and long black hair. What they disliked even more was the fact that Amber had no idea how pretty she really was.

If not intimidated by her movie star looks, many of the boys were kept at bay by her academic achievements—like consistent advanced placement in math.

Charlie and Stewart stared at Amber as she descended the hillside behind the Doubecks, wearing a short summery skirt over her long legs. She struggled to negotiate the steep hillside path while maintaining some semblance of modesty. Hanging close to Marty, and keeping her hands on his shoulders as they negotiated the hill, helped keep her from falling. Marty balanced himself by holding his arms straight out to each side like a tightrope walker.

Mish Murphy tried desperately to draw little attention, preferring to retreat into the background and observe. But when she spoke, her powers of observation and her creativity often combined in awesome ways.

Though she worked hard to hide it, she was every bit as pretty as Amber. She was artsy, too. Her imagination and talent worked together, often producing clever and beautiful things.

True to her eccentric nature, Mish wore a sleeveless sweater vest and a vintage silk scarf around her neck. Her red hair was piled up on top of her head, where she had pierced it with several delicate bleached and weathered sticks of bent driftwood. In contrast to her woodland-nymph hairdo, white cotton t-shirt sleeves poked out of each side of her vest, calling attention to her well-toned arms.

Stewart greeted them. "Hey, weirdos. What's up?"

Doubeck walked up to him without hesitation. "What are you doing here, Swanson?" He was the only one of the neighborhood kids who was anywhere as big as Stewart.

"I'm going skinny dipping. No nerds allowed."

Doubeck wasn't buying it. "The lake's like sixty degrees, Stewart. It's way too early."

"Plus, seeing you naked would be too traumatic," Mish added with a dash of venom.

Swanson fired back. "You wish."

"Get over yourself, Stewart," she said.

"Get over yourself," shouted Rocky at the top of his lungs. The others laughed at Stewart's being called out by a four-year-old.

Stewart pushed hard on Charlie's shoulder. "I'm not done with you, Skid Marks." Then, he stepped across the creek, walked around some bushes, and headed down toward the lake.

"You don't think he's really going to skinny dip, do you?" asked Amber.

"He's such a jerk," said Doubeck, looking directly at Charlie.

"So, what are you guys doing here?" asked Charlie.

"Well, Amber called Doubeck, and then Doubeck called me. I called Mish, and Mish said we should come over here to see if you wanted to do something," said Marty.

"Yeah. I'm glad you did. I'm soaked. Let's go up to the house and I'll change."

Along the way, they passed the manhole and once again Rocky asked Charlie to tie his shoes for him. It had become a ritual.

"Okay, Rocky," Charlie said, patting the platform. "Can you get up there yourself?"

"Yeah, I think so." Charlie's friends waited patiently.

With a little effort, Rocky climbed up. Again, he reached over and gripped the wheel. Full of himself for making it up to his perch, he rocked it back and forth with his hand.

This time, the wheel moved about an inch. It surprised everyone, especially Rocky, who had tried turning the wheel every time he sat on the platform.

Charlie grabbed it and tugged. It moved another inch, maybe two, but that was all.

"Let me try," said Doubeck. "I want to see what's in there."

"It's toilet water," said Rocky, which made everyone laugh.

Doubeck got behind Rocky, grabbed the wheel, and twisted. He felt the wheel give a little more. Marty went off to find a lever and returned with a cracked baseball bat he found near Rocky's sandbox. Rocky jumped off his perch and they wedged the bat into the wheel. Mish and Doubeck leaned heavily on it. "One...two...three."

The wheel moved.

"Again!" shouted Charlie.

"One...two...three," called Doubeck. The bat strained to the breaking point before Mitch and Doubeck backed away.

The wheel had turned almost a full revolution. They put their backs into it, and soon they could turn the wheel by hand. Around it went, a dozen times, with some resistance—but not from years of rust. Something was happening inside. Gears were turning and parts were moving. Marty and Doubeck grabbed opposite sides of the cover and lifted. A hinge held the heavy steel cover in position, but it swung open—possibly for the first time in many years.

The open cover exposed a large steel tube descending into darkness and silence. They had a sense there was something down there, but no shapes were discernible.

Doubeck stuck his head into the tube. "Oh, this is cool. Don't you wonder what's down there?" The sound of Doubeck's voice reverberated with strange overtones and seemed to be swallowed up by the darkness. He sat up and looked at his friends. "I don't think it's a sewer. I mean it doesn't smell like a sewer."

"You know," said Charlie, "The old lady who lived here before we bought the house left a shit ton of papers and junk here when she died."

"Was she killed?" asked Doubeck.

Charlie wrinkled his face at the question. "No. She was just really old, like a hundred years old, or something. There's a lot of stuff written in German—letters, postcards. We even found a box of really old Christmas ornaments she saved. "

"I heard the Krauses were spies in World War II."

"She sounds like a crapdragon to me," said Marty.

Charlie shook his head. "Nah, I watched that Hoarders show. This is different. Everything's like perfectly filed, boxed, and wrapped. I'm thinkin' there could be something really cool down here."

"Okay." Doubeck was intrigued. "We need to check all of that shit out. Real junk monkeys even save their vom."

Amber stuck her tongue out. "Shut up, Doobs."

"I hear people used to smuggle stuff across the lake. There could be all kinds of great stuff down there. Like dead bodies or treasure. Or Canadian stuff," said Mish.

"What d'ya mean Canadian stuff?" asked Doubeck.

"I don't know. Like maple syrup, or hockey pucks," said Mish.

"Or Tim Horton donuts," said Charlie.

Amber smiled and raised her eyebrows. "That would be called treasure, I think."

They decided they needed to satisfy their curiosity with an expedition and that would require provisions. They made a list and split it up—water, rope, food, phones, whatever they could think of. Everyone, including Rocky, swore to keep it secret, and they agreed to meet back at the tube in a half hour.

"No toilet water," Rocky insisted.

"It's okay, buddy. It's almost nap time for you," said Charlie.

Rocky had a point. If the hole led to a sewer, the adventure would be over very quickly. If not, the discovery might validate some of the rumors associated with the Kraus home. It could make for a very exciting summer.

As Charlie and Rocky headed up the hill, Rocky took Charlie's hand. "Don't fall in, Charlie."

"I'll be careful, buddy."

"And bring me a donut. Okay?"

"A donut? Well, what if there are frogs *and* donuts? Which one should I bring back?

"A frog, I think."

"Good choice, buddy. I'll see what I can do."

THE LAST U-BOAT

DEEP
INTO
DARKNESS

The flashlight started a dizzying spin the moment Mish lowered it into the darkness. Instead of providing comfort by revealing details, it felt disorienting.

"Hold it steady," said Doubeck. "I can't tell what I'm looking at."

Marty took the rope. "Here, Mish. Lower it against the side like this so it won't spin." He handed the rope back to her and she continued to let it out.

"Okay, but if I see glowing eyes or anything poofy, I'm jettin," she said.

"What about zombies? Zombies don't have fur," said Charlie. "And I'm pretty sure their eyes don't glow."

"Zombies? Why did you even say that?" asked Mish.

Amber set her hand on Charlie's shoulder and began to chant, "No zombies. No zombies. No zombies…."

The steel tube led to an open space. When the flashlight dropped into the space, it began spinning again.

"I feel like I'm going to fall in," said Marty.

"Well don't stare at the light," said Doubeck. "It'll hypnotize you."

Finally, the light stopped spinning.

"It's on the bottom," said Mish. "And it's not that far down."

Charlie took his hand from the edge of the steel tube and wiped the sweat from his eyes. "Hey, it's dry down there. And, look, there's a ladder in the tube."

"Yeah, this is not a sewer. There's no toilet water," said Mish.

No one laughed. Finding a sewer would have immediately eased the tension they all felt. Instead, the mystery just got deeper, and the ladder leading into it was a dangerous temptation disguised as fun.

As their faces popped out of the hole, the friends stared at each other, until Charlie finally said what everyone was thinking.

"I can't NOT go down there."

His comment started a mad scramble for the expeditionary provisions strewn around them.

Doubeck spoke up. "Wait...wait, just wait! Let's think about this." The commotion quieted. "Let's do this smart." To Doubeck, that meant enlisting Marty's advice. "What's the plan, Brainiac?"

"You're asking me?" said Marty. "Like I sit around thinking, 'What would I do if I found a hole in the ground with a ladder in it?'" Marty waved his hands in frustration. "Okay, I literally have thought about that. Gimme a sec."

He was the group's high-strung genius. His parents were both college professors and all his classes were on the advanced placement track. Marty won the top prize in every science fair since third grade, and he spoke conversational Spanish and fluent Hebrew.

His friends had high expectations of him. As their defacto scientist, he'd made frequent calls on the spot—*I wouldn't touch that plant if I were you; check in your socks for ticks, dude; no, you can't get sperminated from tongue wrestling.*

Everyone stood around him like they were waiting to pick teams for softball. Finally, Marty spoke up. "Well, let's get one person down there first—with a light. Then we'll lower all the stuff. The person at the bottom can untie everything when it comes down."

"Dudes?" Doubeck was frantically looking around for Mish.

Amber pointed at the opening. "Mish! Mish is in the hole."

At once, three faces were staring at Mish's eyes glaring up at them from under her ball cap.

Her voice echoed as she called up to them. "Ancient Chinese proverb—He who deliberates fully before taking a step is destined to spend life on one leg."

Doubeck shook his head "Erm...I don't speak Chinese, Mish."

"It means she got tired of waiting," said Amber.

"What's it like down there?" asked Charlie.

"Are there any rats?" asked Amber.

"No, no rats. It's like a factory or something. I see pipes, and wires, and metal cabinets. It's pretty big. The tube is scary, but once you come down the ladder it opens up."

"Any dead bodies?"

"I hope not. I'm kind of pinned down here."

"What do you mean?" asked Charlie.

Mish sighed. "Well, I had to drop from the end of the ladder. To climb back up, I'm gonna have to do a chin up so my toes can reach a step. I don't want to get hurt trying that, but if someone gave me a boost, I know I could reach it. "

Doubeck was the biggest guy in the group. "I can do it, Mish. I'll come down next."

"Thanks, Doobs. You might have to lift everybody unless we can find something down here to stand on." As she spoke, Mish was crisscrossing under the opening, holding her phone up and checking the display. The crew watched her walk in and out of their narrow field of view.

"It's a dead zone down here, guys."

"Okay. Good to know," said Marty.

"No bueno," said Mish, under her breath.

Charlie called down, "I'll run up to the sandbox and get Rocky's big bucket so we can lower it with all our stuff. Hang on, Mish."

The bucket looked like a giant red beach pail that held Rocky's sandbox toys. They filled it with bottled water, snacks, whatever they'd been able to scrounge up at a moment's notice—then they lowered it into the tube. Doubeck and Charlie stood side-by-side and eased the line out until the bucket stopped, its lip stuck on the first rung. The ladder stood out just enough to catch the lip and block the hole.

From beneath them, they heard Mish's muffled voice. "Sup, guys?"

"Sorry. The bucket's stuck on the ladder. We're working on it," said Charlie.

Doubeck leaned into the hole. He stretched and pulled at the lip to bend it around the ladder. When he did, it quickly dropped to the next rung. Now it was stuck between rungs and just out of reach.

"Pull me up. Pull me up!" called Doubeck. Marty and Charlie strained to pull him back to the surface.

"I can get it down there, but it's going to be slow…and dangerous."

Marty tried to focus on a solution. "No. We're not doing dangerous," said Marty.

"We're not?" It was Amber, pointing into the hole. "Mish is already trapped."

"She's okay. We'll figure it out," said Charlie.

Marty spoke up. "Look. We just need to squeeze the top of the bucket so the rim doesn't catch on the ladder."

"Yeah. Okay, I'll try it," said Doubeck. He turned, braced himself against the steel tube, and slipped into the hole. Only his friends and the toes on his sneakers—pressed tight against the rim—held him in place.

The bucket had a white rope handle and Doubeck was able to get the top of the bucket to squeeze inward by twisting the rope.

"Yeah, yeah…it's working," Doubeck said excitedly. "I need a string or something to tie the handle and keep it closed. Book it, dudes."

Charlie looked around and spotted just what he needed on Amber's neck. She stood in front of him, mottled by sunlight filtering through the trees. Her pretty face glowed, her cheeks were flushed, her brown eyes looked as big as saucers, her lips pinched tight. She looked scared.

"Amber, that cord on your dress. We can use it to tie the handle. Can I have it?"

Amber untied the cord, and as she handed Charlie the foot-long ribbon of flower-print fabric, the neckline of her dress fell open.

Amber never took her eyes off Charlie. She didn't say a word, she simply watched his eyes.

"Charlie?"

It was Doubeck, waiting. Charlie knelt, leaned into the tube, and handed over the cord from Amber's dress.

Doubeck took the cord and began to secure the handle. "Dude, I heard that," he said. "It was way too easy."

"Shup, Doober," said Charlie.

The two were hanging inches apart, nearly upside down in the tight space. Doubeck turned away from what he was doing and looked Charlie in the eye. "She likes you," he said.

"Maybe."

"Dude, she's a snack."

Charlie didn't respond.

Marty leaned into the tube, between the two and whispered. "You know we all have shoelaces on our sneakers, right?"

"Ooooooh," Charlie gasped. "I didn't think of that."

"The question is, did Amber?" Doubeck chuckled.

Marty called down into the depths. "It's coming down, Mish!"

There was no response.

Marty, Doubeck, and Charlie eased the bundle down. Every few inches it would bump the ladder and then with a bit of jostling it would slip past another rung. When it cleared the bottom of the tube, the space below was dark. There was no sign of Mish.

"Mish?"

"Mish, you okay?"

"Mish, say something."

Amber joined the boys, peering into the darkness. Tears welled in the corners of her eyes.

Doubeck noticed. "Come on, guys, let's get down there. Amber, you good?"

Amber nodded.

Charlie put his hand on Amber's shoulder. "Listen, she has a flashlight. I'm sure she just wandered away. You know Mish." The sincerity in his soft blue eyes and his kind smile reassured her.

Marty put his legs into the tube and his feet found the ladder. Everything they needed now rested at the bottom of the hole and descending was easy.

Charlie tied the rope off on the hinge.

"I'm down. Everything's good," said Marty. Doubeck followed, leaving Amber and Charlie above.

"Do you want to go first?" Charlie asked Amber.

"No. I want you to go first, so if I slip you can catch me."

Charlie put his hands on her shoulders, "Don't worry, you can do this. It's not far. I'll be right in front of you."

Amber reached out and pulled Charlie to her. She hugged him tightly and, as she finally let him go, she whispered softly.

"Thank you."

"Yeppers," said Charlie, unsure if he felt his heart racing because he was next down the ladder, or because he had just been hugged by the best-looking girl he had ever seen. But he didn't take time to think about it.

A moment later Charlie stepped into the tube and turned his body to locate the ladder with his foot. He stepped down cautiously, again and again, until he was no longer above ground.

"Okay, Amber. Easy now," he said.

As he looked up, Amber turned her back to the hole, placed her hands astride the opening, and took a step into the tube. As she did, her tiny sundress puffed open. She continued to move closer to Charlie, unaware he had stopped, paralyzed by the view.

This was Amber Garcia, *the* Amber Garcia, the girl that every guy at school wanted to be with.

The distraction quickly sent waves of hormones rushing into Charlie's bloodstream. As the chemicals reached his brain, they instantly took control of his central nervous system. Immediately, Charlie's toes slipped from the rung he'd been standing on and he found himself hanging by only his fingertips. His survival instincts quickly took over and his feet began pedaling in the air, his sneakers squeaking against the side of the tube as he searched frantically for the ladder.

Amber heard the commotion and started calling down nervously, "Charlie! What's going on? Are you okay?"

Charlie's feet found a rung as Amber shouted and he was able to stand again and relocate his grip. "I'm good. I'm okay." He looked up again. "I just slipped for a second, I'm okay now. Really good."She started to step down, but Charlie hadn't moved.

"Hold on, Amber. Let me get out of your way. We're almost there."

Seconds later, Charlie felt his friends steadying his legs, allowing him to put his feet down.

He heard Marty's voice. "We gotcha, Charlie."

Standing at the bottom of the ladder, Charlie took one more look up at Amber. He swallowed, reached up, and steadied her with one hand on her bottom, the other around her legs. He took her in his arms and set her gently on her feet. She turned toward him, her face now as close as her bare legs had been just moments earlier. She brushed her hair away and gave him a soft smile.

"Thank you for being such a gentleman."

Her look told him, beyond the shadow of a doubt, that she had enjoyed being held by him. Their friends pretended not to notice.

Marty reached down into the red bucket and handed out supplies. The crew immediately began shining their phone lights around, examining their surroundings, and trying to make sense of what they saw.

"Look at the pipes!" said Doubeck. "Maybe this *is* a sewer."

"This is so steampunk," said Amber. "It's definitely old."

"I wonder if these levers do anything. Think it would be okay to turn a couple of these handles?" Charlie asked.

"I wouldn't do that, Charlie," said Marty. "Hey, anybody see a light switch?"

Doubeck was exploring a narrow walkway behind the ladder they came down. The others had gathered in the cramped open space that headed in the opposite direction. "It looks like this hallway only runs back this way and toward you guys," said Doubeck.

"There's stuff printed on some of these gauges, but it's not English," said Charlie. "Like, what's a Tie-fen-messer?" Charlie struggled to make a word out of the odd letters.

A sound in the darkness startled the group. They turned their phone flashlights toward the source, just beyond the cramped room where they were standing. Their missing companion appeared out of the darkness, walking toward them.

"Mish!" shouted Amber. "You're okay!"

"Guys, we're inside a machine," she said. "And look what I found."

She stretched her arms wide to allow a brightly colored, folded cloth to fall open, unfurling itself into a large banner. Their lights all centered on the giant symbol in the middle of the black and blood-red field surrounding it.

They'd all seen one before, in movies and on the news. But this was the first time any of them had seen a real one—the broken white Nazi cross called a swastika.

THE LAST U-BOAT

LOST
AND
FOUND

Marty took one look at the Nazi flag and headed back toward the ladder. "Oh, shit. Okay, we're done here." He stood beneath the tube, his hands reaching up toward the light. "Doubeck, how about a boost? Like right now, dude. I don't wanna be here."

Mish's voice was calm and measured. "Hey, Marty. It's okay. There are no Nazis here. There's no one here but us. We have to figure this out, and we're gonna need you to help us do that." She nodded to Amber as if to say, "Can you give me a hand here?"

Amber stepped forward and joined them. She put an arm around Marty's waist and spoke to him calmly.

"If I can handle it, you can handle it, Marty. I know you can. I don't like spiders. I don't like mice. I don't like any bugs. So, I'm like freaking out right now, and I'm expecting to see one at any moment. But see? Here I am."

Marty looked at the group and then back to Amber. He shrugged reluctantly.

"It's all ancient history, dude," said Mish. "Everything in here is old, like a museum. Look around, you can tell. No one's been here for a very long time. Pretty sure nobody even knows it's here, okay?"

"Amber, have you seen any bugs?" Marty asked.

"Ah, no," she said.

"No spiders?"

Amber was emphatic. "No. None, nada, zilch."

"Isn't that a little weird? I mean, whatever this room is, it's built so tight that an ant can't get in." He looked at Mish with concern. "Okay, if you're right and it's a machine, what kind of a machine is it?"

"Heck if I know," she said. "And how'd it get here?"

Doubeck chimed in, "Don't be afraid, but I'm pretty sure it's from ancient aliens."

The comment took a moment to sink in, but from the sound of the reaction it was met with a good deal of skepticism.

Amber was the first to react. "Oh, please, Doubeck. Everybody blames aliens."

Mish stepped in. "It's Doobs, Amber. He means the kind of aliens from Scooby-Doo."

"From outer space?" asked Charlie.

Doubeck pointed a finger at Charlie. "From youranus, dude."

Marty did a double face-palm. "That's perfect. Space Nazis."

"*Space Nazis*?" asked Doubeck. "There are legit space Nazis?"

"Meshuggener." Marty walked away, past Mish, and toward the darkness she had just traveled through. Mish looked at Charlie to see if he had any idea what was going on. He just shrugged.

"Okay," she said. "I guess we don't have a clue what this machine is."

From the darkness, Marty called back to the group, "Come on, guys, let's figure this out." After a few steps, he turned back to his motionless crew and hit them with the beam from his flashlight. "You coming or not?"

The reaction was less than enthusiastic, but, in a moment, everyone moved forward. Marty was now in the lead.

They had to pick their way, single-file, along the narrow passageway. They took care to keep from bumping their heads or elbows on the meters, pipes, valves, and steel supports that crossed close overhead. Levers, metal equipment boxes, and switches hung from every wall and there was only enough space to weave your way along the narrow walkway.

The explorers stopped for a moment to catch their bearings. Roaming flashlight beams revealed leather upholstered seats and benches wedged into occasional gaps in the machine's anatomy. The seats represented real people, people who probably stood or sat right here in this mechanical beast eight decades earlier.

A sharp sweetness drifted in the stale air—the smell of old steel.

"Didn't I say I thought it was real steampunk?" said Amber

"Oh, it's outta-pocket dieselpunk," said Mish. "I love it."

Charlie noticed a device he recognized. "See that thing hanging on the wall?" He pointed his light to direct everyone's attention. "That's a headset, with a microphone."

"Maybe we're like inside the original Nintendo?" said Charlie.

"It's probably just so they could talk to someone," said Marty. "Like someone in the next room."

His flashlight was trained on a closed door with rounded corners at the end of the passageway. The bottom of the door rose a foot off the floor and ended just inches from the ceiling. A guy much bigger than Doubeck would have to be folded over to get through. The wheel on the door looked just like the one on the manhole outside.

Charlie moved ahead and handed Marty his flashlight. "If you'll hold this," he said. "I'll see if it works." Marty took the light and trained it on the wheel.

Charlie placed his hands on the wheel and tried to turn it. He grunted as he struggled to turn it, but it didn't budge. He looked at Marty who was shaking his head.

"Just a suggestion, eejit. Try turning it the other way."

"Oh, yeah. Okay." Charlie turned to the others with his hands up. "Sorry, I'm a little jumpy. I know that's not the right direction. Lefty loosey, tighty whitey...or whatev—"

Doubeck held his hands up to signal Charlie to stop chattering. "Just turn the wheel, okay?"

Charlie looked back at the door. He placed both hands on the wheel and gave it a tug in the proper direction. It turned without much effort. He spun it until it engaged the steel bars that began to move toward the center of the door. As they did, they slipped out of the surrounding latches with a thunk. The door was free.

"It's like a bank vault," said Charlie, as he grabbed the handle and opened the door.

Light spilled into the unknown as each of the friends stepped through the hatch. They stood on a heavy black grate inside the passageway. Amber looked down through the floor.

"We're on a big metal screen and it doesn't look too safe," she said.

"It'll hold us. It's steel. And look, there's more room down there. The screen lifts up so you can get down there," said Doubeck.

"Look at those huge batteries down there, and all those crates," said Marty.

"What do you suppose these ropey things are hanging here for?" asked Charlie.

"They're just twisted, they're not ropes," said Mish.

"She's right," said Marty. "See?" He tugged on the nearest one and it spread open.

"They're some kind of nets," said Charlie.

"I know what they are," Amber said. "They're hammocks. We have one for camping."

"So, people for real slept here?" asked Doubeck.

Marty nodded, "Yeah. I think this is where the Nazis slept. Three here and three over there.

"And there's another door," said Mish as she trained her light ahead.

Doubeck looked at Charlie. "You're up, dude."

Charlie stepped forward and spun the wheel. It worked just as smoothly as the one at the other end of the hammock room. He pulled it open and shined his flashlight in before anyone else could move forward to take a look.

"Holy crapoli," he said.

The room was quiet.

"Ho-lee crap oh-lee," he repeated.

Charlie turned back to his friends with a look on his face they had never seen before—the very serious look of a much older person. "We're in a freakin submarine," he said.

Doubeck squinted. "An underground submarine? You know that's not how they work."

"I really don't want to be in a submarine," said Amber. "I'm getting all flurpy. Maybe we should go."

"Hey, everything's cool. We can go when we're done," said Mish.

"So, what makes you think we're in a submarine?" asked Marty.

Charlie caught his breath, blinked, and swallowed hard.

"Torpedoes."

"Awww, I *gotta* see this." Doubeck blew past Charlie and threaded himself into the room. Mish followed.

Doubeck shouted back to the others, describing the scene. "Holy shiz! It *is* a submarine. There's three gigantic torpedoes, like eight feet long. And you can see the little round doors where they shoot them out. One of 'em's hanging by a chain right in front of the hole so they can swooce it in. I mean, it's ready to go." Doubeck was nearly giggling. "Dudes, it looks like the valves and gauges in here are growing out of the walls like mushrooms. Tons of them." Doubeck pulled himself out of the torpedo room and swung around to his friends. "Take a look."

As Doubeck squeezed back behind the group, the others peered in with phone lights extended at arm's length. The scene left them speechless. The first two feet of the torpedoes were oxidized green. The bullet-shaped payload was bright red like it had been painted that morning. On the other end, each torpedo had two in-line propellers.

One by one, the crew pulled their heads away from the torpedo room and back into the sleeping quarters. What they had seen left them somber and silent.

After a moment, Marty spoke. "This just got real."

Mish ran the back of her hand across her mouth. "Yeah, it's pretty unbelievable."

Charlie pulled open a lower hammock and managed to pull himself into it. Amber opened a hammock on the opposite side and tried to sit but there wasn't enough headroom, so she lay down, too.

"Your apartment's cool, duder, but the beds are for shit," said Doubeck, choosing the hammock above Charlie's. Mish, meanwhile, took a hammock next to Amber. When floor space opened up, Marty sat down. He noticed a handle on the cabinet under the bunks. He pulled it, and a trundle bed rolled out across the passageway. It had a thick green smelly felt pad as a mattress.

"Look at this," Marty said. "No wasted space."

Mish switched her flashlight off. "I'll bet it's really scary in here with our lights off," she said. Then Marty, Doubeck, Amber, and Charlie followed suit.

"I've never been anywhere this dark," said Amber.

"That's not what you told me," said Mish.

"Shup, you," Amber replied with a giggle.

"So, what do you want to do, guys?" asked Marty.

"Well, I'm a little weirded out," said Mish. "What do we know for sure?" "Charlie's a geek," said Doubeck.

"Doubeck farted," said Charlie.

The darkness made their laughter sound very loud, but it also allowed them to laugh unrestrained, to relieve some of the tension and just relax.

Marty tried to interrupt. "Hey...hey, listen to me. I just thought of something. What about air?"

Mish chuckled, "Like Doubeck's going to kill us with his airborne toxic events?"

"No, I'm serious," said Marty. "Really. If there's no way for a spider to get in here, it means the only fresh air is what came in with us."

Mish spoke up, "I brought a candle and matches. I need to light one."

"We know there's oxygen cuz we're breathing," said Amber.

"We just don't know how much," said Marty. "I've got an idea."

He clicked his flashlight on and pointed it toward the ceiling. He was searching for something among the pipes, wires, gauges, and valves.

"Doobs, come with me," he said, and he headed forward again to the torpedo room. He poked his head in and bent over backward through the bulkhead.

"There it is," he said as he stretched himself through the hatch, face up. Doubeck waited to look in until Marty had made room. "I'll go in," he said.

Doubeck squeezed through the opening and looked up where Marty was pointing.

"Wow. It's a door on the ceiling."

The crew wanted to know what was going on, so Marty explained. "There had to be another hatch," he said. "They'd have to have a way to load more torpedoes. He patted the torpedo that was hanging beside him, and then quickly stopped, realizing he was patting a bomb. "Doubeck, climb up there and see if you can open the hatch."

Doubeck put his right foot on one torpedo rack and his left foot on the other. The propellers on the hanging torpedo rubbed against his back as his head stuck up into a short tube with only two rungs. In the tube was a neatly folded rope ladder set into a tray. Doubeck lifted it off its cradle and let it fall. He placed his feet on the wooden rungs and reached up to turn the handle on the hatch above him.

"Mish," Marty called out.

"Yeah?"

"You got that candle?

"Yeah, got it."

"Light it and stick it in here."

Mish lit the candle and extended it and her full arm into the torpedo room. Her hand was shaking and droplets of wax were spitting into the air as she shook.

Marty saw the candle and looked up at Doubeck. "How's it going, Doob?"

"I'm ninety-five percent there."

Marty could hear the latch release and the solid clunk of the hatch falling back against its hinge. As the sound reverberated through the submarine, Mish's candle suddenly flickered violently and went out.

"It went out! There's no oxygen," Doubeck shouted.

Marty called out, "No, no, no. Chill. Try to light it again, Mish. Quick!"

They could hear the scrape of matches on the other side of the bulkhead. One, then two tries, then a third. Silence. A light glowed in the doorway and Mish's hand returned to the torpedo room holding a burning candle between her thumb and forefinger. The flame pointed away from the hatch over the torpedoes. An imperceptible breeze was passing through the submarine. The flickering candle proved it.

"We've got air," Marty announced.

Doubeck slipped his flashlight into his hip pocket and stepped down from the rope ladder to the floor. "Looks like a cave out there," he said. "You want to go out?"

They found themselves in a long, narrow room alongside the hull of the submarine. Across the ceiling, heavy boards held up the roof. The walls were bolstered by rough-sawn boards that still had tree bark on their edges. It looked like they imagined a mine might look.

The space was surprisingly dry. Marty suspected that was because it had been carved out of blue Lake Erie clay, which meant rain and groundwater couldn't penetrate it. There was a thin layer of sand on the floor, littered with the footprints of the people who did all this, footprints undisturbed for almost a century.

Doubeck emerged from the U-boat and stepped onto the deck. The others soon joined him. They stood only a few feet from the sandy floor of the dark room because a substantial part of the sub was below the dirt floor, set well beneath their feet like it had been built in a pit. All they had to do to reach the floor was to slide down a couple of feet of the smooth curved hull or head back across the deck to where a boarding net dropped from the deck to the dirt floor.

Their lights revealed a mammoth collection of metalworking tools, welding tanks, workbenches, and metal parts in the cave. Shelves along the perimeter held neatly stowed material and tools.

"What do you suppose that is?" Charlie asked. He was pointing his flashlight at a metal shroud shaped like a giant crown. Large blue, gray, and black blotches of camouflaged paint covered its surface.

Marty walked over and stood behind it. It rose nearly neck-high. "I think it goes on top of the conning tower, Charlie.

"I think the conning tower is where we came in," said Mish. "It was the highest point."

Doubeck walked over to Marty, standing behind the shroud. "What do you think Doubeck? Someone built this whole sub right here—right in this spot—didn't they?"

"Yeah, but I wonder if the Nazis ever finished it?"

"It looked finished inside," Charlie said. "I wonder if it floats."

"It's not supposed to float," said Amber. "It's supposed to sink."

Marty chuckled, "Yeah, true. But the water's a long way away and like fifty feet down." He scratched his head. "I don't get it. Why did they pick this spot? How'd they figure they'd get it out of here and into the water?"

"Maybe it was s'posed to just stay here," said Mish.

Amber put one hand on her hip and used her flashlight to survey her surroundings. Ever since she exited the sub, she acted more and more at ease. After sizing up their situation for a moment, she posed a question to Charlie.

"Any idea where we are? I mean, are we like under your house?"

"I'm not sure," said Charlie.

"Me either. I think I'll see where this room goes."

Amber began to explore by herself, no doubt comforted by the nearby voices of her friends and emboldened by Mish's fearless foray into the sub when they first arrived. She realized she was actually beginning to enjoy the adventure, the risks, and the excitement. It was evident the way she walked confidently farther into the darkened room.

Mish steadied herself against the hull of the sub as she carved an X on the floor with the toe of her Timbs. "Let's say this is the tower we came down," she said. Then she walked six feet away and drew a line. "And here's the lake. Okay? So, Marty, show me where *you* think we are."

Marty walked up to the "X" and looked ahead to the mark for the shoreline. He started carving lines into the dirt floor with his heel.

Charlie caught on right away. "So, the big room runs alongside the sub?"

"Yeah, they *had* to build a room underground to put it together. No way they could do it out in the open. And, it had to be close to the water because they couldn't put it on a truck and schlep it to the harbor."

Marty put his toe on the map. "I think the sub is here running right along the hillside. We haven't seen the engines or the captain's quarters. We haven't seen bathrooms. Betcha there's as much sub behind the tower as we already saw up front."

Charlie looked at Marty and scratched his head. "I still don't get it," he said.

"Don't get what?" asked Marty.

"How were they going to dig this out and take it down to the water? I mean, it's not going to get there any other way, right?"

"I don't know, Charlie. I really don't," Marty admitted.

Doubeck spoke up, "I say we finish looking around. I'm starting to feel like I'm in the Upside Down. Plus, we don't want anyone to come looking for us."

"Wait a second, Marty, before we go," Charlie walked over to the X on the floor. "Show me where my house is."

Marty motioned to an area between the sub and the lake. "It's in here," he said.

"Show me," said Charlie. So, Marty traced the outline of a big square box, representing Charlie's house, onto the dirt floor. As he did, the corner of the house came very close to the edge of the underground room they stood in.

"I think the house is connected," said Charlie. Marty studied the lines.

From the darkness some forty feet away, Amber called out.

"It's for real connected, Charlie. Come say hello to your mom."

THE LAST U-BOAT

GARBOLOGY

A mber stood with her hand on one hip. She waved her flashlight like a laser pointer. "Come with me," she said. "There's a stairway at the end of the room. I could hear your Mom talking."

Charlie felt a chill go down his spine. He didn't want their discovery to get out, at least until they got the answers to a few questions. Like, why did the Nazis abandon a submarine in his backyard? Would it actually work if they could start the engines? How did the Nazis plan to get the sub into the lake? Who owns the sub now?

He could imagine that if the secret did get out, his house and the hillside would be surrounded by FBI and Homeland Security. He'd be a prisoner in his own home for weeks. They'd haul away all the boxes of Mrs. Kraus's stuff, and he'd never hear another word about it. All the evidence would vanish. He'd never solve the mystery of the U-boat.

On the other hand, Charlie didn't want anyone to get hurt. Balancing the risks and rewards in his mind was a real challenge. He just kept reminding himself that the sub had been buried there a long time and there was no reason to rush into revealing it. This was a huge deal and the significance of the decisions he was facing made him feel like he was being thrown into the adult world without any warning.

He also noticed the effect on Amber, and he realized he cared how it was affecting her. This Amber, the confident one, acted a lot different than the girl he had held in his arms an hour earlier. He hoped she could keep it together. While their friends examined the shelves full of tools and materials, Amber stood alone. Charlie thought it might be a good time to check on her, and maybe explore what it was that happened between them as they came down the ladder.

"Hey, you look a lot more relaxed now. I mean when we were up on top you seemed pretty shook. You okay?"

"I am. Thanks," she said. "When we got out of the sub, it felt like stepping off a roller coaster that you really didn't want to go on in the first place. But, you sorta did, you know?"

"Like Cedar Point," said Charlie.

"Exactly. Just like the Iron Dragon. I hate it! But when it's over..."

"You can't wait to go on it again," he said with a smile.

Amber just pursed her lips and nodded. Her determined look softened for a moment as she looked at Charlie. She leaned toward him and then stopped. Their friends were coming.

She looked past Charlie's shoulder and called out. "Hey everyone, you're going to want to see this."

Once the others gathered around, she hustled them deeper into the darkness. "There's a light switch up here. I tried it, but it didn't work."

"So, the cheap-ass Nazis didn't pay their electric bill," Marty sneered.

The crew had to hustle to keep up with Amber, whose long legs covered the ground quickly. The beam of her flashlight found the end of the room. "There, see the stairs? They're pretty steep. Try to be quiet. This is where I heard Mrs. LeClair."

Their flashlights trained on the top of the stairs. The light caught a sign hanging over Mish's head that read, *Der Tiefe Raum*.

"*Der Tiefe Raum*. I'll look that up as soon as I have bars," said Mish.

Marty and Doubeck stepped onto the stairs to test them. They didn't squeak or bend under the boys' weight.

"I'll see where they go," said Marty.

He climbed to a landing about ten feet above the floor. There, the stairs turned and went straight up to a wide door. He could hear Charlie's mom talking.

The door had only a wooden peg for a handle. As Marty pulled on the peg, he heard a latch release and the entire door swung away with ease. He turned toward the others and put his finger to his lips. They could all hear Mrs. LeClair clearly now.

Marty motioned for the group to come up quietly, to follow him through the doorway. He stepped forward, out of view, into a pantry. They followed, being very careful not to make a sound.

Charlie was the last to enter the pantry. Inside, there were two doors and stacks of boxes piled a good five feet high. Old household appliances, and pots and pans along the wall, made the room look a lot like a garage sale in progress.

His mother's voice was coming from behind the kitchen door at the top of a small staircase right in front of them.

Light poured through windows facing the side yard. A dark curtain had once covered them, but both the curtain and the rod holding it had fallen to the floor. The room was filled with canning jars of various sizes containing a variety of what must have been food that all bore the same deathly brown color. As they shut the wide door behind them, a ceramic crock labeled *Gherkin* tipped back flat on its base. The movement made Charlie jump and reach out to catch it. But it was glued to a hinged base connected by a cable to the door latch. Tipping the crock unlatched the door.

It was a secret entrance.

"Where do you think we are now?" Amber whispered.

"We're in my basement," said Charlie. "This is where we keep most of the junk that old Mrs. Kraus left behind."

"We were in The Deep Room," said Mish, looking at her phone. "That's what that sign said."

Amber picked up a sheaf of papers from a nearby box. She looked back at Mish. "When I heard Deep Room I just got creeped."

"Me too," said Doubeck.

"The Deep Room sure is an oogy name," said Mish.

"I think we should each take a box and start going through this stuff for clues," Amber suggested.

"That's a great idea," said Marty. "Your rents are gonna be trashing everything, Charlie. What if they threw away something that explained what went on here? Old lady Kraus had to know what was happening right under her nose."

"Like who built a submarine in her pantry," said Amber.

"So, I guess nobody thinks we should go upstairs and tell my mother there's a Nazi U-boat down here," said Charlie.

"No," was the unanimous answer.

"Okay, then we have to go back to the gully and shut that hatch on the conning tower before anyone finds it open. Our rope is tied to the hinges, remember?"

"Charlie's right," said Mish. "Let's get outta here. And then let's figure out what we're going to do. Everybody grab a box and follow me."

The plan was to walk out right in front of Charlie's mom like nothing had happened.

Charlie started to say something about the questionable audacity of their plan when Amber tapped him on the shoulder. He turned and she handed him a big cardboard box with a heavy braided twine cord tied tight around it.

He took the box in his arms and followed everyone else up the basement steps to the kitchen. As the crew walked in, Sharon turned.

"Hi, Mrs. L." They each said hello as they passed her. Charlie's friends rushed to exit the house.

"Hey-hey, Mom," said Charlie as he passed by.

Mrs. LeClair had a confused look on her face. "Hang on one minute, can you?" She pressed the phone to her side. "Charlie? Where did you come from?"

"Well, according to Dad, when two people love each other very much…"

"Charlie."

"We were just in the basement. We found some cool magazines and more of Mrs. Kraus's garbology. We wanna check it out before you guys toss it."

"Why?"

"I don't know. Cuz it's fun? There might be something interesting. I'll let you know if we find anything important."

"Well, what about lunch? It's almost one-thirty."

"Oh, I completely forgot."

"You forgot *lunch*?" Mrs. L shot him a sketchy look. "Did you see the sub?"

Charlie felt his face grow warm. He blinked hard. "Whut?"

"I bought subs yesterday. They're in the fridge on the bottom shelf. Take them for your lunch. Grab some pop, too. Dinner's going to be late today, anyway."

Charlie's heart was racing.

"Ahhhhh. Okay. Yeah, thanks. I'll go out and see what everyone wants."

"Your face is all flushed, Charlie. Go get some fresh air," she said, as she raised the phone back to her ear.

By then, the rest of the group was outside, happy to be out of the house and away from any cross-examination. They couldn't wait to hear what happened when Charlie was questioned.

"I think I'm gonna hurl," he said, as he approached the crew sitting on the lawn near Rocky's sandbox."Where's Doubeck?"

Marty nodded toward the hillside. "He went down to shut things up and make sure everything's copacetic down there. What's up with you?"

"So, listen. You won't believe what my mom just said."

All eyes were glued on Charlie.

"She said, and I quote, 'Did you see the sub?'"

"Wot?" said Mish.

"How did she know?" asked Amber.

"Maybe she's one of them," said Marty.

"Bruh?" Charlie was more surprised by the sudden paranoia than the comment his mother had made. "Guys, she was talking about sub sandwiches. She offered us lunch, but I thought she was talking about the...the other sub. So, I'm like, oooohhhhh, I'm dead. How could she know? But it was most definitely about lunch."

His rambling was met with blank stares.

"It was very stressful and you weren't there, so jess shup. Now do you want a sandwich or not?"

"Yayer. Kurkey sammos."

"Yomp, Dude."

"I'm fammed."

"Sammiches!"

The free lunch meant the accusations against Charlie's mother were suddenly dropped. "You buttheads suck like the CW," said Charlie.

Amber followed Charlie back into the kitchen to put their picnic together. As they left, Doubeck appeared, climbing up the gully from the creek below. He gave everyone a thumbs-up.

When Charlie and Amber returned, they all got down to business.

"Why here?" asked Marty. "And how the hell did the Nazis build a submarine underground without anyone noticing?"

"Submarines don't work underground, right? So they had to have a plan to get it in the water," said Charlie.

"I know. But there's no ramp, there's no way to pull it out and hulk it all the way to the lake," said Doubeck. "Maybe the shoreline was up here back then."

"Naw," said Charlie. "But think of the damage they could have done sinking ships, like iron ore and coal freighters. Blocking ports. Nobody would have expected a Nazi submarine in Lake Erie and there probably wasn't a single ship around that could have sunk it."

"They only had three torpedoes," said Mish. "That must mean they knew someone who could bring them more."

"Probably only took five minutes to load one," said Marty. "Say you're out in the middle of the lake on a cloudy night and there's nobody in sight. You've got all the time in the world. Nobody's going to get close enough to see you."

Charlie was still bothered by the idea the Nazis had decided to build the sub in a place that would make it useless. "I don't think they screwed up and built the sub underground by accident."

"Right," said Marty. "Like they finished the sub, climbed out onto the hillside, grabbed the guy with the tape measure, and said, 'Dude, you had one job. What were you thinking?'"

Doubeck and Mish started laughing.

Amber remained serious, deep in thought.

"I'm telling you," she said. "We'll find a clue in these boxes. We just have to check every single piece of paper, every folder." She looked at Marty for confirmation.

"Yup. It could all be here right in front of us. But also, we have to get back in there and nose around. We haven't found the captain's room. The answers could be there, in the sub."

Charlie finished his sandwich and dropped to his knees in front of an open box. "Look, we're all going to have to go home in a couple hours or so. Let's go through as much of this as we can now, and then let's meet back at my house after dins. We'll go down to The Deep Room, a couple of us can go back into the sub, and whoever wants to can go through the boxes in the pantry."

"I'm in."

"Like eight o'clock?"

"Okay, it's on."

Amber tossed an empty box aside. "Guys, look. This box was full of German stuff." Several brown leather binders lay around where she sat. "These definitely look technical. This one has a note paper-clipped to the cover."

Mish grabbed Amber's wrist. "Amber, you can't be Velma, I have to be Velma. It's the hair."

Amber shook her head. "Sometimes you are so derp."

Doubeck picked up a bound notebook and read the cover with a phony German accent. "*Operation Seehunde, Heimlich behandeln.*" Then he handed the notebook to Marty. "Okay, Marty, I get *Operation and Heimlich.* Like Heimlich Maneuver. Think it's a medical book?"

"Negatory," said Marty. "This book's full of drawings of the sub."

"The actual sub?" asked Amber.

"Hey, you know what?" Doubeck said. "I just realized, we captured a freakin U-boat."

Mish interrupted. She was reading her phone.

"Anyone want to know what Heimlich means in German?" she asked. "It means *Secret.*"

THE LAST U-BOAT

HOW TO
HIDE
900 TONS

Mike LeClair answered the doorbell. "Hey, Michelle, how are you?"

"Peachy, Mr. LeClair. How you doing?" Mish stepped in, offered her hand, and though a bit surprised by the gesture, LeClair shook it. "Ah, good. Your Mom and Dad okay?"

"Uh-huh. Dad's traveling again. Mom's on a *Below Deck* binge."

"A what?"

"She's like watching *Below Deck* all day long."

"*Below Deck*? That's a TV show?"

"Sort of…Charlie around?"

Rocky came running down the hall when he heard Mish's voice. He stood behind Mike and curled his arms around his dad's leg.

Mike patted Rocky's head. "Oh, yeah. Everyone's in the basement."

"Hi, Rocky." Mish gave the little guy a warm smile and bent down when he wouldn't come out from behind his father. He didn't answer her greeting.

"Need a hug, Rocky?" she said.

Rocky looked up at his dad for approval.

"Never turn down an offer like that, buddy."

He spun around his dad and wrapped his arms over Mish's shoulders.

"Wow, Michelle. You have a real fan there," said Mike.

Rocky was still hanging on, so Mish looked up with her eyebrows raised and her arms held wide.

Mr. LeClair recognized her plea and intervened. "Okay, buddy. Anything more than a few seconds gets weird."

Rocky let go and stepped back, a giant smile plastered from ear to ear.

"I like you, Mish," he said. "Can you be my girlfriend?"

"Sure, Rocky." She extended the palm of her hand and Rocky slapped it. Then he did the same for her and they touched their fingertips. It was a greeting the two had obviously rehearsed before. Rocky giggled and ran out of the kitchen.

"Okay. Good talk. Laterz." Mish made a getaway toward her friends. From the top of the basement steps, she surveyed the scene. Marty and Amber were on their hands and knees poring through documents scattered across the floor.

"Hey, posse. Find anything?"

Marty looked up and smiled. "Hi, Mish. Not much. Once we're done here, we still have all the stuff we took home. So, we're a long way from being finished."

"How 'bout you, Amber? Anything interesting?"

"Naw. It's all normal bills, old newspaper clippings, and like general garbo."

Mish stepped down and settled in with her friends, surveying the unopened boxes.

"Marty's right. There's a lot more to go through," she said.

Amber nodded in agreement. "You know, I don't understand why anyone would save all this." She held up a wrinkled, yellowed envelope.

"Maybe we should focus on what we've got and not what we don't," said Marty.

Mish wrinkled her freckle-covered nose. "Erm?"

"I mean, instead of looking for submarine documents and just ignoring everything else, maybe we should look closer at the garbo and see if it means something. Maybe there's a pattern, like a code, or some clues to this whole mystery."

While Marty spoke, Amber looked over a letter that was in the envelope she'd held up. "This envelope has Canadian stamps on it. Two thirteen-cent blue stamps. Maybe that's a clue."

"Did you read the letter?" asked Marty.

"No, it's German, I think. Some of the alphabet is even different than English."

"Can I see it, Amber?"

She reached across Mish and put the letter into Marty's outstretched hand. He unfolded the paper as the girls leaned over him and studied it.

"Where's Charlie and Doobie? Have they already been here?" asked Mish.

"They went down to the U-boat to check out the back half—the stuff we didn't see yet," Marty replied.

"It's called the stern," said Amber.

Marty drew a check mark in the air with his finger. "Oh, that's right. I forgot the Garcias have a sailboat."

Just then, the gherkin crock tipped and made Amber jump. The wall of shelves started to open and she called to whoever was opening the door.

"Hang on! Let me move the stuff that's in the way," she said, as she swept a space for the door to swing free.

"Okay, it's clear."

Charlie's head appeared around the side of the secret door. "We found it."

"What?"

"What did you find?"

"Show us!"

Charlie and Doubeck entered the basement pantry, then shut and latched the secret door. Charlie was holding a large briefcase in one hand and a large leather-bound book in the other. They sat on the floor and Marty opened the book to the first page.

"Mish, get your phone ready to translate this, okay?" He held the cover open and swung the book around so the others could see it. The page had a bold title and a Nazi symbol—an eagle holding a wreath with a swastika.

She tried to read the words out loud as she typed the letters into Google Translate. "Geheim, exclamation point. Tauchvorschrift, whatever that is, für Unterseeboote."

That phrase was unmistakable.

"For under-sea boat, right? That must be where U-boat comes from!"

"You got it," said Marty. "Anything else?"

"Yeah," said Charlie. "Berlin 1940, Oberkommando der Kriegsmarine. And it's stamped U-22, and signed by someone named Jenish or Yenish."

As Mish tapped in the last letter of the title, the translation flew onto her screen. "It says, 'Secret! Diving Regulations for U-boats. Berlin 1940 Naval War High Command.'"

The group was quiet, stunned by what they had just heard. Charlie flipped the binder around and was leafing through it. "I can't read German, but it sure looks like a workbook—kinda like one we'd get in school," he said.

Marty's eyes opened wide as an idea slammed into the front of his brain. "Mish, copy-paste that English into your search engine."

"Okay, got it," she said, after a few keystrokes.

"Now, check results in the images tab."

Mish selected 'Images' and the page refreshed. "Krud. This is awesome. Someone already translated the whole thing," she said as she scrolled through page after page of drawings and instructions.

Marty grinned. "Anybody want to learn how to drive U-22? We've got the manual."

"Drive it where, Elon?" said Doubeck.

Marty shrugged.

"I can't even get a license to drive a car," said Charlie.

"I bet you could park a car better than the Nazis parked their sub," said Doubeck.

"Y'know," Marty said. "This book is really helpful, but I'm not a mechanic. I mean, there's a million things I'd need to know about engines, generators, and who knows what else. I understand the principles, but I've never even worked on an engine. The book is great, but it isn't enough. "

Doubeck slapped Marty on the shoulder. "That's all valid. But we'll get there, dude. What you have right there is the owner's manual. Let's print the sucker out, go back down, and figure it out."

———————

For everyone except Charlie and Doubeck, it was the first time back in the sub since morning. Finding out how the Nazis planned to launch it and make it go were just two of the many mysteries left to be solved.

Everyone's curiosity gradually overwhelmed their fears. Still, as the crew walked past the conning tower ladder they were reminded of the morning's tension and a couple of them shuddered.

"Doobs," Mish called Doubeck's attention to a metal frame sitting just beside the walkway. "Look at this, it's the bottom of the ladder to the conning tower."

Marty called Doubeck over. "Cool. Let's hook it up."

Charlie and Doubeck lifted the ladder extension as Amber held the rope. It hooked firmly into place. No more jumping up to grab the ladder.

"So, let's head aft and see what's back there," said Amber.

Phone lights shone into the darkness toward the first hatch. Everyone had improved their agility when traveling through the sub by grabbing the handles welded above the hatches to vault through as quickly as possible. It wasn't easy to move through the boat, especially when the whole crew was aboard. The cramped quarters made it easy to collide with obstacles along the way, and there were lots of very solid obstacles.

"This is the captain's quarters where we found the briefcase, and it looks like maybe two more people could have crashed here, too," said Charlie. He pointed at a second berth and hooks for a hammock.

"Maybe, this was the officer quarters," said Marty.

Doubeck pointed his light toward the other end of the room. "We went through to the next room and that's all there is," he said.

"I just thought of something," shouted Doubeck. "You know what? We didn't see a periscope."

"He's right," said Charlie.

"It's got to have a periscope, right?" asked Amber.

"Only way they can see where they're going," said Doubeck.

Marty aimed his flashlight forward. "Well, we can look for it on the way back. It should be in front of the—whatever you call the place the captain stands—next to the ladder we came down."

"Let's call it the Control Room," said Amber.

"You know, Amber," said Marty. "I'm glad you're putting names to everything. We need to start learning the lingo, and using it like a crew would—like a well-oiled machine."

"Aye-aye," said Charlie, casting a smile toward Amber.

"Aye-aye," the crew repeated.

Doubeck led the way, and they entered the engine room as a group for the first time. "So, this is the last room. Lots of machines. Lots of valves."

"Doubeck, look. These are diesel engines. On each side. How could you miss them?" asked Marty.

"How would I know they were engines? She-it, they're huge."

Marty raised his eyebrows. "These engines gotta be like ten times more powerful than a Peterbilt semi."

Charlie looked skeptical. "Naw. Really?"

"Think about it. They have to push 900 tons of steel through water. It's way harder to move through water than air."

Charlie shrugged. "Okay. I get it. I just expected them to look different, more like these metal boxes back here, I guess."

Marty patted the rounded sheet metal boxes behind the diesels. "These are the electric motors."

"That's what all the batteries are for," said Amber.

Marty, the science officer, was in the zone. "Yeah, diesels need air, so they only use the diesels when they're on the surface. When they're under water they use the electric motors."

"Do you think the diesels work?" asked Mish.

Marty shrugged. "I don't think they can be started now because they need water to cool them off. I mean I understand how they work in theory but I never even stood this close to a diesel engine before."

"It's kind of a waste of time then," said Mish.

"What is?" asked Doubeck.

"Well, we can't get it in the water and we can't move it without the water," said Mish.

Doubeck extended his hand. "Tell you what, Mish. You figure out how to get it in the water, and I'll figure out how to make the engines work."

THE LAST U-BOAT

SUBTERRANEAN

School was winding down and summer vacation was just a few days away. Between the time-wasting activities the teachers invented to fill the hours, and the glorious distraction provided by the beautiful weather beaming through the classroom windows, nothing important could possibly happen during the last week.

It was just as well. The need to explore and investigate the mystery of the U-boat consumed the friends like nothing they had ever experienced.

Between classes, Doubeck ran into Stewart Swanson in the hall. Their previous meeting down at the creek had been mucho tense, so Doubeck thought he'd try to smooth over any ruffled feathers. He started with a knuckle knock.

"Hey, Stewart."

"Hey, Doubeck."

"So, Stewart, did you go swimming after we saw you?"

"Yeah. It wasn't so bad, maybe sixty-five."

"Too cold for me," said Doubeck.

"You have to get used to it. Takes a couple of minutes. But I'm trying to get as much beach time in as I can cuz I have a summer job at the marina and it's getting busier every day."

"Cool. What do you do?"

"Pretty much everything. Gas up boats, wash 'em, keep the docks clean and stuff. I've been working on engines, too, outboards, inboards, whatever Oleg tells me to do."

"Oleg?"

"Yeah, he's some guy who bought the marina from Mr. Daglian over the winter. I think they're related."

Doubeck smiled as he remembered old Mr. Daglian. "He was a good guy. He used to let us take boats out without a security deposit."

"Oleg's all right, I guess. He's kinda quiet. I think he's a little nervous about taking over with no experience. When he found out I worked on cars he hired me right away. I got the diesel working in his boat and he's been like my best friend ever since. He's paying me twenty-five dollars an hour, too."

"Yow! That's amazing. Full time?"

"Yeah, overtime, too, if I want it."

Doubeck thought it sounded too good to be true. "You fixed his diesel engine? Aren't they really diflicated?"

"Naw, they're actually simpler than gas."

The bell rang just as Charlie was coming around the corner to grab a book from his locker.

Swanson couldn't resist trying to embarrass him. "Hey, Skid Marks!"

"Hey, Doubeck." Charlie ignored Swanson, scooped the book, and sped away as the other two headed for class in the opposite direction.

Doubeck again defended his friend. "Check it out, Stewart. You may think Charlie's a nerd but a lot of people think he's a great guy, so maybe you could back off just a little."

He looked away. "I can't figure out why you hang out with those geeks."

"Geeks? They're my squad, and they're just like you, dude." Swanson didn't like that and he reacted by pulling up straight-shouldered and tilting his head like he didn't hear what he just heard. Doubeck kept it up. "Look, you're a motorhead—a genius with cars. Well, Marty's a science whiz, Mish is a badass artist, and Amber is totally smexy."

"Yeah. So, what's Charlie?"

"He's my friend."

Stewart turned away, resisting the idea of letting go of his bad attitude.

Doubeck saw it but decided to drop the subject. "Hey, I gotta cut." He ducked into class, gliding past his teacher who stood in the doorway eyeing him, waiting for stragglers.

Stewart lumbered on down the hall—late, but in no hurry.

After school, Marty waited on the corner for the rest of the crew, as planned. Mish showed up first and made herself known by coming up behind him and swinging her shoulder into his.

Marty stumbled forward before catching his balance. "Oh, It's you, Mish. Shoulda figured."

"Hi, Marty. Listen, Amber's on her way. She had to talk to somebody."

"Okay."

Mish leaned in close to him and whispered. "I couldn't focustrate on anything all day."

"I know!" Marty's eyes grew wide. "It's like I wanted to shout *Guess what, we found an awesome German U-boat and it's in Charlie LeClair's backyard and nobody in the world knows about it.* But I had to sit there and look like I was interested in whatever the heck was happening in class."

"We're really obsessed with this, aren't we?" said Mish.

"Yupp." Marty looked around to make sure no one was close by. "I'm pretty sure nothing like this is ever going to happen to me again. I think I need to make something out of it while I can."

Mish slung her arm over her friend's shoulder and gave him a squeeze. "I feel the same way. It's all very cool."

Marty nodded. "Yeah, but it's awful hard to keep it a secret."

"It's crazy." Mish sighed.

"So listen," said Marty. "I went through all my boxes and I found some interesting things. I think there's definitely some secret code wordage in here because the letters, some of them, anyway, are full of just stupid stuff you wouldn't waste your time writing if it wasn't a code."

Mish wrinkled her nose. "I'm guessing as they built the sub, and more and more pieces of it showed up, there was probably a lot of communication with their Nazi homies in Canada—a lot of coded shit going back and forth."

"Canada?" Marty asked.

"Yeah. I found like a heap of mail from Halifax. So, I Googled it, and

Halifax is right on the ocean. Could be where they unloaded the parts for the sub."

Marty wasn't enthusiastic. "Maybe so. But that's like another piece of the mystery we probably don't really need to spend time on right now."

"Why not?" Mish asked.

"Because I have a feeling the clock is ticking, and sooner or later someone else is going to find out about the U-boat. If that happens before we get it out of the ground, they'll confiscate it. The Coast Guard, the state of Pennsylvania, or some museum will just take it. I'm pretty sure the only way to keep that from happening is to figure out how to make it run and, you know, get it into the water. I just have the feeling that as long as it's in the ground, it's a lost puppy—up for grabs."

Mish didn't want to believe him. "So, the government could just take it?"

"*We* couldn't stop them. But if we sail it into the bay at high noon on a Saturday, it's over. The government is totally owned."

Marty saw Doubeck, Amber and Charlie coming.

Doubeck waved. "Sup, guys?"

Marty and Mish returned the greeting.

"Hey guys!"

"Hey, sailors!"

"Shhhhh," said Charlie. "We're under cover."

"No shit," said Mish.

"Sub-terranean, dudes." Marty gave himself a thumbs-up for creativity.

"Ooooh. Good one," said Charlie.

"Amber." Marty shifted into leadership mode. "Did you find anything besides that secret code in your stuff?"

"Yeah, I found technical manuals, pictures, some newspaper stories, and I found an old VHS tape in a padded envelope but I didn't have a way to watch it."

"Any return address? Who was it for?" asked Doubeck.

"Oh," Amber squinted as she tried to remember. "It was addressed to Mrs. Kraus from somewhere in Canada."

Marty and Mish spoke at the same time. "Halifax?" they asked.

"Yeah, I think it was."

Marty turned to Mish. "Don't get too excited. There were no VHS tapes during World War II."

Mish rolled her eyes. "Ya, sure?" She turned to Amber. "What about the newspaper stories, anything cool?"

"Oh, yeah. Lotta U-boat clippings." Amber opened a well-worn scrapbook and flipped right to a strip of paper that marked an inside page. "Listen to this. *The War Department reports four German spies were captured in Chicago, Illinois, and Cincinnati, Ohio after disembarking from a Nazi U-boat in Ponte Vedra Beach, Florida. The men had infiltrated into the interior of the country using disguises and falsified identification. Two of the four were captured with weapons on their person. They have been transported to the Federal Penitentiary in Leavenworth, Kansas, and will face a military tribunal.*"

"Whoa. She kept all this stuff?" asked Charlie.

"I'm not surprised," said Marty. "The Nazis documented everything. Even the incriminating stuff. They didn't care."

"Well, listen to this one," said Amber. "*Four German spies were arrested after infiltrating into the country via New York City. They freely confessed to Civil Defense and FBI authorities that they had been delivered to the shores of Long Island, New York by U-boat. The War Department reports the pair were so overwhelmed by New York City and the freedom they found in the United States that they sought out FBI authorities in order to confess and turn themselves in.*"

"I wonder what happened to them," said Charlie.

Amber turned the page. "Well, as a matter of fact, here's a clipping from August 9, 1942. *Six Nazi spies who were convicted of espionage last week in a Military Tribunal in Washington, DC were executed yesterday in the electric chair on the third floor of the District of Columbia jail. President Roosevelt commuted the sentences of two of the defendants, noting they had surrendered themselves and provided information on the others.*"

"Sheesh. You think the Nazis who built the sub were part of this?"

Amber nodded. "I do. The story goes on to talk about their secret mission, the hydroelectric power stations in Niagara Falls, ALCOA aluminum factories in Illinois, and railroad lines in Pennsylvania. They were planning sabotage all over the middle of the country, like right around here."

"We still don't know very much about the U-boat," said Marty.

"Maybe the tape has a documentary about the sub on it," said Doubeck.

"I might have pictures of our sub," said Amber. She unwound a burgundy thread that held the flap closed on a yellowed envelope. "There's the back of a submarine sitting up on a wood platform."

Marty reached for the envelope. "Can I see?"

Amber handed the package over, but she kept the photo and pointed to a sign on the wall of the drydock. "Look, this says *MV Praetoria. MV* means Motor Vessel and back then it was a term mostly used in the US. When I'm sailing, I hear ships hailed all the time with MV. In Europe, they used SS, for steamship, so I'm pretty sure this picture was taken in North America. Anyway, I looked up *MV Praetoria.* It was a double-hulled oil tanker built in the Netherlands in the 1930s."

"What do you need a double hull for?" asked Doubeck.

"Merchantshipping.com said the double hull was there in case a hole got punched in the boat. The inside hull might still be okay."

"There could be another reason," said Marty. "You could open the back end of the boat, flood the double hull until the ship sinks a few feet, and sail a boat right in. Pump the water out, the boat you loaded is dry, you close the back door and no one knows what's going on inside the hull. I think your picture was taken from outside the boat. Maybe standing on that back door."

"So if you had a floating dry dock, you could slice that sub just like a loaf of pumpernickel. And no one would know," said Doubeck.

Marty nodded, "Yeah, and then you smuggle the pieces across the lake."

"Fam. Listen up. This is really scary. It fits kinda perfectly with what I found out," said Doubeck.

"Like how?" asked Marty.

"I looked up U-22 on Wikipedia." Doubeck looked surprised by the stares he was getting. "They don't know where it is."

"I know where it is," said Charlie.

Amber nudged Doubeck. "So, what else?"

"Well, they think it disappeared where it was last spotted in the North Sea. But I looked at a map. The North Sea is up by Sweden and, you know, it's way up there. Anyway, it's like a straight shot from there to Canada, which is like only twenty miles from right here."

Mish pulled her phone out. "So this really could be U-22."

Doubeck took a deep breath. "I'm pretty positive it is. See, there's something else. I was thinking, so if this is U-22, what about U-21 and U-23? What happened to them? So, I looked them up. It turns out U-19, U-20, and U-23 were cut into sections."

"No shit, why?" said Mish.

Amber handed the photo to Marty. "

"They had to cut them up so they could be moved secretly to the Black Sea, where they were put back together and used to patrol the inland waters. It's all documented. Oh, and the Black Sea is a lake, dudes, just like our lake." Doubeck shrugged and took a deep breath. "That's it," he said.

"Doubeck, do you know what happened to 19, 20 and 23?" asked Amber.

"Yeah, they were just found like three years ago at the bottom of the Black Sea. It's really deep, so they've been hard to find."

"That leaves 21 and 22," said Marty.

Doubeck shook his head. "No. U-21 was cut up for scrap in 1945. It only leaves U-22."

Mish shuddered. "Doobs, I just got a freakin chill down my spine."

"Me, too," said Marty.

"The VHS tape," said Mish.

"Y'know," Charlie interjected. "Mrs. Kraus left a lot of cool shit. There's an old record player, a radio with an amp and speakers that's like as big as a microwave. There's an old TV. There's definitely a VHS tape player. I know we still have it."

"I've gotta watch that tape," Mish insisted.

"Okay, I'll bring the tape over," said Amber.

"Yeah," Doubeck grinned. "I'm pretty sure it's a TED Talk on how to build a U-boat in your basement."

"Or how to get it out of your basement," said Amber.

Charlie had been cooking on all the mysteries swirling around in his head, so the idea that they might easily get the answers they were looking for really appealed to him. "Wouldn't that be great? I mean, if somewhere all the plans were right there. We could just take everything step-by-step."

"So, Charlie? What time do you want us there? Just wondering because I have to take off and do some shopping with my mom."

"Oh, yeah. I guess we could get together at seven. Does that work?"

Mish nodded. "Yup!"

Doubeck cleared his throat. "One other thing before everyone jets, okay? So, I ran into Stewart Swanson this afternoon. I don't know how we could make this work, but he knows a lot about boat engines, and he's working at the marina this summer. He might be a good contact."

"He's a dick," said Charlie.

Mish pointed at Charlie. "What he said."

Amber pretended to stick her finger down her throat. "Stewart. Eww, nerts."

Marty jumped in. "Hey, come on. We can talk about Stewart tonight. Let's plan to watch the tape and then let's decide what our main focus is going to be, and who's going to do what. We need major finesse."

Doubeck, Mish, Amber, and Marty all showed up together and on time. The LeClairs were at the kitchen table just finishing dinner, so Charlie got up to answer the door. Charlie's mom, dad, and little brother Rocky all greeted the group as they filed past and headed down the stairs to the pantry. Mish had a red gift bag in her hand and she hung back as her friends made their way down.

"Hey, Rocky. I was at the store today and I got you a present."

"You did?"

"Hey, we're all famalam, right?"

She looked up at Mr. and Mrs. LeClair. "I hope it's okay. I saw something I thought Rocky might like."

"That was very thoughtful of you, Michelle," said Sharon. Mike just nodded and smiled.

"Here, Rocky. Open it up."

"Thanks, Michelle!" he said.

Rocky reached into the bag and pulled out a foot-long, red plastic submarine that brought a huge smile to his face.

"It's super, Michelle." Rocky almost shouted the words, as he whirled it around in the air like an airplane.

"You know, it's a boat that goes under water, right?" she asked.

"Like Captain Nemo!" he said.

"You got it, bruh. Happy sailing!"

"Thanks, Michelle," he repeated. "Thank you!"

"Wow. Three thank-yous," said Sharon. "I think you hold the new record."

Michelle waved to her happy young friend as he continued to twirl the sub in the air over his head. Then she turned and disappeared down the stairs, in the direction of a much more lethal submarine just yards away.

Mike turned to Sharon. "Famalam?"

The squad was sitting in a circle on the floor of the pantry. Marty waited until Mish got settled. He excelled in organization and planning, and he had already begun taking notes.

"Okay," said Marty. "Here's what I'm thinking. First, we need to figure out how we're going to drive this boat. Then we need to figure out how the Nazis planned to get it into the water. And, above all, we need to keep anyone from confiscating it when the word gets out."

No one disagreed.

"Okay. Let's look at the first problem. We have to figure out how the engines work. Doob, you said you'd work on getting the diesels going."

Doubeck looked at Mish. "I did?"

"You know you did," said Mish.

"Okay, I guess." Doubeck found it very easy to tease Mish—and a lot of fun.

"Look," said Marty. "There's an awful lot to read and learn before we're going to be able to make this work. Honestly, it might never happen. I mean, we're way in over our heads here. We're going to have to develop some awesome skills, so we can't be afraid to take on the challenges."

Marty then turned to what he viewed as the next element of the operational challenge. "Okay, let's say Doubeck figures out how the engines work, then we'll have to figure out how we're going to drive the boat, too. It's got to be very complicated. And remember, it doesn't just go forward, reverse, left, and right like a car. It also goes up and down. So, we have to study that diving instruction manual and know it forward and backward. You know what I mean?" Marty looked at each of his friends until he set his eyes set on Amber.

Her family owned a huge sailboat and Amber had a reputation as an excellent sailor. She was a natural choice to drive the sub.

"You want the job?" he asked.

"I'll take it," she said.

"And, finally."

"Finally?" Mish asked.

"Yeah, finally for right now, anyway. We need to figure out a way to get the U-boat in the water, and, honestly, I don't even know if that's possible." Marty was looking directly at Mish as he spoke.

"I'm on it," said Mish.

"You don't sound too sure," said Marty.

Mish shrugged.

"Mish, maybe Doubeck and I can help," said Charlie. He looked at Marty. "Nothing's off limits, right?"

Marty tried to give a thoughtful answer. "Well, no dynamite or anything like that, alright?"

"Well, forget it, then," said Doubeck. "I'm only in this to blow shit up."

Charlie smirked. He and Doubeck slapped their hands together while everyone else chuckled.

"Yeah, I'll work on it," said Charlie.

Mish stood up. "What do *you* want to do, Marty?"

Marty checked his notes. "I wanna help any way I can. Plus, I'm going to handle the documents. So help me collect anything you guys think is important—you gotta keep going through the boxes. I want us to know everything we can about the U-boat. Finally, I'm going to see what we can do to make sure no one takes it away from us."

The group accepted the plan without further comment. Mish looked around and offered Amber a hand getting up off the floor. The others all stood, as well.

Marty held his hand up to get everyone's attention and to make a final comment. "This is a big deal. It's historic, it's sick, and it's all ours. I really think we have a shot at making this work and, someday soon, sailing right into the marina."

"Guys," Charlie said. "I'd like to go down to the sub. We keep running our phone batteries down using the lights so I rounded up a bunch of flashlights to take down. I was thinking about just hanging out there to think about my job for a while and take some more time just to look around. Anyone want to go along?"

"Wait. Wait a second," said Doubeck. "There's one more thing."

Marty looked quizzically at him. "Like what?"

"We need a name for it. We need a name for the sub."

Marty shrugged. "We could name it after my aunt in Cleveland."

Doubeck scrunched his face up. "What's your aunt's name?"

"Doris."

Mish cracked up and Marty shot her a scowl.

"I love it," said Amber.

"It's very cool," said Charlie.

Marty raised his hand. "All those in favor?"

Doubeck waved his arms, "No no no no no. That's just headass!"

That started everyone laughing.

Charlie nudged his friend. "Doobs. We'll give it a name in due time. Just relax."

Doubeck calmed down. "Then you're not serious about Doris?"

Charlie patted him on the back, "Let's all think about names and see what we come up with. There's no rush."

"Yeah, I suppose. But we need to be thinking about it," said Doubeck.

Marty started to fidget. "Okay, everybody, grab a box and keep going through Mrs. Kraus' files."

Mish stood and checked her phone. "Look, I promised I'd be home five minutes ago. I'll see you dudes later." A chorus of ciaos and goodbyes followed her up the stairs to the kitchen.

Sharon LeClair was just pouring an iced tea when Mish opened the basement door. "Going home?"

"Have to. I promised my mom I'd help do some chores before dark."

"Good for you, Michelle. See you soon."

About fifteen minutes later, it occurred to Sharon that there wasn't a sound coming from the basement, and there hadn't been since Mish left. So, she decided to go downstairs and check on Charlie and his friends.

THE LAST U-BOAT

FACE TIME

Marty was looking away, holding something in his hands, but the picture wasn't clear. It played back with the characteristic garbo static of a VHS recording from B.N., Before Netflix. He fiddled impatiently with the controls, trying to stabilize the image.

Doubeck whacked the top of the TV. "Pretty f'n cheugy, if you ask me."

Marty shook his head "Oh, yeah."

As he turned one of the dials, the picture centered itself and the streaks disappeared.

The man on the tape was holding a Nazi U-boat uniform, exactly like the uniforms they found neatly folded and stowed on the sub.

"He's one of them," said Doubeck.

"Bet," said Amber.

A voice spoke up from behind. "What are you watching, Charlie?"

Everyone had been so intense watching the video, that they never saw Charlie's mother walk into the room.

"Mom! Ahhh, it's a VHS videotape that Mrs. Kraus left."

Sharon furrowed her brow and looked at the crew, sitting around the old TV, looking jacked up like they were watching the Super Bowl.

"Is it really that interesting?" she asked.

"Yeah. And maybe a little creepy, too," said Charlie. "We're just curious."

"Aren't you eavesdropping, like invading her privacy?"

"No."

"Huh-uh."

"Nah."

"Not really."

"She's dead, Mom."

Sharon was outvoted.

"Well, okay. Let me know if she confesses to being a spy or something."

Five faces suddenly became ashen and their mouths fell open.

Sharon saw it happen. "I'm just kidding. Have fun."

She left the room, but only Charlie moved during the next few moments. The others were still frozen, staring at the spot where Sharon LeClair had been standing.

"I'm telling you, dudes, that's so sus. She knows something," said Doubeck.

"Oh, stop it." Charlie put his hand over his face. "You're just reading all kinda shit into what she says."

Amber grabbed Charlie's shoulder and pointed at the TV. "Hey, the Nazi dude is talking. Listen." Marty reached over and turned the volume up on Mrs. Kraus's TV.

The man was facing away, so his voice sounded muffled. Marty turned the volume up again and the words became clear.

"*Mutter, Du kennst Ich liebe dich. Es tut mir Leid.*" Then, in perfect English, he said, "I'm so sorry, so very sorry we had to abandon the U-boat."

"Ho-lee crap," said Doubeck.

"She knew," said Amber.

Mish was furiously searching for a translation app on her iPhone as the man in the recording began to sob. "*Es ist alles meine Schuld. Meine Schuld!*"

Mish hit the speaker on her phone and the AI voice on the app spoke, "It is all my fault. My fault." The video played on as Mish's phone listened and translated.

"I should have stayed with Hans. I could have helped, but instead, I killed my own brother, my dear brother Hans. Had we stayed home to wait for the storm, we could have changed history."

Then the man turned toward the camera for one last word. As he did, the group's curiosity was replaced by revulsion. One side of his face was missing. Where there should have been an eye, an eyebrow, an ear, or a cheek, there was nothing but patchy skin stretched tight. As the man continued to turn, they could see a slight ridge and nostrils, the remnants of his nose. In a moment his left cheek and his left eye appeared.

"Oooh. I'm shook," said Mish. "Gag."

"Serious cringe," said Doubeck.

The video continued. "*Verzeih mir, Mutter.* Forgive me, Mother."

Rocky was outside screaming at the top of his lungs. His dad, Mike, once said Rocky's scream was like having someone pour boiling water in your ears. His mother was trying to console him as the crew, fresh from viewing the VHS tape, filed out of the house with blank looks, their chins down like they were returning from a funeral.

Sharon called out. "Charlie, do you know where Rocky's red bucket is?"

"Ah, it might be in the woods, Mom." But it wasn't. Charlie knew he'd left it in the U-boat.

"Then could you bring it up and give it back to him? All his toys are scattered around and I'm trying to teach him to keep everything picked up."

"Okay. We're headed down to the beach. I'll bring it back with me."

"Thanks, Sweetie." She turned to Rocky. "You have such a nice brother. He loves you very much." Behind her, the kids disappeared into the woods as they quietly made their way down the hill to the creek, each of them very aware that a pristine German U-boat, more than eight decades old, lay just inches beneath their feet.

The trunk of an ancient black locust tree lay along the lake shore just above the beach. It straddled the creek like a bridge and made a perfect bench for watching the waves, the passing boats, the sunset, and the occasional bonfire. It must have fallen long ago because bark no longer covered the wood.

This was a peaceful place. A place to chillax, to work out problems, to admire the beauty of the world, to hold someone else's hand, and maybe even to cry. Each of the crew had come here at one time or another for at least one of those reasons. In light of their amazing discovery, it seemed right that they were all here, united by an incredible secret.

"I hate the fuckin Nazis," said Marty. "Still, that tape was really sad. I don't know what happened to make him that way, but I'm feeling a little scared."

"I am, too," said Charlie. "We need to know if something happened here that caused those injuries."

"Maybe a torpedo exploded in his face," said Doubeck.

Mish slapped his arm. "Seriously?"

"I think I know what happened," said Amber.

"I found news clippings from 1941. They were all about an explosion and fire at the old steel plant. They found these shredded shoes from five people. But, the paper said the remains only accounted for four."

Amber looked at her friends.

"I think the man without a face was number five."

"That would explain why Mrs. Kraus kept the clippings," said Marty. "But it means it was probably no accident. They were up to something."

"He worked on the sub. That's gotta be why he had the uniform," said Charlie.

Amber wagged her finger. "Then so did his bruh. The one he said he killed."

Marty jumped off the log, turned, and faced his friends. "It didn't look like there was any kind of fire or explosion around the sub. Maybe there isn't anything to worry about, after all."

Nobody could say for sure.

"Hey," said Marty. "It's another piece of the puzzle." He picked up a flat stone tossed it into the lake and watched it skip three times before disappearing.

There was a brief silence before Mish changed the subject. "Doober's right. We need a name for the sub."

Doubeck scratched his head. "Okay. I've been thinking about it. How about the Sea Pickle?"

"Doosh. This is why you have no clout," said Mish.

The others looked at him like he'd lost his mind.

Doubeck held out his hands. "What's wrong with that?"

"Doobs. The Sea Pickle? Seriously?" asked Charlie.

Amber started brainstorming. "Well, what's another name for a sub?"

"A gyro," said Marty

"A hoagie," said Mish.

"A grinder," said Charlie.

Doubeck threw his hands up. "Okay, enough. I was trying to help and you guys are jerking me around."

"I don't think you understood the assignment," said Marty.

"Hey, didn't all the U-boats have numbers," said Amber.

Marty nodded. "The paperwork said this was U-boat number twenty-two."

"Should we call it U-22?"

Charlie stood. "But that's not really a name. U-22 needs a name."

It was beginning to get dark. Charlie was looking back at the house, thinking about how he was going to get Rocky's bucket back to the sandbox without going through the basement. His eyes casually drifted down the face of the cliff toward the locust log lying at the foot of the embankment.

"Hey guys, why's there a pipe coming out of the cliff below the house?" he asked.

The group turned to look. Charlie pointed and soon everyone could see the stub of pipe emerging from the hillside.

"It's your bathroom, buddy. Go back up and drop a deuce. I'll tell you what happens." said Doubeck.

Marty turned and looked at him. "Doubeck? That's literally whacked."

Doubeck grinned because this time he was kidding. "That pipe's always been there. I've seen it ever since I first started coming down here."

"Maybe it's an air vent into the basement. I'll bet that's right where the lower level is," said Mish.

Minutes later, the crew entered the conning tower, crawled out the torpedo room hatch, and slid down the hull into the basement. Along the way,

Charlie grabbed Rocky's red bucket.

They headed toward the place where they thought the pipe came through. An old tarp covered an unknown object the size of a sports car.

"Amber, grab your end," said Charlie. "I'll get this side. You guys all stand back." Charlie handed his flashlight to Doubeck and grabbed the heavy, oilcloth tarp with both hands. Together, he and Amber lifted it up and off, tipping it toward their friends. As it dropped, their lights revealed a machine painted industrial pea-green.

"It's an engine," said Marty.

Doubeck immediately set his hands on the machine and started following its contour, as though looking for something.

"What's it for, Doobs?" asked Mish.

Doubeck walked part way around the device. "It's geared up to this big empty spool with that cable coming out of it. Here's the lever to engage it."

"It's a winch," said Marty. "Maybe they were going to use the cable to pull the sub out of here." Then he thought better of the idea. "No, that's not it. The cable's not big enough to pull a sub."

"The fuel tank's all gunked up. The gas is like wax," said Doubeck wiping his finger on his jeans.

"If it's a winch it's supposed to pull something," said Charlie.

"But the cable disappears into the wall," said Amber.

"Look. The exhaust pipe coming out of the engine." Charlie grabbed a cleaning rag and a stick from a pile of scrap wood on the floor. "Doubeck, pull that exhaust pipe out and shove this through the wall? Let's see if we see it from the beach."

"Yeah, okay." Doubeck popped the joints apart and handed the pieces to Marty so he could fish the rag through the wall.

"You guys go. I'm going to stick around and clean it up. I won't try to start it until we're all here," said Doubeck.

Marty agreed. "Go for it, man. Let's see what it does."

The crew helped Charlie boost Rocky's bucket up the conning tower and out onto the hillside. From there it was only a short walk to the sandbox.

The others climbed out of the sub and took the trail through the woods, along the creek, and back down to the lakeshore. The sun was setting, and a glorious orange, pink, purple, and gold blanket spread across the western sky.

A minute later Charlie joined his friends as they walked carefully around the greasy old wooden steps that held the bank back. They hopped up onto the old fallen locust log and moved single-file across the surface. They dodged underbrush and mosquitos, balancing like gymnasts, all the while scanning the hillside for a sign of the rag on a stick.

"I see it," said Mish. "It's straight up over our heads."

"Wait a second," said Charlie. "The cable's up there, too. See, to the left of the rag and down about four feet. It looks like a vine, but I'm sure it's the cable." The setting sun made the cable glow golden yellow.

"I see it, too. So can we get outta here? The mosquitoes are killing me," said Marty.

"Me, too," said Amber. "Let's get down to the beach."

Everyone scrambled away from the bushes and escaped to the safety of the water's edge.

"Look, the cable goes all the way to the bottom of the steps." Charlie followed alongside the creek to where the water rushed over the old wooden retaining wall they called the steps.

Charlie called out, "Marty, you gotta see this." Marty hustled up the path and joined Charlie on the locust log looking down into the narrow crevice between the log and the retaining wall.

"Do you see it, Marty?"

"Yup, it's the end of the cable with a rusty old thing hooked to it."

"It's called a clevis pin. We have one on the back of our lawnmower so we can pull a wagon. It means they planned to hook that cable to something and I'm betting it was this wall."

Marty didn't see the logic behind the idea. "Why would the Nazis want to pull the wall down?"

"I don't think they did. Look, we can't even walk on it it's so slippery. Why is that? And look how each timber is grooved."

Marty held his hand over his face while trying to make sense of it, trying to find answers to Charlie's questions.

"I have a feeling the man without a face had something to do with this," said Charlie. "If he was alive we could have learned so much."

"Charlie, I have no idea if the cable's supposed to pull the wall down. Maybe you're on to something," said Marty.

"Hey, Fam. Before I forget," said Mish. "I found a video game we need to buy. It's called Wolfpack and it's all about operating a U-boat."

"What?" Amber's jaw dropped. Getting the team ready to drive the boat was her job. "That's outstanding," she said.

"I've heard of it, too," said Marty. "I didn't know it was still out."

"Bet. I just found it. It's been around a long time and they've kept updating it. I watched some YouTube videos of the new game and it's so authentic, it's like an actual video of our U-boat. If we can learn to play that game, I think we can learn how to make ours work."

"Seriously," said Charlie. "You mean, diving and torpedoes and everything.

"Yeah, and it's good for five players. I mean you can do it yourself as the Captain, and the game will create avatars for everyone else. But, otherwise, we're a crew—captain, helmsman, dive officer, radio man, and navigator."

"So we play online?" asked Amber.

"Yeah, like MK," said Mish.

"Okay, let's do it," said Marty. "When you've got a Wolfpack account, let everyone know."

<hr/>

The squad turned and headed back along the creek where they would each take a different path toward their homes. Charlie trudged up the hill past the conning tower. He saw the hatch was closed but not locked down. That meant Doubeck was still inside.

As Charlie emerged from the trees at the edge of the bank and stepped into his yard, he saw Rocky making a mess in his sandbox. Charlie set the big red bucket in front of him and looked toward the house to see his mother's face in the window. She waved and he waved back. Meanwhile, Rocky had tossed his red plastic submarine into the bucket and started shoveling sand in until the sub was covered. He lifted a garden hose dribbling a slight stream of water and squirted a bit on Charlie's leg as he did.

"Whatcha' doing, Rocky?" asked Charlie.

"I'm floating my submarine,"

"Ahh, where is it?"

"It sunk cuz I buried it."

Charlie's eyes widened. There was no possible way Rocky knew about the U-boat.

"Where'd you bury it?"

"In my bucket." Rocky spoke with a sense of accomplishment.

Charlie looked into the red bucket, but all he saw was sand.

"It's in there?"

"Uh-huh. Ten, nine, six, three, one," said Rocky, counting down as he lowered the hose into the bucket.

Charlie started to laugh but suddenly caught himself. Rocky's connection between the toy and the real buried U-boat was like a science experiment. He watched the swirling brown water rise in the bucket within an inch of the top, and as he stared, Rocky pulled the hose away.

The sloshing water slowly stilled.

A bubble rose to the surface and popped. Suddenly, a bright red plastic toy submarine jumped up through the murky mix, bobbing upright and proud, floating on its own little pond.

Charlie's mouth fell open and a big smile grew across his face.

"Rocky! That was amazing!" He hugged his dirty, wet little brother. "You're a genius!"

THE LAST U-BOAT

A STEP
CLOSER TO
ANSWERS

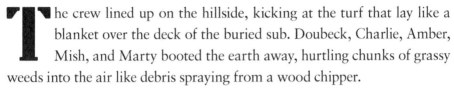

The crew lined up on the hillside, kicking at the turf that lay like a blanket over the deck of the buried sub. Doubeck, Charlie, Amber, Mish, and Marty booted the earth away, hurtling chunks of grassy weeds into the air like debris spraying from a wood chipper.

"Hold it. Hang on," Charlie shouted. "Under the clay here there's nothing but sand."

"Same here," called Marty.

"It's all sand," said Doubeck. He held a shovel in one hand and a clump of grass in the other. Beneath the grass hung a big clod of blue-gray Lake Erie clay. "I mean, the grass and stuff all had dirt and clay under it, but everything below that, it's just sand."

"That's it, then," said Charlie. "Sand doesn't belong up here. The only way to get sand up here is to haul it up from the beach."

Marty walked over to Charlie. "Then you're right. The Nazis planned for the sub to pop out of the sand when water covered it. But that means this whole gully has to fill up. That's a lot of water."

"The storm," said Amber. "Remember the man without a face said he should have stayed home for the storm."

"There have been plenty of storms since the U-boat got buried. It would have happened by now," said Charlie.

"No, it'll take more than just a storm. It has to be totally under water," said Marty. "There's this thing called displacement," he said. "When the U-boat's under water it takes up the space of more than five thousand tons of water. But, it weighs like nine hundred tons. So it floats because it weighs less than the water it displaced."

Everyone nodded, but their faces said they weren't sure.

Marty pushed on. "Okay. So, it would take maybe five hundred tons of sand and dirt to hold the sub down when the water flooded over it."

Charlie wasn't convinced, and not too proud to admit it. "I think it's more complicated. Like how much does sand weigh? How much sand is on top of the sub? How much sand equals five hundred tons?"

"Hang on." Marty raised his hands to hold off the onslaught of questions he figured was about to be released. "A car weighs about a ton, Charlie. There's no way the weight of five hundred cars is laying on top of that sub."

Everyone agreed. If Marty was even close with his math, the U-boat would be unable to resist floating out of its sandy berth.

"You really think that was the plan, Marty?" asked Doubeck.

"It's the only thing that makes sense. Add the weight of the ceiling, the sand and the clay, and they were nowhere near the limit. But there's something else that makes this solution a sure thing, guys." Again, Marty could see the group looking skeptical. "Oh, no. This is something good. It's called specific gravity."

"I've heard of it," said Mish. "What's it got to do with the sub?"

"A lot." Marty wiped his face with his hand as he thought for a moment.

"Doubeck, remember late last summer before Charlie moved in, we had that storm, and the next day the sand bar had those big boulders on it?"

"Yeah."

"And remember you reached down and you moved them out of the way?"

"Cuz we were tripping on them under water," said Amber.

"And how much did they weigh, Mish?" Marty asked.

"I don't know, but I lifted one off the bottom that Doobs couldn't even lift."

"I remember that. You lifted it while it was still under water. But Doubeck tried to lift it *out* of the water," said Marty.

"That's right," said Doubeck. "So what?"

"So, that's specific gravity. It's why things seem to weigh less in water."

"How much less?" asked Charlie.

"'Bout half," said Marty. "It means that when the dirt on the sub is under water, it'll weigh half of what it did when it was dry. It means that sub's going to pop out like a cork.

Doubeck turned and looked at Charlie. "Oh my gosh. It's gonna work."

"But what about the ground that's built up around the conning tower?" asked Mish.

"We could loosen it up at the last minute," said Marty. "Might be a good idea just in case roots have grown around it."

"I'm going down there right now," said Doubeck, and he headed a few feet down the hillside with his shovel to see if he could find the optimal spot to undermine the hull.

Mish had been listening carefully. "Okay, hang on. The only way the Nazis could do that—to make the water come up to here—would be to build a dam this high." She pointed as she held her arm out level. As she spoke, she turned slowly and traced a line across the far side of the gully and to the nearby edge of the cliff that overlooked the lake. There, the retaining wall everyone called the steps emerged from the hillside.

"...and that means the dam would have to start right over there."

"The steps?" said Amber. The revelation hit everyone at about the same time.

"Mish, you nailed it. The steps are a dam," said Marty.

Charlie nodded in agreement. "That means the Nazis built the steps."

"Sheesh, you're amazing Mish," said Doubeck, climbing back up the hill.

Mish didn't look directly at Doubeck, but Amber and Charlie both saw her smile just a little.

"Anything there, Doob?" asked Marty.

"Yeah, there's a greasy black tarp under the clay and I whacked it with the shovel. Pretty sure it's right over the hull. It's all covered with sand and then it's packed with clay." Doubeck dropped the shovel and brushed his hands on his pants. "The sand just poured right out. It wouldn't take us long to open up that whole side. Less than an hour."

"Doubeck, you and I need to figure out how the steps turn into a dam," said Charlie.

"Not just that," said Marty. "But once the sub's floating, we still have to get it out from behind the dam and into the lake."

"Torpedoes!" said Doubeck.

"I knew you were going to say that," said Mish. Everyone laughed.

Marty wanted to make sure there was no misunderstanding. "No torpedoes. Okay, Doubeck? There's got to be another way that doesn't blow shit up. You know the Nazis have to have some engineering solution in place. That's how they roll. Blowing the dam up is a bad idea."

For the next few days, it rained a lot, so the gang took advantage of the time to practice learning how to drive a U-boat. Because the sub wasn't functional, they had to practice the best way they could—with the video game *Wolfpack*—and, for a simulation, it was very real. *Wolfpack*'s animated sub looked exactly like the inside of their own U-boat, except the virtual boat was much bigger.

During the war, the Germans would have stationed two dozen crew members in a full-sized U-boat. But the U-22 crew wouldn't need cooks, security officers, and enough extra people to cover two shifts. Five was probably too few for a real sub, but they didn't need to do all the jobs a crew did during the war. And anyway, it would have to do.

The crew often stayed awake late at night and got up early the next morning to boot up their game consoles, get online and play *Wolfpack* together. The game trained them to use the same gauges and controls that were in the real sub, and it penalized them if they made mistakes.

"Look at the Papenberg meter, Mish. That's the main depth meter. The other one is a fine depth meter. Don't get them mixed up." Amber ordered.

"Got it."

"Call out our depth."

"Five meters."

"Mish, I want to submerge to periscope depth, how much water do we take in?"

"Ahhh. It doesn't say. I don't know."

Amber shook her head so hard her headphones almost fell off. She was feeling the pressure. "Marty, help me out."

"We don't know until we do it because it depends on how much fuel, and crew, and cargo we carry. Just let the water in easy and watch the gauges. It's like steering only we go up and down."

"Nothing to it, right? Doubeck, you there?" Doubeck was on the bow planes and propulsion.

"Here. I'm just listening to you guys adulting."

"Doob, this is serious. Just hold the planes steady. Mish, take her down easy to ten meters."

"Down ten meters."

"I don't like this. We're a sitting duck, half out of the water." The crew could hear the anxiety rising in Amber's voice. "Don't drop below ten, Mish."

"Aye-aye," she replied.

"You really said that?" There was a smirk in Amber's voice.

Mish shot back. "Yes, Captain, I did. I am officially adulting. I said *aye-aye* and I liked it."

"See?" said Doubeck.

Amber whispered into her microphone. "You're so f'ing weird, g."

"*I'm* weird? Have you been listening? Doubeck's right. We're talking to each other like we're different people. It's like freakin' real."

Amber, cross-legged and alone in her room, sitting on pillows stacked in the middle of her bed, sensed a mixture of humility and responsibility wash over her. It lasted only briefly before her attention was called back to the task at hand.

"Ten meters, Captain."

"All right, let's try ten more. Make depth twenty meters."

"Twenty meters," Mish replied, as she tapped the yellow button on her controller.

The needles on the depth meter began to move.

Immediately Amber regretted her order. "Belay that. Maintain five meters."

"Five meters," Mish repeated. The needles on the gauges rose again. "What happened?" she asked.

"Maintain course two-seven-zero, Charlie." Amber ignored Mish's question.

"Course two-seven-zero," he repeated.

"Maintain ten knots."

"Ten knots," Charlie replied.

Amber straightened her back, looked up, and took a deep breath. "Well, I messed up. I just realized I don't know where the bottom is. If we only have fifteen meters I could drive us right into the sand, or a rock pile, or a wreck." Amber was legitimately angry with herself. "My fault, guys. I wasn't ready."

Marty was impressed when Amber caught her own mistake. "It's okay, Amber. We're all learning."

"It's not okay." Her voice sounded shaky. "If I crash this boat we start over. If I crash the real boat we die. So it's *not* okay. "

Marty pushed back. "If you crash your sailboat you could die, too. So you learned how to sail, how to be a great sailor. You learned how to be safe. That's why we're practicing. Come on, you're one of the best sailors around, Amber."

Positive vibes began filling her headset.

"Amber, we're with you."

"You've got this, Amber."

"Vaya, chica."

"Proud to serve with you, Captain."

Then, it grew quiet.

"Amber?" called Charlie.

Amber never acknowledged the praise or Charlie. "Where's the bottom, Marty?" she said.

"Forty meters, Captain."

"Planes down five degrees," she ordered.

"Down five degrees."

"Make our depth twenty meters."

"Depth twenty meters," Mish answered.

"Change course to zero-one-zero."

"Changing course to zero-one-zero. We'll slip off course in the turn, Captain," cautioned Charlie.

"Not under ten knots. We'll lose forward speed as we turn. I don't know how the real boat will handle until we drive it, but I'm betting it's a lot like coming about."

"Fifteen meters"

"What's our heading, Charlie?"

"Three-six-zero."

"Okay, ease it back, don't go past zero-one-zero. Learn to make all your movements smooth."

"Coming up on twenty meters."

"Okay. Maintain twenty meters. All stop." Amber immediately took a deep breath that everyone could hear in their headsets.

"All stop," repeated Charlie.

"Marty, keep your eye on our depth. Let's see if we can figure out how to get to neutral buoyancy. Zero bubble."

"Oh, yeah. We're already starting to float," he said. "We're tilting up from the bow."

"Do we have bow tanks?"

"Yes, we do," said Doubeck. "Left and right."

"There *is* no left and right," said Amber, and she waited for Doubeck's response.

"Sorry, Captain. Port and starboard."

"It's okay, Doobs. I couldn't resist."

"No problem," he said. "I want to get it right, too."

"You're doing great. Now, blow some ballast aft so we can watch the tilt meter. Easy does it."

Doubeck tapped the blue button on his controller and the tilt meter dropped like a rock.

"I said easy, Doubeck. Charlie, all ahead fifteen knots."

"Ahead fifteen knots."

"Marty, look at the gauges, the engine's acting wonky. What's going on? Planes up ten degrees."

"Up ten degrees."

"When we're level, Doubeck, use the planes to maintain depth. We'll slow down again and see what happens. It's really hard to maintain depth when we're not moving. Charlie, I said give me fifteen knots. Doubeck, let's keep doing this until we learn how to keep our balance."

"Amber?" It was Charlie again.

"Hang on, Charlie. Marty, question. How deep is Lake Erie?"

"Ahhhh, Lake Erie? Well the middle's roughly nine miles off the beach. Maybe a hundred-fifty feet. That'd be forty-five to fifty meters."

"Yikes, that's shallow."

"There's something else, Amber…Captain. We're maybe thirty feet tall from the keel to the periscope. To hide, to completely submerge, we'll have to be a half-mile offshore. The only place we can get closer is in the channel to the harbor. The maps say that's dredged to thirty-five feet and barely wide enough to turn around."

"So we can't park the boat on the bottom?"

"Nope. It could jam our vents—including the toilet. We're going to have to drop anchor at just the right spot and use a boat to get back and forth."

"Marty, you need to think about that problem. Where do we hide in the daytime?"

"Amber?" Charlie sounded anxious.

"One second, Charlie, okay? Marty, what about if we wanted to float as close to shore as we could get? You know, like a regular boat."

"Well, we probably draw six or eight feet at the bow, maybe ten in the middle. The deepest approach to shore is probably right in front of Charlie's house where we swim. The gully the creek cut goes out under water a long way."

"I'll bet we could almost lay the nose on the beach like a pontoon boat. You think the Nazis knew that, Marty?"

"I sure do. They beached U-boats during the war, I read about it."

"Amber?" Now, Charlie's voice had a real edge to it.

"Yes, Charlie."

"We're not moving. You forgot to tell us to close the exhaust vents and turn the diesels off before we dove. We just ruined the engines."

THE LAST U-BOAT

RACCOON
BAY

"**S**tewart! Get ass in here." Oleg Petrosian had a habit of screaming from his office instead of walking out to the docks and speaking like a normal human being.

"One second, Mr. Petrosian." Stewart had just lifted a fifty-horse out-board onto the transom of a small Boston Whaler and he still had to tighten the last clamp.

Petrosian didn't impress Stewart. Oleg had a much different work ethic than his cousin, Armen Daglian, who sold the marina to him at the end of last season. Petrosian had explained that he and Daglian grew up together in Armenia but they weren't close anymore. He said Armen didn't even stay to hand him the keys. Instead, he arranged for Oleg to pick them up at the Shore Good Diner, a half mile up the marina access road where it met the highway.

"Now, Stewart! I not have all day."

As the new owner of Raccoon Bay Marina, Oleg left all the real work to eighteen-year-old Stewart, and spent most of his time on his phone, secluded in his office.

That was just fine with Stewart. He loved his job. Though Petrosian tended to be unpredictable—he'd treat Stewart kindly, bring him lunch, maybe shove a wad of cash in his hand after a hard day. But a couple of days later, he'd be all over Stewart for some stupid little thing.

The best days were the ones when Oleg let Stewart drive his thirty-two-foot Nordic Tug, *Ararat*. Stewart planned to ask Petrosian to let him take the *Ararat* to Canada, not a hard slog for the boat's diesel. Cruising at ten knots put the beaches of Long Point within two hours.

Swanson appeared in the office doorway before Petrosian's shouts stopped reverberating off the walls.

"Stewart. Did I call? Is so long I don't remember." Petrosian hadn't yet mastered sarcasm in English. But he was working on it every day.

"Sorry. I was just hooking the Merc onto that Whaler. It's ready."

"You fix Merc?"

"Yeah, a little rubber ball got stuck in the water intake. It had a bell in it."

"Was for cat playing maybe? That weird thing to find."

Stewart shrugged. "I'm just glad it wasn't a cat. That would've been messy."

Petrosian's eyes suddenly bulged, his cheeks turned red and he burst out laughing like Stewart had never heard him laugh before.

"That funny. Listen, Stewart, friend of mine come later to look at boats. I want you show him what we got. You do for me?"

"Sure, I can do that."

"If he want go on water, you take him, okay?"

"Okay."

"That it. Thanks, Stewart."

Oleg had dismissed him, but Stewart had something on his mind. He stepped toward Petrosian's messy desk. Crumpled McDonald's wrappers, paper clips, scribbled notes, a moldy remnant of bread, and a stack of unopened bills represented only the top layer of garbage covering its surface. The stack of unpaid bills he remembered from his job interview a month earlier.

"Ah, Mr. Petrosian. You know how I take the *Ararat* over to the harbor, to McCutcheon's for parts and stuff?"

"Yah."

"Could I take it to Canada sometime? On a clear night, I can see lights over there and I'd just like to say I did it."

"Whoa! That big trip." Petrosian's eyes darted around the room. "You think you can drive boat into middle of big lake?"

"Oh, sure. I know I can."

"And when you want go?"

"Since I have Saturdays off, I was thinking any Saturday the weather's good."

"So, I go out with you first, see how you handle boat."

"Of course."

"Okay, we talk." Petrosian looked away and Stewart took that to mean the conversation was over. He didn't get a yes, but he didn't get a no, either.

Stewart headed back to hook up the Merc's fuel lines and steering cables. He'd only taken a few steps before he heard someone call his name.

"What up, Stewart?" Doubeck leaned his bike alongside the marina's workshop and hustled down the dock toward his friend. "Just wanted to see where you're hanging out, dude."

"Hey, Doubeck. Well, this is it—Raccoon Bay Marina."

Doubeck took a good look around while Stewart pointed out the facilities. It had been a few years since he last saw the cove and things looked a lot different to him.

"Very cool. So, what do you do here, dude?"

"Everything."

"Like what?"

Stewart pointed toward a floating boardwalk. "I added that forty feet of dock last week."

"Wow. That's beautiful. You still working on engines?"

"Yeah. Just fixed that one on the back of the Whaler. Come on over while we talk. I still have some lines to hook up."

"What about diesel, Stewart? Have you ever worked on any diesels?"

"Uh huh, Mr. Petrosian's boat has a big diesel. It was a repo the owner had trashed. I got it pretty much fully restored now. Wanna see?"

They stopped beside a beautiful deep blue tug with a smart, stylish cabin and plenty of room below for the galley and berths. Swanson took Doubeck through the companionway and below, where he opened the engine compartment behind the stairs that descended from the wheelhouse. He revealed the engine like he was unveiling a painting.

"That, Doubeck, is a two-hundred twenty-horse Cummins diesel."

The engine glistened bright red in the light of a single overhead bulb. There was not a drop of dirt, grease, or oil to be seen.

"It's new?"

"Nope. I cleaned the whole thing up and pretty much rebuilt it. It was all rusty, and ugly. Pretty sad."

Doubeck was amazed. He knew the guy worked on his own car. But he had no idea that Stewart Swanson, the big, dumb, neighborhood bully, had such an aptitude for mechanics, and such skill. His desire to bring Stewart onto the U-boat crew was growing stronger. But the risk was huge.

Doubeck watched while Stewart hooked up the fuel and control lines on the outboard. He was still hoping to find an opening to invite Stewart to look over the sub.

"Stewart!" It was Petrosian yelling from his office.

"Yes, sir?"

"Come here and meet my good friend."

"Hey, if you gotta go, no problem," said Doubeck.

"Hang out a while. This won't take long. You can chill out on the dock."

"You got it. Thanks."

Doubeck knew no one in the squad had the expertise to get the engines started, but it sure looked to him like Stewart did. Plus, they'd found another diesel engine in the Deep Room, and they still hadn't figured out how it might fit into the Nazis' plans. As he watched Swanson head back to the marina building and Petrosian's office, Doubeck felt more strongly than ever that Stewart could hold the key to unlock all the remaining mysteries. But it would only work if the crew dealt with this responsible, skilled, and hard-working Stewart, not Stewart the jerk. Stewart the jerk would blow their cover in an instant, just to do it.

Doubeck had put himself in a tough position, acting on his own, and he felt the pinch. He had to be very sure before he shared the secret. Even then, his friends might see it as a betrayal.

"Yes, sir," Stewart said, as he approached the two men standing in the store. Oleg and his guest were both large, unshaven, black-haired men wearing almost identical clothes. Each wore a pale blue turtleneck with gold necklaces and shiny black polyester dress pants. Petrosian sported a leaf-green Orvis vest he was unable to button, and the stranger wore a plaid sport coat. As he approached them, Stewart was slapped by the pungent smell of after shave.

Petrosian put his hand on Stewart's shoulder. "Stewart, this my old friend Frik Nazarian. Say hello."

"Frik?" asked Stewart. The man nodded.

"Frik?" Stewart repeated, looking at Petrosian.

Petrosian interrupted. "Yes, Frik Nazarian. I said this. Is good Armenian name. Now, say hello."

"Hello, ah, Mister Nazarian."

"Hello, Mister Stewart. Is good to meet."

"There, good," said Petrosian. "Now we go."

Petrosian pushed Stewart back toward the doorway. Stewart obliged, walking back to the docks with the two Armenians in tow. As he crossed the threshold, he caught a glimpse of Doubeck coming off the far pier and heading around the building toward the bathrooms, like a customer. That was good, he thought. The Armenians didn't need to know he had a friend visiting him at work.

"Stewart, show Frik boats. He want new boat." Stewart nodded. "Frik, see blue boat. That *Ararat*. Is my boat. You like name *Ararat?*"

"Is big boat. Nice looking. Good name for boat."

"Yes. Listen, Stewart. I call boat *Ararat* for mountain in Armenia where Noah Ark found."

"Noah's Ark?"

"You don't know from Bible?" asked Frik.

Stewart turned and smiled. "Oh, I know the story. I just didn't know they found it."

Frik saw this as a teaching moment.

"Yes, they find...they find the bone of it. This part." Frik spread the stubby fingers of his massive hands across his chest as he searched for the word.

"The boobs?" asked Petrosian.

Frik looked embarrassed. "Not boobs. I no have boobs. Oleg, you don't change. I see you after five years and you still *apush.*"

"Then say right word, cousin," Petrosian pleaded.

"I think you mean ribs," offered Stewart.

"Yes! Ribs." Nazarian lit up and he repeatedly slapped Stewart on the back. "The bone part."

Stewart smiled politely.

"Ribs was exact size to be ark," said Petrosian. "Maybe you go Armenia and make sail again."

Stewart took the little joke as a compliment.

"Frik, this boy take *Ararat* when it stinking pile of shit and make it beautiful, and comfort. He good, this one."

"If Oleg say you good, you very, very good because he is *apush*—Armenian idiot. Not say nice thing ever. So you know is good he say this."

Stewart thought this might be a good time to try his salesman's wings. "Do you want to take a ride around the cove in one of the boats?"

Frik looked past Stewart at Oleg and Stewart saw Oleg furrow his brow and shake his head ever so slightly.

"No, Mr. Stewart. I want go fish."

"Sure. We could do that. We'll get you a license. There's gear on Mr. Petrosian's boat and we can go any time."

"Tonight, then."

"Ahh, I've been here since six this morning. I...I promised my mother that I would do some painting. I'm headed out at 6 p.m. "

"Then we leave at sunset time. Is 8:30."

"I'm sorry, I just can't make it tonight. But I can go tomorrow."

Immediately, Frik showed the strangest look on his face. His dark eyes were pinned to Stewart's, but he showed absolutely no emotion for a good ten seconds. Stewart thought, just for a moment, that Frik was going to suddenly choke him or something. Then, in an instant, Frik was animated again.

"Okay, then. Some other time." It sounded insincere.

Frik turned his back on Stewart and looked at Oleg.

"Do you have flares, Oleg? Coast Guard say I need flares or get big fine."

Then he winked. Stewart couldn't see it because Frik had his back to him. But Doubeck was standing two aisles away, watching everything from behind a display rack. He had wandered in unseen through the open side door near the bathrooms.

"How many you want, Frik?" asked Petrosian, pulling a card of three flares from the shelf beside him.

"How much?"

Oleg looked at the sticker on the package "Ten-fifty for three."

"Okay, I take three," he said.

Petrosian looked at Stewart. "Ring him up, Stewart."

Stewart stepped around the counter and pressed the keys on the old cash register. Frik Nazarian already had his wallet out and held a twenty in his hand. Before he handed it over he pointed to a display on the wall behind Stewart.

"Could I also see key chain on wall. Orange one with floater."

Frik exchanged a glance with Petrosian. "I see you later, Frik," he said, and he walked back to his office.

As Stewart turned, Frik slid a bill across the counter and let it drop to the floor at Stewart's feet. Stewart was stretching to reach the key chain and never saw the bill fall.

He looped the chain around an index finger, lifted it from the rack, and turned back to Nazarian, handing it to him. Nazarian looked over the key chain as Stewart made change for the flares and closed the cash drawer.

"I'll take two of these. Just take out of my change."

"Okay," Stewart secured a second key chain. "That's fourteen. I have nine-fifty. Another five would do it."

"Another five? But I give you one hundred dollar bill."

"No, you gave me a twenty."

Frik's indecipherable look returned.

"Sir," Stewart swallowed hard. "You gave me a twenty-dollar bill. The flares were ten-fifty…"

"What going on?" demanded Nazarian.

"…that leaves nine-fifty."

"You cheating me. You think you pull something?"

"No, I'm not." Stewart started taking shallow breaths. His face was becoming bright red. "You only gave me a twenty. I'm sure of it. I never saw a hundred. No one's *ever* paid with a hundred."

Nazarian lunged across the counter and pinched both of Stewart's arms just above the elbow. Stewart winced.

"I want money now or I call police."

Stewart collected himself and assumed a zen-like composure. He took a deep breath, his shoulders relaxed and he showed Nazarian a look of such ambivalence to his predicament that Nazarian let go of his arms.

Stewart called toward Petrosian's office. "Mr. Petrosian? Can you please come out here?"

Nazarian stuck his fat lower lip out with indignation and they waited for Petrosian to appear.

"What you need? Frik, what's going on?"

"He is stealing hundred dollars from me."

"What?"

"Mr. Nazarian says he gave me a hundred-dollar bill but he didn't—he only gave me a twenty."

Petrosian moved around to stand beside his employee, a gesture that Stewart appreciated.

"I give hundred for twenty dollar worth of crap and he say I owe him five more dollar. He is crook."

"Stewart, show all pockets open."

Stewart dutifully agreed and emptied everything, including his shirt pocket.

"Now who's *apush*, Frik?" Petrosian told his friend off, looked at Stewart and smiled. As he did, something caught his eye. Something on the floor.

"Stewart, pick up." Petrosian pointed at Stewart's feet. There lay a one-hundred-dollar bill. Stewart brought it up and set it on the glass counter in front of him.

Petrosian wagged his index finger.

"This not look good for you, Stewart," he said.

"Why not?" Stewart asked.

"If you stand on money to hide, then at right time you pick up."

Nazarian pulled out his phone. "I'm calling nine-one-nine."

"You not call nobody, Frik."

"Look. I didn't do anything. I never saw the money until Mr. Petrosian spotted it. It probably just fell out when you handed me the twenty," said Stewart.

"That right, Frik. You make accident big deal."

"And you still owe another five dollars for the key chains," said Stewart.

Stewart's refusal to back down struck Nazarian funny and he started laughing. Stewart looked at Petrosian and he started laughing, too.

"I like you, Mr. Stewart. You tough guy. You can take it."

Petrosian leaned toward Stewart's ear. "I think tonight, you and I take Frik to fish, this be forgot, okay?" Stewart clenched his jaw.

As the two Armenians walked out of the store and back to Nazarian's car, Doubeck came out from behind the displays.

"You were set up, man. I saw the whole thing."

Stewart scowled. "That guy's shady."

"Oh, they were both in on it. Your boss winked at him. He watched when the guy dropped the bill beside you."

"You saw that?"

"Yes. I'm telling you, they wanted to make you owe them this fishing trip."

"Yeah?"

"You gonna go?"

"I have to. I need this job."

"Listen, I gotta talk to you about something important. Is there a time tomorrow?"

"Can I call you when he leaves? He goes to his club for cards and then he'll be gone all afternoon."

Stewart had the *Ararat* ready to go at 8:30 p.m. when the Armenians arrived.

To Stewart, the only disconcerting part of boating at night was the quiet. Sometimes it got creepy. He had the feeling it would not be a quiet night.

Nazarian had insisted on a specific heading where he claimed he knew for sure they would find fish. It was nowhere near the mountains. That's what the local fishermen called their perpetual hot spot, a group of deep holes that looked like inverted mountains on the fish finder. Instead, *Ararat* ran west about fifteen miles and then north, ten miles more, out to the middle of the lake—over a sandy bottom, with no structure. It was a terrible spot for fishing. As he neared the coordinates, Stewart slowed the boat.

"I think we need go that way just a little," said Frik as he pointed into the darkness with an open bottle of vodka.

"We very close."

Stewart looked over at Petrosian who was sitting in a deck chair against the opposite gunwale. Petrosian tilted his head, lifted his palms, and shrugged his shoulders.

Frik peered out into the darkness.

"Look, someone lost life jacket," he shouted.

Something was floating in the water. "It might be a body, grab a flashlight from under that seat," said Stewart.

The Armenians leaned over the rail as Stewart stayed at the helm. Oleg grabbed a boat hook and lifted the orange life preserver. There was no body.

"False alarm," said Frik. "Is caught on fishing string."

Frik lifted the life jacket from the water, wrapped the monofilament line it was caught on around his huge hands, and broke it without much effort.

Stewart held the boat's position while he tried to make sense of the fact the Armenians had never bothered to pick up a fishing pole on their fishing trip but had navigated out to find a lifejacket that had been left anchored in this location in the very middle of Lake Erie.

"Why not keep," said Petrosian. "Can use on your boat."

"I think so, too," said Frik. "Okay, we go back now."

THE LAST U-BOAT

MEETING
THE ENEMY

"**W**here you been? You texted me a half hour ago." Charlie said."

"Sorry I'm late. I'm trying to get my headset on."

Doubeck's trip to Raccoon Bay had taken him longer than expected, so he was the last to log in. The crew saw him arrive when his icon popped up on the *Wolfpack* game's crew list.

In his bedroom, two hundred yards across the creek from the LeClair's house, Doubeck spoke through the *Wolfpack* game like they were all in the same room.

"Okay. I'm good. So, listen, I went over to see Stewart."

"Did you say Stewart?" asked Amber. "Gack."

"Yeah, he works over at Raccoon Bay Marina and I wanted to talk to him."

"What for, dude?" asked Marty.

Doubeck anticipated an interrogation, so his answers were ready.

"Well, we've looked at those diesel engines and we can't figure out what to do with them, how they work…"

"Wait a second," said Mish. "You didn't say anything to Stewart, did you?"

"Hell, no."

Speaking Stewart's name was like lighting a fuse. Their headsets exploded with reactions.

"Thank goodness."

"That's good."

"Nobody likes him."

"He's such an asshole."

"Hey…hey, just chill. Sheesh." Doubeck paused and took a breath before moving on. It was the reaction he expected. "You don't know him like I do. He's just a little insecure, that's all. He doesn't know how to relate to people."

"That's for sure," said Amber.

"He relates by pushing you around," said Charlie.

"Dudes, let me finish, okay?" He waited for silence. "I need you to trust me on this. But, if you're gonna get all salty about it, okay. It saves me from having to worry about how I'm gonna tell him there's a U-boat buried in Charlie's backyard."

"Bullshit! What are you talking about?" said Charlie.

"What I'm talking about is this. Is there anybody here who can get those engines going? Anybody?" Doubeck waited. "Bueller?"

No response.

"I didn't think so." Doubeck took another deep breath. "Stewart works at a marina. With boats. He slays as a diesel mechanic. I saw it for myself. Anyway, I'm supposed to go over there this afternoon and I'd like you guys to come with me."

The crew continued to object. They reminded Doubeck about their history of encounters with Stewart—how he had abused them verbally and physically, and threatened them.

"Look, when I said you didn't know him like I do, I meant it. He and I share a vibe. I think he feels threatened by you. You're all smart, and I get the feeling he thinks he's just mid. But the guy's a real CEO with mechanics. He really is. I'm telling you, we need him—or I'm not sure we're ever going to launch the sub."

"I can't believe you're on that jerk's side," said Mish.

"Come on, Mish. I'm on *our* side. I'm trying to tell you he can help, and if he doesn't help, we're no worse off."

"We're worse off if he turns us in to the Coast Guard," said Marty.

"Or calls the cops," said Mish.

"What if he starts pushing Charlie around again?" said Amber.

"Listen, don't worry 'bout me," said Charlie. "I want this to work out as much as you do. Maybe more. But I don't trust Stewart."

"Me either," said Amber.

"He's such a doosh," said Mish.

"But," Charlie said. "I do trust Doubeck."

His comment ended the debate.

"Thanks, dude," said Doubeck. "I know we're all pressed. But we can't let this fail just because we didn't try. I mean, I thought a lot about it. The only person we know who can possibly get those engines working is Stewart. That's why I have to go over there."

He waited for comments, but he heard only the game's background sound effects. "Who's coming with me?"

Still, no one spoke. The bad feelings for Stewart ran deep.

"Okay, fine. Well, he's going to call me after lunch. I'll text everyone the time and place in case you change your mind. Right now I gotta blast. See ya."

"Hang on," said Marty.

"What?"

"Aren't you going to practice with us?"

"What's the point? Without engines, we've got nothing."

Doubeck took some comfort in knowing he could put off the decision to reveal the secret to Swanson until the very last moment in case the discussion fell apart. However, the moment of truth was fast approaching. The text Doubeck sent an hour later was simple and direct.

Raccoon Bay marina 2:30 p.m.

Doubeck and Swanson sat side-by-side on the lid of a white steel dock box, talking and watching the boats in the cove glide past the marina. Doubeck nervously pulled the fluff from the end of a frayed rope and tossed it into the air.

Stewart's story about his trip with Oleg and Frik was sick. For sure he was telling the truth, but Doubeck couldn't make sense of it.

"Maybe there were drugs packed in the life jacket," said Doubeck.

Stewart shrugged. "I don't think so. After he took it out of the water, he handed it to me before we got underway. I looked it over real good. It was buckled and strapped like it just came off the shelf. It seemed like a normal Type 3 life jacket. If someone packed anything in it, I'd have felt it. Plus, it still had a price tag on it."

"Why'd he give it to you?"

"I guess he didn't want it to blow away. We were running full-out, and he picked it up when the wind knocked it off the seat beside him."

Doubeck put a hand to his chin. "How did he find it? Did he like know it had been left there?"

"Sure looked that way. He kept checking an app on his phone."

"And it wasn't just floating loose? You're sure it was anchored?"

Stewart raised his hands, palms up. "Yeah, he pulled the line in and snapped it. I saw him do it?"

"Sounds like they wanted to see if they could find it in the dark. Like maybe it had one of those GPS chips on it, or they knew the coordinates."

"Well, we were in the middle of the lake and he steered me right to it."

"Yeah. I'd call it a test, Stewart. I think they were testing you to see if you'd freak."

"Maybe. It just started out like a fishing trip."

"Just a fishing trip? You ever see Godfather Two?"

"Nah. Never did," said Stewart.

"That's probably a good thing," said Doubeck, as he tossed a big tuft of rope fibers into the breeze. "Well, listen. I said I had something I wanted to talk to you about."

"Oh, yeah. Like something important?"

"It kind of is. You know the geeks?"

"You mean the dipshits? What about 'em?" Stewart tipped his head like he had zero interest.

"Well, they might be coming over here."

"What for?"

"Cuz we need your help."

Stewart squinted and wrinkled his nose. "My help?"

"Yeah, and you gotta know it wasn't easy for them to ask, either, because they're pretty sure you don't like them."

"They're right."

"Well, maybe you could cut 'em a break and just listen."

The sound of footsteps on the boardwalk interrupted. They turned to see the crew coming toward them. All of them.

Doubeck could easily read their attitudes. Their hands were shoved into their pockets, their eyes looking down. Reluctance screamed from their faces, frozen like solemn portraits.

"Thanks, guys. I'm glad you're here," said Doubeck.

"Did you tell him?" asked Charlie.

"Tell me what?" Stewart checked his watch.

Doubeck looked up at his friends.

"Go on," said Amber. "We talked, and we agree with you."

Stewart stood and took a step back like he was about to leave. "What's this all about?"

Doubeck took a deep breath. "Well, we found a boat. It's at Charlie's house and it's a big boat. It's historic."

Stewart studied the faces around him. They showed zero enthusiasm, and that seemed very odd.

"If it's historic and important that's good, right?" he asked.

"Yeah, it's all good, except it has diesel engines and we can't figure them out. We'd like to know how to start them, or even find out if they will start."

"Engines? There's more than one?"

"Ahhhhh, yeah. Two," said Marty.

Stewart looked at Charlie. "Is this like your family's boat?"

Charlie had expected a confrontation, and when Stewart spoke to him, he recoiled. But the insults never came. No pushing, no verbal assault. It struck Charlie as the first time in a month Stewart had spoken to him without calling him 'Skid Marks.' Maybe there really had been a change in him. Maybe Doubeck had it right.

Charlie swallowed hard. "See, we discovered this boat, but it's still hidden. My parents don't even know about it."

"Do they know they have a car?" Stewart asked, grinning at Doubeck.

Doubeck shook his head. "Yeah, I know, you got jokes. But Charlie's right. You could walk by it maybe a hundred times and never see it."

"Why don't you tell your parents? Did you steal it or something?"

Charlie waved his hand dismissively. "No. I'm trynna say...this is something I want to do for me—for all of us, Stewart. If we can get this boat going, then they'll be the first to know. But I don't want them to help. I don't want them to be worried and interfere. I just wanna do this myself."

Stewart looked at Doubeck, and Doubeck nodded.

"Listen, Stewart," said Charlie. "We'd like you to come over, take a look, and tell us if you think you can bring it back to life."

Stewart folded his arms over his chest. "I don't know. You're saying you have a boat—it's gotta be a big boat if it's got twin fucking diesels—it's at your house, and your parents don't know about it?"

"Yeah, it's at Charlie's house," said Doubeck.

Stewart looked at him with skepticism written all over his face. "What's going on, Doubeck?"

"It's just what we said. This boat is very special, and we've been trying to keep it a secret until we can get it seaworthy and surprise everyone."

"Plus," said Charlie looking around at the faces of his crew. "We want this to be our boat, not something our parents gave us permission to do."

"Well, somebody's gotta own it. So' you're going to need to register it with the state of Pennsylvania."

"We have to tell the state?" Marty asked.

"Duh, yeah," said Stewart. "Wait. It's not salvage? I mean, it's not under water is it?"

"Not yet," said Charlie.

"Listen, I'm workin a lotta hours. But I could come over Saturday morning around 8:30." He looked at Doubeck and shrugged. "That okay?"

"That's perfect. Thanks, dude. Based on what you showed me at the marina, I think you're gonna love this."

The crew looked stunned. Doubeck's gamble might actually pay off.

Stewart turned and walked away, mumbling under his breath. "Yeah, we'll see,"

Saturday morning, the crew gathered around the manhole, where they had already opened the hatch to the conning tower. They were uncharacteristically quiet as they waited and considered their next moves. After all, this was a big deal. It would be the first time they had revealed the U-boat's discovery to an outsider, and the outsider, in this case, happened to be someone none of them liked or trusted. But, if he didn't give them up, and if he didn't freak out, he could be very helpful.

Promptly at 8:30, Stewart appeared on the path beside the creek bed. They called from the hillside for him to come up and meet them.

"Isn't the boat down here?" he shouted. "The water's down here, you know."

They waved for him to come up the hill.

"What the heck is a boat doing up there? Is it in your driveway, or what?"

Marty answered. "It's hidden like Doubeck said. We'll take you to it, but you've gotta come up this way."

The scowl on Stewart's face, clearly visible as he climbed the hill, showed he'd already tired of the cloak-and-dagger. As he approached the crew, he spoke only to Doubeck, ignoring the others.

"What's up, Doober. Where's this boat you're talking about?"

He pointed at the manhole. "We get to it though here. Follow me."

Stewart shot him some nasty side-eye.

Doubeck let it go. He handed Stewart a flashlight and climbed into the conning tower shaft without waiting for a question or objection.

"You coming?"

Stewart checked the faces of each of the others. Satisfied they were acting in good faith and hadn't planned to murder him, he entered the tube.

"You gotta be fuckin kidding me. There's a boat in the sewer? This better be good." His voice echoed metallic and cold against the steel.

The only response was the squeak of sneakers on the ladder's rungs as the rest of the team followed behind. Regardless of his immediate misgivings, it would be a matter of moments before their new confidant would either approve of their mission or scuttle it.

When they reached the floor, Doubeck stepped forward into the control room area, keeping his flashlight down, both to help Swanson find places he could safely put his feet, and to prevent him from seeing his surroundings until the moment was right. At the periscope, he stopped. Stewart stood barely three steps behind him. Doubeck's light shone in his face, so Stewart shielded his eyes. "I always thought this was a sewer down here," he said. "Doesn't smell like a sewer, though. I smell oil. Where's the boat?"

"I'll show you," said Doubeck. He switched off his flashlight, reached up, and turned on the LED lantern they'd hung on an overhead cable.

Stewart looked around at the maze of pipes, gauges, switches, and valves. He turned full circle, and when he again faced Doubeck, his eyes were bulging and his mouth hung wide open.

Doubeck grabbed the handles on the periscope, snapped them down, and spun the eyepiece in Stewart's direction. "Welcome aboard, Stewart. How would you like to be chief engineering officer on the last U-boat?"

THE LAST U-BOAT

GUN RUNNING

"**E**verything in the U-boat runs off these batteries." Marty tried to explain the complex power distribution system to Doubeck as they knelt in the hold. He trained his flashlight on a stack of black boxes connected by cables. Each box was topped by copper bars that made the space look like it held a giant glockenspiel. Overhead, the cables traveled first to steel cabinets with handles marked *Ein* and *Aus*, on and off, and from there, wires spread out into the darkened boat in every direction.

Marty looked toward the ceiling and brushed his hair back. "All these wires probably feed the lights."

"Yeah," said Doubeck. "But not just the lights. Anything with a motor—like compressors, pumps, fans—everything needs a wire, dude." He opened the latch on a panel and looked inside. "Man, this shit is complicated."

Marty nodded. "Well, Stewart's heading this way. Maybe he can figure it all out."

Doubeck smiled. "I'll bet he didn't sleep all night. He was completely blown away yesterday."

Stewart arrived ready to work. The shock had worn off. He had dropped his attitude, and he began to hyper-focus on the U-boat and its inner workings. Machines were his sweet spot. And the U-boat, after all, was just a big machine with some room for a crew.

He started the day examining the engine room, aft. By the middle of the afternoon, he had made it to the control room, amidships.

Soon, he appeared on the metal grate above Doubeck and Marty, smelling of oil. He set a rolled-up rag carefully on the small tabletop beside the periscope.

Doubeck stood in the cramped hold, the upper half of his body rose just above the metal deck into the control room. He turned when Stewart approached, pulled himself up, and sat on the deck.

Stewart wiped his face with a clean rag as he spoke. "Guys, I'm done. I need to head home now. I'm working at the marina tomorrow 'til three. How 'bout I come back after work?"

"We'll be here," said Marty.

Doubeck leaned back against a bulkhead. "Stewart, you've been here pretty much all day. So, what do you think?"

Stewart handed Doubeck his flashlight and wiped blue-black grease off his hands. "What do I think?" He snorted and started grinning. "I think it's about the most fucking awesome incredible thing I've ever seen in my life."

Doubeck started shouting and jumped to his feet. "Yes! Yes, it is! I told you. I told you, you son of a bitch. Didn't I tell you?" Stewart grinned and just kept nodding as Doubeck slapped his back and laughed.

"Listen, guys. I know I can fix this boat. I mean the engines look pretty good. There are some problems with the electric motors. The terminals on the panel to the batteries are all corroded. Plus, I saw rust on the ductwork coming off the manifolds, and almost every gasket has to be replaced. You can't have carbon monoxide problems in a sub—it'll kill ya. I could install battery-powered CO detectors, though, come to think of it. Oh, and I want to mount waterproof GoPros on the hull so we can see underwater."

Stewart pulled a small notebook out of his shirt pocket. He flipped the cover over, along with the first few pages, and started reading from his notes.

Doubeck and Marty sat wide-eyed at Stewart's command of the situation. They looked at each other, grinning as Stewart wrapped up his to-do list.

"Yeah, we need all-new batteries. We should use car batteries, like three dozen at least. These old batteries would work, but they have to be filled with sulfuric acid, and that makes poison gas when they run. Nowadays, car batteries are sealed, so they're safer. More amp-hours, too."

"I figure it'll take five to ten grand," said Stewart. There followed a moment of silence.

Doubeck rubbed his neck. "What?"

"But we don't have any money," said Marty.

"Actually, I think you do," Stewart said.

Doubeck stared quizzically. Stewart picked the rag up from the tabletop. He unfolded it and held it out for Doubeck to see. A German Luger pistol glowed softly like a bar of silver in the near darkness of their surroundings.

"Yikes. Where'd you find that?" asked Doubeck.

"There's a whole crate of 'em. Maybe more. You wouldn't believe what's in that hold. I haven't checked the internet yet, but I'd guess they're probably worth at least a couple thousand each."

Marty peeked at the weapon, his head squeezing in between Doubeck and Swanson. Marty gasped, raised his hands and started toward the crew quarters. "Guys. I'm going to walk away now."

"Is that normal?" asked Stewart.

"Yeah," said Doubeck. "That's Marty. He's normally paranoid."

"Okay, if you say so." Stewart shrugged. "Oh, and this is important. There's an envelope with paperwork on top of the box. It has all the serial numbers so you can prove they're the real thing. They're in such good shape people aren't going to believe they're real." Stewart picked up the clean Luger.

"See? This pistol was completely covered in grease so it looks brand-new. Heck, it *is* brand-new, it's never been out of the packing. It's so clean, though, a collector might not even believe it's real without the paperwork."

He wrapped the pistol in the rag and handed it to Doubeck. Then he opened his wallet and pulled out a piece of paper the size of a dollar bill.

"This is a deposit slip for my checking account. If you want, you can pawn the gun or sell it and Zelle the money into my account. Then, I'll buy what we need. I have all the catalogs."

Doubeck held the Luger with both hands like he was holding a baby kitten. He just stared at it wide-eyed, and then his eyes rose to the deposit slip.

"Oh, and there's this," said Stewart. "It's a boat registration application

I picked up at work. I already filled out most of it. You guys can finish it up and I'll send it in with the application fee—probably a hundred bucks." Stewart gave the guys a thumbs-up. He moved toward the ladder but stopped and turned around.

"By the way, I'm going to quit my job, so hold out for all the guap you can get. Keeping this boat in condition is gonna be a full-time job. I'd like it to be my job if you'll let me—but I gotta live on something. Mr. Petrosian, my boss, he's getting strange. I think he's got something illegal going on."

Doubeck's eyes widened. "You serious?"

"'Fraid so. I mean, that life jacket thing? That was way too weird."

"Okay, dude. Be safe. We'll figure out where to sell the guns and I'll text you as soon as the money's deposited."

"Thanks, Doubeck. I mean that. Thanks for bringing me into the fam. You were right."

"I was right?"

"Yeah. You guys are cooler than I thought. Way cooler." Stewart offered a fist bump to Doubeck, who smiled. Doubeck thought it might have been the first time he'd ever seen him really smile.

"A damn submarine. I would *not* have believed it," said Stewart. "No fuckin way."

Charlie's phone vibrated on his bed. He muted his laptop and picked it up. It was from Doubeck:

> *Found place to sell our antiques.*
> As You Were *on Perry Blvd*
> *OK? LMK*

Charlie texted back:

> *Monday?*

Doubeck replied:

> *KK TTYL*

Monday morning, Charlie and Doubeck walked into the military surplus store, As You Were. Racks of merchandise on every wall surrounded a spacious open area with heavy oak tables filling the floor space. Their eyes became overwhelmed by the ubiquitous camouflage in green-brown, blue-black and white, and even more in sandy desert tones. Once they adjusted to their surroundings, though, military hardware seemed to emerge from the background.

There were knives with matte-black, foot-long blades, machetes the size of tennis rackets, folding shovels, and water purification stills. Charlie counted a half-dozen different ways to start a fire without matches, and about everything you could need to fight a war—except firearms and explosives.

"Can I help you, men?"

The boys turned toward the skinny blonde clerk in an olive t-shirt. He had a narrow face that rose above a scruffy graying beard confined to his chin. His arms were covered with ink.

Doubeck's eyes were transfixed by a dagger running from the man's elbow to his wrist. The dagger's handle was adorned with the letters USMC. Charlie was trying to ignore the body art and keep eye contact.

The man's name tag read "LACEY" and it looked exactly like the name patch you'd see on a uniform.

"We saw your ad," Charlie said. "It says you buy World War Two guns."

The clerk's eyes drifted to the bag in Charlie's hand. "Yeah, sometimes. You have a weapon to sell?"

"Yes, we do."

"Well, you'll have to talk to Gunny." Lacey picked up a green walkie-talkie that was lying on the counter and triggered the microphone.

"Merle to Gunny."

A voice that sounded like a blender full of gravel replied, "Go."

"Two friendlies here carrying."

"Eyes on the weapon?"

"Negative."

Doubeck and Charlie squinted at each other when they heard the unfamiliar jargon.

Before LACEY could set his walkie-talkie down, the drapes covering the doorway behind the register lifted like wings to reveal a man of otherworldly scale and proportion. He could have been designed by Stan Lee. His head looked like a piston, flat on top and cylindrical, not football-shaped like most people. His neck was only slightly smaller than his skull, supported by muscular buttresses that descended from the back of his head to the tip of each shoulder.

His chest stretched his shirt so tightly it looked painted on. It had to be a triple XL, struggling to prevent its own self-destruction with every breath he took.

The name tag on his chest read GYSGT COLT. He stepped toward the counter and the doorway drapes wafted behind him like a cape. His hands gripped the edge of the ten-foot glass showcase in a way that looked like he was ready and able to push it over.

"Gentlemen. What can I do for you?"

"We have a collectible gun," said Doubeck.

"A gun?" Colt raised his eyebrows.

"Yeah, it's a…a gun," said Doubeck.

Colt looked at Charlie who nodded in agreement. "I'd call it a gun."

"You've got a pistol, a side arm. A weapon—not a gun."

Charlie and Doubeck's wide-eyed faces showed they understood the lesson.

"Is it loaded, men?"

"No. No, it isn't loaded," Doubeck answered.

"Then you can set it down right here in front of me." Colt folded his arms and waited for the boys to present their treasure. Charlie reached into his paper bag and withdrew the weapon, still covered by the rag. As ordered, he set it on a piece of carpet sitting on the glass countertop.

Colt took one hand and gingerly lifted a corner of the oily rag. He repeated the move with another corner, then peeled away the overlaid fabric, revealing the Luger. He stood motionless for a good thirty seconds and then, without moving, he said, "Merle, get me a pencil." He held his hand out to his side. In the blink of an eye, Merle Lacey slapped the pencil into his hand, like a nurse passing a scalpel to a surgeon.

Colt threaded the pencil through the trigger guard and lifted the weapon to his face. He studied it like a jeweler, rotating it in front of his eyes. The boys never saw him blink.

"I'll give you $5,000. Not a penny more," he said.

"What?" Doubeck thought the number was astronomically, miraculously high and he practically shouted. He surprised himself so much by his outburst, that he immediately adopted a sour look, thinking he'd embarrassed himself.

Colt glared at him with his brow furrowed and completely misread Doubeck's schizo reaction. "Okay, $7,500. But that's only with provenance." He leaned on the counter and looked down at the boys. "You know what provenance is?"

Charlie took a chance. "The capital of Rhode Island?"

Colt glared at him and suddenly burst out laughing. "Okay, I'm gonna guess this is a first-class reproduction. I shoulda spotted it. Nobody walks in here with a pristine Kriegsmarine Luger with a Nordsee stamp. I mean, I've never even held a busted one. Wow," he chuckled, "You almost got me, guys."

Doubeck pulled a paper out of his pocket and unfolded it. It was a typewritten list of serial numbers printed on Kriegsmarine letterhead. "Maybe this will help." He set the paper on the counter.

Colt studied it, then turned the Luger upside down and checked the barrel. His eyes darted back to the document. Then they slowly rose to the boys again. Only now, his eyes had narrowed and filled with suspicion.

"How did you two acquire this weapon?"

The friends looked at each other. Charlie spoke. "We found it."

"Bullshit you found it."

"We *found* it," Charlie insisted.

"And see those serial numbers?" Doubeck pressed his finger to the column of two dozen twelve-digit numbers. "We've got every one of these, too. In a case. In grease. Each one's wrapped with parchment paper."

Charlie blurted out his words like they were being fired from a shotgun. "The woman who used to own the house we bought died. And it turns out she was a German spy, but we didn't know that until my friends and I found a shit-ton of secret documents. And then we found the guns, I mean the weapons. We found them after we moved in, and…"

The Marine crunched his jaw back and forth like he was troubled by what he heard. "You found them in…"

Charlie interrupted. "In a wooden crate. With the holsters…" He motioned diagonally across his chest because the holster he had seen was worn belted across the chest.

"Yeah," Colt said. "That's exactly the way the Kriegsmarine wore them. Hmmmmff."

The boys noticed Colt relax. He was quiet as he thought about what he'd heard. They decided they'd passed his test, so they fist-bumped.

"You look like good guys. Too bad you're going to jail," said Colt, without making eye contact. "You gotta be eighteen to carry in Pennsylvania."

"I'm eighteen," said Doubeck.

Colt looked at Doubeck and nodded. "Yeah? Well, you still can't conceal-carry until you're twenty-one, unless you're hunting, and you ain't hunting downtown."

Charlie was crestfallen. "We're in trouble."

Colt set the Luger down and glanced back at Lacey.

"Merle?"

"Yes, Gunny."

"Go polish your howitzer."

"Copy that." Merle headed for the front door. Once he stepped out, Colt spoke one word. "Relax."

"You guys are going to leave this with me so you don't go to jail. You got no choice in this. Then, you get your dad to come back with you and I'll pay you. Do that and you'll be fine."

"My dad doesn't know," said Charlie.

"Then you're gonna have to grow a pair and tell him."

"I'm not afraid to tell him. It's just bigger than that." Charlie's forthright reply softened Colt's expression.

"It's pretty complicated," Doubeck added.

Colt turned his head askance. "What'd ya mean bigger than that? You find something else, guys? Is that what's going on?"

They looked at each other thinking *U-boat* and hoping Colt wasn't a mind reader. But when Charlie answered "Yes," and Doubeck said "No," Colt scowled.

Charlie got flustered. "I just can't talk about what we have."

"We'll figure something out," said Doubeck.

"Okay, men. Good decisions make good leaders. Do this right and you'll be just fine." The boys nodded. Colt wrote his phone number on a Post-it and handed it to Charlie. "Put this number in your phone and leave that piece of paper here," he said. Then he picked up the shrouded pistol, the list of serial numbers, and walked back through the drapes and disappeared.

The two friends left the store without saying a word. Outside, Lacey looked at his phone as he leaned against the building. When the boys appeared, he held the door for them.

"Gunny must like you guys," Lacey said. "He's taking a chance not turning you in, you know. He goes by the book." They glanced at Lacey as they passed, but they kept their feet moving and their mouths shut.

They rode their bikes back to Charlie's house. Five miles without uttering a sound. The events of the morning had been too stressful for them to sort out just yet.

They were feeling much older than their years. Especially Charlie. Overwhelmed by the power of the U-boat's secret, Charlie had become more withdrawn and sensitive, as the burden of power began to settle heavily on his shoulders. He was beginning to see that his secret could change lives, perhaps bring him wealth and an exciting future. Today also showed him that it was only when he or his friends had revealed the U-boat, or even hinted about it, its power suddenly came alive.

The crew would have to learn quickly to control that power, and Charlie wasn't at all sure they could do it.

THE LAST U-BOAT

ALWAYS
HAVE A
PLAN B

Over the next few days, Oleg Petrosian and his cousin Frik spent very little time at the marina. If they were up to something, they didn't let on. Instead, they left Stewart alone and when they were around, he kept his distance. His goal was to quit as soon as possible and work full-time on the U-boat, but timing would be critical. His job provided important resources the crew could use and he needed that access.

Oleg appeared early Wednesday morning to tell Stewart that he and Frik wanted to go fishing after sunset. Stewart bargained for the rest of the day off, claiming he had some things to do for his mom. Wednesdays weren't usually busy, so Oleg agreed. When he finally clocked out, Stewart made a beeline for Charlie's house and the sub.

Mrs. LeClair answered the door. "Is that you, Stewart?"

"Yes, Ma'am."

"My goodness, you look much older, so grown up since I saw you last. I hardly see any of Charlie's friends anymore. It's like you've all gone underground."

Stewart's eyebrows shot upward

Just then, Charlie appeared in the hall behind his mother. Surprised to see Stewart, he blurted out, "What are you doing here?"

"Charlie, that's rude." His mother looked appalled.

"Sorry. Sorry, Stewart. I just meant I thought you'd be working." Charlie looked at his mom. "Stewart works at Raccoon Bay Marina."

"Oh, that's nice."

Stewart nodded and addressed Charlie. "I took the day off. You doing anything?"

"No, I'm good." Charlie grabbed his Vans from the hall closet.

Mrs. LeClair backed away, allowing Charlie to squeeze through the doorway. "It was good to see you again, Stewart. Gotta check on Rocky. You boys have fun, okay?"

"Thanks, Mrs. LeClair. Good to see you, too," said Stewart, as Charlie's mom disappeared down the hall.

"Sup, Stewart?"

"I've got a lot of parts in bags and boxes in the car. I could use help getting it down the hill and into the sub."

Charlie stepped out and closed the door. "I didn't get the money, Stewart. There was a problem. The guy at the surplus store says we can't transport guns because we're under twenty-one. Oh, he offered us $7,500 for each one. Can you believe it?"

"Really? That's amazing. What're you gonna do?"

"I don't have a clue. He said I should tell my dad." He rolled his eyes. "But I can't. Not right now. He'd kill me."

Stewart casually swatted Charlie's shoulder with the back of his hand. "Sure, just say, 'Hey Dad, I found an old gun. Is it okay if I sell it and use the money to buy parts for my U-boat?'"

For the first time, Stewart and Charlie laughed together.

"Not gonna happen, Stewart."

"You and Doubeck will come up with something. Meanwhile, I grabbed a lot of stuff we needed and put it on my store credit. Just pay me when you figure it out."

"You can do that?"

"Yeah. I'm practically running the place." As the boys headed down the drive, Stewart described Petrosian's work ethic. "He never checks anything—the inventory, repairs, the schedule. He just grabs a handful of twenties from the cash drawer once in a while and takes off."

Stewart eventually stopped complaining, and after three trips to the car they had finished transferring all the supplies into the sub.

Stewart remained below and Charlie headed back up to his house for a scheduled *Wolfpack* session, eager to report that Stewart was already hard at work.

No sooner had the door closed behind him than a dark figure emerged from the bushes, almost a hundred yards away, on the hillside below the hatch. It moved cautiously under the trees without a sound, timing its movements with the breeze, gliding from shadow to shadow, and eventually reaching the hatch.

Stewart had started checking pipe joints inside the control room. He had just turned a wrench on a coupling when he thought he heard rubber soles squeak on the metal rungs of the ladder behind him. "What did you forget?"

There was no answer.

"Charlie? That you?"

A strange gravelly voice cut through the darkness. "Don't move."

Stewart froze, silent.

"That's good. Now just lower your arms to your side."

Stewart complied. "What do you want?"

"I'm a friend of Charlie's," the voice said.

Stewart swung around in one swift motion, rolling up onto his knees, brandishing the pipe wrench in his right hand, and a flashlight in his left. Before him, stood a real-life version of the Incredible Hulk wearing full camo and a Marine utility cover.

"I'm Gunnery Sergeant Colt. Who are you?"

"Stewart Swanson, sir."

"Don't call me 'sir,' Stewart. Call me Gunny."

"Gunny?"

"As in Gunnery Sergeant."

"How did you? Did you follow me?"

"Nah, Charlie and his buddy came to sell me a Luger. I tracked him down because I needed to know what was going on before I bought such a valuable piece of history. Know what I mean?"

"Yeah, I do. I'm the one who told Charlie and Doubeck to sell the Lugers."

"Charlie showed me the receipt. I count twenty-four pistols signed for by the captain of the German sub, U-22."

This was the guy Charlie had told him about. "You own As You Were?"

"I think I see what's going on—boxes of spare parts, a roll of bell wire, hydraulic oil. You guys were trying to get some cash to fix this thing up."

Stewart nodded.

Colt smiled for the first time since their encounter. "Most guys your age work on cars, you know."

The smile didn't erase Stewart's suspicions. The Marine's story made sense, but he still didn't know whether Colt was a good guy or a bad guy, and not knowing was risky.

"There was nothing on that paperwork about the sub. How'd you find it?"

"I figured it out." Colt relaxed and dropped to the floor. He sat cross-legged a few feet from Stewart, who was still squatting, holding his wrench like a hammer. Colt motioned for Stewart to sit, too, which he did.

"I looked online. Commander Jenish captained U-22 for eight months before the date on the receipt for those Lugers. That means Jenish didn't need the pistols for his crew. They already had sidearms. They're probably locked up in here somewhere and I'll bet you haven't even found them yet. So, the only reason he'd take more pistols would be as cargo. And I'm guessing there's even more."

"So the guns are cargo?" Stewart shook his head. "I still don't see how you could find the sub from that."

"A few years ago, Stewart, there was a guy who left his factory job every night with a tarp over his wheelbarrow. The guards didn't want to start a grievance with the union by accusing him of stealing without any evidence, so they always looked around after he left. But they never found anything missing."

Stewart looked quizzical. "Yeah?"

"Well, they finally said to the guy, 'Listen, just tell us what you've been taking and we won't press charges.' So, the guy says, 'Okay. I've been taking wheelbarrows.'"

"Wheelbarrows?" Stewart asked.

"I'm saying the Lugers weren't the only cargo, Stewart. The cargo was the whole fuckin U-boat. The Lugers were the breadcrumbs I had to follow to find the real answer. So, how'd I do?"

"I'm impressed." Stewart pursed his lips and nodded his head. "So, are we in trouble?"

"Hell, no. I'm not here to get anybody in trouble."

"Why don't I believe you?"

Colt rose and took a full step toward Stewart. He pointed a finger at the younger man's chest. "Now, you listen to me. You can believe I'm telling you the truth because I'm a Marine. You got it?" Colt's broad chin protruded like a battering ram.

Stewart took a second to think and swallowed hard. "Yes, Gunnery Sergeant."

Colt backed off. "Let me tell you something, Stewart. Unless you're the enemy, I will never tell you, or Charlie, or Doubeck anything but God's honest truth. You got it?"

Stewart nodded in agreement. "Understood," he said. Then Stewart set the wrench down. His hand was cramped from squeezing it for so long.

Colt relaxed and leaned back against a rail. "I know I could really make a good buck in the surplus and collectibles market—and Charlie and you guys would get the lion's share. I don't want to screw that up. But there's more to it than that.

When your friends came to see me, they weren't nervous, they weren't cocky or smart-ass. They wanted to obey the law, to follow the rules. They just didn't know what the rules were. They never asked me to look the other way or cut them a break."

"They're good guys. I found that out myself," said Stewart.

Colt took it down one more notch and continued. "The damn law never crossed their minds. When I told them they were committing a felony, they were ready to take the consequences." Colt stood and shifted his weight. "Not everybody understands accountability anymore, and those of us who do, we need to stick together. So, I'm in. If I can help you men out, I'll do whatever I can."

Stewart stood and leaned back against the rail running alongside the walkway. He cocked his head and looked Colt straight in the eyes. "We sure could use it."

The secret was out now. But maybe, Stewart thought, by confiding in Colt, he could do some damage control and persuade him to keep the secret from spreading further.

Colt leaned on the rail next to Stewart. "I am curious about a couple of things. Like, why the hell are you working on a sub that's buried in a hillside? You know you're not going anywhere."

Stewart just grinned a grin that told Colt a lot more was going on than he was aware of. So, they talked. Colt's questions covered all the bases. How old are you? How do you know Charlie and Doubeck? How did they find the sub? Why don't Charlie's parents know? How many people are in on it? Who are they? How do they plan to launch it? How does the crew figure they can ever drive the sub?

They talked for over an hour. Stewart offered the best answers he could and, they seemed to hit it off—though Stewart remained skeptical.

They were about to take a tour when Charlie came down the conning tower ladder. When his feet hit the deck, he turned to see his friend standing next to Colt.

Charlie's chin dropped and he looked down at the deck. "Shit. We're dead."

"No, Charlie. Come on. Gunny wants to help."

"Gunny? Did you know him before?" Charlie pointed at Stewart like he'd been double-crossed.

"I just met Stewart. I came down the hatch and he was here."

Stewart stuck his hands into his pockets. "Charlie, Colt tracked you down. He came down the ladder and surprised me while I was working."

Colt waited silently, hoping the friends could work it out.

Charlie shrugged. "I'm telling you, Stewart, we're dead. Too many people know about this. It's not a secret anymore. We're going to lose the damn boat, we're going to get into huge trouble, and we'll end up in jail."

"Ain't gonna happen," said Colt. "You didn't do anything."

"Right," Charlie whispered. He looked up at Colt. "How did you find it?"

"I got your address from a friend who helps me find people who don't want to be found."

"Are we in trouble?" asked Charlie.

"That's what I was wondering," said Stewart.

"Not as far as I'm concerned," said Colt. "I want this to work out as much as you do. I love history. I mean, come on, I own a military surplus store. This is a big fuckin deal. I'm not going to steal from you, or turn you in, or cheat you. I want to help. Just tell me what you need."

Charlie sat down, his body language shouting exhaustion.

"Okay. But, you know, I feel like I'm fighting a losing battle. I'm trying to keep this a secret and here you are, one more person who knows about it. It's just…it's getting to me, okay?" He turned and faced Colt. "Are you telling me you wanna buy the rest of the Lugers?"

Colt smiled. "Sure do. And you don't have to break the law by carrying them off your property. I'm here now—I can take 'em with me."

"Alright. But I want your promise you'll keep this boat a secret. Do I have that?"

"Aye, aye."

"And I need a bank account."

"Done. I've got a friend at Coastal Bank, Pat Ryan. We served together. I'll tell him to fix you up with an account and take care of all the legal stuff."

"Legal stuff?"

"There's always legal stuff. If I vouch for you, he'll help you work around it."

Stewart and Charlie exchanged glances and nodded.

"Oh, and you'll need a company since you're underage. You can stick Stewart on the board and then the two of you are legit. Divide the shares. Keep control, share control. You can make all those decisions. Ryan'll do that for you and he'll keep it confidential."

"Sounds complicated," said Charlie.

"It is. For five minutes. Then you're done. Listen, Charlie, nowadays, unless you're Elon Musk, you can't even put money in your own damn account without getting interrogated. So, right now, you need a way around that."

The idea of owning a company with Stewart triggered old uncomfortable feelings, but Stewart seemed to be like a different guy, and Charlie was quickly learning to be pragmatic.

"Okay, you can tell Ryan—if you can keep the sub out of it."

"Aye-aye."

"And we need walkie-talkies, too, for inside the boat," said Stewart.

"Got 'em," said Colt.

Charlie took a step toward Colt to get his attention. "So, Gunny. You wanna buy a deck gun?"

"Sonofabitch. Seriously? You have a deck gun?" Colt's voice sounded a bit like a kid on Christmas morning.

"Wait a second." Colt peered into the distant darkness. "Does this sub have…torpedoes?" Colt's eyes darted from Charlie to Stewart. They stared back without emotion.

"No shit." Gunny grinned and pointed a finger at Charlie and Stewart. "I mean, I know guys with all kinds of ordnance. But you, you're the only guys I know with their own torpedoes, and a U-boat to launch 'em."

To Charlie, the torpedoes were nothing more than a frightening menace, so Colt's euphoria did not rub off. "Stewart, how you fixed for time? If we take a tour, you gonna be here when we get back?"

"Oh, yeah. I have a few hours before I have to blast. Oleg and Frik want me to take them fishing again tonight."

"Seriously?" said Charlie.

"Yeah, I have a bad feeling about it."

"Who's Oleg and Frik?" asked Colt.

Stewart described the Armenians, and how strange they acted in general.

"They could be Armenian mafia. Can you get out of it? Make an excuse?" Colt asked.

Stewart's eyes rolled up with a look of resignation. "I don't think so."

"Got your phone?"

"Yeah."

"Unlock it and give it to me."

Without hesitation, Stewart fished his phone out of his pocket, unlocked it, and tossed it to Colt, who caught it with one hand."

Colt tapped and swiped at the screen as he spoke.

"You've got my number now. If you need anything, call me. Day or night. Got it?"

"Yeah, I got it. But why'd you do that?"

"It's my training. Always have a Plan B. Do you have someone to call if you can't call 9-1-1?"

"No."

"Now you do."

Stewart shot a glance at Charlie. Charlie just shrugged and Colt picked up on it.

"Give the number to my business partner, too," he said, nodding toward Charlie.

Colt flipped the phone through the air and back into Stewart's waiting hands. "Will do," he said, as he slipped his phone back into his pocket and looked over at Colt and Charlie. "Enjoy your tour."

"Oorah!" was the reply. Something Stewart and Charlie were destined to hear a lot more in the coming days.

They started in the engine room, making their way toward the bow. When they returned to the control room Stewart had moved farther forward, so with the space available, Charlie invited Colt to jump into the hold under the steel floor.

"The rest of the pistols are down there in crates. And you'll see a heavy pipe over toward the bulkhead. I'm pretty sure that's the barrel of the deck gun."

Colt trained his flashlight on the bulkhead.

"I can't carry that through the woods. Where's the nearest road?"

"My driveway. But if my mom or dad, or if my little brother, Rocky, sees you…it's all over."

"Don't worry about that," said Colt.

"Yeah. Okay. Too late now, anyway, I guess," said Charlie.

"Listen, Charlie. This is what I know. Adapt, improvise, and overcome.

That's what Marines do."

"I get it, you live on the edge."

Colt didn't respond. He was thinking about when he came down the ladder and saw the sub. He was sure these kids were in way over their heads. But then they turned him into a believer, impressing him with their seriousness, their decision-making capability, and their intensity. Those were attributes Colt held in high esteem. In his estimation, their chance of success had gone way up.

He bent down to lift a wooden crate with heavy rope handles and set it on the metal grate over the hold. He opened the cover and through a translucent layer of blue-black jelly, he could see the Lugers glowing in the beam of Charlie's flashlight.

"Charlie, we need to get your bank account opened. I'm going to have $175,000 for you on Monday."

"No shit?"

"I have a feeling that's just the beginning. There are a lot more crates down there."

FISHING
WITH
FRIK

Frik knelt on the *Ararat*'s seat cushions and spread his belly over the top rail. His massive gut sloshed up and down as the bow repeatedly slammed into the waves coming hard and fast out of the north.

"In a couple minutes I'll turn west," shouted Stewart. "Then it'll get easier."

"Don't worry about it. Frik is big baby," said Oleg. "He's okay."

"Good, because this is our heading. It's the same one we were on last week looking for the life jacket."

"Yes. This where we go. Keep it up." Oleg gave Stewart a slap of approval across his back.

The trip to the center of Lake Erie took about two hours, full-throttle. Fortunately, during the last half hour, the wind slowed and the waves subsided, becoming great rolling swells that caused the boat to rise and fall like a teeter-totter.

Stewart throttled down and switched off the ignition. Immediately, the boat began a gentler, rhythmic rocking, slowly turning broadside to the oncoming breeze.

Frik had brought a fishing pole, and as the boat bobbed up and down, the pole click-clacked against the bow rail. But he wasn't fishing. He peered through a pair of binoculars, constantly sweeping the dark horizon looking for something.

"This place good, Oleg?"

"Yes, Frik. This where you find life jacket."

"I don't see nothing."

"Relax, Frik. Night is warm, stars out. Air clean and fresh. Maybe should catch fish."

"I go in water. You get string ready."

Frik moved to the seat next to his fishing pole. He removed his shoes and then his pants. When they dropped to the deck around his ankles, he stood up and turned toward Oleg and Stewart who were standing slightly above him on the bridge.

"You think I skinny dippy? I fool you. Look, swimming pants."

Stewart had been raised to believe it was impolite to laugh at someone's clothes or body shape. But Frik's ensemble put Stewart's self-control to the test. He wore a red, blue, and orange Speedo, a straw Borsalino hat, and a loud Tommy Bahama shirt—adorned with giant blue macaws—that draped across his chest and bloated belly like a tent with a front porch. Stewart wanted to look away, but he couldn't. If the Armenians didn't creep him out so much, it would have been hilarious.

Stewart glanced at a thermometer on the dashboard. "The water's only about sixty degrees, Frik, I wouldn't…"

Frik blithely removed his hat, shirt, and watch, revealing his avoca-do-shaped torso, adorned only by a clutch of gold chains hanging from his neck and his skimpy bathing trunks in the colors of the Armenian flag. He stood for a moment with one foot on a bench and one on a gunwale, then he jumped rather awkwardly from the safety of the *Ararat* into the dark, frigid waters of the lake.

"Oh, boy. He's going to get a cramp and sink like a bowling ball." Stewart grabbed a flashlight from a tray under the console, took three steps from the bridge onto the main deck, and headed to the rail. Petrosian joined him, and in a moment Frik reappeared.

"Is more warm than Lake Sevan, Oleg. Not bad."

"Good, because they come now, Frik." Oleg reached down and placed something into Frik's outstretched hand. "You okay?"

"Yes, yes. Very good. You should try catch fish now." Frik's head disappeared below the surface and he was gone.

Petrosian wheeled around. "Stewart, throw line out. Already you put worm on?"

"No, but I can," Stewart offered.

"Yes. You try catch breakfast."

"Fish for breakfast?" Stewart asked.

"Smoked salmon and toast. Is delicious. I buy some, you try."

"Should I just throw the line in?"

"Yes, throw. Let string fall out. We have no hurry."

As Stewart tossed the line into the water, he saw the red and green lights of an approaching boat, red on the port side and green to starboard. Stewart knew the position of the lights showed that the boat was headed directly toward them. He left the line to spool out freely and laid the rod back against the rail.

"Mr. Petrosian, are you expecting someone?" he asked.

"Yes. Visitors. Meeting first time. You stay here." Oleg pulled a large steel toolbox out of a bench seat back by the cabin. He opened it and withdrew a compact black machine gun. He set the gun on the adjacent seat and covered it with a striped beach towel. Oleg looked at Stewart whose eyes were wide open and fixed on the gun. "Is Uzi."

Oleg nodded toward the oncoming boat. "Like I say, have not met before."

Stewart's heart began pounding in his chest, and he seriously considered jumping off and swimming back to shore—ten miles due south, unless he drifted a little off course. If he did, the next familiar site would be Niagara Falls.

But Stewart, a strong swimmer, thought he might be able to make it ten miles—if his life depended on it. Still, water temperature presented a big problem. After mulling over the prospect of abandoning ship, he decided he'd jump only if someone started shooting. He'd throw the keys overboard and swim for it. Maybe it was crazy, but at least he had a Plan B.

It seemed events were converging toward an end that Oleg and Frik had not seen fit to disclose. The mysterious boat Oleg had been expecting bore down on them while Frik floated somewhere on the swells rising and falling over the deepest part of Lake Erie. Oleg had just hidden a machine gun within arm's length, there were no landmarks in view, and only the ship's compass could tell them the way home for certain. The random thoughts that blew through Stewart's mind as the boat drew close had the ring of madness—none of them comforting.

Oleg stood precariously on the bow, in the halo of the visitor's running lights. He grabbed the rope they tossed to him as they glided alongside, and he tied it tight to *Ararat*'s starboard bow cleat. He looked back at Stewart and pointed a finger.

"You stay put, stay by ass of boat," he said, before stepping gingerly off the *Ararat* and onto the other boat. Oleg carried a briefcase Stewart had not seen until that moment.

Stewart backed away and headed for the stern, shaking his head in disbelief. *I shouldn't be out here with these numbskulls. What kind of frickin mafia doesn't even know the back of a boat is called aft, not ass?* As he reached the transom bench seat, he looked into the water and saw a blue-tinged, round face staring back at him. It was Frik, motioning frantically for Stewart to look away. Stewart obeyed. A moment later he glanced back, but Frik had vanished.

Stewart could hear arguing aboard the visitor's boat, but the words were not in English.

The Swansons were first-generation Americans, and when he was a kid, Stewart heard his grandparents speak Swedish, German, and Russian at home. This was none of those.

Petrosian continued to shout at the visitors—there looked to be six—and they shouted back at him. Things were heating up.

Stewart remembered the Uzi and, for a second, the thought crossed his mind that he might have to use it if things went south. There would be a safety, probably a slide on the side of the gun near the trigger. He'd have to make sure the safety was off. If the other boat fired first, he'd shoot for the water line at the bow to try to sink it.

Then he remembered. *Oh no, we tied up to them. We can't get away. What a stupid mistake. I'll have to shoot the cleat off the bow. If that doesn't work I'll have to ram their boat—probably while they're shooting at us. They just have a big outboard, maybe twenty-four feet. Ararat would win that fight. I can't believe these guys got me into this.*

Then he remembered having Colt's phone number. He wished Colt was with him. He'd know what to do.

If they saw me get my phone out they'd know I was calling for help. Oh, man. I think I'm going to throw up.

Stewart crossed over to the starboard side of the transom, hugging the gunwale in case he got sick. From there, he could see into the visitors' boat and hear them more clearly. He also saw Frik, on the port side, climb *Ararat's* swim ladder and roll aboard like a harbor seal, hidden from the visitors by the cabin.

Frik dressed quickly and moved cautiously across the stern to get closer to Stewart while remaining out of sight of the visitors.

"What you see, Mr. Stewart?" he whispered.

"They keep waving their arms at Mr. Petrosian. Someone's shaking a finger in his face and threatening him. It's not looking good."

"Okay. You get up now. Go to front. Lift up fish pole and do fishing."

"Really? Fishing? I'm not going to get shot or anything, am I?"

"Probably no."

"Probably? Forget it. I'm not going up there."

"Do not go and you definitely be shot."

Stewart felt his blood run cold. Happy-go-lucky Frik wasn't smiling.

Oleg and a middle-aged, bearded man were still shouting, but the yelling and screaming was a far cry from the threat of lethal weapons, so at this moment, Stewart's risk seemed small.

Regardless, he had already committed himself to jumping overboard if he had to. Stewart stepped forward and reached for the fishing pole.

Petrosian turned and looked at him, then back at the visitors. He pointed at each one as though threatening them. He turned, stood on the back of their boat, and casually stepped back onto the *Ararat*. Stewart watched transfixed.

"Bewa qufa'an," said Petrosian, and he waved the back of his fist like a curse toward the other boat. Then, he snatched up the rope binding the boats and threw it back at the visitors with clear disdain.

The boats drifted apart for a few seconds before the visitor's engines started. Petrosian moved back to Stewart's right side. As he did, Frik walked up on Stewart's left and said, "Mr. Stewart, I think you have fish on."

Stewart hadn't even been conscious of holding the pole.

"Pull fish in before string gone," ordered Frik.

Stewart knew he didn't have a fish on the line. He had seen the shimmer of the heavy nylon line passing into the stern of the other boat before it pulled away. *What's Frik up to?* Stewart's heartbeat began to slow when it seemed like the danger had passed. He could not wait to head home. Frik and Petrosian were acting more bizarre all the time.

They watched the visitor's boat turn a tight one-eighty back toward where it came from. Stewart looked down at the reel and spun the handle, closing the bail. He began to reel in the line that had spilled out while they were adrift.

Suddenly, the line started to play out again.

"Pull fish. Pull now!" shouted Frik.

Stewart didn't move fast enough, so Frik grabbed the pole, lowered the tip of the rod, and prepared to pull up hard.

Stewart held out his hands toward the line, knowing there was a very good chance the lure would spring from the water and come flying back in their faces.

Frik yanked the rod. The end of the line came flying out of the darkness and slapped Stewart hard on the chest. He peeled a steel pin off his shirt. It had a loop on one end. The shape was unmistakable.

The flash seemed to wrap around them as the visitor's boat exploded in a brilliant yellow burst. Two seconds later the sharp crack of the blast reached their ears. He reeled faster while his mind tried to come to grips with what happened. At the end of the line, the leader appeared. Tied to it was a heavy wire loop.

Frik had yanked the pin on a grenade from 300 yards using a vintage six-foot Shakespeare Ugly Stick spinning rod and thirty-pound-test Berkley monofilament line, killing a half-dozen men instantly.

As debris rained down on the swells in front of the *Ararat*, Oleg and Frik were laughing and dancing like football fans celebrating a touchdown. Along with the fluttering debris were bits of paper—money—intact large denomination bills and hundreds of smaller pieces.

Stewart slipped the wire loop off the snap swivel and slid it into his shirt pocket.

"What did you do? You maniacs! Aren't you going to help those guys? Their boat blew up."

"They big boys," said Frik.

"So you just murdered those guys in cold blood? Are you fucking crazy?"

"They come to kill us, Stewart. But I pay them off with ten thousand dollars while Frik put grenade in back of boat."

"Why the hell would they want to kill us? What did you do to them?"

"They work for bad guys," said Oleg.

"Very much bastards," said Frik.

"We say we not help them. So they come to kill us."

"So you killed six guys and blew up ten thousand in cash?"

The Armenians ignored Stewart's questions.

"Oleg, they took bait." Frik laughed and even Oleg chuckled.

"Money was fake, Mr. Stewart. But very good fake," said Frik.

"Let them swim home," said Oleg. "They would do same to us."

"They're not swimming, they're dead." Stewart sat, his sweaty hands cradling his head. "You killed them and we're all going to prison now." Oleg and Frik looked at each other and shrugged.

Out of the silence, Oleg spoke softly and patiently to Stewart. "Why you not hear? These sons of bitch plan to kill us. Also you."

"How can you be so sure they were going to kill us?" Stewart looked Oleg in the eyes. "Who were those guys?"

"Bratva. Russian Mafia, Stewart. If they go home alive, there is war we not win. Do you agree, Frik?"

"No more Bratva," said Frik.

"Da. No more Bratva," said Oleg. "We save your life, Stewart."

Frik walked over and put his pudgy hand on Stewart's shoulder. "This good night's work, Mr. Stewart. We have very successful negotiation with competitor. Now we go home."

"Are you going to kill me, too? Cuz it feels like you are." He glanced over toward the bench seat where the Uzi lay covered.

"Stewart," said Oleg, with a Cheshire cat's grin. "You like son. You good at business. You drive boat good. You keep mouth quiet." Oleg put his hand on Stewart's other shoulder. "You one of us now. Come on. Take us home."

"Yeah," said Stewart. "Let's do that, because I'm fucking done with it."

"Oleg, Mr. Stewart is done," said Frik, with a smirk.

Both men looked at Stewart and began to laugh. They were laughing at his fear, his morality, and his loss of innocence. As Stewart looked back at them, he realized he was looking at faces of evil. He started the engine, slammed the *Ararat* into gear, and made a sharp turn to 130 degrees south-southeast.

The Armenians slipped and fell to the wet deck as the boat wheeled around underneath them. They hit hard, but instead of reacting angrily, they began laughing and slapping each other on the back, as though blowing up a boat full of men had left them euphoric.

Oleg retrieved the Uzi and the Armenians disappeared below deck. Minutes later they reappeared with drinks and a bottle of vodka in hand, somewhat subdued, but still giddy.

They approached Stewart at the helm and stood on opposite sides of him.

"Now, what this about being done?" asked Petrosian.

Stewart ignored him, maintaining an emotionless face.

"This not fun for you, Mr. Stewart?" asked Frik. "Vodka help you relax. You not drink with friends?"

But Stewart didn't react. He just gripped the wheel, kept the engine running full-out, and searched the horizon for any lights that might reveal the shoreline. Oleg and Frik walked away.

"This is thanks to us for saving his life, Frik." Petrosian egged Stewart on as though he was showing off for his cousin. "You part of this now, Stewart."

Stewart throttled down so fast the wake slammed into the transom. He turned and looked back at the men who were now sitting on the bench at the back of the cabin.

"What's 'bewa qufa'an'?"

Frik got an exaggerated look of confusion on his face. "This I don't know. Is not Armenian word."

"Why you ask this?" said Petrosian.

"I want to know what you were telling them before you killed them."

"We talk Russian. So, you not hear good. Is not even spell like English. Is acrylic language," Oleg replied.

"Stewart, we must go now. Soon we run out of vodka." Oleg laughed. Frik reached out and Petrosian passed the bottle to him. "I hope you thank us for saving life, or we be most insulted." It sounded a lot like a threat.

That was the last time they spoke to Stewart on the trip home. By the time they reached the docks, the Armenians were so drunk they couldn't stand up to leave the boat. Stewart walked past them, tossed Oleg the keys, and said, "I'll see you tomorrow."

In truth, he had no intention of returning, though he was pretty sure they let him leave the marina only because they thought they had him on a leash. Stewart felt trapped, an accomplice to murder, and he knew Oleg and Frik thought they had their hooks in him.

But they didn't know about Gunnery Sergeant Colt.

THE LAST U–BOAT

WHAT THE DEAD GUY SAID

Gunny's phone rang three times, waking him from a sound sleep.

"This better be good, Stewart. It's half-past balls."

"It's bad, Gunny. I'm in trouble."

A half-hour later, Stewart and Colt were sitting at the kitchen table in Colt's apartment over the store.

He handed the young man a cup of coffee, hot and black. Stewart's hands were shaking so badly the coffee splashed like the chop on Raccoon Bay. Colt could see the trauma in his eyes, so he let him settle and collect his thoughts. The kid needed to feel safe, to relax, and Colt was in no hurry. He just stretched his legs out under the table and squinted a bit under the harsh blue light of a bare fluorescent bulb. After a good long swig, Stewart opened up.

"I helped blow up a boat with six guys in it tonight. I think they're all dead."

"No shit?" Colt stroked his chin. He left his hand there and leaned on his elbow. *Don't overreact and don't push too hard. Let him tell you when he's ready.* He studied Stewart intently. "You okay? You hurt?"

"Huh! I'm not okay. I mean, I'm…I'm not hurt or anything. The explosion was a long way off."

"So tell me."

"Well, they asked me to take 'em fishing in the middle of Lake Erie. After a while, this big motorboat pulled up. So we tied up to them, to the other boat, and Petrosian, my boss, he gets on their boat and right away starts yelling at these guys. Then Frik, he's with us, he's Petrosian's cousin, he swims behind their boat while Petrosian's yelling at these guys in some foreign language. So, while he's screaming at them like he's a fuckin lunatic, Frik hooks a fishing line onto a grenade, drops it in their bait well, and swims back behind our boat. The pole with the fishing line on it was right there. Petrosian swears some more at these guys or something—I don't know what they were saying. Then he steps back onto our boat and casts off." Stewart swallowed hard and stopped to catch his breath.

"Damn, Stewart, I shoulda' made decaf. Slow down. We got all night, buddy."

Stewart nodded.

"Who are these guys? This Frik guy and Petrosian?"

"Oleg Petrosian bought the marina this winter. Like I said, he's my boss. He and Frik Nazarian grew up together in Armenia. Frik just showed up in the past couple of weeks. Danny Doubeck...you know Doubeck?"

"Yeah, Charlie's friend?"

"Uh-huh. He's a friend of mine, too. Doubeck was at the marina one day and he saw Frik accuse me of stealing money. Frik dropped the money on the floor by my feet, then he said I was stepping on it to hide it, so I could claim he never gave it to me."

"No shit. Why did he do that?"

"Doubeck thinks they were trying to suck me into their scheme by making me feel like they let me off the hook."

"Does it have anything to do with what happened tonight?"

Stewart thought for a second. He took another long gulp of coffee and a deep breath. Then he sat back in his chair.

"Yeah, I think it did. I think they were planning this all along. The day they pulled that trick on me, they asked me to take them fishing at night on Petrosian's boat. They had me navigate to specific coordinates in the lake. It's not a fishing spot, either. It's like dead center in the lake."

The emotion in his voice, as Stewart described the events of that night, gave Colt great empathy for Stewart's predicament. "So, it was a rendezvous?"

Stewart considered the question for a moment. "Yeah—had to be."

"I'm still not clear. How is it you helped blow up that boat?"

"Well, because when the other boat took off, I was holding the pole. I didn't know about the grenade. Honest. I didn't know, Gunny." Stewart was starting to choke up. Tears welled up in his eyes and spilled down his cheeks.

Gunny didn't flinch. He just sat, listening. Caring.

Stewart cried as he took on the guilt that rightfully belonged to Frik and Petrosian. Watching this young man grieve, Colt's eyes narrowed and the corners of his mouth turned down. If Petrosian could have seen the transformation in Colt's demeanor, it would have shaken him to his core. The Marine had been trained to deal with violent men, and, in that moment, he resolved to deal with these Armenians.

Stewart wiped his face with the palm of his hand and continued.

"Frik. He grabbed the pole away from me. When the other boat was a hundred yards away, he reeled in the loose line and yanked the pin out."

Stewart reached into his pocket and retrieved the pin. He set it on the table in front of them. Colt's eyebrows shot upward.

"Yep. That's a grenade pin. Damn, these guys play rough," said Colt.

"Yeah, Petrosian kept saying, 'No more Bratva."

"Bratva?" Colt snorted. "You telling me they blew up a boatload of Russian Mafia?"

Stewart looked sheepishly at Colt and shrugged his shoulders. "I guess."

How were they dressed?

"It was kinda' dark. I saw some hoodies, Nike I think. Gray and brown jackets."

"No leather? You didn't any see shiny leather? I mean, real expensive leather jackets?"

"No, the main guy, the one Petrosian was yelling at, he had a big beard, like a lumberjack. But he was wearing, uh, you know, a nylon jacket. I remember a stripe on the sleeve, like Adidas."

"Hmmmm. I'm kinda surprised the Armenians let you go."

"They were drunk when we got back. Plus, they think I'm in too deep to get out. They made that clear."

"Do you feel like you're in danger?"

"From them? No, not right now. Not really." Stewart swallowed hard. "I mean, I did. But they just let me go like I was part of everything—like I was in on it. Still, I don't want to go back, because those bastards are crazy. But

I don't think they plan to hurt me. It's almost like they sorta like having me around for some reason."

"It's cause you're doing their dirty work. Listen, you gotta go back to the marina. They'll come get you if you don't. Get intel. Keep your eyes and ears open."

Stewart's head dropped as he thought about the prospect of spending more time with Oleg and Frik. Colt shook his shoulder to snap him out of it.

"Hey. Stewart. I'm not going to let anything happen to you, but you need to be prepared."

The young man's jaw tightened just a bit. "Okay."

Colt pulled his chair over directly in front of Stewart to command his attention. "You know what situational awareness is?"

"Ah, I'm not sure."

"It's being alert to where you are, what's going on, what's out of place, anything unusual, dangerous or otherwise. It means noticing anything that doesn't sound or smell right. You can't relax and lose focus for a second. If you get that sense, that feeling, right here." Colt tapped hard on the top of Stewart's skull. "You evaluate, engage, or evacuate. Got it? Evaluate, engage, or evacuate."

Stewart nodded.

"Listen to what your brain's telling you. Make a quick assessment, and act decisively. That little warning you hear is a hundred thousand years of evolution trying to preserve the species. So, when you get that feeling, remember, you evaluate, engage, or evacuate. Got it?"

"Yeah, Gunny. I got it."

"I'm betting your Armenians are Mafia. If they met the Russians by boat, I'm guessing it's about turf. The Russians are probably coming over from Canada looking for some action in the States, and this Petrosian guy is trying to keep them out. That means he's got an organization here. He wouldn't be doing this with just one other guy.

"There had to be at least one Russian muckety-muck on that boat. The rest were probably soldiers. I've got some buddies in intel who can do some checking." Colt took a big swig of his coffee. "Petrosian did some damage tonight, but the Russians will be back. They're not going to let this go unpunished. They're badass."

Stewart lowered his head and squeezed his forehead. "How did I get in the middle of this mess?"

"Wrong time, wrong place, Stewart. Don't dwell on it. Right now, we need to know what you're up against. I'll have a tactical bag packed in case you call me. You know how to handle a weapon?"

"Yeah, deer hunting. I had a whole summer of NRA courses and competitive target shooting when I was thirteen."

"That's good. But it's a lot different when the targets shoot back."

"I thought about that tonight."

"Well, I have an idea. Instead of giving you a gun, let's put an app on your phone."

"An app?"

"Yeah, there's an app that streams audio to the cloud. Anyone with the password can listen." Colt tapped his right ear lobe. "Once you open the app, I can hear everything your phone hears."

Stewart nodded. "Okay. But it's not going to help you much if they start yammering in Armenian. You speak Armenian, Gunny?"

"No, but if Petrosian was shouting at those guys, he might have been speaking Russian. I picked up a little Russian during two tours in Afghanistan. I'll know it if I hear it."

Stewart finished his coffee and set the cup down on Colt's Formica table. "My gramma and grampa used to speak some Russian, but I didn't recognize any of what these guys were saying."

"Yeah, it could have been Chechen."

"Petrosian yelled something at 'em. Baywah coof...baywa something..."

"Was it bewa qufa'an?"

"Yeah, that's it. That's what he said, I'm sure of it."

"That's not Russian, Stewart. That's Pashto. Those guys were Taliban."

The next morning, Stewart was late for work for the first time. When he arrived, Oleg was alone and waiting for him. The man looked haggard and pale. His voice was dry and raspy.

Petrosian called from his desk as Stewart walked through the store and turned on the overhead lights. "Stewart. Get ass in office."

Stewart walked to the doorway, stopped, and leaned against the door frame. He didn't want to enter the room and make everything normal, because nothing was normal anymore.

"Yes, Mr. Petrosian?"

"What you doing today, Stewart?"

"I have to order fuel and some parts. There's a lot of trash in the cans around the pier. And I wanted to trim the weeds under some of the junkers sitting behind the building."

"You are busy today."

"Yeah, lots to do."

"Listen." Petrosian stood and walked around to the front of his desk. He tried to sit on top of the desk, but as he leaned on it, it slid back under his weight. Despite how Stewart hated him, he found it funny—and even embarrassing—to watch Petrosian chase his desk around with his ass. Nevertheless, Petrosian wouldn't stop trying until he managed to get his plump butt up and onto the desktop.

"Stewart. These killers, they make plan to attack. They not leave. When we turn around they come back to kill us."

"You don't know that for sure."

"Yes. I do. I have ears."

"You mean inside information?"

Petrosian nodded. "For sure I know this."

"Then they're going to come after you, aren't they?"

"I no think so. When men no come back. The bosses call me. I tell them I pay fifty-thousand and boat leave. Maybe their guys steal money or boat sink."

Stewart didn't buy it. But, he remembered what Gunny told him to do when something was out of place, when it didn't make sense—evaluate, engage, or evacuate. He decided to engage.

Stewart grinned and looked into Petrosian's eyes. "So the bosses think they got double-crossed by their own guys." Stewart shook his head like he was impressed. "Very clever. But you're right, if those killers had turned their boat around and come after us, we'd all be dead. I wouldn't have looked back over my shoulder once I started to head home. Why would I?"

Petrosian became very animated when Stewart seemed to accept his story.

"Exactly, Stewart. It save our lives."

"I sure wish nobody had gotten hurt. But I guess I should thank you for doing what was necessary."

"Of course, Stewart. You good person. I know this. You have big heart. So, I say you take *Ararat* for ride to Canada. Remember, you ask for fun trip with friends? You go Saturday. Is no problem."

"That's very generous of you, Mr. Petrosian."

"Also, you should…keep quiet about…accident. You safe because Frik, and me, and you, we see what happen."

Oleg pointed his fat finger at Stewart's face. "No one but us."

"I understand. It's just between us."

"Do you? Because interesting thing. You safe because it only us there last night. For same reason, maybe you not safe."

"I'm not safe?"

"Not if someone hear about accident. This why you keep quiet."

Stewart nodded slowly.

Petrosian slid his broad rear end off the desk and executed a clumsy pivot to return to his chair. When he turned his back on Stewart, their meeting was over.

As Stewart walked away, he heard Petrosian behind him, struggling to push the desk back into place across the old, warped planks of the wooden floor.

The Armenian's unsettling words gave him a lot to think about. Most likely, "Keep quiet" was how Petrosian figured he could put Stewart in a box—so he could keep him around as long as he was useful—without having to worry about getting ratted out.

Then it dawned on him—their brief conversation had been a negotiation, a chess game. Petrosian was using the marina as a cover and he needed Stewart to make the marina work, to maintain the *Ararat,* and to keep the business running. Petrosian desired Stewart's skills and, in exchange, Stewart had to accept Petrosian's lie. That arrangement constituted the bargain: *I know you know the truth, but I'm overlooking it.*

Check.

At Stewart's suggestion, only Doubeck and Charlie boarded *Ararat* at the marina. There was no sense in exposing the others to the Armenians. They shoved off and headed west along the shoreline for the five-mile ride to the beach off Charlie's house. Stewart was able to take the boat to within fifty feet of shore just beyond where the waves were breaking. He anchored and waited while the rest of his passengers swam out to the boat.

Colt climbed aboard first and scanned the *Ararat* with a device designed to find electronic bugs. The boat was clean.

"We can talk, guys. It's all clear."

The yacht eased backward until the sandy lake bottom was six feet under the keel and Stewart could safely head for deeper water. He cruised past the marina to let Colt check it out, which he did using a 12-power Leupold rifle scope. Colt watched two obese men on the dock in a conversation that included a lot of pushing and shoving.

Stewart made the ID. "That's Frik in the plaid jacket, Petrosian is the one with the rust-colored pants." As the boat passed, the scope's reticle eased across the chest of one and then the other. The men were so wrapped up in their discussion they never looked toward the boat.

Ararat was soon concealed by the thick grove of poplar trees along the shore east of the marina. When he was clear, Stewart turned north toward

Long Point, Canada. They would be on the beach in less than an hour after a quick check-in at customs.

Once underway, the crew convened in the cabin and shut the door to block the noise.

Charlie looked serious. "So, except for Rocky, everyone who knows about the U-boat is right here. Since we're all together, Doubeck and I thought it would be a good time to check in and see where we stand, what we have to do, and so on."

"So, Gunny sold the Lugers and the deck gun," said Doubeck. "We have enough money now to buy a damn house."

"I made a couple of calls and found a buyer the same day you guys brought the Luger to my shop. They're very valuable and very collectible," said Colt.

Charlie continued, "And, you arranged with Mr. Ryan for me to get a bank account going, and Stewart's using the money for parts and stuff."

Stewart set the autopilot and turned to join the conversation. "That reminds me, I'm ready to fill the fuel tanks. Marty calculated it out to eleven-thousand gallons."

The Marine just shook his head. "Ain't gonna happen."

"Why not? We've got the money," said Charlie.

"Where would you put the fuel?"

Charlie shook his head. "Shit, you're right. The gas filler's buried, isn't it?"

"Yeah," Colt scratched his ear. "And it's oil, not gas. They call it bunker, and it's loaded just forward from the torpedo hatch where we can't quite reach. That says to me that the Nazis planned to fuel her after she was launched. I mean, they probably could load a couple hundred gallons on board so they'd have enough to rendezvous with a tanker. But just enough to get out and charge the batteries."

"What if we get out there and something happens we didn't expect?" Doubeck looked worried.

"I fully expect something to happen that we don't expect," said Colt.

"Aww, I feel like I'm gonna throw up," said Charlie.

"Gunny, if we use all our fuel charging batteries and filling our air tanks, we're gonna be cutting it close," said Doubeck.

"And if we run out of battery power," said Marty. "We're real likely to get grounded and sunk. We won't be able to dive, we won't be able to…"

"Marty, that's enough." Amber took a step in Marty's direction. "Listen, we can think of scenarios all day long. Good ones and bad ones. But just taking us into a dark place isn't helping. I'd suggest you use your scenarios for planning."

Marty shook his head. "Can't run without fuel, that's all there is to it."

"Then we got no choice. We'll have to rendezvous with a tanker. Right, Gunny?" asked Stewart.

"I'll see what I can do," he said. It wasn't a promise, but it offered some hope.

Amber walked past Stewart and leaned into the corner of the cabin. She pulled a captain's hat off the back corner of the shelf behind the wheel and slapped it on her hip to dust it off. Then she snugged it onto her head.

"Looks good on you," said Charlie. He could feel his breathing speed up.

Mish stepped between them, turned toward Amber, and must have made a face because Amber rolled her eyes and removed the hat. Mish turned and looked at the group.

"So, what about the water," she said. "How do we float the boat?"

"I'm sorry. I think my parents must have thrown a lot of Mrs. Kraus's notes out before we started searching them because we never did find any plans for a dam, or any way to fill it," said Charlie.

Mish patted Charlie's back. "It's okay. We'll figure it out."

"Well, I calculated the volume of the gully from the creek up to the top of the sub." Marty leaned back against the cabin instead of hanging onto a railing. "It's like five frickin million gallons. Based on the trickle that comes down that little creek, we'd need a rain like the Great Flood to fill it. Plus, the whole thing probably would have to happen overnight."

"Then that's it?" said Doubeck. "We're S-O-L."

Marty threw up his hands. "Sheesh, Doubeck. I'm just saying it would take a month of monsoon rain to turn that gully into a pond, and someone's bound to notice it's dammed up. We gotta come up with something besides hoping for a storm."

"Guys, think about this," said Colt. "You know the Nazis had it all worked out. They had to have a plan to fill that hole with water like overnight. They couldn't have a dam with a sub floating around in it for a few weeks where anyone could spot it."

"Maybe they already had the pond," said Doubeck.

"You mean they might've had a pond here once? I don't think so," said Marty. "Some of the trees are a hundred years old and a pond woulda killed 'em."

Heads were shaking around the cabin as the enormity of the problem sunk in. The lack of energy in the room was bringing everyone down.

"There's the duck pond," said Amber.

"The duck pond? The duck pond is a mile away," said Charlie. "It would be easier to get the sub down to the lake than up to the duck pond."

"But what if we moved the duck pond?" asked Mish.

"Come on, let's not waste time with bullshit philosophical stuff," said Doubeck.

Colt waved his hand high. "Hang on, hang on, guys. Tell me what're you thinking, Mish?"

"I'm thinking that our creek, the one right down here, starts at the duck pond up by the airport, like a mile away. The duck pond is huge, it's probably the size of a city block."

Colt pointed south, toward the duck pond. "So, you're sure that's the same creek that comes down the gully at Charlie's house?"

"Yeah, I think so. But I'm not sure cuz it disappears. It goes into some huge pipes right beside the pond."

"We gotta know if it's the same creek that runs past the sub."

Mish shrugged and looked to Charlie for an answer.

"I mean, it's the only creek around," he said.

"If it's the only creek, then I think we've gotta go with it," said Colt.

Mish pointed a finger at Marty. "You and I need to check it out. Let's take a hike up to the duck pond."

Mish wasn't the only one encouraged by the thought that a solution to the launch might be possible. Heads that had been bowed and sullen just moments ago were suddenly up and animated. A whole new vibe had entered the cabin.

"This could work. It's really genius, Mish," said Doubeck.

Charlie agreed. "It's almost like it was designed that way."

"I think it was, dude. I think maybe they had it all set up," said Marty. "We just have to figure out how to get that water from up there, all the way down here."

The sound of the engine soon replaced the chatter. When Stewart noticed people had stopped talking, he turned his head away from the oncoming waves and looked down to see the entire group staring at him. They had moved on to the next issue—how to make the machine come to life.

Stewart grinned. "I guess the ball's in my court, huh?"

The progress they'd made and the optimism they felt about the duck pond suddenly moved everything else from the bottom of the list and squarely onto Stewart's shoulders.

That was a concern to Colt. He was more aware of the pressure on Stewart than the others were, and he knew this was not a good time to add more.

He patted Stewart's shoulder. "How's the U-boat looking?"

"I think everything's ready. Batteries are hooked up. I ran the electric motors and they run smooth and quiet. There's a little bit of ozone but I think if I can get some copper cleaner on the commutators that'll go away."

"That's exactly what I was thinking," said Mish, rolling her eyes and bobbing her head.

Everyone chuckled.

Stewart seemed embarrassed by his skills. "Okay. Well, it's a machine. The parts have to be clean."

"That we understand," said Marty.

"But I also won't know how good the boat's plumbing is until it's actually in the water. I mean, for sure we're going to have leaks. We just are. We're going to have to find them fast and fix them. If they're too bad, well...you know."

"Yeah, we'll sink like a literal rock," said Doubeck.

"Were you thinking you'd have to be on board when we launch?" Colt asked.

Stewart shrugged. "Uh-huh. I figured I would."

Amber stepped out of the corner and put a hand on Stewart's shoulder. "The captain will be there right with you."

"Thanks, Amber."

"You're going to need a helper," said Marty.

"Guys." Gunny scratched his cheek. "I'm as excited about this as you are, but everything in my gut is telling me you need to think of a way to launch the boat without being in it. It's the feeling of self-preservation. It's the same feeling that helped get me home from Afghanistan."

The crew was listening. Colt had never talked about his service.

"I can't think of a single reason anybody has to be in that boat when it goes into the lake. But I can think of a lot of reasons you shouldn't be there. The damn thing has never been floated. Remember, it was sawed into pieces and then welded back together. It could crack in half when it hits the water. It could."

Colt's concern reminded Amber of the anxiety she felt the first time she took the helm of her family's sailboat. But driving the sub would be a lot different. There would be no horizon to watch, no stars to steer you at night. You would feel no wind in your face, and no smell of rain from distant storms would fill your head.

She felt a chill.

Colt took advantage of the silence and continued. "Listen, I know you've all been reading about these boats. I hope you read that eighty-five out of a hundred German U-boat sailors never survived. That's not even close to reasonable odds. Serving in the Kriegsmarine on a U-boat was a death wish. Now, I'm not saying it was the boats, but that might be part of it. And, shit, it's eighty years old. Why don't we just button it up, let it fly and we'll swim out and board it after we're sure it survived the launch? It's not going to sail away without you."

The crew, all of whom had been looking at Colt from the moment he started his speech, now had their heads hung low again.

"I'm with Colt."

It was Charlie, and his opinion carried a lot of weight. "Amber, Stewart, and I will stay aboard until she floats to make sure everything is buttoned up and secure for launch."

"Doubeck," said Colt. "Once she's floating behind the dam, you and I need to stay on the lines until she goes over and into the lake. It's going to take both of us to jockey the cables around the steps, run that winch, and then trigger the dam to open all at once so it flushes the sub like a doggone toilet."

"Hey," Stewart pushed Colt's shoulder. "Show some respect for my girl."

"She needs a name, guys," said Doubeck.

Mish threw her hands into the air. "Doobs, will you give it a rest?"

Amber stood and moved toward the ladder. "Just get me my fuel, Gunny."

"Oorah," was all he said. It was just enough to let everyone feel they were almost there.

THE LAST U–BOAT

DAY
AT THE
BEACH

As the sun set over the lake each evening, the wind shifted almost imperceptibly from offshore to onshore. Alone on the sand, sitting on a big beach towel, Amber and Charlie felt the air begin to warm their backs as the breeze gently rolled off the land, carrying with it the heady fragrance of newly mowed grass and blossoming lilacs. In front of them, the lake rocked lazily, offering not so much as a splash as the water moistened the rocks along the shoreline.

Amber reached over, took Charlie's hand from his knee and held it. "I'm worried about you," she said.

"What d'ya mean?"

"Something's bothering you. Is it about working with Stewart?" she asked.

Charlie sighed. "No, I'm over it. Actually, I kinda like Stewart. He's okay. It's just that we can't keep the U-boat a secret much longer, and I have this awful feeling I'm going to be in big trouble. We all are."

"We haven't done anything wrong, Charlie."

"It's not gonna matter. Someone's going to want to take the sub away from us and if they don't have a reason they'll just come up with one. I keep thinking how my Mom and Dad are going to feel when they find out I had this big secret and I didn't tell them."

"But if this works, they'll be amazed. We'll all be amazed."

Charlie squeezed her hand. "I never told you I remember seeing you the first day I went to McCullough High. I mean where you were, what you were wearing, everything."

Amber smiled. "When was that?"

"It was after a game, in the gym. I tried to think of ways to meet you before I knew you lived right across the creek." He motioned back up the hill behind them.

"Surprise! I'm your neighbor."

"You're like some kind of therapy. I mean you really calm me down and help me relax."

Amber rested her hand on Charlie's back. "You'll like this, Charlie."

"What?"

"My cousin, Elena, went out on a date last week and her boyfriend asked her if she wanted to go watch the submarine races."

"Huh?" His back stiffened. "Submarine races?"

It surprised Amber how quickly the word 'submarine' put him on edge.

"Charlie," she grinned at his naivete, "he was asking her if she wanted to make out."

Charlie turned toward Amber with a quizzical grin. *Really? I don't get it.*"

As she spoke, she traced the features of his face with her index finger, barely touching his cheeks, his neck and his chin. He thought it was odd that her light touch didn't tickle. It felt like electricity.

"So, if you and I drove down to the lake and parked at Powell Avenue in that turnaround...?"

"Yeah."

Her finger brushed across his lips. "...we could look out at the lake and see the submarines race."

"Oh, okay. I get it. There are no submarines."

"Well, not yet," said Amber. Charlie took her hand and kissed it.

"So they made out?"

"I don't know. I asked, but she wouldn't tell me. She just giggled."

"She wouldn't tell you? I think she would if she did something," said Charlie.

Amber tipped her head to one side. "Oh, Charlie, sometimes I think you might be too innocent for me."

"Me?"

She put her arms around him and squeezed hard. It was the first time she had hugged him when they were alone. "Yeah, you," she said. "But we can fix that."

"Oh, really!" he said, laughing a bit nervously. He dropped his head back onto the sand and held his arms wide. "Do what you want. Just don't hurt me."

Amber lowered her voice to a whisper and imitated a familiar movie line, "Be afraid," she said. "Be very afraid."

She lay against him and closed her eyes. Her face was perfect, soft and smooth.

Charlie put one hand behind her waist, the other behind her head. He drew her close and softly touched her lips with his. Amber rolled back onto the sand, taking him with her. She sighed, looked up at him, and then pressed her mouth harder against his.

When they stopped, Charlie kissed her cheek and whispered in her ear.

"You know, I don't want to be *too* innocent."

Amber took Charlie's free hand, wrapped her fingers around his and held it tightly to her. She looked softly in his eyes as she turned toward him. "Yeah, that wouldn't be right."

She pressed his hand hard against her body and left it there as she caressed his face. He could feel their hearts pound, and with his fingertips, he felt the heat of her bare skin.

A feeling of happiness grew deep within him, an immediate antidote to all the stress in his life, and it felt very good.

Neither wanted to say it first, but after a few minutes they knew it was time to go. The crew would be gathering at the sub.

Amber's fingertips wandered slowly down Charlie arm. She slipped her fingers between his and brought his hand back to her cheek. Then, they sat, watching silently as the sun painted the clouds in orange and purple pastels until it disappeared beyond the horizon, and doing so, pulled the darkness down with it.

Colt, Stewart and Marty were in the factory room looking at the old green diesel engine.

"This diesel's been run before," said Stewart. "Looks like it's in okay shape. I'm concerned about the fuel filter. See, it's inside the little glass jar here. You can see the filter's dirty. It looks like the fuel has all turned to jelly."

"Then it's shot?" asked Marty.

"Ehhhhhh, it probably just needs to be cleaned out." Stewart buffed the glass as he spoke.

"Maybe, once they built the sub, they didn't need this engine anymore," said Colt, as he walked to the front of the massive diesel and looked down at the floor. He reached toward a steel plate fastened to the slab to see if he could shake a bolt loose. The plate had two three-inch circular holes in the middle and a bolt on each corner. "Why do you think they poured concrete here, Stewart? Why didn't they just set the thing on a pallet, or right down on the dirt floor?"

"I'm not sure, Gunny. But they sure wanted it anchored. That's a deep foundation."

"Let's pull this plate and see what's down there." said Colt.

The Nazis had left an amazing collection of tools and hardware. Stewart handed Colt an open-end wrench. He took a socket wrench for himself, and the two of them began removing the four nuts that secured the plate at the foot of the old engine, handing each one to Marty as it came off. The steel plate covered only a portion of the slab under the engine. The concrete ran all the way to the lake side, the north end of the factory room. It looked like a sidewalk leading to the wall.

As soon as they had removed the steel, they trained their lights into the pit.

"Look at those gears," said Colt.

Stewart leaned over the edge. "That's a long way down."

"Yeah, it's like looking into a well," said Colt.

Marty leaned in and looked into the darkness below. "I think I know what it is," he said. "It's how we're going to launch the sub."

Doubeck lay on his back in a hammock on one side of the crew quarters, and Mish stretched out in the hammock on the opposite side, holding a flashlight so she could see him as they spoke.

"Doob, you think Charlie's okay?" she asked.

"He's pretty stressed. A lot of it's my fault, too," he said.

"How do you figure?"

He took a deep breath. "I pushed him about talking to Stewart, even when I knew he had good reasons to dislike the guy. I could have given him more time—more time to think about it and work it out in his head. I just pushed way too hard."

"Personally, I think Colt and his money might be the problem," she said.

"Naaahhh. Colt's a good guy. I'm sure of it," said Doubeck. "I mean, Colt's out there right now working his butt off. Plus, we need his money to get the U-boat running."

Mish kicked one leg over the side of the hammock. "So, what's Colt's deal? I get the feeling he's like counseling Stewart."

"He's keeping Stewart in line, that's for sure. And he's helping with the heavy work."

Doubeck and Charlie had agreed to keep Stewart's problems under wraps until they resolved. His personal troubles didn't have anything to do with the sub, so Stewart had asked to keep it a private matter. Doubeck wanted to tell Mish but he just couldn't.

"What are they working on?" Mish asked.

"They're looking at the diesel engine in the factory room, following up on your theory, Miss Genius."

"My theory?" said Mish. "You mean the dam?"

"Uh huh. Closing up the steps and making a pond in the gully will definitely float the U-boat. It's perfect."

She returned a very sweet and uncharacteristic smile when Doubeck acknowledged her. "But what if we close the dam and the duck pond doesn't fill it up. I mean, we need a major flood. How do we make sure that happens?" Mish asked.

"Like you told Marty. You two should go look at the duck pond and figure it out. I haven't been there in years."

The U-boat suddenly went dark.

"I think I'd rather stay here," she said. Doubeck felt her hands wrap around his shoulders as she pulled herself into the hammock with him.

———————

It was almost 10:00 p.m. as Charlie and Amber walked up the path along the creek, headed back to their homes. Charlie heard some movement and saw lights up ahead. It was very unusual for anyone to be down at the creek after dark, unless they were heading home from the beach. He motioned toward the light, put his finger to his lips and pulled Amber off to the side of the path where they crouched behind a giant oak.

Charlie could make out a figure, a lone man, wearing a gray suit and a tie. He wasn't trying to hide. He made a lot of noise as he picked his way along and he swept his light back and forth. It was clear he was unfamiliar with the path.

As he came close, Charlie recognized him. "Mr. Ryan?"

Patrick Ryan, who worked at South Shore Bank had set up Charlie's bank accounts that currently totaled nearly three-quarters of a million dollars.

The man froze. "Who's that?"

"It's Charlie LeClair."

"Charlie! Where are you, Charlie?" Charlie motioned for Amber to stay hidden as he stood and stepped out from behind the tree and toward the light.

"Right here."

"Hey, Charlie, I'm glad you're here. Listen, I'm looking for Gunny. I've been calling him for a couple hours but he's not answering. Do you know where he is? He said he'd be down by the beach tonight."

"I really don't know where he is. I haven't seen him since the day he introduced us at the bank. I was just at the beach for the last hour, so I can tell you for sure he's not down there."

"Okay. Well, listen, if you see him, ask him to call me right away. It's important. Oh, and tell him his phone's busted."

"Will do, Mr. Ryan. I'll see you."

Ryan turned and retraced his steps back up the creek. Charlie watched him retreat and then made his way back to Amber.

"It's okay," he said. "That's Mr. Ryan from the bank. I know him."

"I heard you say something about Colt," said Amber.

"Yeah, they're friends. Ryan's looking for Colt because Colt's been ghosting him."

"He's probably underground. Maybe we should go up to the sub and see if he's there," Amber suggested.

They crossed the creek to the well-worn trail winding up the hillside and toward the manhole. Soon, they had descended the ladder and were making their way forward to the torpedo hatch where they would exit into the Deep Room.

Just before entering the crew quarters, they were surprised when a flashlight suddenly snapped to life.

"Hey, come on. That's bright," said Charlie. Amber grabbed Charlie's arm to steady herself.

"Yikes, dude." It was Doubeck's voice.

The flashlight revealed Doubeck and Mish, sitting next to each other on one of the padded leather benches under a hammock, acting way too casual. They stood when their friends reached them.

Charlie could hardly hide his surprise. "Doubeck, what's wittchu and Mish?"

Amber's fist hit Charlie's right kidney from behind. The jab made Charlie realize he might have made it sound like making out with Mish was a bad idea.

He tried to change course. "No, I mean, why here?"

Amber smirked, "That was awkward."

"Can we move on?" asked Mish.

"Yeah, we sure can. Charlie, we're looking for Colt, remember?" said Amber.

"Pretty sure Colt's in the Deep Room," said Doubeck.

"Sorry, you two. I wish our phones worked down here. We coulda called," said Charlie.

Amber pushed Charlie along, "We gotta go. See yah!"

As he passed, he yanked on Doubeck's untucked shirt. "@ me next time, doosh." Doubeck smiled and clapped back with a shoulder bump. It took Charlie off-balance and turned him around. As he grabbed a hammock to steady himself, his light caught Amber and Mish exchanging smiles behind him.

Colt saw Charlie and Amber slide off the hull onto the floor of the Deep Room. Marty and Stewart were with him, bent over an opening in the floor next to the diesel engine.

"Hi, Charlie. Hey, Captain." Colt saluted Amber and she returned it.

"Hey, Gunny. We ran into Mr. Ryan down by the creek. He's looking for you. Said it was important. Oh, and he said he's been calling your cell but didn't get an answer."

Colt checked his watch. "Dammit. I had no idea it was this late. Listen everyone, I have to go topside to make a call, so I'm just gonna take off. "

Colt dashed to the hull of the sub and climbed up the boarding net like Spiderman before turning around and calling out. "You all need to get home so no one sends out a search party." He quickly disappeared down the forward hatch.

"He's really strong," said Amber.

Before Charlie could respond, Marty walked up.

"Charlie, I haven't had a chance to ask you, and Colt's not here now, so I was wondering. Are you really against us riding the sub into the lake when it's launched?"

Charlie had been thinking about it because that decision was one of those more important life calls Colt had been talking about.

"Yeah. That's a good question. Here's what I think, Marty, and I'd appreciate your opinion."

"Of course."

"I think the sub needs to be running when it hits the lake so the waves close to shore don't wash it aground. If it springs a leak from the launch, who'd fix it? Anyway, she needs a crew. I say we have a crew when she's launched."

"Well. It's dangerous. Colt's right. Anyone in the sub could die."

"Yes. That's a fact, Marty. No question. So what's your opinion?"

"My opinion is a lot could go wrong. I think there's about a thirty-percent chance whoever's in the sub could die. It could hit hard, blow up, crack and sink, you could get knocked out, a hatch could get jammed so you couldn't get out. A torpedo…"

"Marty…" Amber stepped toward him.

Marty swallowed but ignored her. "…I mean, a torpedo is a major weapon. It could kill us all."

"Chillax, Marty…" Now, Stewart was trying to talk him off the ledge.

"I'm just sayin…" Marty looked around at the faces of his friends.

Stewart held a hand out, like he was pleading for restraint. "He asked your opinion, dude. We all know what could go wrong."

"Yeah, okay. In that case, I guess it's better if there's a crew."

Charlie looked over at Amber. Then they both looked at Stewart. It would be them.

Marty nodded. "Yeah. Well I'd suggest we keep this on the DL for now. Cool?"

"No shit," said Doubeck. It remained quiet for a time as the impact of their decision sunk in.

"So what is this hole in the ground, Marty?" asked Amber.

As Marty pointed into the hole, Mish and Doubeck appeared.

"Sup, dudes?" asked Doubeck.

Charlie turned when he heard Doubeck's voice. "Not a clue, Doob."

Marty faced the crew. "Well, in order to make the steps into a dam and float the sub, the steps have to close up. I'm pretty sure the gears and cables down here are what the Nazis were going to use."

"How's that supposed to work?" asked Charlie.

"Think of it like lacing a shoe," said Marty. "The cable goes through a pulley tied to a tree on the far side of the creek and hooks onto a timber on this side. Or, the cable can hook to a timber on the other side of the creek that has to slide this direction. Either way, when the diesel pulls, they come to the middle. We're still figuring it out, but it'll work."

Charlie stuck his hands into his pockets. "Well, while you're working on that, you can figure out how the duck pond, or a thunderstorm, or some miracle is going to fill the gully? I mean, we need to know where we're gonna get like ten million gallons of water overnight."

Marty nodded and slumped back against the diesel as his friends left for the pantry. He rubbed his eyes, his head bowed in thought. Under his breath he whispered, "Noah got a flood. Moses got a flood and it saved his tuchus. Can I maybe get a flood here, please?"

THE LAST U-BOAT

T
IS FOR
TALIBAN

Stewart had never spied on Oleg. From the time he was hired to help out at the marina, he had respected his boss's position and his privacy. After Oleg casually murdered a boat load of strangers, that respect morphed into fear. Stewart chose the safety inherent in keeping his distance and ignoring Petrosian's comings and goings.

Today was different.

Stewart was on a mission to search Petrosian's office for anything he could find about his nefarious alliance with the Taliban.

Pat Ryan said the bank had picked up some intel indicating that something big was happening on the Canadian border. They'd been told to look for suspicious activity.

Thanks to Colt, Charlie had become a millionaire in just the past six weeks, and his sudden wealth matched what the Feds had told banks to look out for. Ryan wanted and got Colt's assurance that everything Charlie was into was above board. Truth be told, Colt may have embellished things a bit.

"Pat, the kid's a genius. Long story short, I'm helping him buy and sell surplus using legit online auctions. He's written an algorithm that tells him when to bid or sell, and we're killing it. Some of our transactions involve very valuable antique guns, but he's under age, so I do the transactions for a commission and everything goes through on my Federal Firearms License. It's all on the up and up, man."

His story was mostly true. There wasn't any written algorithm. But Colt did unload the weapons through online auctions, and he did take a commission. Ryan knew Charlie's deposits were all checks written by Colt, and Colt's corresponding deposits were ten percent of Charlie's. Ryan, of course, had already carefully checked the activity on both Colt's and Charlie's accounts and everything Colt told him added up. The only question that would be hard to answer was, where did Charlie get the weapons they were selling? Colt hoped no one would ask.

Once Colt confirmed what Ryan already knew, Ryan willingly shared with him everything he'd heard about the alert. The absence of key details, like bodies washing ashore, told Colt that he and Stewart probably already knew a lot more about what was happening than did Homeland Security, or whoever had sounded the alarm. It also meant that Colt and the gang probably had only a short time to launch the U-boat before the Feds found some leads, moved in, and covered the lake shore like ants at a picnic.

Colt agreed to Stewart's spy mission because he sensed it wouldn't be long before the Armenians would be in the government's crosshairs. At that point, Stewart would surely get swept up in their surveillance. They'd connect him to the rest of the kids and then all hell would break loose. Time was of the essence.

Stewart stepped behind Petrosian's desk. He had no idea what he was looking for. Colt had told him he might not recognize a clue if he saw it. It might be something ordinary, something nondescript. He also told Stewart to immediately send any photos he took, and then erase them from his phone.

Stewart played back Colt's speech in his head: "Question everything you see," he said. "Why's it there? Could it have another purpose? Is there something on the desk that he'd never ordinarily use? Check the garbage cans. Think creatively. It's all about the difference between looking and seeing.

"Once you're standing there, looking at his desk, you will be looking at something incriminating, I guarantee it. The trick will be to see it."

Stewart stood beside Petrosian's chair and stared at the chaos in front of him. It looked like nothing had been moved for weeks. Where no trash or papers lay strewn about, there was a layer of dust. McDonald's wrappers filled the waste can and a few dried french fries had taken refuge between stacks of papers and unopened mail.

Stewart was going to search the desk the same way he'd troubleshoot an engine. He'd cover every square inch until he understood what he was looking at.

He decided to begin at a corner of the desk, isolating a square foot of surface and looking carefully at each item within it. He would be suspicious of anything and everything until he could dismiss it and move to the next square foot.

In his mind, Stewart broke the desk down into a grid pattern, so he could efficiently search every square foot until the job was complete. Colt was standing by, monitoring the entire process.

Stewart took a deep breath and focused his eyes on the far left corner of the desk.

The sun would be up soon. Marty and Mish had expected to be at the duck pond by now. A heavy, early morning fog drifted down from the warm pond waters as they approached. Through the milky haze they saw red and orange lights flashing. They could hear men shouting and the growling of truck engines. As they drew closer, they could see a squad of orange and yellow-vested workers had blocked the access road with barricades, and were unloading heavy equipment.

"This isn't good, Mish. Let me see what's going on." Marty walked around a barricade and casually approached the only worker holding a clipboard. He looked to be twenty-something, probably a college kid with a summer job. "Is it okay if we walk around the pond?"

"Yeah, no problem. Just stay clear of the trucks."

Mish's pretty face caught the young man's eye and he took a step in her direction. The fog obscured everything around her like a painting. "Hey, do you have a sister at Algonquin College?" he asked.

"No. I have a cousin who went there. Look, my name's Michelle. You could have just asked." The guy's eyebrows lifted to the middle of his forehead.

Marty covered his face with his hands. Mish's unfiltered reply was so Mish.

"Hi, Michelle. I'm Bud Staley. Nice to meet you. We're going to start work here next Tuesday. If you come back, make sure you stop and say hello. I'll be here."

"Okay. We'll be back."

"What are you doing with all this equipment?" asked Marty.

"We're cleaning years of muck from the bottom of the pond. We have to drain it, build a ramp up to it, excavate a few feet of mud off the bottom and then let it fill up again."

Marty's heart sank. The solution to launching the submarine was about to be taken away from them.

"How do you drain it?"

"Through the outfall control down there at the far end. It's the thing that looks like a big guillotine." Staley motioned toward the north side of the pond where the earthen berm grew concrete shoulders. It formed a spillway, designed to allow the controlled release of the pond's waters.

"We tried to open it up a couple of inches last week and it jammed cuz it's really old. Now we're taking it slow, since it's all rusted. If we try to open it any more, it could let go and send a huge flood down the culverts. They're six feet in diameter, so they can hold the water. But we don't know what might happen below West Lake Road where the culverts end. Down there it's just a creek bed with houses on either side. Could be disastrous."

"That's where we live. You're not going to flood us out are you?" asked Mish.

Staley pointed to a huge machine that had just been set on the roadside along the berm surrounding the pond. "That's our pump right there. It'll take twelve days, running full-time, to empty the pond. We're going to go nice and easy." He seemed proud to be able to recite his understanding of the project.

Marty thought he'd test him. "Twelve days? So, how many gallons is that?"

"This pumps going to run full-out. That's a thousand gallons a minute. Comes out to just over twenty-million gallons. Could be less. Depends on how much muck is in there."

"How'd you figure that out so fast?" asked Mish.

Staley grinned. "I didn't. They ran the numbers back at the office."

"Yikes," said Marty. His heart rate picked up. He had figured they'd only need half that volume of water to launch the sub.

"When does this all start?" asked Mish.

"They're doing some grading and site prep today, and we'll be back in a week to start pumping. Next Tuesday." Staley smiled. "You gonna be here?"

Mish held her hands up palms out. "Hey, if the pond's still here, I'll be here."

Staley face showed he was trying to make sense of her comment. "Oh, it'll be here, Michelle."

"We'll see," she replied, and with her index finger to her forehead, she saluted the young man in orange. Marty took her by the elbow and turned her away, heading toward the gate in the direction Staley had pointed.

"Mish, what are you doing?"

"I want him to wonder how I knew the pond would disappear before he got back."

"Ah, no. Trust me, you don't."

"You're so freakin paranoid, Marty."

"Mish, when we take that water, they're going to come looking for it."

***

Colt stood on the crest of the hill beside the well-greased steps, far above Lake Erie's breaking waves. He planted his left foot on the highest timber, bending his knee. The offshore breeze blew his coal black hair straight back and pinned his T-shirt to his chest. He looked a lot like a ship's captain commanding from the forecastle, watching the infinite sea before him, awaiting the adventure to come.

The crew had mastered the mystery of the wall, figured it all out, and it was pure genius. Half-inch cables meant to draw the timbers together, exited a cast iron pipe on the exterior of the lake cliff.

With the help of a couple strong men, clevis pins, and a pulley, the diesel would retrieve the cable and drag the timbers, left and right, until they met in the middle. Then, the process would be repeated with the next pair, and the next, until the gap closed and the creek bed was dammed.

The Nazis had drilled holes through the tops of the timbers where big pegs were meant to be inserted. Colt figured the pegs would stiffen the wall against the weight of water pushing against it.

But to launch the sub on a pillow of rushing water, there had to be a way to crack open the dam in an instant and spill its contents all at once into the lake below.

Colt thought he had the solution. He wandered down to the steps for some recon. After an hour, he spotted eye bolts installed in the ends of the eighth timbers, left and right. They would be just eight to ten feet above the floor of the creek when the dam closed. That suggested to Colt that the eye bolts were located at points where Kraus had figured the dam would need to be supported.

Between the reinforcement provided by the pegs inserted into the wall, and a couple of steel cables connecting the eye bolts to two of the giant oak trees in the gully, the tons of water behind the dam would not be able to breach it.

But, if they rigged the cables with quick release hardware, when it let go, the pegs would start to snap, transferring all the weight of the water to the unsupported walls, assuring the rapid, cascading destruction of the dam.

It was one of the last pieces of the puzzle and, as long as the dam held when they needed it, he knew it could be breached—even if he had to use an explosive. And as a trained sapper, he knew just where to get one. Or two.

It was a safe and sure solution guaranteeing success, especially now that the crew had agreed to let the sub launch unmanned.

As he watched a distant sailboat tack against the west wind, his phone began to vibrate. It was Stewart.

Stewart didn't even say hello. "I think I found it, but I don't know what it is."

"Where are you?"

"I'm out on the pier."

"Is Petrosian there?"

"No, not yet."

"Okay. What did you get?"

"It's a little paper address book, but it's weird. I sent you a picture."

"What's weird about it?"

"Well, first, it's just A through D. I mean, if I had an address book and I didn't have E through Z, I'd throw the damn thing away."

"Good point. I'll look at it."

"Well, there's something else."

"Yeah?"

"So, all the names are written in English and then right next to them it looks like another name in some different language. It's a whole different alphabet. But the names that start with A aren't in the A section and the Bs aren't in the B section. Well maybe there's one or two, but it's just nuts."

"Yeah? Like how?"

"Like, why put a bunch of names under a certain letter when they don't even start with that letter? And there are no phone numbers or addresses with the names. Nothing about it makes sense."

Colt thought about that for a second while Stewart waited in silence.

"Gunny!" Someone was calling to him from the hillside.

"Stewart, hang on."

Colt turned toward the voice. "Marty?"

"Yeah. Mish and I are here. We need to talk. It's important."

"Be right there. Get below, I'll see you there."

He put the phone to his ear. "Stewart, can you get home, pack a bag and get to the sub like your life depended on it?"

"Yeah, Gunny."

"Then, get outta there. Now."

THE LAST U-BOAT

STEWART
GOES
UNDERGROUND

Mish and Marty filled Colt in on the activity at the duck pond as they met in the U-boat's engine room. Clearly, the crew was running out of time. When they finished talking, they headed topside. Mish and Marty left to round up Charlie and Amber, and Colt had his own list of chores to finish before dark. Once he cleared the hatch, Colt's phone went back on line and started vibrating. It was a series of text messages from Stewart.

Colt read the texts and called Stewart.

"Gunny?"

"Stewart. You can't stay at home."

"I know. I'm just grabbing a few things."

"Is your mother there?"

"My mother? Ah, no, she's not."

"Well, she's not safe. You've got to get her outta there."

"She's gone and she won't be back, Gunny. I'll explain when I see you."

"Okay, sure."

"I have a duffle bag packed. I'll be heading down the creek in a few minutes. You around?"

"Yeah, I'm at the hatch and about to go below."

"Okay. I'll meet you there in fifteen minutes."

"Just go, man. You're going to be hunkered down in the U-boat for a while. If you need anything, we'll get it for you. Just get here." Colt ended the call without a goodbye.

Twenty minutes later Colt and Stewart were sitting on the floor of the control room. Colt leaned back against the cold steel tube that housed the periscope, facing Stewart who sat across the narrow walkway. The remaining crew was expected soon, but this was their first chance to talk since

Stewart hustled out of the marina earlier that day, never to return.

"So, where's your Mom?"

Stewart took a deep breath. "My mom's been dead for over a year, Gunny. She was away visiting family in Sweden when my aunt called to say she had a heart attack and passed away. She was cremated in Stockholm. Nobody here ever knew, I mean no one, and I was afraid to say anything because I didn't know what would happen to me if I did."

"What about neighbors? Didn't they wonder where she was?"

"Neighbors? She never even talked to them. She had a thick accent and she was self-conscious about it. Mom really only went out to garden. She didn't have any friends except my father, and he died years ago." Stewart wiped the backs of his hands across his face. His palms were stained with grease.

"I only had a year of school left, so I didn't want to leave, and I figured since I was eighteen I was pretty much on my own. Our relatives in Sweden called me after it was all over. I didn't even get to go to her funeral."

"You mean you've been holding down a job, paying your bills and keeping house on your own for a year?"

Stewart thought about it for a second. "Year and a half."

"Sheesh, Stewart. Your friends didn't know?"

Stewart's chin started to quiver. "I didn't have any friends, Gunny."

Colt leaned over and put his hand on Stewart's shoulder. He spoke softly and deliberately. "You do now, Stewart. And don't ever doubt it. They're friends who respect you enough to put their lives in your hands. You hear me?"

"I hear you, Gunny," he said, as he wiped his eyes again, this time with his sleeve.

Stewart's story answered a lot of questions Colt had harbored about the young man's history.

He had suddenly found himself an orphan. Life had robbed him of a family, and left him with no one to share his grief. He became angry, and people who had normal lives with brothers, sisters, mothers and fathers became targets of his resentment.

His loss helped Colt understand Stewart's bullying, and the chip on his shoulder. It also helped explain why, when he finally responded positively to the group's cautious offer of friendship, it turned him around. It explained Stewart's work ethic, demonstrated some real character, and revealed a level of maturity beyond his years.

Colt stood, grabbed a rag from the table next to the periscope, and tossed it to Stewart to wipe away the grease. Putting an arm around his neck, he patted Stewart's back like a proud father comforting his son. "I'll keep your secret. But, someday, you probably should let the others know. It'd be a way of showing them you trust them. It's up to you."

"I'll think about it." Colt gave Stewart's back one more firm pat, as if to say he knew Stewart would do the right thing.

Colt tapped on his phone. "So, here's the picture you sent me."

"Yeah, so see that letter B. This was the last page of the Bs and the first page of the Cs. There's this kinda' scribbling and then right next to it a name. Like here it said Dwayne, and then beside it whatever that scribbling says."

Colt scratched his chin. "Dwayne's a first name, right? Well, I bet Dwayne's last name starts with a B in Afghan."

Stewart tapped his finger on the screen of Colt's phone. "So, why does Oleg have these names? Who are these people?"

"I'll do some checking and see what I can find out."

Colt slipped the phone back into his khakis as a light shone from above them. The hatch was opening topside. He spoke softly.

"Sounds like they're coming down. Let's keep this phone directory thing just between us."

"Yeah, sure," said Stewart.

"Meanwhile. This is your home until the Petrosian matter is settled."

"Cool." Stewart stood and made his way toward the engine room. "I'll go turn on the lights."

"Really? Lights? That's great."

In a moment, tungsten filament light bulbs began to glow from every corner of the control room.

The sub came to life. Its internal organs, circulatory system and sinews were bathed in a pleasing warm light, courtesy of a reliable electric current supplied by an array of brand-new automobile batteries. It was the first time the group had been able to see the complexity of the machine so well, much of it now painted, polished, oiled and shining. They had grown familiar with its dark corridors, but most of the boat had remained in darkness, with only brief glimpses under flashlight beams exposing its deeper secrets. To see it now, fully revealed, inspired awe and terror at the same time.

The group entered the control room one or two at a time, in silence.

First in were Mish and Marty. Marty reached out to every nearby pipe and cable, feeling its texture and temperature. A lot of the pipes had been painted so often they had acquired a bumpy, slick surface, like a lizard's skin. Marty remembered watching Doubeck touch the diesel in the Deep Room. He thought it was odd then, but in hindsight, it made sense. Touching was just another way to study the plumbing and electrical systems. To know them by their heat and feel, and to follow their routes with your eyes. It was much more revealing than just reading about them.

Mish was clearly looking beyond arm's length, her designer's eyes scanning entire sections of the sub. It was amazing to see it lighted up. It was much smaller than she had realized.

Charlie and Amber appeared next. He walked, without hesitation, to the leather stool installed in front of the diving plane controls where he sat. He looked at the ceiling above him.

"Something's wrong, Stewart. There should be a big red vent valve right here over my head. It's in *Wolfpack*. I have to open and close it when we dive and surface."

Stewart remained by the ladder. "They moved it. You're sitting at one of the places where they sawed the sub into pieces. When they welded it back together I think they made some adjustments. The pipe is still there. Just follow the…"

"…I see it now. Thanks."

Amber stepped to the table by the periscope and turned to face the room.

Doubeck appeared last. As he moved through the passageway, he tapped his hands on the pipes, rails and bulkheads like they were bongo drums. It was annoying, but he wasn't trying to be obnoxious. He was just fidgeting.

They were sitting, now facing each other, looking at the machine that surrounded them. The moment they'd dreamed about approached like a predicted celestial event—destined in the distant past, unstoppable, inevitable. They could not be certain of the outcome, except that it would surely change their lives forever.

Colt cleared his throat to get everyone's attention. "Listen, before we get started. I want to say how proud I am of all of you. I'm a lot older than you guys."

"A *lot* older," said Doubeck.

"Thanks. But hear me out. You've already accomplished something very few people could ever hope to do. You've worked like a team. You've put petty differences aside. You've stayed on mission, and you've kept an amazing secret that was screaming to get out. You've solved some incredibly tough problems.

"I'm not saying this just to blow smoke. I'm saying it because, from here on out, it gets really dangerous. Now, there are things we can and will do to minimize that. But there are no guarantees. So, here's my point."

Colt stopped and looked at the floor, carefully considering his next words. "This is a perfectly reasonable time to just walk away with our heads held high. This is when it might be smart to say we've done everything we can."

There were plenty of quizzical looks.

Doubeck popped off. "You're shittin me."

"I know. I'm probably wasting my breath. But you need to think about it. I've lost friends who would be alive today if they hadn't pushed their luck just a bit too far. In their case, it was because we were fighting a war. But you're not. You're here for the adventure. Nobody's sayin you have to be here.

"Like I said, I'm not really trying to talk you out of completing your mission. I don't think there's any quit in you. So, if you're staying, I'm going to insist on one rule. Just one—don't die. That's it. Don't die." Colt stared right into Charlie's eyes as he said the words. He saw Charlie swallow hard.

At first, Charlie found it strange that Colt would say something so obvious. But "don't die," had a deeper meaning, and as Charlie thought about it, he began to understand what he thought Colt was driving at. 'Don't die' meant make good decisions. Think first before you act. Don't take unnecessary chances. Have a 'Plan B,' or an escape route. Have each other's backs. Don't ride the sub off a cliff, nose-first into the beach.

Colt was right. They were about to try to launch a ninety-year-old submarine that had been buried in a hillside since the middle of the last century. What could go wrong? Still, no one walked out.

Charlie's knee started bouncing up and down, something he did when he was getting anxious. It was time to bring the mood back up.

"Let's talk about the duck pond," he said.

That ended the discussion about quitting.

Charlie looked at Mish and Marty who were sitting together under the periscope. They hadn't yet told everyone what they found on their hike.

"We've got until Tuesday," said Marty. "That's when they plan to start pumping a thousand gallons an hour down the creek. I have a feeling they'll be here a lot checking to make sure they're not causing a disaster."

"Okay. It's got to be before Tuesday morning then," said Doubeck.

Marty nodded. "Yeah, and they messed up the spillway—it's a steel door that holds the whole pond back. So, I think if we put a chain on it, wrap it around the trailer hitch on Gunny's jeep and, yeet, it'll fly right outta there."

Colt was shaking his head. He clearly didn't like the idea. "You're not messing with my jeep. Besides, you need a half-track, not a jeep. Plus, how the hell are you going to get out of the way when twenty-million gallons are headed up your ass and you've got a steel plate hooked to your tail?"

It grew suddenly quiet, until Mish spoke up. "I'll take care of it."

Everyone looked at Colt like they expected him to throw a flag.

Colt shook them off. "You heard her."

Everyone looked at Mish.

"Okay. You wanna tell us how you're going to do it, Mish?" said Charlie.

"Nope. I need Marty there with me. That's it. We'll get it done."

Marty tipped his head toward Colt. "Gunny, you good with that?"

"Oorah!"

Mish pulled her hands out of her pockets and headed toward the ladder. "I gotta go, guys."

Amber and Charlie exchanged questioning glances and Charlie turned back to the crew. "Stewart, is the sub ready?"

"Engine wise, we have electric power and we can probably load enough diesel in jerry cans for four hours run time. I can pop a vent and pour it into the tanks from down here.

"We still need to rendezvous with a tanker and fill up pretty soon, or we'll end up dead in the water, bobbing around until someone finds us."

"What about the ballast tanks and the hull?" asked Amber. "Are we sure it won't leak?"

"Are we sure we can come back up once we're down?" Doubeck added.

"No, we're not." Stewart did not sound like he was kidding. "In fact, I'm almost certain when we get in the water, we're going to find all kinds of leaks. I won't know if the compressor pumps work, or if the ballast tanks are sealed, or if there might be holes in them. All the other welds look amazingly good, so I'm hoping the stuff I can't see is good, too."

"Can we fix things if we're out on the water?" asked Amber.

"Or under it," Mish added.

"Sure, if the leaks aren't too bad. But remember, in a sub, sooner or later, everything is below the water line. I don't have the tools or the training to fix anything outside the hull. I mean, I can order a set of hull plugs, and we might be able to dive in and fix small leaks with some special underwater putty. But if the leaks are too big or in the wrong place, we won't be able to stay buoyant. If that happens, we open the hatches and go for a swim."

Amber's eyes narrowed and her expression was grim. "There's a lot on you, Stewart."

He looked Amber straight in the eye. "Yeah, I know."

"Good. That tells me you're the right person for the job."

It was an affirmation that Stewart needed, and a statement of fact that no one could disagree with.

Marty's thoughts had moved past concern into tactics, and he still had a lot of questions. "Once she floats, we'll need to get her positioned dead center behind the dam. How do we do that?"

Amber offered a suggestion. "Let's tie the bow up to the spot where we want to be when we launch. If Gunny can put a peg on the top of the wall, right near the middle, we could toss a line over it and secure the other end to a cleat on the bow. Then we'll run our stern lines to each side of the gully to keep the boat lined up square."

"Couldn't we ram the wall to help launch the sub?" asked Mish.

Colt shook his head. "We can't without someone in the sub. Plus, you really do need to start the engines before you're launched, don't you think? You'll have plenty of time to prep the sub once you're floating behind the dam—I mean, if you even need to. If you're still behind the wall, then at least we can get you out if we have to."

Stewart agreed "Yeah, that's a good idea. We need to know they'll run. As soon as I have water under the boat I'll check pumps, load a little ballast and see if I can start the diesels. If everything's in good shape, I can shut 'er down and head down to the beach for the launch."

"How do we pull the quick release hardware on the dam?" Doubeck asked.

"I'll do it," said Colt. "I'll be on cables behind the sub. When we put the lines in, I'll attach them both to a single cable and I'll bring it over toward the driveway. One tug will pop both releases."

Charlie looked around the control room at the faces of his friends. He could see the excitement, the fear, the hope in each. "What are we forgetting?"

"Torpedoes," said Doubeck.

The crew laughed again at Doubeck's obsession with the boat's three underwater missiles.

Colt interrupted the chuckling. "Doubeck, you, Stewart and I are going to inspect them and make sure they're not armed and they're tied down solid. We don't want an accident if she drops hard into the lake. Then I want you two to do a complete inventory of all the weapons aboard. We haven't gone through a lot of the crates, and the hidden compartments. You know they used every available space to stow cargo. We need to know where all the dangerous stuff is so it doesn't kill us. Old explosives can't be trusted."

"What else are we forgetting?" asked Charlie.

"Pegs," said Colt. "Yeah, we need about forty wooden pegs to drop into the holes when we pull the timbers tight."

"How's that supposed to work?" asked Marty.

Colt thought for a minute. "Remember your butterfly collection?"

"How'd you know I had a butterfly collection?"

Colt raised an eyebrow and grinned out of the corner of his mouth. "Come on, Marty. I know you. Never was there a guy more likely to have a butterfly collection."

Marty shrugged. "Yeah, I remember it."

"How were the butterflies mounted?"

"I stuck a pin through them."

Mish and Amber issued a simultaneous "Eeeeewwwwww."

"And then what?" asked Colt.

"Then I pushed the pin down into balsa wood."

Colt nodded. "That's right. The pegs pin each timber to the one beneath it. That way, they distribute the weight of the water across the wall. They need to be almost as big as your wrist—and hard—but they need to snap like twigs when the quick release lets go and the sub hits the wall."

There were blank stares all around.

Colt surveyed the group's faces. "Any ideas?"

Doubeck had a question for Charlie. "Hey, remember when we broke your baseball bat opening the manhole?" asked Doubeck.

"Yeah." said Charlie.

Colt stood up. "Baseball bats. That's perfect."

"How many do I need to order?" asked Charlie.

Colt and Stewart replied at the same time. "Forty-eight."

Charlie smiled. "I should have known, you already counted."

"There's something else," said Amber. "Tomorrow's already Wednesday. We need to pick a day."

"We're supposed to have a big thunderstorm on Friday night. Maybe Saturday's best," offered Marty.

"It needs to be Friday." said Colt.

"In the rain?" asked Doubeck.

"Exactly. We're going to be making a racket so we could use the cover. The rain, the thunder—it'll help. Plus, we're gonna leave one helluva big hole in the side of the hill where the sub used to be, so we can blame the storm."

As the image of the torn hillside emerged into everyone's imaginations, their eyes turned toward Charlie.

He winced and put his hands on top of his head. It had never once crossed his mind that with the sub gone, there'd be nothing between his basement and blue sky but sixty feet of dirt floor. As he shook his head, he pictured himself trying to talk to his parents.

"I'm going to have a shitload of explaining to do."

THE LAST U-BOAT

COLT
BUYS A
BAYLINER

Colt had only seen Petrosian from a distance. Walking from his jeep to the marina store, he snugged his Smith and Wesson .38 Special to nest it securely in its Kydex sleeve. Colt sported a gaudy orange and violet Tommy Bahama shirt deliberately untucked to conceal the weapon.

He walked to the counter to wait for service and played nonchalantly with his phone. Oleg soon appeared, wearing his smiling salesman's face. Colt set his phone down on the counter and smiled back at the portly Armenian.

"Yes, sir. What help you need today?"

Colt had decided he'd take on the persona of a beer-drinkin' good ol' boy.

"Eye-talian, am I right?"

"What is Italian?"

"You sound Eye-talian. You Eye-talian? My girlfriend's Eye-talian. Gorgeous women, those Eye-talian girls. You all are really lucky." Colt punctuated his comment by pointing at Petrosian with his hand imitating the shape of a pistol.

"No, not Italian."

"Oh, I thought you had the Eye-talian accent. I apologize." Colt feigned embarrassment.

"Is okay. I Armenian. Also, we have lots of beautiful women in Armenia, so don't feel bad for me." Oleg's grin held firm.

Colt nodded. "Don't worry, I don't." Petrosian didn't flinch at the acerbic reply so Colt soldiered on. "I stopped in cuz I need a junk boat, a fix-up project for summer. Thought it might be fun. You got anything like that?"

"Hmm." Oleg whined and shrugged. "We don't got no junk. But we have some boat in back that need work."

"That'll do. Show me."

Colt wasn't looking for a boat. He was looking for a disguise. They needed something to conceal the conning tower when the U-boat was parked in the shallows or running on the surface. It needed to make the sub look like just any other boat on Lake Erie.

Of course, Stewart knew every boat in Petrosian's inventory. He told Colt to look for the thirty-two foot Bayliner with a big hole in the bottom and no engine. Stewart had scrapped it after it sank while tied up at the marina docks.

Colt's plan was to gut the Bayliner, cut the bottom out, spray urethane foam inside the hull to make it buoyant, float it out, and bring the sub up directly underneath it. It would be just wide enough to cover the tower. The top of the conning tower had never been installed, so the Bayliner would also provide cover for entering or exiting the hatch.

When submerged, they'd simply pull the whole boat down with them. Even at close range, the sub would be well camouflaged.

"That Grady-White looks perfect," said Colt.

"Yes. It make very fine boat when fixed up."

"But it doesn't have any outboards on it."

"No, I sell."

"What about that Bayliner. What kind of engine does it have?"

"It not have engine."

"Oh, that's a shame."

"Tell you what, I give away."

"Yeah, you're giving it away?"

"Say, two thousand dollars."

"Seriously, I could buy a boat that runs for that."

"Okay, one thousand five hundred. But not less."

"That includes the trailer?"

"No trailer."

"Well, come on. I have to be able to get it outta here."

"We go back to two thousand. You take trailer."

"All right, I can do that. Grab the title for me and I'll pull my jeep in and hook it up."

"Papers inside. You hook up boat. You come in."

Colt walked outside as Petrosian headed back to pull the paperwork. As soon as he disappeared, Colt pulled a small black cube out of his pocket, turned around and headed toward the store instead of his car. As he walked in, he raised his voice to be sure Petrosian knew he had entered the store.

"Hey, I forgot I left my phone here. I'll be right back after I hitch up the trailer."

From his office down the hall, Oleg replied, "No problem."

Colt grabbed his phone from the counter with his right hand, and with his left, thrust the two blades on the back of the cube into an electrical outlet behind the counter near the cash register. The cube, a USB phone charger, also contained a one-inch CMOS color camera with 4k resolution and a miniature microphone. Colt had already set the wifi password provided by Stewart. The camera now had its own IP address and it could be seen and heard on any browser anywhere in the world.

Five minutes later, Colt re-entered the store with a check for $2,000 and handed it to Petrosian.

Oleg looked at the face of the check. "What As You Were mean?"

"Oh, I buy and sell military equipment and surplus. 'As you were,' is a military term. It means, 'relax.' It's the name of my store."

"Military supplies?" Petrosian wanted to hear more.

"Yeah, anything to make a buck."

"Maybe sell things like rucksack and boot, but not things for fighting."

"You mean weapons?" Colt raised an eyebrow to suggest some level of interest.

Petrosian grinned. "No, I think not possible. Laws not permit serious weapon."

Colt smiled. "Some guys in my line are more concerned about that than others."

Petrosian furrowed his brow and his pasted smile cracked a bit. "Of course, sometimes making money is against law. Seems unfair."

Colt turned the check on the counter top back toward him and wrote a series of numbers on the memo line. Then, he spun it back to Petrosian.

"That's my cell phone. Call me if there's anything I can do for you."

Oleg's eyebrows jumped and the smile returned. "Maybe. We see," he said.

Back on the hillside near the U-boat, Stewart had been watching the hidden camera on his phone since Colt first plugged it in. "Oleg's such a weasel," he thought. "I really hate that guy."

Friday morning dawned a dreary gray. The air was heavy with humidity. A northwest wind kicked up four-foot swells dotted with whitecaps, and tossed the leaves in the trees that towered along the shoreline. All signs foretold the coming storm would be ferocious.

Rough weather had chased the pleasure boats off the water, and most sightseers had abandoned the beaches. There would be no curious eyes watching the team at work.

In the Deep Room, preparations were underway.

"Are we ready, Stewart?" Colt asked.

He didn't reply. He just held his hand up asking for more time to check the old stationary diesel out.

Marty clenched his teeth with concern. "What about the noise?"

"The wind's screaming out there. Waves are crashing on the beach. Nobody's going to hear us." Colt spoke with great assurance, a leadership skill he had practiced over many years.

"Look, Marty. The diesel's going to be running the whole time." Colt grabbed the shift lever. "This is neutral." Next, he stepped on a clutch pedal and slammed the rod forward until it slid home between the teeth of a massive gear. "This is forward. That's all you gotta know. Just step on the clutch before you shift.

"When I call you on the talkie, you shift from neutral to forward, forward to neutral. And confirm it to me. These cables could cut us in half if we're in the way when you put her in gear. You follow me?"

"Yes, Gunny."

"Good man."

It was not yet noon when the rain began. The stones underfoot, the greasy steps and the grass all became slippery hazards, making work even more dangerous. Charlie thought it would be a good idea to remove as much overburden from the sub as possible, so he and Doubeck shoveled everything they could away from the hull, figuring it might help ease the sub into the rising waters. Large chunks of turf and layers of oil cloth were beginning to fall away, giving the boys their first look, in the dim light of day, at the skin of the beast they were hoping to awaken.

Charlie stopped for a second and looked around. He and Doubeck were alone on the hillside. "I talked to Stewart, Amber and Mish."

"Ah, yeahhhh."

"Amber, Stewart and I are going to ride the sub down."

"You're shitting me."

"You can't tell Colt, Doob. He'll pull the plug."

"Yeah. He would."

Meanwhile, Amber and Mish were inside the sub. Amber had revised and re-arranged her checklist for the launch.

It helped to prepare. She had forgotten, for example, to add to her checklist that the periscope must be in the down and locked position. If the U-boat rolled when it launched, an up periscope could get caught in debris.

Mish was busy creating what she called "cocoons."

The crew aboard would experience about the same forces as riding a barrel over Niagara Falls. The cocoons offered some protection—snug, padded capsules made from sleeping bags, bubble wrap, pillows and all the soft blankets they could lay their hands on. These were strung through the pipes and duct taped in place.

When the time came, Colt would be on shore with the quick release lines, Doubeck on the far stern line, Mish on the near stern line, and Stewart, Amber and Charlie would sneak on board instead of leaving for the beach where they'd supposedly be waiting for the launch.

The plan was to do as much preparation as possible. Then, in the afternoon, everyone would head home to spend time with family, partly to make an appearance so the parents wouldn't wonder later why they hadn't seen their kids all day. The other, unspoken reason, involved a growing awareness of their own mortality. Nobody knew for certain that they would ever see their parents again after the launch. Today might be a time for goodbyes.

Stewart and Colt didn't break for lunch. Colt brought slickers and rubberized overalls, so they worked as the storm grew. He pulled cables on the wall crossing the creek bed, and Stewart swapped jobs with Marty at the Deep Room diesel.

By 1 p.m. the wall was just over ten feet high. High enough to attach the quick release hardware. When he came out of the sub to take Stewart's place on the wall, Marty saw that a shallow, swimming pool-sized basin of water had already collected.

It took quite a few tries to get the ropes up into the trees. Tying them to the quick release levers would allow the cables to be disconnected from a distance with just a firm tug. Finally, the cables were secured to the steel hooks in the wall of the dam, and turnbuckles on the cables drew them taut.

Colt heaved a sigh and wiped the rain from his eyes with his sleeve. It left a broad smudge of grease across his face. "Marty, you and Mish need to head up to the duck pond at 9 p.m. With this cloud cover, it'll be dark by then. Any earlier and you risk being seen."

Marty agreed, "The second we're done here, Gunny."

"I don't know what Mish has in mind but you guys are the geniuses. Just be careful."

"Will do," said Marty.

Colt grabbed his shoulder and spun him around. "Will do?"

Marty looked surprised.

"You can give me an 'oorah,' you know. It's okay."

Marty let the words go loud and clear. "Oorah!" All the guys wanted to be like Gunny, and Marty had just been invited to oorah by the man, himself.

For the next thirty minutes he couldn't wipe the smile off his face.

Once the wall was in place and the baseball bats had been inserted, there would be nothing left to do but watch the water rise and hope the U-boat would launch itself. That meant, of course, that Stewart, Amber and Charlie had climb aboard as the water neared the hull. As the sub floated on the temporary pond high above Lake Erie, it would be a strange time of calm. There would be plenty of time to make certain everything was ready for the launch. But that lull would give way to chaos as soon as Stewart threw the engines full ahead and Colt pulled the quick release rope.

Lunch turned out to be anything but quality time with family. Charlie's mom and dad had taken Rocky to 'Dinosaurs on Ice.' Charlie was invited, and he couldn't stop laughing when they told him what the show was called. When he declined the invitation, his dad briefly flashed him a look of envy.

Charlie felt bad for him. Whatever the outcome, his adventure would be much more exciting than watching a Skate-o-saurus.

Before Charlie left the house, he grabbed the day's mail from the hall table and started looking through it. The second envelope was addressed to him. It was from the Pennsylvania Fish and Boat Commission. His pulse quickened. He stuck it in his pocket and set the remaining letters down.

He never saw that the rest of the stack included five more envelopes for him, each one holding a monthly statement for a checking account in his name. Four of the accounts had reached the FDIC limit of $250,000, so, according to his arrangement with Mr. Ryan, the bank started a different type of account whenever he reached his insured deposit limit. Charlie was just shy of seventeen years old and already starting on his second million.

Amber's parents had embarked on a day-trip to a mall halfway to Pittsburgh. Mish's parents were watching the Golf Channel and she was unable to distract them. Marty's Mom and Dad left early for the synagogue to help out with a rummage sale. They'd left a note telling Marty he was expected to show for Shabbat services. He felt bad, but he'd explain his absence somehow.

By 2 p.m., the crew had begun to arrive back at the sub, each bringing with them a strange mix of foreboding and acceptance. Within the boat, its closed and quiet environment felt oddly comfortable. There, they were separated from the world and its problems, drawn together as a team, supporting and encouraging each other, solving their own problems and sharing their sense of satisfaction.

With a little luck, by this time tomorrow, they would be captain and crew of the last operating U-boat.

Colt showed up after everyone else, giving the crew time to compare notes and prepare a distraction for Colt so they could slip the crew aboard. They were all set by the time he opened the hatch. Rain poured in and splashed at the foot of the ladder, it was followed by a black garbage bag, and finally, a soaking wet Marine.

"I brought you guys a little something," he said. "I apologize for not wrapping it." He tossed a small paper bag to Mish. She opened it, reached in, and withdrew a soft piece of dark twill with a firm band around one edge. It was a navy blue sailor's cap, a beret, with two wide grosgrain ribbons trailing from the back. He tossed a similar bag to each of the crew, except Amber.

Colt reached into the bag again and withdrew a captain's hat, complete with gold embroidery on the brim, culminating in a huge flourish rising above the forehead. It looked absolutely authentic. "This one's for you, Amber."

"These aren't hats, folks. You will call them your 'cover.' Got it? Oh, and there's nothing Nazi on any of these. They're just a cover. Because they resemble the originals, they're also a tribute to the sailors who served. And you can tell that to anyone who suggests otherwise."

The crew donned their berets, Amber her captain's hat, and even though they were gifts, there was a feeling among the crew that they had earned them.

"One more thing, guys." said Colt, reaching back into the bag.

"I had a pin made up for the boat. All the U-boats used to have their own sorta mascots—like devils and sharks. Anyway, I got to thinking about it and, you know, In the Battle of the Atlantic in World War II, all the U-boats gathered and hunted together wherever there was a huge convoy of merchant ships or warships. That's where they first called them a wolfpack—like the game you guys trained on.

"They were opportunistic, deadly and cunning just like wolves. This crew, you guys, have that quality. You're gutsy, smart, and for-sure opportunistic. By the way. It's just a coincidence, but the man who engineered and built all this, Mr. Kraus. His first name was Wolf."

Opening a small cloth pouch, he said, "There's one in here for each of you."

Hands reached in, each taking a small gold box with an enameled pin bearing a stylized howling wolf's head. They clipped their pins to their berets and admired each other's new look.

"I just want to point out that she still doesn't have a name," said Doubeck.

"Doobs, we'll get there," said Charlie.

"Just one last thing," said Colt. "I want you to know I'm grateful to be included in this. I'm proud of what you've accomplished and I thank you."

"Where's *your* cover, Gunny?" asked Charlie.

"I have one provided by the United States Marine Corps and tomorrow, when we ride this boat together, I guaran-damn-tee you I'll be wearing it."

Marty had imagined it would be a long time before he'd get a chance to do another 'oorah,' but he was wrong. He started them off, and the control room erupted.

Outside, in the sky above the glistening grass that still remained over the submarine, all that could be heard was rain slapping the leaves high in the trees, and occasionally, the distant rumble of an oncoming storm.

THE LAST U-BOAT

STEALING
A
POND

The intense rain sounded like popcorn as it slammed onto the rubber hood of Marty's slicker. It was dark, after 9 p.m., and every speck of light caught by a drop of water was magnified and tossed about like the light in a kaleidoscope.

"So what are we doing, Mish?"

"I'm going to knock the shit out of that dam and dump the duck pond into the creek."

Marty was already squinting to keep the rain out of his eyes but Mish's comment made him squeeze them shut and blink.

"How're you gonna do that?"

"With the excavator."

"You don't know how to run an excavator."

Mish turned her head toward Marty and gave him a look.

"You do?"

"I do now."

"How did you learn to run an excavator?"

"My new boyfriend, Bud Staley taught me. After I left you guys the other day I came up here and asked him to show me how everything worked."

"That's really like espionage, Mish. It kinda creeps me out."

"Yeah, well it was fun."

"But don't you need a key?"

"No problem."

The walk from the neighborhood to the duck pond took almost fifteen minutes. Mish eventually shut off Marty's questions and for most of the walk, they didn't even talk.

When they reached the pond, Marty watched Mish climb onto the big yellow machine from along the edge of the duck pond, hoping none of the cars speeding by on the nearby road would notice.

She lifted the seat, picked up a pair of keys, turned and sat in the driver's seat.

Staley had been eager to show Mish how much he knew about running equipment. After his workers left, he even let her operate the controls. She remembered everything.

The bright lights that came on when the key was turned bothered her. She sure didn't want to attract any attention. After throwing a few switches, she was able to turn off the cab and side lights, but she needed the two elevated headlights to find the plate that held the water back.

Mish tracked awkwardly toward the spillway, the treads of the excavator squawking beneath her. Within eight feet, she stopped, raised the hydraulic shovel over the berm, rotated the boom arm within a foot of the plate, backed the arm away like a batter getting ready for a pitch, and stopped.

"What's wrong?" shouted Marty.

"Can't see! I'm looking for the windshield wipers."

It only took a moment and the wipers flew into action. The glass was clear. she had positioned the shovel right where she wanted it.

"Stand back, Marty. Here goes nothing!"

Mish leaned back, cocked her head, extended two fingers, and pushed the joystick firmly all the way to the left. The steel bucket at the end of the boom jerked from its rest and flew in a smooth arc across the open water of the duck pond colliding with the top half of the steel gate with a crack. The plate exploded from its mounting, sparks flying from the edges of the frame that had held it in place. The thick steel rectangle flew end-over-end down the sluice, propelled by a four-foot high wall of churning water that blasted unabated from the gaping hole left behind. The throaty sound made by tons of water cascading into the massive concrete culverts below the dam shook the ground.

"Shit!" The word rose simultaneously from both the excavator operator and the young man standing at the edge of the raging waters. There was a lot more water pouring from the pond than they had expected.

"Marty, watch yourself. I'm gonna back up. Get to the street. We need to outrun that water and get back to the sub."

Mish raised the boom and tracked back to the excavator's original position. In a flash, she and Marty were running down the road toward Charlie's house, a flood of water coursing along with them, out of sight, somewhere just beneath the sidewalk.

Charlie and Doubeck were there to meet them as they came limping into the driveway. They headed over to the hillside while Marty did his best to describe what happened, and all five crew members trained their flashlights on the water's surface.

A large quiet pool had formed behind the wall. The incoming stream was calm and unremarkable. A few million gallons of water were missing.

"We should be looking at Class III whitewater right now," said Marty.

Mish looked at him. "Do you think we got here first?"

"Not a chance," said Marty.

"Then..."

"I don't know. But something strange is going on."

A odd churning sound mixed with the noise of the wind in the branches and the rain pelting the leaves. There were added overtones that sounded a lot like snarling and growling.

"It sounds like the bowels of hell," said Doubeck.

The noise rose from deep in the gully, so everyone aimed their flashlights into the darkness near the back of the gathering pool of water, hoping to see what it was.

The lights caught a flotilla of red dots skittering like lasers across the water's surface. Then there were more. A squeaky chatter echoed across the water.

"They're raccoons," said Charlie. "Dozens of them."

"Rabies!" Mish screamed. "Don't let them bite me!"

The lights that had been trained on the wall were suddenly all following the scattering animals as they swam through the pool toward the safety of the shallows. One or two managed to catch the branches of trees that rose from the water. Close behind them, driftwood and tangled masses of vegetation, trash bags and broken tree limbs started to appear, floating toward the larger pool.

"It's not rabies. They're just scared," said Charlie.

Colt bumped Marty's shoulder to get his attention and pointed toward the oncoming debris. "I think the water from the pond just busted up a big clog in the culverts. Those raccoons wanted outta there bad. If I'm right, we're about to get pounded. Grab the talkie, go get on the winch, and I'll start pulling cable."

As he finished talking, a deep, bubbling upheaval rose from the top of the gully a block away. A moment later, a small tsunami traveled down the pool and crashed against the wall where Colt had returned to pull timbers.

The depth of the pool had visibly increased. The flood was on its way.

Marty took a step away from the group, heading to his post at the winch in the Deep Room. "No one's home, Marty. Just go through the house," said Charlie.

"I'm on my way," he said, and he scrambled up the slippery hillside.

Doubeck and Mish had been watching the onrushing waters. "You know, until the water reaches the sub we're kinda useless," Doubeck said.

"Hang on." Charlie started fishing in his pockets. "I just remembered something. I got a letter." He handed his flashlight to Mish. "Hold this for me, okay?"

He found the envelope he'd stuck in his pocket earlier and unfolded it. He carefully pulled the water-soaked flap open and withdrew the letter—a form letter with an attachment. With his flashlight in one hand he read the notice.

"Dudes! This is the registration for the U-boat, and the stickers for the bow. Can you believe it?" Charlie started laughing uncontrollably.

"Let me see that," said Mish, taking the papers from Charlie's hands

"Oh my gosh. It's true. Pennsylvania gave Charlie's boat a birth certificate." She laughed and handed the papers to Doubeck.

The three friends huddled together. They laughed and danced for joy despite the rain and the wind, despite the cold and the tension. They had passed another critical milestone. Because now, even if the sub sank like a rock when it entered the lake, it would be almost impossible for anyone to reverse the state's decision. Charlie had won an important victory. He was the registered owner of the last working U-boat on earth, and he owned it free and clear.

Charlie carefully folded the papers, replaced them in the envelope and put them back in his pocket.

"I gotta go tell Gunny," he said.

To reach Colt, Charlie carefully picked his way around the rising waters and found a path to the edge of the cliff. Then he descended the greasy steps that remained to be winched into place. Colt saw him coming.

Even over the screaming wind and the crashing waves below, Charlie could hear Colt yelling. "Careful Charlie. It's not safe up here."

From the rising water in the gully, a sound like firecrackers drew their attention. Quickly the popping became sharper and louder—like rifle shots—then even deeper like explosions. The tree limbs pushed by debris were being crushed and compressed by the weight of the water driving them forward. Dead branches as big around as a man's arm were being snapped by the water's force as they encountered the ancient oak trees standing in the gully.

The overall level of noise was terrifying. On the beach, waves pounded rhythmically, incessantly, and shook the ground with their force. In the air, the oaks and maples shrieked as the wind blew through their branches. Below, water from the duck pond was rapidly filling the basin and the low growl it produced as it pounded into the little valley was amplified and reflected off the hillsides.

Worst of all was the lightning and thunder pummeling the crew from the skies. Each blast rocked them, and there was often only a heartbeat between the flash of brilliant blue light and the shock-wave of thunder that followed. It was that close.

Colt worked steadily on, as though immune to the distractions. When Charlie reached into his pocket to find the envelope, his cold wet hands were shaking so badly his flashlight slipped and fell into the rising pool of water.

He and Colt watched the light sink into the turbid, swirling mix.

Colt tilted his flashlight up and pointed it at Charlie. "What's going on?"

Charlie was holding his hand up, a rain-soaked envelope between his fingers. As Colt waited for him to answer, a blast of wind sucked the envelope away, and tossed it into the murky pool.

"I hope that wasn't important," Colt shouted.

Charlie screamed back. "That was the registration for the U-boat. I can't believe it. What am I going to do now?"

"Forget it. Don't lose focus. We'll figure it out."

"I gotta go back."

"You can't go back until you have a light. It's too dangerous. Stay here and help me and we'll have someone bring a light out to you."

"Okay." Charlie wrapped his arms around a small tree limb that steadied him against the wind and the chaos swirling around him.

Colt lifted the talkie that was slung around his neck. "Marty, stop what you're doing and get a flashlight to Mish. Tell her to come down to the steps and bring it to me. When you get back to the winch, let me know. We've gotta keep going."

Charlie heard Marty reply with an 'oorah'. Despite the conditions, it made Charlie smile.

The rain stung his eyes, the noise was deafening, and the danger was very real. This was the adventure Charlie had been waiting for, and it was even better than he ever could have imagined.

Colt dropped the talkie and shined his light back in Charlie's face. He saw the grin.

"That's a sign, Charlie."

"What is?"

"All hell's breaking loose and you look like you're enjoying it."

"Yeah? Sorta. What's wrong with that?"

"Not a damn thing. It's just not everybody has that in 'em. Least not until they've been through boot camp. Hell, after that, nothing fazes you."

Charlie felt suddenly calm and unaware of the crashing and roaring of the forces of nature around him. Colt was right. He had definitely crossed a threshold.

"What can I do to help until Mish gets here?"

Colt swung around and grabbed a cable. "Here, wrestle this thing over to the next timber. There's a pulley on it. Slip the loop over the hook on the pulley and let me know when you're done. When Marty gets back to the winch, I'll have him pull the cable. So back away to the next timber when you're done and just wait there. Got it?"

Charlie surprised even himself when an "oorah!" came out of his mouth.

Colt didn't even look in his direction. "You, too, huh?"

"You have only yourself to blame, Gunny."

Colt just smiled, although Charlie couldn't see his face in the pitch-black night.

Mish appeared after two more rows of timbers had been secured. There were only four more to go and the pool was rising rapidly. She delivered a flashlight to Charlie, and they hurried back along the edge of the cliff, leaving Colt to finish the wall.

When Charlie got back to the sub, he stopped abruptly.

"Mish, look." He directed his flashlight to the edge of the rising pool. It was so close to the sub, they couldn't walk past the downhill side of the hull without walking through several inches of water. As long as the water kept coming, they would soon learn soon if their crazy plan to launch the sub would work.

"I'm guessing less than an hour and it starts to float," said Mish.

Charlie pulled his sleeve up to check his watch. "What time is it, anyway?"

"About ten," said Mish.

"We have to find everybody and get into position. My parents are going to pull in the driveway any minute and we can't be out here."

"Okay, I'll go in through the tower hatch. Doubeck took off for the sub when I left to get you. You want to get Marty?"

Charlie took a step toward the house. "I'm on my way. Let's meet back in the control room."

"We'll see you as soon as Colt and Marty wrap it up," she said.

Charlie came around to the front door and started up the steps as the headlights of his parents' car threw his silhouette large against the front of the house. There was nothing he could do but wait, so he walked to the far side of the steps, hoping that his parents would keep their heads turned toward him and away from the gully where a flashlight beam could occasionally be seen darting through the trees.

Rocky was the first one out of the car. He came running full-tilt to greet his big brother. "Charlie, I saw a Tyrannosaurus wreck!" he shouted.

"What did he wreck, Rocky?"

"He wrecked a jungle, and he wrecked a city, and he wrecked a bunch of monkeys, too."

Charlie's mom came around and gave Charlie a hug. "Monkeys and dinosaurs together was a little weird," she confided. "The whole way home we were trying to explain how something from ages ago could suddenly come alive."

"Yeah, could happen," Charlie sighed.

"Listen you. Get out of the rain and tell me what you've been up to." She ushered her sons to the front door as Mike LeClair locked the car and followed behind. Rocky entered the house as Sharon opened the door. Charlie and Mike followed.

"Nice outfit," said Mike, looking at Charlie. "You look like the guy on the fish sticks box." Charlie just raised a hand and pulled the hood back from his wet head.

"Where did you get that rain gear?" Sharon asked, as a clap of thunder crackled nearby.

"Did you get it on the submarine?" asked Rocky, who then immediately put both hands over his mouth as he realized he had broken his promise.

"No, Rocky. A friend of mine loaned it to me because we were all going places and doing things in the rain."

Sharon hung up their jackets and shut the closet door. She grabbed the stack of mail from the table by the stairs, crossed the hall and sat at the kitchen table.

Mike took Rocky's hand. "I'm going upstairs to change. Come with me and we'll do baths. You're up way too late."

"Call me when it's time for goodnight kisses," said Sharon, as she thumbed through the mail. She smiled at Charlie. "Sit," she said, and so he did.

"Anyway, Mom. I might hang out with Doubeck tonight."

"That's odd."

"Not really. He stayed over here last time so it's kinda his turn."

"No, I mean this letter from the South Shore Bank. Why are you getting mail from the bank?"

Charlie suddenly felt dizzy.

"CL Enterprises, LLC? LeClair Online, LLC? Charlie LeClair Trust? What is this?"

She inserted a fingernail under the flap and sliced an envelope open in a well-practiced motion.

He knew that any letter from the bank could compromise his secrets. This was it, then. Moments before the sub was to be released from the grave, it was over.

"It's a bank statement," said Sharon.

Charlie's face went pale.

Before looking closely, she opened the next envelope. "Charlie, why are you getting all this mail? You never get mail."

"Mom, you realize you're opening my mail."

"I just want to see what they want..."

She didn't bother to open the last envelope. Instead, she lifted the cover sheet from the first statement and her eyes fell on the balance at the bottom line.

This time, Sharon's face went pale.

Suddenly, she was clearly having trouble drawing a breath.

"Mom?" Charlie got out of his chair.

He patted her back and pumped her arm until he heard a rush of air enter her lungs. It was something they used to do if someone had hiccups. It wasn't exactly CPR, but he didn't know what else to do. Sharon sat motionless.

"Sit, young man."

Charlie returned to his chair. Sharon stared at him like a jungle cat—still, intense, and ready to pounce.

"I found some buried treasure, Mom."

"What?"

"Yeah, a lot."

"Like coins and jewelry?"

"More like historic items. And I've been selling them online. I hope that's okay."

Assessing the imbalance between Charlie's highly reasonable approach to her questions, and the near impossibility of his story, made Sharon's mouth twist like she was sucking on lemons. Her eyes squinted nearly shut. But then she assumed her special pose again. Her panther pose.

"How much are these *historic items* worth?"

Sharon asked first, then realized she held the answer in her hands. She began frantically pulling bank statements from their envelopes and gaping at the numbers. "Oh my god! ohmygodohmygodohmygod. Is this legal? Well of course it's legal, a bank wouldn't do anything illegal. Not that you *would*, Charlie. I mean, you're as straight-laced as they come. I know you wouldn't do anything illegal. Ohmygodohmygodohmygod. This must be..."

"It's one million, one hundred thirty-two thousand dollars, Mom."

Sharon gagged. Then, suddenly, she stopped breathing again. Charlie stood, patted her back, pumped her arm up and down, and waited for the sound.

As the air returned to his mother's lungs, Charlie sat. Sharon picked up the papers and, this time, looked at them more thoughtfully.

Then she looked up at her boy. His thick auburn hair flopped over his forehead in wet curls. His cheeks were blushed from the wind. His brown eyes were wide and without guile. He was starting to look like a man.

"This is all on the straight and narrow?"

"Uh huh."

"You're amazing," she said, and Charlie's heart soared.

THE LAST U-BOAT

MAKING
HISTORY

"Where did you find a million dollars worth of treasure around here?" Sharon was trying to hide her excitement, and her curiosity, by appearing to be preoccupied with putting today's dishes away. "Was it on the beach? You've been spending a lot of time down on the beach. I thought maybe you were... I don't know...I don't mean you were in trouble. I was thinking more about how much time you spend with Amber." Sharon wasn't even looking at the cupboard shelves anymore. She was searching Charlie's face for any sign of emotion. "You know, maybe you two were getting too friendly. I mean, I don't understand why you didn't say anything to us sooner. Honestly, I think Amber's a sweet girl. She's really pretty." Sharon took a breath.

"Mom. That plate's dirty. I don't think you ran the dishwasher yet."

Sharon realized Charlie was right. All the dishes she had put away were dirty. Without missing a beat, she started pulling all the dishes back off the shelf and re-stacking the dishwasher.

"All your friends seem so nice. They are nice, aren't they?" Realizing she wasn't making any progress she sat down again at the table. "So, tell me. What's going on? No, wait. Don't say anything. Let's get your father, and you can tell us both at the same time."

"Mom?"

"I don't think he started Rocky's bath. Wait here, I'll call him." Sharon started to stand up, but Charlie reached out with his open hand.

"Mom. Please listen."

Sharon LeClair shook her head and spoke a little too loudly as she finally focused on Charlie. "What?"

"Mom. Chill. I'll tell you all about it, but it's a long story, so I'd really rather tell you tomorrow when it's not so late, and we're not tired. Plus, I told

Doubeck I'd hang out at his house tonight."

"Oh." Sharon sounded disappointed.

"I'd really like this to stay our secret until tomorrow, so I can see Dad's reaction when I tell him. Can we do that?"

"Just tell me this. Did you find gold, jewels, what was the treasure?"

"They're antiques."

"Oh. Antiques. Well, I can't imagine anyone getting in trouble for selling antiques." Sharon visibly relaxed. "I want to trust you. Promise me everything is alright and you're not in trouble."

"I'm okay. Everything is amazing. All my friends are good, too. Oh, I also asked them to keep it a secret from their parents, too. That includes the guy you met who's working underground in the hill."

"You know him?"

"Yeah. Doubeck introduced him to me. He's a really great guy and he's got a lot of contacts. We call him Gunny cuz he was a gunnery sergeant in the Marine Corps. He owns a military surplus store downtown and he does everything by the book."

"Why did he say he was working for the county?"

"I made him promise me he would keep our business a secret. Believe me, he's been on my case about not telling you."

"I don't like secrets, Charlie. You can get in big trouble keeping secrets."

"I know, I know. This was just something I wanted to do on my own, and since it was legal and I had good help, I didn't see the harm in keeping it a secret at least until it worked out."

"I understand that. But I worry about you. I always wonder if you are doing anything that could be dangerous or get you into trouble."

"You shouldn't worry, Mom."

"So, you said you were hanging out with Danny Doubeck. What are you doing with him?"

"Ahhh. Not much. Probably playing *Wolfpack*."

Sharon resumed her frozen attack-cat stare.

"Mom, Doubeck's my friend, we hang out all the time."

Desperate for an acceptable explanation, Sharon reanimated. "Oh, of course. I am just so excited for you! I can't wait to hear all about it. Okay, it's late. It's our secret until tomorrow morning, then we talk to Dad," she said, wagging a finger at him.

"You got it." Charlie jumped out of the chair and stepped around the table. He said, "Thanks, Mom," as he gave his mother a kiss on the cheek and disappeared before she could think of something else to ask.

Charlie quickly headed down the hill. Colt was still on the steps, popping pegs into place. Charlie went down the hatch and found the others had already gathered there, standing in a huddle inside the U-boat, for one final group meeting. The air was heavy with moisture and the temperature in the boat was warmer than anyone could remember. The lights burning inside the boat were warming the air.

Amber flipped Charlie's cover to him from across the cramped space. Charlie caught it and snugged it onto his head. "Thanks," he said, smiling at her.

"Sorry I was late, guys. My Mom found a bank statement and I had to confess that I'd been selling…well, I called them antiques. She knows about Colt helping me, too."

"You okay?" asked Amber.

"Yeah, I think so. I sure hope we can pull this off. I'd hate to come this far and end up with nothing to show for it. We have to make this happen tonight because tomorrow I'm probably going to have to tell my parents everything."

The crew exchanged concerned looks. Everyone always knew this time would come.

Amber stepped to the middle of the huddle. "If this crazy plan is going to work, it's going to happen within the next few minutes. It's time to get to work. Hands in!"

Amber extended her right arm and the entire crew followed suit.

"Wolfpack on three!" she shouted and with their hands all touching, they drew their arms up and down three times.

"Wolfpack!"

As they brought their arms to their sides there was a grinding sound like a weight being dragged across a stoney beach.

"Did you feel that?" Marty asked. Some did, others looked quizzical and frightened.

"The water's coming up. We moved a little," said Charlie.

Amber reached out and grabbed Charlie's shoulder with her left hand. With her right hand she grabbed the back of Stewart's jacket. "You two, with me. Everybody else, head topside and get to your stations. If we start floating away, don't let the lines drag you in. Just tie up to a tree or let go. It can't go far. Take your time and think before you do *anything*."

"While you're thinking, think of a name for the sub," said Doubeck.

As her friends left the sub, consigning her, Charlie, and Stewart to their fate, Amber remembered Colt's one rule. But she didn't speak it because she figured everyone else was remembering it, too.

"Charlie, head on up and secure the tower hatch. Stewart, secure the forward hatch."

Both young men scrambled to fulfill their tasks, but Amber stopped them in their tracks. "Guys. Hold it. When I give an order, repeat it so I know you heard it the way I said it. That's protocol on this boat. That's how we communicate."

"Aye," said Charlie.

"Aye, Captain," said Stewart.

"Securing the forward hatch, Captain," said Stewart.

Amber gestured like a hitchhiker. "Go!"

"Securing the conning tower hatch, Captain," said Charlie.

"Do it, and take flashlights," she said.

To save battery power, Amber ordered the boat's lights to be turned off. As she stood in the darkened control room, her eyes grew wide and her pulse quickened. She could feel a drop of sweat trail from her forehead to the tip of her nose.

It was getting late and everyone was exhausted—a bad time to make decisions. She would have to be very cautious.

Charlie was sitting near his cocoon at the dive plane controls. He turned his flashlight on and pointed it toward his feet to minimize the light entering his eyes. He looked toward Amber, standing just a few feet away, as the darkness closed in. Light from the scattered beam fell softly on her. Her deeply tanned face glowed and her t-shirt clung tightly to her skin. A few curls of moist hair lay against her forehead.

She looked into Charlie's eyes with a gentleness he could feel, and his heart pounded in response. He wanted so much to hold her again.

He knew, somehow, everything was going to be alright.

The small speaker of the walkie-talkie hanging in the control room crackled. It was Colt.

"Captain, do you copy? Over."

"Yes, Gunny. I hear you fine. What do you see? Over."

"It looks like the water's about two feet deep around the hull. Over."

"Understood. We've got plenty of time. Please give me updates at ten-minute intervals, or whenever there's a change I need to know about. Over."

"There is one change, Captain. The rain has stopped and there's a break in the storm."

"I'm glad, for your sake. With a little luck we'll all stay dry tonight. Out."

As she released the push button on the talkie, the silence within the U-boat was overwhelming. She let the solitude wash over her briefly.

With a single flashlight providing the comfort of illumination, the three crew members inside the sub sat on the floor to await the next update.

Outside, Colt stood near the conning tower hatch holding the quick release line. The water's edge was just a few feet away. Mish was ready with the near stern line and Doubeck was standing with her on the hill just above Colt.

They weren't sure how Doubeck would get his line from the far side of the gully. He might have to walk a half mile, all the way to West Lake Road and back down the other side of the gully.

Colt fished for the talkie still hanging around his neck when he saw a large blanket of turf fall off the low side of the U-boat. It had been ripped out of the hill, which had to mean the stern had pivoted again.

The rear half of the sub was now completely visible, including the lower half of the sail, the oval structure that rose from the deck in the middle of the sub. The U-boat was definitely sliding right where Charlie and Doubeck had been digging. It appeared that the stern had eased toward the water while the bow remained a pivot point. Most of the weight was aft, ballast vents were closed and the ballast tanks that would counterbalance it were filled with air.

"Colt to Captain. Over."

"Go ahead, Colt," said Amber.

"Just had a thought. Your tail end is going to hang low in the water until Stewart can balance the ship with the ballast tanks. It'll probably feel like your back end is sinking, but don't be concerned. You're making progress. Over."

"We felt the boat slip a couple of times, Gunny. We're definitely sliding backward. Over."

"That's all I got. Can see some stars now. Stay dry. Over."

"Captain out."

Amber stood and looked down at Stewart and Charlie. "Time to get to our stations, guys."

As the water rose, it became easier to identify the shape of the submarine, as the topsoil fell away and water hugged its contours. Colt and Doubeck began to attack the oilcloth and sod covering the props. Marty shoved some sticks in the ground near the water's edge so they could measure how fast the water was rising.

"Doubeck, we have to get this uncovered so there's nothing holding the sub back. A lot of little roots have grown in here and I think they're hanging onto the sub like tentacles."

They worked furiously, and within five minutes, the massive bronze blades were visible. The props rode high, so although much of the stern was underwater, the props were exposed.

"Look, Gunny. We can really see the props now, and more of the hull."

As Doubeck spoke, the aft end of the boat slipped downhill a good six feet, pivoting in the mud on the stem of the bow. A large section of the Deep Room collapsed, filling the space where the sub had rested for over eight decades.

Amber almost lost her footing. In the engine room, Stewart fell forward but managed to grab an overhead pipe to steady himself.

Topside, Doubeck pointed at the stern. "It's moving, Gunny!"

Colt keyed his talkie. "Captain, you okay? Over."

"We're good. We felt it. What's it look like? Over."

"Props are almost submerged. The forward third of the boat isn't really in the water yet...Hey, if the props get submerged, you could back the boat up. I mean, it could pull itself off the hillside, right? Over."

There was no response.

"Colt to Captain. That could work, right? Over."

A few moments passed.

"This is the Captain. Stand by."

Colt stood looking at the stars, waiting while Amber assessed the proposal. Almost a minute went by before she spoke again.

"Gunny, you there?"

"Go."

"Gunny, we're going to open aft ballast tanks just enough to drop the stern. If there's no debris or trees behind the props, we're good. If we bend a prop, we're in trouble. Give it a good look and tell me what you see. Over."

"Stand by."

Doubeck handed Marty the stern rope for a safety line so he and Colt could make their way to the water's edge. Doubeck held on to the shroud around the props for security, and searched the water below them with his flashlight. Colt checked farther out behind the boat to see what it might hit if it successfully backed up. It looked clear for many yards, presuming the U-boat would continue to slip down into the pool. Even if it backed up its full length, it would easily clear the only tree anywhere near the stern.

"We're good here, Gunny." called Doubeck.

Colt grabbed the talkie. "Captain?"

"Yeah, Gunny."

"Captain, you are clear..." As Colt spoke, Doubeck fell headfirst into the water. The pond had continued to rise, and the stern had suddenly slipped another six feet into the pool, submerging the props and dragging Doubeck—who had a death grip on the shroud—along with it. Doubeck's wet hands could not hold on and he slipped silently between the hull and the hillside.

Colt keyed his talkie. "Don't move, Amber. Doubeck's behind the props."

"Doubeck!" Colt shouted.

If the sub slipped again while Doubeck was under it, it could crush him, or block his way to the surface. Colt grabbed the stern line from Marty and ran to the water. As he tied the line to his belt, Doubeck's hands popped up by the props, reaching for anything to hang on to.

Marty spotted the splashing. "He's up, Gunny."

Doubeck's head popped quickly out of the murky water, and he shot Colt a thumbs-up. Colt grabbed the walkie talkie slung around his neck.

"Captain, that last slide put the props under. You're clear, and I think the stern is actually floating. Over." Colt eased his way over to Doubeck and helped him up.

When Doubeck was clear, Colt keyed the talkie. "Doubeck's with me. He's okay. It's time for Stewart's magic, Amber."

In the engine room Stewart rigged for electric motors. He closed the diesel vents and intakes. He disengaged the main clutch and the diesel engine clutch. He engaged the heavy three-bladed copper switch that connected the batteries to the engines. The E-motors speed and direction were controlled by a rotary switch, with a different position for each command. Stewart put the drive gears in neutral and moved the telegraph to full stop. It was now the captain's boat.

A muffled bang announced when the bank of solenoids came alive and the sweet smell of ozone drifted through the engine room.

The wolf's heart was beating. Again.

Stewart keyed his talkie. "Captain, breakers are holding. We have power to the electric motors."

"Thanks, Stewart." said Amber. "Colt. Let me know when you're out of the way, we might throw a lot of prop wash. I want you to shout out any warning so we can react in plenty of time. I'll hear you. Over."

"We're getting out of your way right now, Captain. Do *not* engage until we're clear. Repeat. Do *not* engage motors until you hear my all clear. Colt out."

Marty took Doubeck's free hand and, together, he and Colt dragged their water-logged friend to the safety of higher ground.

"Engine Room? Stewart, you got that?" said Amber.

"Yes, Captain."

"Colt, we will wait for your all clear. Captain out."

Amber didn't even take a breath. "Stewart, when Gunny tells you to start I want you to pump reverse and keep doing it until he tells you to stop. We'll start with low revs and we'll keep ramping it up if we have to. Hear me?"

"I hear you."

Colt's voice came through the talkies. "We are clear."

"Gunny, Stewart's ready to pump reverse. Call it for him."

"Aye, Captain. Stewart, 3... 2... 1... Now."

For five seconds the sub shuddered.

"All stop."

"All stop," Stewart replied.

"Reverse half speed, Stewart. Ready? 3... 2... 1... Now."

The sub shook and Amber could feel it rotating around her. Something was happening.

As she tried to interpret the motion, Colt's voice intervened "All stop."

"Aye. All stop," replied Stewart.

"Hang on." Colt sounded frustrated. "Your bow's still in the dirt, Amber."

Amber had an idea why they weren't moving out. The forward bow planes were way below the water line. They could be jammed with dirt.

"Charlie, check the bow planes and give me the angle."

"They're 10 degrees up, Captain." Charlie tried turning the wheel that tilts them. "They're stuck, too."

Amber slammed her hand on the varnished black walnut desktop next to the periscope. "Dammit. Should have thought of that sooner." She keyed the talkie.

"Colt, we're stuck in the mud. The bow planes must have picked up some dirt when the roof collapsed. They're jammed and pointed up 10 degrees. Can you shovel them out? Maybe push them level?"

"On it, Captain."

Colt grabbed a shovel and jumped up onto the turf remaining over the bulbous hull. "Marty, get a shovel and get up here. We have to dig the bow planes out."

While Doubeck shivered in his water-soaked clothes, Colt and Marty tore at the turf like they were digging survivors out of an avalanche. The bow planes were soon exposed, and they were able to rock them slightly up and down. Within ten minutes, the planes tilted more or less level, where they would offer little resistance to the motors as they strained to back the boat up and off the muddy shoal.

Colt tossed his shovel onto the hillside and clutched his walkie talkie. "Doubeck, Marty. Get up the hill. Up to the top. Go go go!" Colt jumped to the ground and scrambled right behind them.

They sprinted, slipping on the wet grass as they charged uphill. At a level spot, Colt fell to his hands and knees and rolled onto his back so he could sit up and get a good look at the action. He keyed the talkie.

"Captain. You're good to go."

Amber reacted immediately. "Stewart. Make it happen. Full speed reverse for three seconds in 3… 2… 1…"

The sub shuddered again, the hull started pulsing rhythmically. Then it all stopped.

"That was three seconds, Captain."

"Thank you, Stewart. Charlie, trim the ballast, add a little weight to the stern. I want zero bubble. We need to lift the bow off the hillside."

"Aye, zero bubble."

Charlie was the first to notice the change. He walked back to her from the front of the control room and whispered. "Amber. Can you feel that?"

Amber looked at Charlie with an intense stare. "We're not tilting forward."

She raised an arm to place her open hand against the tube containing the periscope. Then, she reached out and held an overhead water pipe in her other hand. She could feel her weight shift slightly in her knees. As every second ticked, her smile grew wider.

"I feel it, Charlie. I feel it! We're floating!"

"We're floating! Son of a bitch! We're a real boat," said Charlie. He reached out to take Amber in his arms, but she stepped back and held up a finger that clearly said, "Wait."

"Are you ready for what's next?" she said.

"Damn right I am. I know we're taking a chance, but I really want this."

She smiled. "I wasn't talking about the U-boat," she said.

"Neither was I," said Charlie.

She turned away, lifted her talkie to her lips and squeezed the mike. "Stewart, check the bilge and let me know if there's any water coming in."

"Aye Captain."

Amber waited. Then Stewart's voice returned with a snap.

"The boat is dry," You could hear the smile in Stewart's voice.

Amber and Charlie looked at each other and smiled. Amber tilted her head, as if to say, "That's one hurdle." She keyed her talkie.

"Thank you, Stewart." She released the microphone and whispered to Charlie, "Hold that thought."

The talkie crackled again and startled everyone. It was Colt.

"The wolf is on the prowl. Congratulations, Amber. You're now the only living U-boat Commander—piloting the last U-boat. And, you're the first American woman to have command of a military submarine in US waters. I wanna get some pictures. Come on up. We have some lines to tie and then the crew needs to get down to the beach to catch a ride. Colt out."

Amber heard some cheering on the talkie before Colt let go of the mike. Stewart came forward and he and Charlie slapped each other on the back, high-fived and stood to applaud Amber.

She didn't smile. Instead, she raised her open hands and looked somberly at the two crewmen in front of her.

"Men, we have a lot of work to do. Charlie, head topside and help Colt with the lines. Stewart, check the bubble, the boat feels heavy on the bow to me. It's probably Doubeck's stupid torpedoes weighing us down. Let's go! We need to learn how to do a few important things real fast."

"Aye, Captain."

On the surface, the night was quiet. Water had risen to the very top of the dam and had begun a picturesque cascade over the wall and onto the beach below. The U-boat floated effortlessly on the pool, high in the water and near the hillside from which it had just emerged. Charlie exited the forward hatch, walked aft and caught the stern line as Mish tossed it to him.

"I like your boat," she said. "Where'd you get it?"

Charlie smiled. "I found it."

THE LAST U-BOAT

OUT
WITH
A BANG

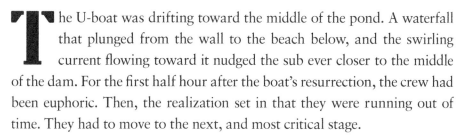

The U-boat was drifting toward the middle of the pond. A waterfall that plunged from the wall to the beach below, and the swirling current flowing toward it nudged the sub ever closer to the middle of the dam. For the first half hour after the boat's resurrection, the crew had been euphoric. Then, the realization set in that they were running out of time. They had to move to the next, and most critical stage.

It wasn't long before Charlie called Colt's attention to a problem.

"We're caught on a cable."

Colt's flashlight revealed a shiny quick release cable pressed against the unfinished conning tower. He powered into command mode.

"Everyone get to your stations. The conning tower's caught on the quick release cable. If it snaps, the wall could collapse. This is dangerous, guys. Hustle."

Charlie went below to tell Amber and Stewart the news, closing and sealing the forward hatch behind him.

Amber keyed the talkie. "Colt, let's take the sub down while Doubeck pulls the stern line until we're right between the left and right quick release cables where we need to be."

"Should work," he replied.

Stewart didn't like it. "We haven't really tried the ballast tanks yet. I'm pretty sure we can take the sub down, but I don't know if we can come back up."

Amber heard the problem loud and clear. "Better to find that out now and not when we're out a mile and under water."

Stewart hadn't considered that. "Okay, good point. Let's go for it."

"Colt, how deep do we have to go to clear the cable."

"If you drop where you are, it's six or eight feet, Amber. That means your decks will be maybe a foot below the surface. If you can't come back up, you can always evacuate out the conning tower hatch."

"Alright, Charlie, open the forward hatch, then come back to the control room so you're near your cocoon, just in case. Stewart, when Charlie reports the hatch open, start the compressors and fill our tanks."

"Forward hatch unsealed, Captain. Opening it now."

The crew heard only the throbbing of the air compressors aboard the sub until Stewart spoke. "Captain, I'm guessing from the looks of the gauges, we're going to need a half hour to fill the air tanks."

"That's too long." Amber knew time wasn't on their side. "How much pressure do we need to surface?"

"Not a clue," Stewart answered

"Marty?"

"Yes, Captain."

 "If we're shallow, it's easier to push the water out of the tanks, right?"

"Ah, yes. Close to the top should be easiest."

The talkie went silent for a minute. On the surface, Marty, Mish and Colt waited from the near shore where they were surprised to see Doubeck suddenly climb out of the water and onto the deck of the sub, a few feet forward the conning tower. He had just paddled in on a pool float that looked a lot like a glittery unicorn.

"I found a boat!"

Colt slung his head and laughed. "Improvise and overcome," he said to himself.

Mish called out to Doubeck. "Doobs, tie the stern line and get back to shore. They need you to pull the boat over. Plus, you're embarrassing yourself."

"Not possible, Mish." Doubeck was already on one knee, looping the line around a cleat. "Okay. I'm good—it's done."

Doubeck ran back to his unicorn, set it on the slope of the bow, climbed on and slipped into the darkness of the pond, taking the stern line with him.

It was very strange and disconcerting for Colt, Marty, Mish and Doubeck to watch the U-boat sink quietly beneath the surface of the pool, knowing their friends were inside. Only the odd-looking conning tower stood above the water, the tube containing the ladder to the control room rising over it like a chimney.

Colt directed the action. "Mish, hang on to your line so the sub doesn't drift too far across and get tangled in the other quick release."

They needed to line up the boat up squarely between the two cables where the dam was designed to collapse.

"Marty, Mish, keep your flashlights on the sub. Make sure we can see all of it. Doubeck. Pull on your line. It's going to feel like it's not moving, but it will."

Doubeck looped the rope around his left arm and pulled with his right. Hundreds of tons of steel began to float slowly toward him.

"Mish. Get over to a tree and wrap your rope around it a couple times so the sub can't go too far."

"Got it." Mish ran along the edge of the pool until she found a sturdy maple.

"Now, Mish!" Colt watched as the boat drifted between the quick release cables and then stopped. He grabbed his talkie and keyed the microphone.

"Captain, take her up. You should be exactly where you need to be."

"Thanks, Colt." Amber replied. "Charlie, blow the ballast tanks."

Colt, Mish and Doubeck watched from the crest of the hill as the U-boat's stern rose out of the water until the tops of the propellers could be seen reflecting the moonlight just below the surface. The bow was still underwater.

"Charlie, you can't do one tank at a time. Try turning fore and aft valves at the same time."

"Sorry. The valves are really stiff, but I can turn one and then turn the other a little... I'll just go back and forth."

"They haven't been turned in 80 years. They might loosen up as you use them. Just keep your eye on the bubble, Charlie."

"Aye, Captain."

It was exciting to watch the boat rise above the surface of the pool, even in the dim light cast by flashlights.

"Colt, we're ready as we'll ever be. Give us five minutes to get to the beach, then let's launch this boat."

"Aye, Captain. I'm headed down to pull the cable out of the way. I'll check with you in five."

Amber set her talkie down and stepped the few feet to Charlie's station in front of the diving plane and ballast controls.

She reached down and took his hand. "Charlie, come with me."

They turned and walked back through the control room just past the tube containing the ladder to the hatch. As they passed behind the tube, Amber stopped and turned. Charlie was just a foot away. She put her hands on either side of his head, drew his face toward hers, closed her eyes and kissed him.

It was a serious kiss, long and gentle. Charlie reached up and put his left hand behind Amber's head and his right hand behind her waist. He pulled her to him and leaned her backward against a wall of pipes and cables. There was a hand rail behind her. He lifted her, sat her on the rail, put his arms around her, and drew her close. Her ankles pulled tight against the back of his legs.

When the kiss ended, Charlie's eyes were still closed. She watched as he slowly opened them. Then, she swept his curly hair across his forehead and smiled.

"You know I'm crazy about you, don't you?" she asked.

Charlie returned the smile. "Oh, Captain, my Captain," he said.

She grinned. "Submarine races, anyone?"

Amber took Charlie's hand and said, "Let's go see Stewart."

They made their way along the narrow path in the control room and stepped through the bulkhead hatch to the engine room. Stewart was there, winding one of the springs that powered the flywheels used to start the diesels.

"Sup, Stewart?"

"Oh. I wanted to have the diesels ready, so after the launch we can just move out and recharge the batteries. We've been using them a lot."

Stewart's cocoon allowed him to reach the engine controls.

"You ready?" asked Amber.

"I think so," he replied.

Amber held her hand out to Stewart and he shook it. Then she kissed his cheek.

"What's that for?"

"It's for being amazing. I didn't really know you before. I thought you were an igit. But I was wrong and I'm sorry."

"I *was* an igit." Stewart dropped his head and stared at the deck. "My mother had just passed away and for a long time I took it out on anyone who tried to be nice to me. At least until you all came along." He lifted his head and looked at Charlie. "I'm sorry for the way I treated you and your little brother."

"Thanks, Stewart. You're a good guy. You're fam now." As they shook hands, they put their arms over each other's backs and gave them a pat. When they did, Stewart picked up the unmistakable aroma of Amber's perfume on Charlie's neck. He looked at Charlie, then at Amber. She read the look on Stewart's face and just smiled. "Stewart, time to get into your cocoon. We're going for a ride," she said. "Charlie, let's go forward. When you're in, I'll tell Colt we're set."

Less than a minute later Amber made the fateful call.

"Colt?"

"Aye, Captain."

"We are ready."

"Okay. Listen up everyone. When I pull the quick release cables. There's going to be a huge crack and this pond will empty in seconds. Let go of your lines as soon as the sub starts moving."

There was no more waiting.

Inside the sub, Amber put on her cover. "Helmsman?"

There was no response.

"Charlie."

"Aye, Captain."

"You're our helmsman."

Charlie turned on the leather upholstered stool and looked at Amber over his shoulder. "I am?"

"Yeah. You're steering the boat, right?"

He turned back. "Uh huh."

"Helmsman, stand by to take us to Lake Erie."

"Standing by, Captain."

Outside, in the still darkness, Colt reached up and pulled hard on the quick release cables. The connections separated and the cables fell into the pool, splashing in the water on either side of the boat.

But nothing happened.

"What's happening, Gunny?" shouted Mish.

"Hold your line." Colt keyed the talkie as he ran along the edge of the water toward the wall. "Doubeck. Hold your line. Don't let the ass end of the sub move sideways."

Colt quickly reached the wall at the edge of the pool, he leaned over the side and found a pair of wires hanging over a nail on the wall. "Doubeck, Mish. Let go of your lines now and get down. Get back up the hill, Marty. Run!"

Colt put the butt end of his flashlight in his mouth. With both hands, he started gathering the wires until a black box appeared, covered by a plastic sandwich bag. Colt pulled the bag off the wires and threw a toggle switch on the box. A red light came on. A second later the light turned green. Colt brought his thumb down hard on a fat red button under the light. Then he tossed the box back over the wall and dove for the weeds

Blasting caps inserted into the two Bangalore torpedoes Colt had placed under the bottom timbers ignited before Colt hit the ground. Those charges were connected to another two that Colt had set in the mud behind the wall. All four explosives, 160 pounds of TNT, exploded at once. Under the weight of ten-million gallons of water, it felt like no more than a thud under their feet. But the pressure wave generated by the blast immediately collided with the wall, shattering the timbers nearby, blasting a broad, irregular hole above the floor of the creek bed.

Immediately a river of water began to escape. As the force of the blast continued upward, it tore the pegged timbers apart, sending shards of wood flying into the lake. The wall ripped apart like it was being unzipped. As the blast reached the sub floating directly above the explosion, it lifted the bow six feet into the air. Beneath the wave, a massive dome of hot gases shot upward. The boat dropped hard into the giant bubble.

The explosion had also pushed nearly half the reservoir back up into the gully. It returned like a tidal wave and drove the sub forward like it was pushing a child on a swing. The sub shot over the falling tower of water and slipped forward like a surfboard, propelled by the wave behind it. It rode the slope of the falling water down to the lake and then disappeared into the darkness.

It was all over in less than ten seconds and then, just as suddenly, the air grew eerily quiet.

Colt stood and looked down where the wall and the pool had been. He never saw the sub flushed out of the gully. Mish was standing nearby. He walked to her side. She grabbed his arm and shouted. "They're gone."

"What happened, Mish?"

"There was a huge explosion."

"What happened to the sub, Mish? Who's gone?"

"I don't know what happened."

"What do you mean, you don't know?"

Mish couldn't answer. She had fallen to her knees, sobbing.

Colt reached for his talkie, but it had swung around to the back of his neck. He grabbed the sling and pulled it forward. Clutching the talkie with both hands, he keyed the microphone. "Amber? Charlie? Stewart?"

There was silence.

Colt's eyes searched the shoreline, then the lake. He took a few steps down the hill and then stopped.

All of a sudden, there was no plan B.

As Marty stepped onto the beach, Doubeck had just reached the creek bed. He walked out of the gully, through the gaping hole where the wall stood just moments earlier, past the debris and chaos the rushing waters had left behind The two giant locust trees, sprawled in the same place on the beach for as long as he could remember, had been brushed aside like twigs. He climbed up on one of the trunks and walked out to its end. It had been thrust toward the lake and lay cantilevered in the sand, pointing upward like a cannon protecting the coastline.

He stood on it, staring out over the darkness of the lake's waters, searching the silence for his friends.

Colt arrived a minute later.

"Do you see anything, Doubeck?" Colt was still looking for answers. Something that would tell him what happened when he hit the dirt.

Doubeck was not happy. "What did you do Colt? Did you blow it up?"

"I blew up the wall. It wasn't breaking up on its own. It was a possibility I prepared for."

"How do you know you didn't blow up the sub? How do you know?"

"Doubeck. Take it easy," said Marty.

Colt knew this was not the time to argue.

Mish arrived in time to grab Doubeck's arm and try to calm him down. He pushed her hand away.

"Gunny doesn't know, Doubeck. I didn't tell him."

Colt spun Mish around and took her by the shoulders. "They were on the sub?"

Mish looked down and nodded slowly.

Colt turned his back on his three companions and looked out over the lake. "It's okay. They're safe in that sub. It's built for war and it can take a punch."

Doubeck walked up behind Colt. "You fucking blew them up, you maniac."

"Stand down, Doubeck."

"What the hell were you thinking."

"You know what I was thinking. That sub was going nowhere and I had planned for that. They took the risk on their own. Listen, hot shot, you're the guy who always wants to blow shit up. But I'm the guy who's trained to do it. Got it?"

"Really? Were you trained to recover bodies, too?"

"Don't you say that. Don't you dare give up on them. I laid a pressure charge to rip the wall open—an old wooden wall with ten-million gallons of water pushing against it. It did not blow the sub apart. I'm telling you, they're fine. Give them time and get outta my face."

Doubeck and Mish turned from Colt toward the waves, now rolling gently and slowly toward the beach. Except for the rolling water softly falling and dying on the shore, it was quiet. In front of them was only darkness.

THE LAST U-BOAT

GONE

Colt sat on the locust log that pointed out over the lake, watching a half-moon set in the western sky. Marty, Mish and Doubeck stationed themselves next to him toward the very end of the log.

Colt kept quiet and waited. He learned long ago it was a weak leader who put his concerns on display. At this moment, it was imperative that he exude unwavering confidence. But the longer they waited with no word from the crew, the weaker his firm convictions would appear.

He checked his watch. "We've got about five hours before all hell breaks loose." The comment was a deliberate attempt at distraction.

The three didn't take the bait. They were still very angry following the discovery that Colt had used explosives to help launch the U-boat. Mish was staying close to Doubeck to act as a damper, but the continuing quiet finally got him so stirred up, she couldn't keep him restrained any more. He stood and turned on Colt.

"Why aren't you doing anything?"

"I am doing something," Colt replied calmly. "I'm waiting."

"That's not helping."

"Doubeck, listen to me. Getting mad at me changes nothing—but it clouds your reasoning. And right now, you and I—all of us—we need to think clearly."

Marty tried to break the tension. "Listen, they're in a steel tube—probably submerged. I wouldn't expect to be able to talk with them right now."

Colt kept his mouth shut and let Marty's words sink in.

Doubeck looked at Colt. "What did you mean when you said all hell was going to break loose?"

"I mean some model citizen, doing her civic duty, is going to call the township when the sun comes up, complaining that the ducks in her neighborhood don't have a home any more. The township will check the duck pond, and when they do, they're going to come right down here—right where we're sitting—looking for their pond."

"Oh, crap." Marty felt the unease of remorse in the pit of his stomach. "Do you think they'll figure it out?"

"Maybe. But not right away. Remember, they were planning to do this all along. We just expedited the process."

Doubeck shook his head, unamused by Colt's usually charming arrogance. He looked back to where the now scattered timbers once held back ten-million gallons of water and a U-boat. In the moonlight, he saw a few broken bat handles, metal cables and cracked timbers scattered everywhere. To anyone coming upon the scene it would look plainly like the aftermath of a flood. There was no way anyone could know it was actually two floods and neither the one at the duck pond nor the one at the beach was natural.

"Would I go to jail, Colt?" asked Marty.

"You didn't do anything."

"I wrecked the dam," said Mish.

"Yeah. Well, ducks don't make good witnesses."

The conversation was interrupted by a hissing coming from Colt's walkie talkie. It only lasted a few short seconds. Everyone froze. A moment later, the hiss of white noise returned and a voice could be heard only faintly discriminated from the background. With a pop and a click, the sound cleared.

"Colt? Doubeck? Anyone? Come in."

Mish screamed, "It's Amber!"

Colt keyed the mike. "Amber. We hear you. What's your condition? Over."

"We're okay. We're banged up pretty good. I got a bruise on my chin and Charlie cut the back of his hand, but it's not bad. Stewart got burned on his left arm just a little, but we're good. Is Mish there?"

Colt handed the talkie to Mish. She spoke through tears of joy. "I'm here, Amber."

"Mish, your cocoons saved our lives. Just want you to know that."

Amber's comment left her friend speechless.

She handed the talkie back to Colt just as it sputtered again. "Colt?"

"Stewart, how you doing?"

"We're good. Hey, I'm sorry we didn't tell you. We were afraid you'd call a red light."

"Well, there's something I didn't tell you, too. I blew up the wall when it wouldn't collapse. I didn't know you were in there."

"I wondered what that was. We got smacked pretty good. We popped up when it hit us, but we coasted out of the gully like we were on a snow board."

Colt had a lot of questions. "Amber, do you know where are you?"

"I'm on a submarine, guys. It's awesome!" she said.

Amber's comment signaled that a serious conversation would have to wait until the giddiness passed.

"I climbed up the tower, opened the hatch and took a good look around. I know this shoreline. We're about a mile off the beach. I took her down eight or ten feet because it's smoother than sitting right on top. Our talkies and flashlights hit the floor when we splashed down and batteries went everywhere. We had to use the lights on our phones to find them. Plus, we had some leaks we're fixing. Over."

"Is the hull okay?"

"Stewart says the hull's fine. The leaks were in a few pipes—loose water lines, not fuel. We're going to need fuel, Colt. Don't forget about us."

"Soon. You can have all you want. Just practice driving your boat and save enough diesel to get to the ferry docks at the West Slip. I'll have the fuel truck there tomorrow night."

"You mean we're not going to hijack a tanker?"

"Your life's too normal, right? Listen, is Charlie handy?"

"Hang on." Amber handed the talkie to Charlie.

"Hey, Gunny, it's Charlie."

"Hey, buddy. You know the registration that blew out of your hand? It's in my pocket."

"That's great news. How did you find it?"

"I was on the wall where the water was spilling onto the beach. It floated right over to me. By the way, you can still read it."

Charlie screamed into the walkie talkie. "Yes!"

"Can you put Amber back on, please?"

"Gunny, It's Amber."

"I have an idea, Captain. Stick your flashlight into the eyepiece of the periscope and swing it in our direction. We should be able to see the light coming up through it."

Amber took a moment to reply. "Okay. Charlie's on it—stand by."

Almost immediately the three friends on the shore saw a light on the horizon.

Marty took the talkie from Colt and stepped to the highest point on the log. "We see you, Captain! Oh, man is it good to see you guys…and hear you."

"Stewart unscrewed the antenna on this talkie and hooked it into the original radio antenna down here. We weren't sure it worked until we finally heard you answer us."

"Amber, this is Marty. I have 3:37 a.m. on my phone. Let's connect every half hour at 15 and 45 until dawn, and then maybe back off to every hour. Okay with you?"

"Okay with us. If we need you in the meantime, we'll call. Keep us posted, too, okay?"

"Will do."

"Gunny, Stewart wants to talk to you."

Marty handed the talkie back to Colt.

"Gunny, we're going to try to get some rest, but I think we need to move pretty quickly to camouflage the boat. It's going to be hard to hide. Can we do something soon? Amber and Charlie need to get home. Over."

"Man. We didn't plan this part, did we, Stewart? Okay, we'll get some volunteers and we'll find a way to get out to you. Our next call is in a half hour. I'll have some answers for you then. Get some sleep."

"I have a couple of GoPros I'm going to mount on the deck, then I'm hitting the sack. Here's Amber."

"Gunny, we're going to sign off and start the diesel. We need to charge up. Talk to you later."

"Thanks, Captain. Gunny out."

Colt stood on the lower side of the log, which had the effect of adding several inches to Doubeck's elevation. As Colt lowered his walkie talkie, Doubeck looked him straight in the eye.

"Doubeck. You heard everything I heard. It sounds like we've got a lot of work to do and no time to fight or sleep. Are you in or out?"

"Am I in? I'm not the one that kept secrets from everyone. Do you have any other secrets you're not telling us?"

"Yeah, I do. And melodramatic fits like you're having are the reason why I don't share everything."

Doubeck had literally backed himself into a corner, alone at the end of the fallen tree. Mish was sitting next to him and the Marine blocked the path. The lake and some treacherous rocks lay below. There was no walking away. Doubeck was going to have to deal with his emotions.

"You're the one who always says to keep your senses heightened and be prepared to react. Well, I have the feeling something's wrong. I want to know what you know, Gunny. I want to know if I'm in danger, or if Mish is in danger because *you're* here."

Marty spoke up. "I'd kinda like to know that, too."

"Me, too," said Mish.

Colt nodded. "Okay. I'll tell you what I know. Stewart's in trouble. His old boss from the marina is probably an international criminal. He sucked Stewart into a situation where he felt trapped, and I helped Stewart escape. I did that because I'm pretty sure if his boss can find him, he'll try to kill him."

"What? Then, if he's with us, we're in danger, too."

Colt shook his head. "Doubeck, can you even hear yourself? The guy would have to know about the U-boat to find Stewart. He doesn't know any of you guys."

"I think he saw me when I went to the marina to talk to Stewart."

Marty interrupted, "Doubeck. We're very well hidden."

"Plus," said Colt. "I planted a bug in the guy's office. With a little luck, we'll be able stay a few steps ahead of him."

"You can't go to the cops?" asked Mish.

"No, we can't, and not just because of the sub. It's tricky. Even if they got arrested they'd find a way to order a hit on Stewart."

"Witness to what?" Mish asked.

"Six murders. And they forced Stewart to drive the boat when it happened. He could be arrested for being an accomplice."

"That's unreal," said Mish.

"It was in the middle of the lake and the bodies went down with their boat. Chances are the authorities don't even know about it. But it's the reason Stewart needs to lay low."

"This is all going to catch up with us, isn't it?" Doubeck asked.

"Yeah, it will eventually. But we have some time, and I have some leads I'm working to head them off. I promise I'll keep you guys out of it. I will."

Mish reached up and took Doubeck's arm. "We have to trust him, for Stewart's sake, too."

"There is something else, guys. If I tell you I'll be violating a confidence, but you've put me in a position where if I don't tell you, you'll think I'm holding out."

"Wait a second. There's more you're not telling us?" Marty asked.

"Yeah, there is. It's personal, a family matter having to do with Stewart. That's all I wanna say about it. I'm not going to give any details. It's up to Stewart to share it someday. Just take it easy on him, that's all I'll say. He cares about you guys—you've become really important to him."

"I knew you were keeping stuff from us," said Doubeck.

Colt looked at each member of the crew as he spoke. "Hey, you're all just as guilty of that as I was."

Doubeck had made his point. Now, he was ready to end the confrontation. "Can I go now? You going to let me walk past you?"

"We can all go as soon as we decide how we're going to relieve the crew."

~

Colt, Doubeck, Mish and Marty moved to the sand and settled down behind a small campfire. Despite the rain, Colt managed to scrounge up some driftwood and had the fire going within a few minutes. It helped everyone to dry out, relax, and start working together again.

The radio crackled at 4:15 A.M. "Gunny, it's Amber. You there? Was I supposed to call you or are you supposed to call me?"

Colt picked up the talkie. "Hey, Captain. I'm here. Whatever works, I guess. Everything okay?"

"We're good. The diesel's humming, the batteries have almost topped off, and we're getting rest and cleaning up."

"Need anything?"

"Sleep. Food. My own pillow. Fuel."

"I hear you. We've got a plan to relieve you guys. Doubeck knows a cottage down the beach where they always leave a dinghy turned over on the sand. Give us some time and I'll have some answers for you. Let's talk again at 4:45."

"Sounds good. We're going to take a spin down to the city to look at the lights. I need to see what kind of mileage we're getting on diesel."

"Okay, Captain. Have a good trip. Colt out."

A half-hour later, Mish, Doubeck and Colt were crowded together in a dinghy, drifting a half mile offshore. The moon was high in the sky and occasionally, when fish jumped near the boat, the light traced concentric circles on the water's surface. What started as a chaotic and threatening night had evolved into a peaceful, idyllic, and hopeful new day.

The walkie talkie popped and hissed. Colt turned the volume down.

"Gunny, It's Amber."

"I hear you, Captain. I have your replacements with me and we're waiting to rendezvous. Are you back from your sightseeing tour?"

"Yeah, we're back in the general area. Based on depth, I'm estimating we're a half mile out. I'll leave a light on for you."

"We're on our way. Colt out."

Five minutes later, Mish saw the light. Colt was rowing, so his back was to the direction they were moving.

"I see them, Gunny. Head this way." She pointed off to her left.

Colt adjusted. He put his back into rowing, and soon brought the row-boat to the base of the conning tower. Amber's flashlight beamed down from the tower hatch.

"Hey guys!"

Mish screamed with delight, "Amber! You're my hero. You are so badass!"

"Colt, does that skiff have a flat bottom?"

"She sure does, Captain."

"Okay, grab one of our rails and hang on."

The water around the rowboat began to swirl. Doubeck and Colt each grabbed a rail. A solid bump shook the passengers, and within seconds, the wooden boat sat stranded on a steel island. The fore hatch opened and Stewart emerged. Charlie followed, and a minute later, Amber appeared. There were hugs all around. It was their first chance to celebrate their amazing accomplishment together.

Charlie caught a glimpse of Mish watching Doubeck hug Amber. Her hands were jammed in her pockets and her head was tilted hard to the right.

Colt's shouting broke up the hugs.

"Woo-ooo. Holy crap." Colt had a smile on his face every bit as wide as those of the crew members around him. "This boat is huge. I had no idea how big it was when it was buried. Even when it was floating it looked smaller. But standing on it—actually standing on it—it's scary." He chuckled. "It's awesome scary."

Stewart and Amber laughed, patted Colt's back, and pushed him playfully, delighted to see the Marine admit his astonishment.

Marty lifted two black garbage bags out of the rowboat. "We brought stuff we might need. Towels, soap, swim masks and flippers. We're going to start a list so we can have all the stuff we might need."

Colt was big on planning. "Save the garbage bags, too, so we can carry our trash off."

"Okay, Mom," said Marty, happy to finally get a jab in.

"Mish, I'm giving you the con while I'm home," said Amber. "Stewart's staying aboard but he's going to need some shuteye. I'd recommend you guys take her out and down to forty feet so you can lay low while you rest."

"Alright, Captain. Do I get to wear your hat?"

"No," said Amber. "There are some things I don't share—even with my best friend." She looked at Charlie who blushed for everyone to see, even in the harsh blue glow of their flashlights.

"Look at that sky." Colt pointed toward a bright glow growing in the East. "Amber, Charlie, Marty—into the rowboat. You're coming back with me. Doubeck, Mish, Stewart—get some rest. I want us all standing back here at 4 P.M." Colt drew his phone from his pocket and held it aloft. "You guys need to use your phones, call home. Let your families know you're okay so they don't come looking for you. I'm headed back to the store to cut a hole in the Bayliner. We'll get it bolted on tomorrow. Stewart, I'll see you at the West Slip."

"Gunny, I've got all the tools, stainless bolts, and parts we might need here in the engine room."

"Excellent, and Lacey's going to have a tanker full of bunker there for us. Don't be late."

"We'll be there," said Stewart.

Colt tapped a button on his phone, and it lighted up. "Okay, it's almost 6 a.m., we need to get a move…" He stopped speaking abruptly and raised his phone closer to his face. After tapping on the screen a few times, he lowered the phone and looked at Stewart.

"I thought you said Petrosian never gets to work before 9 a.m.?"

THE LAST U-BOAT

DOUBLE
CHECKING

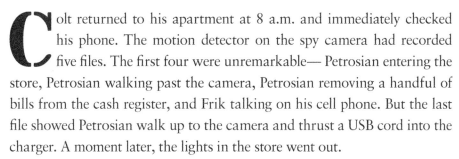

olt returned to his apartment at 8 a.m. and immediately checked his phone. The motion detector on the spy camera had recorded five files. The first four were unremarkable— Petrosian entering the store, Petrosian walking past the camera, Petrosian removing a handful of bills from the cash register, and Frik talking on his cell phone. But the last file showed Petrosian walk up to the camera and thrust a USB cord into the charger. A moment later, the lights in the store went out.

They've left and Petrosian's phone is still plugged into the camera.

Colt tapped his assistant Lacey's number on speed dial.

"Yeah, Gunny."

"Lacey, sorry to call so early. I need a hacker. I've got surveillance on a target who just plugged his phone into my charger camera. If a hacker had the IP address of the charger they might be able to get into the phone and copy the files."

"Yeah, I get it. Text me the IP and anything else I need to know and I'll forward it," said Lacey. "We know just the guy."

"You mean Ming-Ming?" asked Colt.

"Exactly."

Colt snorted, "She's no guy. Call her. I don't know how long we'll have to peek into this phone before they come back to get it." He ended the call, grabbed a screen shot of the setup on the camera app and texted it to Lacey. Then he walked to his sofa and collapsed.

His bliss was interrupted two hours later by the rattling of his phone.

"Yeah."

"Ming-Ming got everything. I forwarded a link."

"Do me a favor. I'm going to be tied up for another hour or two. Look it over and let me know what jumps out at you."

"Yut."

Colt tossed his phone onto a cushion at the far end of the sofa and collapsed once again, falling asleep almost immediately.

Charlie and Amber lay asleep in each other's arms on the beach, just east of the debris that remained from the flood. The voices woke Charlie first. He kissed Amber's forehead and rolled over in the direction of the sound. A small, rocky dune blocked his view. Charlie checked his watch. It was almost 9 a.m.

"Amber, let's fold up the towel. We gotta go. We need to get home."

"What time is it?"

"Almost nine."

Amber sat up with Charlie and they both looked toward the voices. Four men in orange and yellow safety vests were walking around, making notes, and inspecting the aftermath of the flood.

To get home, Charlie and Amber had no choice but to walk past them.

As they turned to enter the gully, one of the men called to them. "Do you kids live nearby?"

"I live right up there," said Charlie, pointing to his house on the hill above them.

"I'm over there, down a few houses," said Amber, indicating the opposite side of the ravine.

"Everything okay?"

"What do you mean?" said Charlie.

"There was a big flood last night."

For the next two minutes, Charlie and Amber played dumb and asked questions. They learned the township had a preconceived notion that the flood took out the wall along the shore. The man called it an *Act of God*. He also mentioned the failure of the duck pond dam, calling that *natural causes*.

The crew wasn't out of the woods, but at least they weren't yet under suspicion. The snooping had begun just as Charlie thought it would. First the township crew, then his parents, then the FBI. That's how he imagined it would happen, little by little. Charlie felt the weight of his success fall heavy on his shoulders as he climbed the hill to his house and the coming inquisition.

Sharon LeClair bustled about in the kitchen while Rocky sat in his high chair shoveling Fruit Loops into his mouth, playing with an iPad. The aroma of coffee steamed from cups on the table, a frying pan sizzled with bacon, and the smell of toast was in the air. "Your father's on his way down. Would you like some scrambled eggs, Charlie?" Sharon was trying to stay nonchalant.

"Sure. Thanks, I'm starving."

She began cracking eggs into a bowl as her husband walked into the kitchen with his favorite golf sweater in his hand.

"You golfing, Dad?"

"Morning, all! You bet I am, Charlie. Hope to get eighteen in before it warms up. What are you up to today?"

"A bunch of us have a project we've been working on."

Sharon had waited for this moment all night. She didn't have any patience for the banter.

"Can I interrupt?"

Mike and Charlie turned to her.

Sharon was looking over her shoulder as she spoke so she could cook and talk at the same time. "Mike, I asked Charlie to talk to us this morning because I found out yesterday he has his own checking account, and he's been working and making money."

"Good for you, Charlie. I had a paper route when I was your age. You need to learn how to manage money, so when you get older you'll have some put away for a rainy day."

"Mike." Sharon interrupted.

"I still remember how great it was to get paid after collections on Fridays.

I had so many dimes in my pocket I couldn't pedal in a straight line."

"Mike, please."

"I'm just kidding. A couple bucks was a lot of money back then. But you have to start somewhere."

"*Mike?*"

"Yeah, honey."

"Ask Charlie how much money he's made."

Mike looked at Charlie.

"So far, I've made just over a million, one hundred thousand."

Mike LeClair smiled and blinked twice. He looked up at Sharon and back down at Charlie. Then he giggled. "A million what?"

Sharon grabbed the bank statements and dropped them in front of Mike. His smile remained pasted firmly to his face as he picked up the first page and looked at the bottom line. Then the second page. Then he examined the third page, and his expression never changed.

He set the statements down, lifted his chin and turned to Charlie.

Charlie looked Mike squarely in the face, and watched helplessly as his dad's eyes rolled upward, his head tipped back and he fell limply out of his chair.

Rocky laughed. "Daddy fell down."

———————

Colt had three missions to accomplish before the end of the day. Getting control of the Petrosian situation was top priority. Next came fueling the U-boat at the West Slip, and last, but equally important, was getting the Bayliner mounted onto the U-boat's sail to disguise it. Colt reminded himself to stay on task, protect his team, communicate effectively, maintain situational awareness—and to take a weapon with him. He spun the dial on his gun safe and pulled out his 9mm SIG M17. He grabbed an ammo pouch, slapped the magazine into the grip, clipped his Kynar holster onto his belt in the middle of his back, and pushed the barrel home until it clicked.

Colt latched the chrome handle on his gun safe, spun the dial once, and walked over to his couch. His phone was buzzing as he approached. Lacey was right on time.

"Lacey, what've you got?"

"I'm on with Ming-Ming. I'll transfer you."

Colt waited for the phone to click. "Ming-Ming, *ni hao, wo de pungyou.*"

"*Ni hao*, Missa Gunny. How you been?"

"I been bad and I been good, how 'bout you?"

"No, you bad all time. You sneaky man. You got big talent to find bad guys."

"With your help, huh?"

"This one very bad, Missa Gunny. He fight with Red Army in Afghanistan in 1980s. But he have many dodgy contact on his mobile."

"Any conversations?"

"Yessiree, many conversations, most about money and secret mission. Many secret mission."

"Well, he may have just neutralized a half-dozen TB. Any idea why he'd do that?"

"I know 'bout that. They not Taliban. They soldier of warlord with name Ismail Noor."

"I remember Noor. What are Noor's soldiers doing here on Lake Erie?"

"Lake no have border. Easy to do terrorism. He think he become next Bin Laden."

"So, Petrosian was just being a good citizen, going out and killing bad guys?"

"Nooooo. He get big money to kill them."

"It was a hit?"

"Yeah-yeah, he like John Wick—*pew pew*—you see John Wick, Missa Gunny?"

"Ming-Ming, who paid Petrosian to kill the Afghans?"

"I tell you but you no believe it. Shura Council pay Petrosian."

"You're telling me the ruling council of the Taliban hired that idiot?"

"Yessiree. In war, Petrosian quit army for opium money, make friend with Mujahid name Rashid. Rashid big shot now in Shura Council. He send many assassin to kill all translator. Why he do that?"

"Probably to get even with them for helping us during the war. But why did Rashid want Noor's soldiers dead?"

"Noor send terrorist same time Rashid send terrorist. Rashid tell Shura Council Noor gonna screw everything up. So, they hire Petrosian to kill Noor's soldier."

"I guess I'm glad he did, but I still hate the Taliban."

"Yessiree. Taliban crazy people. Remember Sun Tsu. He say not do revenge. Revenge always make more war."

"He was right. But if what you're saying's true, it means there are Taliban assassins heading this way. The Taliban may not be all that smart. But you damn well better believe they're dangerous."

———

Mike squinted. "What happened?"

Sharon held a wet dishcloth to her husband's forehead. Mike was back in his chair looking pale.

"You passed out, honey. You need to eat some breakfast. It was Charlie's good news. He's made a lot of money, Mike"

"Oh, I remember now...Charlie, are those real bank statements?"

Charlie was fixed on his dad's distress and just a little slow to answer. Mike didn't notice, he was still trying to pull himself together.

"I...I need some coffee."

Sharon had already poured some. "Here you go, honey. Now, Charlie, tell your dad about your business."

"Oh, sure."

Charlie stared at his father. He looked like he'd just been beaten up. "You okay, Dad?"

"Yeah. I'm good. Just got dizzy for a second. What's this about a business?"

Charlie took a deep breath. "Well, you know how me and my friends have been going through all the boxes Mrs. Kraus left?"

"Mrs. Kraus?"

"She's the woman who owned our house," said Sharon.

"Oh, right," said Mike, emerging from his fog.

"Anyway, we did a lot of research and it turns out, Mrs. Kraus was the leader of a group of Nazi saboteurs during World War II."

"What! Where?" Mike asked.

"Here. In our house. I mean, it wasn't our house then. But, yeah, right here."

"That's nuts! How do you know that?"

Charlie thought for a moment. "Hang on." He jumped off his chair and ran down into the basement where there were still a few boxes of the Kraus's memorabilia. He knew right where to go, and in less than a minute he returned with a leather-bound portfolio. He set it in front of his father with a thud that raised a small cloud of ancient dust.

"What's this?"

Charlie pulled a leather cord and flipped the cover open. A big red swastika adorned the first page.

"What the heck?" Mike's jaw dropped. "Where'd you get that?"

"Remember when we asked if we could go through all the stuff before you threw it out?"

"Yeah."

"This binder has been right here since we moved in, Dad. It's all Nazi propaganda."

"That doesn't prove she was a saboteur."

"Well, when I went down the manhole on the hillside, I found crates of greasy stuff they'd left behind…"

"Why would you go into a manhole?"

"We thought it was rusted shut but Rocky turned the handle a little, and Doubeck opened it the rest of the way. I mean we just wanted to see what was down there."

"It's a submarine," said Rocky. But everyone ignored him.

"Charlie, you lost me. How exactly was Mrs. Kraus involved?"

"The crates were full of German Lugers, Dad. Pistols…We also found machine guns."

Mike's jaw dropped. "Lugers?" Mike pictured the iconic German pistol from a hundred classic World War II movies. "Lugers *are* kinda cool."

Sharon pulled up a chair. "Ohmygod,ohmygodohmygod. My son sells weapons of mass destruction."

Mike raised his palm to get control. The fog was clearing and he wanted to hear more. "Honey, please. Charlie, did you tell the authorities?"

"No. Why would I do that?"

"Because you found dangerous weapons."

"Actually, what I found was a box of root beer-colored snot with guns in it that couldn't shoot."

"Snot," said Rocky, chuckling.

Sharon reached over in a delayed reaction to cover his ears, but Rocky pulled back and said it again. "Icky snot.'"

Overwhelmed by the story, the craziness of the moment, and his light-headedness, Mike put his forehead in his hands. "So, what happened to the guns?"

"Doubeck went looking for someone who knew about antique guns and he found a Marine who owns a surplus store downtown. His name is Gunnery Sergeant Colt, and he told me how to handle the sale so I wouldn't be breaking any laws. He's been really helpful. Mom met him."

"You met him?"

"Yeah, Mike. I told you, didn't I? I'm sure I told you. Maybe I forgot."

Mike just tilted his head quizzically so Charlie kept going. "See, I work the internet side and Gunny handles the sales for a ten percent commission. He has a Federal Firearms license so he can buy and sell guns. He had to come here to get them because I can't legally go anywhere with one."

"So, it's all legal. Well, that's a relief. Didn't he ever tell you that you should tell your parents?"

"First thing he said. But things happened fast. Oh, he also knows Mr. Ryan who manages South Shore Bank. They served together in Afghanistan. Anyway, Mr. Ryan set up my accounts for me."

"So, the guns are gone. Good. Is that it?"

"Well, it's the short version."

"You know, it feels to me like you didn't share this sooner because you didn't trust us. I mean maybe you didn't trust us with the secret, or maybe you thought we'd want the money."

"Dad, I had no idea they were that valuable. No clue."

"Listen, it's fine. I don't begrudge you the money, but I wonder, since you didn't come forward right away, if you maybe deep-down you think it isn't rightfully yours."

"Dad, I found it. It always felt like it was mine."

"Okay, fair enough. I hope this gets your mother and me off the hook for college."

"Yeah, I'm pretty sure I can handle that now." Charlie smiled and his dad sighed.

"I mean is there anything else that's, I don't know—important—that your parents should know?"

"Ummmm, well, yeah." Charlie swallowed. "We found a boat down there."

"You found a boat in the ground?"

"It's a submarine," said Rocky.

"Enough with the submarines, Rocky," said Mike.

"Yeah, there was a flood last night and it washed away a bunch of the hillside and took the boat with it. So, we're going to fix it up."

"Can you do that? It's like abandoned, isn't it?"

"Actually, I already got a registration for it."

Mike LeClair's eyes were narrowed. His brow was furrowed and he, more or less, was glaring at Charlie.

"I'm sitting here, Charlie, thinking there's gotta be something wrong and I'm not coming up with anything. But I am disappointed you didn't tell us before now."

"I know. I guess since I discovered it, I figured it was up to me to work it out. I just took it on and made it like my summer job."

Mike put his hand on Charlie's shoulder. "Did you really make a million dollars?"

Charlie nodded. All Mike could say was, "Wow."

"Well, we want to see your boat." said Sharon.

"It's a submarine," said Rocky." "And it's under ground."

Mike chuckled. "No, Rocky. Submarines go under water, not under ground." He turned back to Charlie. So, when do we get a ride?"

"Ahhh, soon, I hope. Stewart's still fixing it up. It's kind of become a community project so all my friends are sharing it right now."

"Good. That'll keep you outta trouble. Honestly, I'm still in shock. It's pretty incredible," said Mike. "I wish I could have been a part of it. It sounds like a real adventure. But, apparently you handled it well. Good job. Beats a paper route! Anyway. I really am proud of you. I've always been proud of you."

Then Mike LeClair did something he hadn't done in what he imagined was months. Actually, it was years. He opened his arms and invited his son to hug him, to be held and squeezed and loved, for nothing more than being who he is. As he put his arms around Charlie, Mike realized he was going to have to do a better job telling his boys how wonderfully awesome he thought they were. He also thought he caught the distinct smell of perfume on his son's shoulder.

DORIS
AND THE
WOLF

They were about to cut the bottom off the Bayliner. Two extension cords snaked their way out the back door of As You Were and coiled under the boat. On each coil rested a reciprocating saw with a protruding blade so full of teeth, it looked like the smile on a barracuda.

Colt and Lacey stood side-by-side studying the boat. Colt tossed a Sharpie onto the jacket he'd left lying in a heap on the pavement, next to a stack of fresh two-by-fours. A neat black line now traced the perimeter of the boat. Everything below the line would be removed, so that the Bayliner could be set in place and bolted to the top of the sub's superstructure. When the sub traveled just below the surface, the Bayliner would be the only thing visible, and no one would ever suspect a submarine hid beneath it.

"Okay, Lacey, let's start at the bow." Colt moved toward the front of the boat.

"Let's push some two-by-fours underneath and set them on cinder blocks. That'll hold the hull up while we pull the pieces out."

"Roger that," said Lacey.

With that, Colt picked up his Sawzall, and as the blade screamed, he sliced through the stem of the bow. Lacey took the starboard side, Colt the port, and they carefully dissected the hull precisely where Colt's Sharpie had marked.

Once the bow and mid-section were steady, Lacey grabbed the tongue of the trailer and pulled it out from under the Bayliner. He tossed a can of spray foam to Colt, they ducked under the hull and came up inside the boat.

Colt raised his hands. "I have no idea how much foam it's going to take to float this beast."

Lacey looked around. "It's not looking like that case of spray foam is going to cut it."

Colt chuckled. "Nope. I don't think so. But we're committed now. We have to come up with something."

The words of a song had been playing in Lacey's head all morning and, as he thought about the problem, the tune returned.

"Hey, Gunny. You know "Buy Me a Boat"?"

"You mean the song, "Buy Me a Boat"? Uh, huh. Good song. You want me to sing it or what?"

Lacey snorted a laugh. "No, I got an idea. You know those coolers we've got on display in the store?"

"Sure do. We've got Yeti one-tens, too, just like the song."

"They're water-tight, right?"

A "yeaahhh" flowed slowly out of Colt's mouth as he got on board with Lacey's vision.

"I'd put a week's pay on eight of them puppies being able to hold this boat up."

"Oh, hell yes! Lacey. You think like a damn Marine, boy!"

Lacey continued with growing enthusiasm. "If we lag-bolt two-by-fours across the seats, we can bungee the coolers underneath. Then, once the boat's bolted onto the sub, we just undo everything and fill the coolers with beer."

"Yeah, yeah. That's the way to solve a problem! Let's get some coolers out here."

They ducked out from under the hull and headed for the back door. As they entered the store, they heard a knock at the front entrance.

Colt looked at Lacey. "You had the Out to Lunch sign up, right?"

Lacey nodded.

Colt headed toward the door. He could see a familiar profile through the glass. "Lacey, you carrying?"

"Always," said Lacey.

"I need you to close and lock the back door. And lay low."

"Roger that."

Colt flipped the deadbolt on the front door and turned the handle.

His visitors took it as an invitation to walk in.

"I bet we surprise you, Mr. Colt."

"Mr. Petrosian, is it?"

"Yes, you remember. But call me Oleg. This my cousin, Frik Nazarian."

Nazarian didn't speak. A cigarette hung limply out of his fish-like lips. He lifted his chin and looked down his nose at Colt. It was a look laden with disrespect. Colt was unfazed.

"What can I do for you?"

"Frik and me, we have…friends…who need supplies. They want hunting safari, so they need big gun. Also, they might run into big dangerous animal, so they need grenades, also."

Frik interrupted, "They hunting in jungle. Is very dangerous."

Colt played along. "Yeah, I've done that. It is dangerous. You can run into poachers, too, who might mistake you for a tiger or a crocodile."

"That is problem."

"Of course, gentlemen, I can't help you myself. That would violate my Federal Firearms License. But I know people who might be able to help and I'm willing to work with them to get you whatever supplies you need."

"We need in ten days, next Wednesday," said Frik.

Petrosian reached slowly into his jacket pocket and withdrew a folded piece of notebook paper. Lifting his lapel expelled the stench of years of tobacco smoke, loosely held by the fibers of his plaid jacket. "Here shopping list. I need know cost and I need delivery guarantee for 10 days. Call number on bottom of paper."

Petrosian and Nazarian turned and walked back to the door. Petrosian put his hand on the door handle and turned back to Colt.

"One other thing, Mr. Colt. Make delivery on lake."

"Out on the water?" Colt looked Petrosian in the eye. Frik watched the street, as though standing guard.

Petrosian nodded, "Yes. On water."

"I don't think so," said Colt. "You'll need to find someone else."

"What is problem?" said Frik. "We come with good offer. We pay good money. I think you not serious."

"My 'no' is serious. I don't know you guys, so I don't want to be put in a position where I can't protect myself."

"And we need place that have a good secrecy," said Petrosian.

"We should go," said Frik.

"You need boat? I give boat to use," said Petrosian.

"*Apush,* why do you do his job?"

"Relax. He need boat to meet us."

"Okay." Colt rubbed his chin. "Here's how it's going to go. The munitions and explosives will be locked in crates. You'll get the firing pins and the keys when we get back to shore. I'll fill your shopping list on those conditions."

"Call me soon," said Petrosian. "Let me know you meet schedule." He pushed the door open and walked away with Frik at his side.

Colt bolted the door behind them and headed back toward his office. Lacey met him at the back of the store.

"I made a sale," he said, as he handed the list to Lacey.

Lacey scanned the paper and looked at Colt. "Holy balls. This is getting real interesting."

———————

Stewart was standing on deck as Amber, Charlie and Marty rowed up alongside the U-boat. Amber gave Stewart a big smile as she brushed her hair back over her shoulders. "What did you dudes do while we were gone?"

Mish and Doubeck emerged from the forward hatch and joined the rest of the crew. Stewart tossed a line to Marty. "We did a negative pressure test looking for leaks."

Amber raised her eyebrows. "That sounds like fun. How's it work?"

"We seal up the sub and start pumping our air out to see if it sucks any water in through leaks."

Amber nodded slowly. "Okay. How'd it turn out?"

"It hurt our ears but it worked great. We weren't very deep so pipe joints and the hull weren't under a lot of pressure—but no leaks."

She patted Stewart's shoulder. "Amazing. We have a good boat here."

"We sure do. We also practiced loading a torpedo tube and we installed fresh batteries in the fish," said Doubeck.

"The fish?" Amber's eyebrows drew close together. She looked at Doubeck, aware that the torpedoes were his obsession.

His eyes opened wide. "Yeah, that's what they call…"

"Doubeck, I know. It's just…the whole idea of you guys moving those… those bombs around…is kinda scary."

"Stewart did a lot of research on the torpedoes and he says they're safe."

Stewart nodded but Amber didn't even look at him. She had her own opinion.

"They're bombs, Doubeck. The sooner we can shoot them at some shipwreck or rock pile—and get rid of them—the happier I'll be."

Doubeck was ecstatic. "Really!"

"Yeah, really. I'm not going to just abandon a live bomb in the water. I *want* them to explode so they're destroyed."

"Just say the word, Captain." Doubeck gave Amber a fist bump.

Amber couldn't help but laugh. "It takes so little to make you happy, Doubeck." She was looking directly at Mish, whose eyes had opened wide. Mish's face clearly said, "Shut up, Amber."

Amber let it go. She turned to the remaining crew. "Hey, all of a sudden you're all looking clean and refreshed. You guys must have figured out how take a bath in the lake?"

"We took turns," said Mish.

"Good to know," said Amber. "And you shut down the GoPros and dropped the periscope first, right, Mish?"

Mish didn't answer, but she glared at Doubeck as Doubeck looked away feigning innocence. He leaned toward Stewart's ear. "Why's Amber trynna start something? We were good."

Stewart bumped his friend's shoulder. "Doubeck, you're fine. There's something else going on."

Marty sensed he should change the subject. "Listen guys, we brought some more food and stuff, and Charlie brought paint. We though it'd be fun to paint the boat. Plus, it's looking way too Nazi."

"Hey, I have an idea. Let's paint the name on it," said Doubeck.

"He's right," said Mish. "We've been putting it off long enough. She deserves a name."

"What are you thinking?" asked Charlie.

"Remember, Marty wanted to name it after his aunt Doris," said Amber.

"Hey, my aunt slaps." Marty reached for his phone. "Look, I got a picture."

Everyone peered over Marty's shoulder as he spun through his photos and landed on a magazine photo of a gorgeous thirty-something blonde in a thong bikini next to a red Tesla.

"Marty, you've been holding out on us," said Doubeck.

"*That's* your aunt Doris?" said Stewart.

"She's a model. She lives in Cleveland. That's why you guys haven't met her."

Doubeck raised his hand high. "All those in favor of naming the U-22 *Doris* say 'Aye-aye.'"

Only male voices responded.

Amber cleared her throat. "Hang on. I'm the Captain…"

Mish interrupted. "Aye-aye."

"You, too?"

"Sure. Why not? I'll paint the name. And when we get the real top on the conning tower I'll paint her picture in her bathing suit , just like they used to do on bombers. So, whatd'ya say, Captain?"

Amber didn't like being out maneuvered, and she wanted to get to the bottom of the sudden friction with Mish. But this wasn't the time. "Okay, *Doris* it is!"

Before the cheers subsided and everyone wandered away, Stewart got their attention. "Listen guys, one more thing. Colt texted me, and when we surfaced I called him back. He said Lacey's leaving a tanker truck parked along the West Slip tonight after dark. We're supposed to pull in and start the fill-up. We're really going to need it, because all our resources are getting low."

Amber stepped forward. "I really want to practice loading once while we're out here in open water. Loading fuel puts us lower in the water and I just want us to be high in the water with the forward hatches closed, so we can keep our balance while we load. Anyway, we need to practice it before we go in there tonight, so we can get it quick and get out safely."

Charlie was curious about the arrangements. "Hey, Stewart. How'd he get a tanker full of diesel fuel and talk someone into leaving it for us?"

"He told them a research vessel was stopping about midnight on its way from Cleveland and then leaving right away. He paid in advance with your credit card, so they'd agree to park it and give him the keys. Oh, Colt and Lacey will have the Bayliner there, too. They're going to float it off the trailer and pull it over to the sub. They'll tie it to the stern and we can haul it out into the lake to hook it up. Colt said he's coming along."

"Okay, sounds like a plan." She looked around at the crew. "We good?" she asked.

Cheers and a couple of oo-rahs went up.

"Mish, you're up. Let's paint this boat!"

Colt and Lacey sat on the tailgate of Colt's jeep, parked in the lot behind the store. He tapped a number on his burner phone and brought it to his ear. It warbled twice.

"Raccoon Bay. This Oleg."

"Petrosian, it's Colt."

"Yes. What you know?"

"Two hundred fifty grand and I want the Hatteras I saw the day I bought the Bayliner—with a full tank. You'll get it back with the keys and the firing pins. I'll also need your floating dock to tow everything."

"Why such expensive boat? Is worth more than merchandise?"

"I know it is. I figure you'll make sure no one puts a big hole in your nice expensive boat while I'm in it."

"You need learn trust, Colt."

"I take half, a hundred twenty-five grand, the boat and the floating dock on Saturday. I get the rest of the money when we deliver."

"I have no problem with this. You do realize I *can* get firing pins and I *can* break into lock. I think there something you not say."

"Yeah, dirty little secret. You really don't want to try to break the locks. Capiche?"

"I see. This what you call leaving me on back foot?"

"Come on. You know how it's done."

"Yes, I do. Do not show up before noon on Saturday."

Colt pulled the phone away from his ear and turned the power off. The deal was set.

He turned to Lacey. "It's on."

"We'll be ready."

Colt stood. "You got the tanker lined up?"

"Leaving in five to meet him at the West slip and get the key. I put $65,000 on Charlie's credit card." Lacey shuddered. "I never bought that much fuel in my life."

⸺⬤⸺

"It's awesome, guys," said Marty.

Captain and crew had lined up along the fantail to admire their handiwork. They had combined the name Doris with the image of a howling wolf.

"It sure is," said Mish.

Doubeck removed his cover and looked at the silver pin attached to it. "It looks just like the pins Colt gave us. I love it."

The U-boat looked glorious and powerful as the sun's reflections danced off the water and skittered across its gray skin.

Amber leaned on Charlie's shoulder. "It's going to look weird with a boat sitting up there."

"I know," said Charlie. "But I think it's a great way to hide us until

Saturday."

"What's Saturday?" Amber asked.

"I decided I'm going to show my Mom and Dad the U-boat on Saturday. I can't put it off. They already know about the guns and the money."

"They do?" said Marty.

"Yeah. It actually went pretty well. But, the U-boat's gonna be a real shock."

Doubeck laughed. "Ya think?"

"Then I should tell my parents, too," said Amber.

Charlie nodded. "Maybe everybody's parents should be there."

"Our sailboat's big enough for everyone. I'll ask my dad to invite everyone's parents."

"Your sailboat! They'll love it." Charlie smiled broadly. "That'll really help get them in a good mood."

"Okay. Consider it done. Let's stow our goodies below and get ready to dive. We've got places to go." She clapped her hands together and the crew headed their separate ways to their stations. Charlie remained.

Amber turned, faced him, and leaned her hip against the rail.

"What are you going to do with your U-boat, Charlie? I mean after the world finds out about it."

"I'd like to keep it, and actually go places with it. Maybe take it to France. I'm probably the only LeClair who ever captured a U-boat. Maybe I'd get the Croix de Guerre."

"You mean like Snoopy?"

Charlie laughed out loud. "Oh, yeah. Like Snoopy."

Amber kissed Charlie's cheek.

Charlie grinned. "Maybe I shouldn't let my imagination get carried away, huh?"

"No. You're good. We wouldn't be standing on a German submarine in the middle of Lake Erie if you hadn't." She slid close to him, put her arms around him and rested her head on his shoulder.

THE LAST U-BOAT

ADD
TO
CART

Eleven-thousand gallons of fuel, Gunny. You cleaned me out."

"Thanks, Lacey." Colt grabbed the handles on the four-inch hose and hoisted it out of the fill pipe on the side of the sub. "Help me stow this under the truck. We still have to bring the Bayliner over."

The bottomless Bayliner floated smoothly off its trailer, buoyed by six Yeti coolers. Back when ore freighters used the docks, the slip's channel and moorings were dredged to thirty feet, deep enough for the U-boat to submerge alongside the dock. Lacey, Colt, Marty and Charlie walked barefoot, neck-deep on the sub's deck, to guide the Bayliner into position so that it could be ferried out to deeper water.

"Marty, Charlie and I can take it from here. Can you and Lacey lift the rowboat off the Hummer, bring it over to the sub and tie it to the stern? We have to head out ASAP. When we're done bolting down the boat, I'll row back—I need to get some shuteye."

Marty and Lacey stepped up onto the dock and headed for his Hummer as Colt and Charlie finished tugging the Bayliner into place.

Colt whistled to catch Marty's attention. "By the way, guys, before you go. Whose idea was it to name the sub Doris?"

No one answered.

"Doubeck?"

"No, not my idea. She's Marty's aunt and she's a snack."

Colt turned toward shore and cupped his hands in front of his mouth. "Doris is your aunt?"

"Yeah."

"I don't get it."

"I'll text you her picture and a newspaper article about her."

Colt didn't reply. He pulled a wrench out of his back pocket and held it shoulder high. "Sorry, Doris," he said, as he whacked the hull twice. Amber heard the signal and surfaced to bring the Bayliner to rest securely on the deck.

Once the rowboat was secure, Marty opened the torpedo hatch and made his way into the sub. Lacey took off in the tanker truck and Colt headed to the crew quarters for a few minutes of shuteye. With Amber and Stewart below, Doubeck and Charlie put on life jackets and stood at the rails to enjoy the ride to deeper water.

As they headed out into the darkness, Doubeck leaned on the rail with Charlie. "Remember the day Rocky turned the wheel on the hatch?"

"Yeah, I think about that a lot."

"That's when it all started, you know," said Charlie. He turned from the rail toward his friend and shouted over the throbbing of the diesels. "How cool is this?"

Doubeck nodded. "Yeah. Look at that Bayliner. Such a great idea. When we're done with it, I want to torpedo it."

Charlie gave his friend a big thumbs-up. Doubeck laughed and returned the gesture. "I can't freakin wait," he said.

They were soon out more than a mile where they could work without being seen or heard. Amber and Stewart submerged while the remaining crew, in life jackets, floated the Bayliner over the sail.

Colt and Doubeck quickly secured a bolt on each side, and Doubeck banged a wrench on the hull to let Amber know they had the Bayliner in place. When Amber heard the signal, she ordered the sub to the surface and the remaining bolts were easily attached.

Colt walked back to rail at the stern, turned and put his hands on his hips. "It's gonna work, guys. That boat'll fool anyone."

"It's comfortable, too, sitting on these seats," said Doubeck from aboard the Bayliner. "Standing on the sub's deck for a long time is exhausting."

"Speaking of which, I'm wiped out," said Colt. "Wanna do a shift change?" He picked up the talkie he'd clipped to his belt and walked the length of the sub to the torpedo hatch.

"Colt to Captain Amber. We're ready to head to shore. Can you get us close? Doubeck, Marty and I are ready to head in."

"Will do. Stewart's winding the starter on the diesels. Give us a minute to get underway."

The crew on deck stood along the rail watching the stars as the sub eased forward. The diesels throbbed beneath their feet, and the little rowboat bobbed playfully a hundred feet behind them as it hopped over the sub's wake.

Below deck, Mish walked into the control room. Amber was alone at the periscope.

"Do you have something you want to say, Amber?"

Amber was caught off-guard. She tipped her head back and stared at the overhead. A small bare bulb glowed white-orange. It made Mish's hair look even redder.

"I have a question for you, Mish."

"Okay."

"What are you up to?"

"Meaning?"

"Meaning what's up with Doubeck?"

"Isn't it obvious?"

Amber frowned. "No. It isn't obvious. What's the situationship?"

"Hey. Where's this coming from? Why have you been getting so salty with me."

"Was not."

"Yeah. For a couple weeks."

"It's you, Mish. It started with that sneaky link in the sub, and then so much love bombing him after that."

"I'm seriously into Doubeck. What is your problem?"

"It's so sus, Mish. I know you. You're trying to make Charlie jealous."

"Ah, no. I really, really do like Doobs. He's my first boyfriend, Amber. Sheesh. I'm not using him to break you guys up. It just happened"

"Seriously?"

"Uh, yeah. Charlie's nice, but he's a little too mellow for me."

Amber started to offer a rebuttal, but she realized before she uttered a word that selling Mish on Charlie would be working at cross-purposes. She needed to trust her friend.

Mish could see it in Amber's face. "This U-boat has changed things, hasn't it?"

Amber nodded. Her eyes were cast down. "Before Charlie found the sub we used to talk all the time. You and I did everything together."

Mish wrapped her arms around Amber, and Amber hugged her back. Mish whispered in her ear. "I love you and I understand." She pushed Amber away and they wiped their teary eyes. With a big grin on her face, Mish said, "But if you come after Doubeck I'll rip your face off. Deal, bestie?"

Amber chuckled. "Deal."

At dawn, Colt was just warming up the shower when he heard Lacey's Hummer pull into the parking lot. He opened the bathroom window and stuck his head out. "Hey, Lacey. I'm just going to grab a quick shower."

"Take your time. I still have to fix up the Yeti display we tore apart."

"Mind putting the coffee on, too?"

"Aye-aye."

Colt ducked back inside and shut the window. As he pulled his T-shirt off, his phone vibrated. He tossed the shirt aside and picked up the phone. Caller ID said it was Ming-Ming.

"To what do I owe the pleasure?"

"Hey, Missa Colt. I got big news."

"Whatcha got, Ming-Ming?"

"You know, I put app on Armenian phone. Keep you out of trouble."

"You have an app for that?"

"Yessiree. Now everything he say, I hear. You gonna get call from Armenian today. He say no time left, he must get guns Friday."

"How do you know that?"

"He talking to Missa Frik. He say they must keep you on back foot."

"He did, huh?"

"Yessiree. He no want you have time to make trouble."

"Son of a bitch…"

"I think you maybe wanna call him before he call you."

"That's a real good idea, Ming-Ming. Thanks…and keep your ears on."

"You owe me spegedy dinner, Missa Colt."

"With meatballs. I know."

Colt was smiling as Ming-Ming hung up. He tossed the phone down, pulled the shower curtain back, and stepped without hesitation into the steaming waterfall.

Lacey reset the Yeti display quickly. The coffee had begun to warm the store with its familiar aroma. Colt had yet to appear, so Lacey opened his laptop and clicked on his email.

The two retired Marine buddies had developed a close, cooperative network of like minds in the years since their discharge. They were part of a larger group of fellow veterans who loved the country and found ways to help each other, right wrongs, and support their communities from deep in the background. Colt had often found if he needed something uncommon, like Bangalore torpedoes, all he had to do was ask.

Asking meant posting a message on the Listserv, an encrypted bulletin board shared by anonymous members. Once you were admitted to the Listserv, everything was buried under 1024-bit RSA encryption. You knew your own network because they were buddies. Everyone else was a ghost.

Colt came down the stairs in the back of the store ruffling a towel over his wet black hair. "Lacey, Ming-Ming just called. Petrosian's going to pull a switch on us and shorten the time frame."

"Crap. How short?"

"Friday." Colt's tone left no room for negotiation.

Lacey scowled. "Two days! No way in hell. It's all in transit. Best we could do is Saturday morning. The other thing is we've already got a hundred-fifty grand into it."

"We're fine. Just make it happen." Colt folded his towel, tossed it onto a chair, and walked over to the bulletin board corner where patrons posted business cards and the coffee pot stood always at the ready. He poured a cup and headed back to his office. There, he picked up his personal phone and opened the spyware app. The hidden camera was still working, but the store was empty.

Colt put his feet up on the desk. He was glad to have a little time to think.

———————

About 10 a.m., Colt was watching his phone as Petrosian walked past the spy cam. It was probably time to make that phone call Ming-Ming had recommended. He picked up the burner and punched in the number.

"Raccoon Bay Marina. This Oleg."

"It's Colt."

"Mr. Colt. I hope we not have problems."

"Maybe. We're having a hell of a time with a few items."

"I'm too sorry to hear. We also have problem. We must have delivery on Friday."

"Friday? Day after tomorrow? Most of the trucks don't even get into town until Friday."

"So maybe you not right guy for this."

"Listen, you came to *me*. I'm not applying for a job." Colt could hear Petrosian snort on the other end. "So, okay, I'll deliver Saturday morning but the cost just doubled."

"This not good excuse for double cost. Just make some phone calls."

"You're cutting almost a week out of a ten-day plan and you think a phone call is all it takes to make that happen?"

"I thought in America customer always right."

Something about hearing Petrosian speak the word 'America' put fire in Colt's belly.

"Yeah, but in America, the store sets the price, not the customer. So now it's $500 thousand, and I drive the Hatteras to the meet. I'll pick up the boat and half the cash on Friday at sunset. The keys to the explosives and the firing pins will be on your dock when we get back to shore on Saturday."

"I don't like."

"Best I can do. You wanted Friday night—I'm offering Saturday morning. What's the difference?"

"Difference is 250 grand."

"You changed the deal. There are consequences."

There was silence on the line for so long that Colt pulled the phone away from his ear to see if the call was still connected.

It was.

"I see you Friday night, nine o'clock."

The line went dead.

Colt traded the burner for his personal phone and a look at the spy cam. He watched Frik chase Oleg out of the store. Their heated conversation, all in Armenian, looked like it came close to being a fistfight.

Colt texted Ming-Ming requesting a translation. She called five minutes later.

"Missa Colt. You really piss off Armenian. Yessiree, he say again he think he have you on back foot. What back foot mean?"

"It's just a saying, Ming-Ming. I think Confucius said it."

"That no Confucius. Confucius my uncle. He no say that."

"What did Petrosian say, Ming-Ming?"

"He say they pay you, yessiree. Frik say they shoot you. But Oleg knows you buying weapons. He no kill you. He say if he shoot you no one make future deal with him."

"Smart guy. That's why we were so open with our shopping spree."

"Ahhh, didn't I say you smart guy. Now, maybe you find way to get out alive?"

"You know me. Always have a Plan B."

"Yeah, You Plan A never seem to work. You should start with Plan B from now on. Yessiree."

"Thanks, sweetheart. I can always count on you for good advice."

Lacey walked into Colt's office before the call had wrapped up and sat in the old, comfortable, brown leather visitor's chair. He checked his phone and opened the plastic wrap covering a pack of orange-colored Lance peanut butter and cheese crackers—his lunch.

Colt motioned to get Lacey's attention. "I need you for backup on Friday." He found a sharp pencil and turned an electric bill over on his desk to use it as drawing paper. "We're going to Raccoon Bay Marina.

"So look. This is the marina store. There's a customer entrance on the side—another from the docks in front. Here's where I put my camera, right beside the hall to Petrosian's office and the store room. Somewhere back here, the hall connects to the workshop. That's the layout. What do you think?"

Lacey nodded and put his index finger on the drawing near the workshop. "Question. Think anyone's been hired to work in the shop since Stewart left?"

"Not a chance. Oleg and Frik have been way too busy for that."

"Okay, then I'll come in through the workshop. I'll keep your app running on my phone so I've got eyes on both the workshop entrance and the store entrance."

"Perfect. Then when I get the money and the keys to the boat, I'll exit the front, tie a tow rope to the barge, and I'm outta there."

"That's when they could pick you off."

"True. But we'll have comms, and you'll be on my six if anything starts to go south. If I make a clean getaway, I need you to hang out in the building after they lock up."

"I take it I'm not camping out."

"No, there's something else I need you to do. I'll explain when I have time."

"Where you going to be?"

"At the West Slip. Meet me there with the rental when you get away and we'll move everything off the truck and onto the barge. You good with everything, Lacey?"

"Oorah!"

It took a little longer than usual to reach the sub because Marty wanted to learn how to row a rowboat. He learned how to row in a circle almost immediately. He made the usual mistakes—trying to row facing his destination, favoring one oar over another, and pulling the oars clean out of the oarlocks. Nevertheless, by the time Marty, Doubeck and Colt reached the Bayliner, he had mastered rowing and his arms felt stretched out like rubber bands.

After the arriving crew boarded and the rowboat was tied to the Bayliner, the sub descended to a depth where the Bayliner appeared to sit naturally on the surface. Amber assigned Mish to stay on the periscope during the meeting to keep an eye out for visitors. While Mish scanned the horizon, Amber started the meeting.

"We got the word you wanted to talk. What's up?"

"Yeah," said Colt. "Stewart, I need to fill the gang in on where things stand with your old boss, Petrosian."

Stewart nodded in agreement, and Colt continued.

"Stewart's life is in danger because he was backed into a corner by Petrosian and his cousin Frik. You all aware of that?"

Everyone indicated they were.

"Some bad guys got killed while Stewart was there and Stewart was a witness. So, the only way to protect him is to stop the Armenians."

Doubeck put his arm over his friend's shoulders. "We got this, buddy."

Colt looked dead serious as he laid the story out for the crew. "I made a deal to supply Petrosian with weapons, just so I could double-cross him. I have solid intel that he's working with terrorists who've targeted two dozen friendly Afghans—and their families—who were relocated to the US, many in Western Pennsylvania. They helped our side in the war, so there's a price on their heads. We're doing the deal somewhere in the middle of the lake, and for Stewart, and for the country, and those translators and their families—we need to stop Petrosian."

"You want to take the sub out to meet him?" asked Stewart.

"Nope. Petrosian's Hatteras. He's letting me use it. I need you guys to hang back and let the warriors fight the battles."

Most of the crew looked dejected, but Stewart's eyes grew big. "The Hatteras. So dank! I love that boat."

"Sounds dangerous," said Marty.

"It'll all be over fast. I'll signal you to come out and join the party—and whatever you do, make it a grand entrance."

Amber tossed her hair back. "How bout if we make *Doris* jump out of the water like a fish? I've been dying to try that."

Colt grinned. "That's what I'm talking about."

"You got it. Where you gonna be, Gunny?"

"Petrosian's going to let me know. When he does, I'll send you coordinates."

Stewart chuckled and rubbed his forehead.

Colt's eyes narrowed. "What's so funny?"

Stewart grinned, "I know exactly where they're going. We'll see you there."

Amber raised her arms to stop the conversation. "Hang on. Gunny, when is this supposed to happen?"

"Saturday morning."

Amber gasped. "Oh, no. That's when we invited our parents to tour the sub."

THE LAST U-BOAT

HEADING FOR A SHOWDOWN

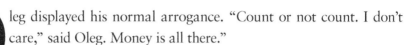

Oleg displayed his normal arrogance. "Count or not count. I don't care," said Oleg. Money is all there."

Frik appeared to be so outraged that his cousin would trust Colt with a quarter-million dollars, that he had to leave the room. He turned as Petrosian stared. The insult made Petrosian's eyes narrow and his mouth form a scowl with his cigarette at its apex. Frik deliberately bumped his cousin's shoulder as he left and cursed him in Armenian. Petrosian cursed him back, dropped his cigarette on the concrete floor and crushed it under his heel.

Colt ignored the drama. He suspected it was a purposeful distraction.

After riffling the stacks of bills in search of blank paper, Colt zipped the black bag closed and slung it over his left shoulder, strategically placing four inches of bundled cash over his heart while keeping both his right hand and his .38 Special available. These guys were cold blooded, so Colt wasn't taking any chances.

With the bag securely over his shoulder, Colt peered coldly at Petrosian. "Keys?"

Oleg reached into his pocket and flipped Colt a single key hooked to a small yellow rubber ducky.

"Not even scratch. Understand me?"

Colt narrowed his eyes. "I'll treat her like she was my own."

"After meeting, I go to marina with you. Frik take *Ararat*."

"When and where do we meet, Petrosian?"

"In rucksack pocket is paper with location. We see you 10 o'clock in morning. Twelve hours from now."

Colt turned and shifted the bag's contents onto his back. Without missing a stride, he opened the door and kept going until he was standing on the steps to the Hatteras.

The yacht was breathtakingly beautiful and Colt whistled involuntarily as he boarded. He turned the key and smiled when he felt the rumble beneath him. Colt stepped back onto the pier, tied up the floating dock that would serve as the barge, and pulled away, his escape executed in less than one minute.

The sticker on the cabin window boldly announced a $1,695,000 price tag. It was the boat Colt had always wanted, and just driving it was a dream come true.

No doubt Petrosian bought it with dirty cash from his Taliban deals. That meant laundered money, a purchase completely off the books. When he sold it, there would be no record, so there would be no paper trail for income and no taxes.

Petrosian was greedy, and greed often causes people to overreach. Colt planned to take advantage of that.

His course took the Hatteras directly away from the marina for three miles. During that time, Colt scanned the yacht for bugs. It was clean.

After a right turn, he traveled east, lights out. If Petrosian was following him, or watching through binoculars, the yacht would disappear, swallowed up by the intense darkness over the lake.

Five miles later, lights back on, Colt made another hard right, and drove straight into the West Slip. As he was tying up the Hatteras, Lacey arrived.

"They left right away," he told Colt. "The little fat guy was shouting the whole time at the other fat guy."

Lacey handed over a manila folder.

"Any problems?" Colt asked.

"Nope. It was right where you said it'd be."

"Thanks."

"I loaded the cargo into the crates so the barge is riding low, but it'll work."

"Perfect."

"Just curious, Gunny. Why didn't we fake this. He's never going to lay hands on it anyway?"

"Not if I can help it. But I figured, Petrosian has a network, too. Ming-Ming confirmed he's been hearing the chatter through back channels about our shopping spree. We had to hook him before we could reel him in."

"Got it."

Colt checked his watch. "We should be done here by midnight. I want you to make those calls we talked about as soon as the barge is loaded. We're going to need reinforcements. While you're doing that, I'm going to mount a couple GoPros on the Hatteras and then take off."

Lacey pulled the list of names and numbers Colt had given him out of his shirt pocket. "You know all these guys?"

"They're buddies of mine who are personal friends with the CO at Great Lakes Naval Station and Surface Combat Training Command. I don't know any of the honchos, but my friends will deliver the message."

Lacey nodded. "Are the kids going to be safe? Have we covered all the contingencies?"

"I think so. They plan to surprise their parents around noon. They'll be out a mile off Charlie's house. I told them to wait until the last minute."

"What about the parents? Is that still happening?"

"Not until noon. Our little adventure will be over by then. I'm actually looking forward to seeing their parents' faces. Can you imagine when their kids come marching out onto the deck of the U-boat? It's gonna blow them away."

At 8 a.m., Colt pulled up alongside an empty Bayliner lolling just off the southern shore of Lake Erie. As he approached, the boat rose twelve feet off the water's surface. Colt grinned as the wolf symbol he'd designed appeared to rise, howling, from beneath the pale blue waters of the lake. His look turned sour when the word *Doris* appeared with it. He'd forgotten about the name.

It took a few minutes for the sub to get squared away, but soon the entire crew was standing on deck. Colt tossed a bow line to Doubeck, a stern line to Stewart, and moved to the rail of the Hatteras to talk with everyone. The faces of the crew were all uncharacteristically somber.

"It's on for 10 a.m. I texted Amber the coordinates. Wait here until I radio that we're clear."

A chorus of oorahs rose from the deck, but there were no smiles to be seen.

"Gunny?" There was an edge in Mish's voice.

"Yeah, Mish."

Her eyes were fixed on the horizon. "We've got two boats coming our way."

Colt looked back and saw two low-profile speedboats approaching at high speed.

"It's okay, guys. Looks like the friendlies I'm expecting. You need to get going. Take the Bayliner for a little run now. Keep the talkies hot and I'll see you when it's over."

Within three minutes, the Bayliner had returned to riding the waves, making seven knots in a big circle. Three minutes after that, two black Zodiac F470s pulled up on the Hatteras, one to port, one to starboard. Colt ducked below the helm, one hand over his head gripping the throttle, the other on his sidearm. He waited for the visitors to identify themselves.

"Gunny?" It was Lacey. "They got your message. I brought the SEALs."

One of the men, in an all-black neoprene wetsuit, walked up to Colt and offered his hand.

"Chief Tom Donikowski. Good to meet you…CO called me out of a sound sleep in beautiful Thoroughgood, Virginia about five hours ago, Gunny. I sure hope this is worth it."

Colt shook Donikowski's hand. "Thanks for coming, Chief. Mark my words, I bet this'll be your all-time favorite mission."

"Hope so. I have twelve men I'd like to bring aboard so you can brief them—and call me Tom."

"Okay, Tom—let's get to it."

The SEALs and their gear transferred quickly to the Hatteras. The men took a seat around the cockpit in the stern, while Colt and Donikowski stood on the riser next to the steps leading to the flying bridge. The Zodiacs sped off, each with a driver and another SEAL, armed with an MK14, on overwatch. The Zodiacs would hang back and wait to be called for the extraction.

"Guys, this is Gunnery Sergeant Colt. The Marines are giving the Navy a boat ride today."

Colt shot a respectful salute to the group. "Gentlemen."

"Gunny, tell the guys what you've got."

"We're meeting two hostiles—Armenians—both in their mid 50s. They operate a marina on the south shore. A young man who worked for them, who I know personally, witnessed them take out a boatload of Afghan mercs. It was a contract killing paid for by one of the muckety-mucks in the Taliban Shura Council. TB started doing business with our targets after they went AWOL from the Russian Army and fell into the heroin business back in the 80s.

"The men they killed were terrorists sent here by Ismail Noor, a pain-in-the-ass Afghan warlord. The hit happened right where we're headed, in the middle of the lake."

"Question, Gunny." Donikowski interrupted. "What the hell does the TB care about Noor?"

"They have their own op running and my source says they didn't want any competition that could fuck things up."

Donikowski continued. "So we're interdicting a Taliban op in progress?"

"Right. The Armenians acquired the identities of a lot of Afghan translators who were resettled here in deep cover. They sold those names to the Taliban. They need weapons for the hunt...and they think I'm their arms dealer."

"That's what you have in tow?"

"It's a ton of lethal shit. Everything you'd need to fight a small war."

"I'm guessing it's not going to be just two, outta shape, middle-aged Armenians waiting for us, is it?"

"I figure six TB can hide on his boat, maybe more."

Donikowski held up eight fingers. "So, eight with automatic weapons, then."

"Roger that."

"Is that it?"

"That's the best intel I've got," said Colt

"Why are *you* in the middle of this, Gunny?"

Colt shrugged. "See something, say something, right?"

The Chief's stare told Gunny he owed the SEALs a better answer.

Colt turned his head and stared across the water in the direction of the sub. "It's the kid. The one the Armenians took to the hit. They wanna kill him. His name's Stewart Swanson. He's smart. Hardest damn worker I've ever known. His Mom died on a trip overseas and he couldn't go to her funeral. But he didn't let it stop him. He hunkered down in the house, got a job, paid the bills and finished school. Alone. A kid like that, he deserves a chance. I am not going to let him die."

"Sounds like our kind of mission."

Colt turned back, tilted his head and grinned at Donikowski. "You're gonna love it, Chief."

Donikowski nodded. "So, the plan is we neutralize the opposition, grab a prisoner for intel, and call it a day. Does that work for you?"

"Aye-aye," he replied, with a nod.

The Chief smiled. "Where's the meet?"

Colt handed the SEAL the paper Petrosian had supplied with coordinates. Donikowski called one of his SEALs over. "Spider, plug these coordinates in."

"I've got it in the Hatteras, Chief."

"Doesn't matter, Gunny. We need to generate the record for the mission."

"Got it." Colt checked his watch. "The rendezvous's one hour away. You might want to have the Zodiacs start following us now. I can't tow the barge very fast, and I want to be just a little late, too, just to mess with his head."

The Chief was about to turn to his men when the SEAL named Spider came back with his left arm held chest high. Velcroed to it was a tablet with a glowing display the size of a mini iPad.

"Chief, we've got a problem."

Amber's mother, Ana Garcia, sat with one hand on her straw hat and another across the cushion behind her friend Fiona Murphy, Mish's mom.

The ladies relaxed behind the port helm, the left-hand steering wheel, watching Fede Garcia steer the family's Catalina 425 from the starboard helm on the other side.

Fede was not only a highly respected plastic surgeon, he was one hell of a sailor. Amber learned everything she knew about sailing during her time behind the wheel of the Catalina that her dad had named *Nip and Tack*.

Deb and Irv Silver, Marty's mom and dad, sat along the bow rails with the jib at their backs. Irv had volunteered to be the lookout, so Fede's binoculars hung from Irv's neck.

Natalie and Peter Doubeck relaxed under the bimini. Across from them sat Sharon and Mike LeClair, and Brian Murphy, Fiona's husband and Mish's dad.

It was July first, so everyone was in their summer finery, except Mike, the advertising guy, who wore red, white and blue.

The LeClairs' group sat in the cubby at a mahogany table, enjoying Mimosas and Bloody Marys. Mike and Brian were already eyeing the Bloody Mary pitcher in its recessed holder, each waiting for the other to reach for more.

Mike leaned back. "Hey, Fede, this is really a perfect Fourth of July treat. We can't thank you enough."

"My pleasure, Mike. Ana and I have been wanting to do this for a long time. You know, since our kids are such good friends."

Peter Doubeck raised his glass. "I'm available to crew any time, Fede."

"Okay, Pete. I'll put you on the list. Anyone else?"

Everybody but Ana raised a hand.

"Okay, you're all in."

"Irv, Deb, in a few seconds I'm going to come about. Careful you don't get whacked with the jib." They waved and started to move.

"You know, there are a lot of boats out today. It might be hard to spot Charlie's Bayliner. We'll just sail around until we hear from them."

Fede spun the wheel, the boat slowed and the mast tipped in the opposite direction. "Coming about." Fede completed his maneuver, and moved to the port helm so he could see past the jib. He tightened the main sheet and the mainsail quickly filled. The boat heeled over as it bore the wind.

Fede looked up at the telltales on the sail and pointed the bow toward the wind and into its sweet spot. He locked the main sheet, grabbed the jib sheet and trimmed the jib until it caught the wind and pulled hard. The Catalina surged forward.

Irv called out from the bow, "What's a Bayliner look like, Fede?"

"Amber said it's a 32-foot fishing boat. A trawler—all white. Is that right, Mike?"

"Not a clue," said Mike.

Fede looked over at Mike "You mean you've never seen Charlie's boat?"

"Nope. Didn't even know about it. He started a business and it went gangbusters, then somehow he found this German boat that dates back to the 1940s. I guess our kids have been working on it for weeks..."

"Mike, Bayliners aren't German, and there *were* no Bayliners in the 40s. Pretty much the only boats the Germans made in the 40s had deck guns mounted on them. Charlie didn't mention guns, did he?"

Mike glanced at the wilted celery in his glass. "Not deck guns."

He threw the celery stalk overboard, grabbed the pitcher of Bloody Marys, poured a tall one and took a gulp. He swallowed, sat back down and took another gulp.

Fede tapped the autopilot, stepped down into the cubby and leaned over the table.

"Mike, where are our kids?"

THE LAST U-BOAT

ALL
SALES ARE
FINAL

"**W**hatd'ya mean we can't go?" Colt's eyebrows were twisted like pretzels and the corners of his mouth were turned down like he was ready to take on King Kong.

"Sorry, Gunny. These coordinates are over the line."

"What fucking line is that?"

"The border, Gunny."

"Since when does anyone give a shit about the border? Our mission is to stop these assholes."

"Gunny. This ain't Pakistan and Afghanistan. This is the Canadian border. Longest peaceful border in the world. I don't want to be the one to change that."

"Well, how far over the line is it."

"Doesn't matter. We can cross for a rescue, but not for hostilities."

"Bullshit. Then I'll go. I'll give you a couple of Armenians to rescue."

"Gunny. It's my command and I can't let you do that. You're not going to do much damage with a sidearm, anyway."

Colt looked off into the distance, across miles of sparkling waves. It was a beautiful sunny summer day with a steady breeze to keep the air cool. Just off the bow, Colt watched a gull dive into the water for a fish. A moment later it popped to the surface with its catch in its beak.

"What if I can get the Armenians to come to us? You got any problem with that, Chief?"

"Hell, no."

Colt grabbed his phone. The chief leaned in to make sure he heard every word.

"Hey, I need *Doris* ASAP." Colt's eyes shot up to meet Donikowski's. He was holding his course.

"Tell Doubeck to get ready."

Donikowski's head tilted and Colt knew he only had a moment before he was going to have to stand down.

"There's a treaty or a law or something. We can't cross the international border unless it's for a rescue." Colt saw the chief's shoulders relax.

"It's gotta be a rescue. You hear me?" Without saying another word Colt tapped the red button and dropped the phone into his pocket.

"Who's Doris?" asked the chief.

"She's a bitch, a tough old broad. She's so fuckin bad she could chew us all up and spit us out and…"

"Colt, what the fuck are you talking about?"

"I'm telling you, if the US Navy can't stop these bastards, *Doris* can."

Donikowski squared up to Colt and shoved a finger into his sternum so hard he flinched. "You damn Marines are always so fuckin jacked up…I don't need your gung-ho bullshit gettin my guys hurt, you hear me? If I see so much as a dinghy out here with a Marine, or a merc, or a pea shooter on it, we're taking it out. You got me?"

"Don't worry, Chief. There'll be nothing to see. Doris is going to bring this little mess right to you. All you're gonna have to do is clean it up."

Towing the barge meant slow-going. The twin 980 hp diesels on the Hatteras purred, bestowing a relaxing foot massage to anyone standing on the deck. The ride had been tense ever since the confrontation, and any sense of comfort or luxury on board changed the moment Colt spotted the *Ararat* five miles out. He alerted Donikowski, crouched near the transom, keeping his eyes on the Zodiacs. The inflatables sliced a straight line through the water a half mile behind the Hatteras, using its towering wake as cover. Even with radar, it would be nearly impossible for Petrosian to see their extremely low profile in the shadow of the seventy-foot Hatteras.

Colt studied the yacht's Raymarine navigation system. "Four miles to rendezvous, approaching at ten knots…less than twenty minutes to contact."

"Roger that," said Donikowski.

Colt's talkie squawked and sputtered. In a moment, Amber's voice came through loud and clear. "Hey, Gunny. You look good on the bridge of that Hatteras."

"Hello, *Doris*. You in the neighborhood?"

Donikowski heard the chatter and almost broke a leg scrambling to get to Colt.

"We are. Amber out."

"Who the hell is that, Gunny?"

"That's *Doris*."

Donikowski scanned the horizon. There were a few distant clusters of fishing boats, but nothing else nearby.

"She said she can see you. So, you have a drone up?"

"Nope. She's in the water, somewhere near Petrosian." Colt turned to face Donikowski. "Listen, there's something you need to know. It's a top-secret op. There's a military vessel in Lake Erie that's completely off the books."

Donikowski pounded his fist against the nearest wall. "Why didn't Great Lakes tell us about this?"

Colt looked straight ahead. "Beats me." He knew the Chief would figure things out soon enough. Still, he seemed a bit touchy for a seasoned Navy SEAL. He was grumpy—like a guy whose sleep had been interrupted.

Colt tried to de-escalate the situation. "Maybe if there'd been more time to plan..."

"I just don't like stuff coming at my guys from out of nowhere. So, if you have any more surprises, I wanna know ahead of time. And I don't care what Doris does, but my guys have orders to stay on our side of the border. You got me?"

"Roger that," said Colt. He keyed the talkie while looking right into Donikowski's eyes. "*Doris*, this is Colt. When you get within a thousand feet of *Ararat*, pop the Bayliner up ninety degrees off his port side."

"Ninety degrees off *Ararat*'s port. Will do."

"And tell Doubeck to get ready. He might get his wish. Colt out."

Donikowski started nodding slowly. "I've got it. It's a remote vehicle, right? You've got a little radio-controlled boat towing a claymore or something."

Colt shrugged. "Good guess, but, like they say, I can neither confirm nor deny."

"Right. So, who's the chick? Is that Doris? She sounds like she's eighteen."

"She's seventeen." Colt smiled at the Chief. "I'll introduce you before you go. She's going to be famous."

"Tom!"

"Whatcha got, Spider?"

"There's a blue water sailor two miles to port. Looks to be heading this way."

"Yep, I see it. Keep an eye on 'em." He turned to Colt. "That your girl, Gunny?"

"No, *Doris* is a warrior. You'll know her when you see her. I told you I'd introduce you. She's pretty cute, too, but I think she's taken."

Colt glanced down at the Raymarine. "Three miles." *Ararat* hadn't changed location, but its bow was now facing the westerlies.

Donikowski had his scope trained on *Ararat*'s stern. "So that's the *Ararat*."

"Yeah, it's Petrosian's pride and joy."

Donikowski studied every detail of the situation. He marked the direction of the wind, the height of the waves, and even the shadows on the surface cast by the clouds racing by. What he saw gave him a low regard for Petrosian's seamanship.

"Look at that. He's anchored at the bow in deep water. Kinda dumb. He'd have to come to the stern to do the deal, and that'd reveal his decks and his cabin. It'll take him ten minutes to bring up all that anchor rope. The guy's a putz."

"He's a half mile over the line, Chief."

"Thanks, Spider."

"Two miles." Colt grabbed the talkie again.

"I'm ordering you to stop this side of the line. You can go right up to it, but that's it."

"Aye-aye, Chief. I will not cross that line unless you order me to do so."

The SEAL just shook his head. He wasn't going to get sucked into a discussion about the propriety of crossing an international border. To him, that matter was settled.

Colt keyed his talkie. "*Doris*, Colt here."

Amber came back fast. "I know why you're calling. *Ararat* did a 180 when they anchored. Don't worry, I won't get fouled. You want me north of him, right?"

Colt smiled. Even submerged, Amber could see the battlefield in her mind's eye. She was one hell of a sailor.

"Roger that. Colt out."

To the south lay the near shore and a gauntlet of weekend fishing boats, day sailors, fish commission patrol boats, and water skiers. Colt and the friendlies were approaching from the east, Petrosian lay at anchor to the northwest, and the U-boat waited submerged to the north. Petrosian could only make a clean getaway by heading west in Canadian waters, into the wind, where safe harbor was over a hundred miles away.

He looked out over the vast Lake Erie horizon, took a deep breath, and bit nervously on his lower lip.

Donikowski let Colt ruminate for a moment before he spoke. "What're you thinking, Gunny?"

Colt scratched the stubble on his jaw. "Have the Zodiacs hold."

Donikowski pushed a comms button on his left wrist. "Red team, Blue team. Hold your positions."

Colt throttled down to idle.

"Help me untie the barge and wrap the tow rope around a cleat. I'm going up to the line and I'm gonna let the barge go. If he wants it, he's going to have to come across the line to get it."

"I like it," said Donikowski. The two men quickly untied the rope, wrapped it temporarily around a cleat, and Colt brought the boat back up to speed.

Donikowski's lookout shouted, "Tom."

"Yeah, Spider."

“That sailboat’s a Catalina 42 and it just turned toward our target. It’s full of people. Could be combatants.”

Oleg handed his binoculars to Frik. “Yes, is Colt. Here, you look.”

“How you know boat not full of Marine buddies, Oleg?”

“Because we give no time for plan. That was point.”

“So, what we do?” asked Frik.

“We pay money, take guns. You take Hatteras, I drive *Ararat*.”

“Something not right.” said Frik, looking away.

“It was always plan.” said Oleg.

“No, *apush*!” Frik grabbed Oleg’s shoulder and turned him around. He pointed his cousin toward the northern horizon. “Why that boat here?”

“You surprised there boat on lake?”

“Oleg, we watch whole time. Boat not here. Now is here.”

“Maybe you not watch good enough.”

“Give me.” Petrosian grabbed the binoculars and focused intently on the stealthy boat off their starboard. “This not good. I think is Bayliner I sell to Colt.”

Marty’s father, Irv, had the binoculars pressed firmly to his eyes. He scanned the horizon, hoping to get a glimpse of the Canadian shore, little more than ten miles away, as three boats entered his field of vision. One of them looked just like Fede Garcia’s description of a Bayliner.

“Is that boat out there, the one in the middle, is that a Bayliner, Fede?”

“Could be. It’s just a bit too far away for me to see. I’ll head upwind. Maybe we can get a closer look.” Fede steered to port and the sailboat began a long arc toward the Bayliner.

Donikowski was calling in his Zodiacs. Colt thought he’d take advantage of the distraction and hail the U-boat. "Amber, Colt here."

"Yeah, Gunny."

"Do you see a sailboat approaching from your ten o'clock?"

Amber was on the periscope full-time. "Hang on, I've been watching *Ararat*. He's been looking right at me…Okay, I see it. That's our boat. It's my dad, Gunny. They're out here tooling around waiting for me to call."

"He's headed right for you—broadside. Does he know about the Bayliner?"

"Yeah, we were going to surface and surprise them."

"Hang on." Colt turned to Donikowski. "Tom, I've got an ID on that sailboat. It's just a some locals." He pulled the talkie back to his mouth.

"Wait a second. You said them?" Colt put his hand to his forehead. "Oh, shit." *All the parents are aboard.*

"Gunny, stand by. We have another problem." Amber set the talkie down and shouted. "Charlie, how deep is the water above our decks right now?"

Charlie sat at the gauges and controls only a few feet away. "I'm going to say maybe seven feet."

Amber considered their situation. The Hatteras sat less than a thousand yards from the rendezvous point where perhaps a dozen Taliban assassins lay in wait. The Bayliner lay exposed above, just off *Ararat*'s starboard. The *Nip and Tack* with all of the crew's parents aboard had just vectored toward the sub, and two squads of heavily armed Navy SEALs lay in ambush on Colt's flank, ready to do what SEALs do best.

While Amber pondered her next move, a familiar old feeling returned to Colt's belly. It was an uncomfortable sense of foreboding he always felt right before a battle.

Colt knew they were running out of time. "What's the problem, Amber?"

"It's the keel, Gunny. If my dad tries to sail past us, the keel's going to hit our deck and crack their hull, probably send everyone overboard. We can't be rescuing people in the middle of your mission."

Colt looked at the Raymarine screen and called back to Donikowski. "Half a mile to the line, Tom."

He keyed the talkie. "Amber, can you call your dad?"

"No. Phones don't work in here, remember?"

"Then you might have to disappear," said Colt.

"If we do, it gives us away."

Before Colt could reply, Stewart appeared in the control room. "Amber, I've been listening and I have an idea. Ya gotta trust me on this. I'm heading to the Bayliner."

Stewart jumped onto the ladder to the conning tower hatch.

"Stewart, you can't go up there. Petrosian will see you."

"Amber, I've got this." Stewart's words echoed within the conning tower tube.

She heard the wheel turn. The hatch creaked and clanked as it opened.

"Gunny!"

"Go ahead, Amber."

"Stewart has an idea, he's getting on the Bayliner."

Colt looked up from the Raymarine screen to see Stewart standing inside the steel tube, disguised by the fiberglass boat mounted around him, waving his arms toward the *Ararat*.

"Oh, shit." Colt pounded the dashboard.

"Where'd that guy come from?" asked Donikowski.

"He was below, I guess. That's Stewart," said Colt.

Donikowski looked quizzical. "Yeah, but where'd the boat come from?"

Colt held his free hand up like he didn't know the answer. "Amber, keep your mike open so I can hear what's going on."

"Who's Amber, Gunny?"

"She's with *Doris*."

"And where the fuck is Doris?"

Before Colt could answer, Amber held her talkie up to the tube and keyed her mike to broadcast the drama.

Stewart shouted toward the *Ararat*, "Hey, you stupid jerk!"

Donikowski prepared his squad. "Lock and load, men. Something's going on. We've got a friendly on the Bayliner on the right. Do not engage. Our

ALL SALES ARE FINAL

targets are only on the *Ararat*. Only the *Ararat*." He touched the comms button on his sleeve. "Red team, Blue team. Stand by. Continue a slow approach. Come up behind us. Nice and easy. Hold your fire."

Stewart's voice was amplified in the tube like a megaphone and Colt could hear every word on his talkie. He throttled down, at the very edge of the US-Canada border, a dashed line running across the Raymarine display.

Stewart had both hands raised, a finger on each extended in a very unfriendly gesture. "Petrosian, you bastard. I saw you kill those guys and I'm not going to let you get away with it. You'll get the electric chair."

Petrosian shouted back, "Look! Is Mr. Stewart. So, we not friends anymore? Now not good time to settle differences." Quietly, he said, "Frik, give me Uzi."

Stewart continued his rant, non-stop. "Screw you, Petrosian. I'm going to get on the radio and call the Coast Guard right now." Petrosian took the Uzi from Frik and pointed it at the Bayliner's hull while Stewart continued taunting.

"You're going to prison. I found you and I'm not letting you..."

Petrosian fired a long burst that emptied his magazine.

Colt held his open hand out to signal his passengers. "Hold your fire. He's got this."

Donikowski leaned into Colt's face. "Do not touch your throttle."

Frik stepped alongside his cousin and repeatedly fired his pistol at Stewart, each shot measured and carefully aimed. Stewart heard a round buzz by as it passed close to his left ear. He ducked behind the open hatch.

Colt watched Stewart drop into the hatch to protect himself. He had to assure the SEALs that the situation was under control. "He's okay, he's okay. He's got this."

The open mike on the walkie-talkie let Colt hear Frik's shots splatter against the hatch.

Colt stepped up to the flying bridge on the Hatteras, he had the walkie-talkie under his arm. He grabbed the mike connected to the marine radio and pushed a preset for channel sixteen, the hailing channel.

"Ararat. This is Colt. Come in. Come in, Ararat."

A moment later the Armenian answered.

"What is problem now."

"What the hell are you doing, Petrosian?" Colt closed his eyes while Petrosian ranted.

Once Petrosian had nearly exhausted his vitriol, Colt brought the talkie to his mouth, and spoke calmly, "This'd be a good time to disappear, Captain. And tell Doubeck to stand by to take out the barge. Oh, and please give Stewart a 'well done' for me. Colt out."

Petrosian slid a fresh magazine into the Uzi and keyed his mike again. "Why you bring Stewart to our deal? Is trick?"

"Look again, Oleg. He's not *with* me. I hired him to fix my boat and now you're putting holes in it. How 'bout I put a few holes in the Hatteras?"

"Is not your fight, Mr. Colt. I settle this, we move on. You buy new Bayliner." Petrosian raised the Uzi and sent a six-second burst into the hull of the Bayliner. As the spray disappeared on the wind, the boat vanished beneath a ring of bubbles.

———

"Listen! Can you hear that? Someone's shooting at the Bayliner...and it's sinking. It's...Oh, my gosh, it's gone." Irv Silver was apoplectic. "I just saw a guy sink a boat with a machine gun."

Deb brought her hands to her face. "It wasn't our kids, was it?"

"No! Hell no. It was nobody. It was like he shot an empty boat—a perfectly good boat. Who does that?"

Fede over-steered and the main began to luff, the boat slowed in the water and the bow quickly turned away from the scene in front of them. "I'm not going over there if some nut's got a machine gun," he said.

As they turned, Sharon LeClair's eye caught the Hatteras. "Look at the guy up on that platform on that big yacht. That's Charlie's friend, the Marine. I'm sure of it."

"What's he pulling?"

Irv focused the binoculars on the barge. "It looks like boxes and metal bins. They're all piled up on a raft. Now he's coming around the other... whoops, he lost the tow rope."

Colt seemed indifferent to what had just happened. "You done now? I'm delivering your supplies. Don't shoot."

Petrosian handed the rifle back to Frik and cupped his hands around his mouth. "You all business, Colt. I like you."

"Marty, I need a firing solution for the barge. It's on the surface drifting maybe two feet per second, right to left. Bearing zero-three-zero degrees, range one-quarter mile."

Doubeck reported from the torpedo room. "Tube one is flooded. Outer doors open. Set for surface running. Waiting for solution."

Marty slapped his own face nervously. *Come on. You do this all the time on Wolfpack. Lemme think. If the game's right, our torpedo travels a quarter mile in...35 seconds. In 35 seconds the target drifts...70 feet. Wait. I need to know how many degrees that is.*

"Captain, give me the bearing and call it out again when I say mark."

Amber shot back, "Target bearing zero-two-four degrees."

The sub went silent, and Marty stared at his watch as 35 seconds ticked away.

"Mark."

"Target bearing zero-two-one degrees."

"Three degrees," shouted Marty.

Amber keyed her walkie-talkie. "Doubeck?"

"Got it, Captain. I'm calling it zero-one-eight degrees, range 440, course 90 degrees, speed under one knot."

A heartbeat later, Amber spoke words she never imagined she would hear herself say. "Doubeck, fire torpedo."

THE LAST U-BOAT

ALL

HANDS

ON DECK

A speeding red flash in the crystal blue water caught Petrosian's eye. He watched the unmistakable shape of a torpedo pass a mere ten feet behind the *Ararat* and just inches beneath the surface. The propellers pushing the dark fish with the crimson warhead churned a frothy white trail of bubbles. It came so close that Petrosian could hear the chugging of the cavitating props and smell the acrid odor of the propellant, spraying into the air around him.

Colt also saw what was happening from his high perch at the helm of the Hatteras. Unlike Petrosian, though, he was enjoying it. His jaw clenched as he watched the torpedo's course converge with the floating platform.

He'd kept it to himself, but from the moment he realized there'd be a confrontation with the Armenians, Colt had always believed there'd be a need to fire a torpedo. Partly because the overwhelming force offered by such a weapon would keep the crew safer than if they got caught in a firefight. But also, because once the sub had fired a torpedo in battle in the defense of the United States, the powers that be would have a much harder time taking the sub away from them. They would become the good guys with a gun that stopped the bad guys with guns.

As the torpedo drew closer to the barge Colt wondered how many ships had sailed across silent seas, on a day just like today, unaware they were being followed in the crosshairs of a periscope. How many sailors, busily manning their stations, writing letters home, tidying their minuscule personal spaces, had been removed from the battlefield in just this way, completely unaware that a waterborne guided missile bore down on them at flank speed?

Petrosian looked toward the Hatteras and back again to the barge as his mind came to grips with the double-cross. He frantically checked the water for a second torpedo that might be aimed at him.

He began to panic, and as he did, his anger boiled over. "You make big mistake, Colt," he shouted. Colt saw him screaming, and could easily imagine what he was saying.

Petrosian turned away from the Hatteras to watch the torpedo's wake meet the barge's drift, hoping against hope the two would not intersect. During the final seconds of the weapon's journey, Colt radioed Amber. "Captain, it's go time. Take *Ararat* out of the water."

As the torpedo contacted the steel drums supporting the barge, inertia drove a lead cylinder through a tube centered in the warhead. At the end of the tube, the weight slammed into a firing pin, igniting a mercury fulminate primer. Instantly, flames from the exploding primer entered the main charge.

The years had degraded the explosive. But it was still plenty powerful enough to destroy the barge and its contents, and rattle both the *Ararat* and the Hatteras.

A frothy white ring rose instantly from the surface of the water and expanded a hundred-fifty feet in the blink of an eye. The faint silhouette of the barge lurched in the middle of the spray, like the bull's eye in the middle of a target.

Petrosian staggered as the barge rose sixty feet out of the water. Its contents disintegrated into a plume that widened across the sky like a Chinese fan. Remnants rained down within inches of *Ararat*. Only shards of wood and bits of styrofoam remained afloat.

He despised the thought of being double-crossed. "You fool! You are the son of a dog, Colt! Those were my weapons. You will die for this, you snake. You think I don't punish?"

The weapons he had promised the Taliban were not coming, thanks to a humiliating screw-up of his own making. Oleg Petrosian had trusted Colt without checking him out. He had let his greed take over and he'd moved too quickly, too recklessly. Naively, a quarter million in cash had been placed in Colt's trust, and now the Hatteras had also fallen into his hands. Petrosian had underestimated his enemy. Even now he believed Colt to be just an ordinary thief who would soon try to make his escape. He had no idea that he, Frik, and the Taliban raiders were Colt's actual targets.

"Shut up, Oleg. Shut up!" Frustration took hold of Frik. Standing behind his cousin, he swung his arm wildly, slapping Petrosian on the back of the head and knocking his hat into the lake.

The blow dazed him and he lost his balance. He stumbled toward the transom and struggled to stay on his feet.

"*Apush.* You were played like balalaika." Frik wagged his finger. "Colt think he get away with this? He dead man."

Doris dropped quickly from periscope depth to 40 meters the moment Doubeck fired the torpedo. Debris was still falling from the sky as Amber saw on her video screen that the U-boat's nose had ducked under the *Ararat.* "Charlie, what's our depth?"

"One-hundred-twenty feet, Captain."

"Stand by to open main ballast blow valves"

"Aye, Captain. Main valves ready."

"Hang on to something, everyone. We're going up. Charlie, EMB! Now!" she ordered.

"Emergency Main Ballast. Aye, Captain."

Charlie pulled the handles on two blade valves and the boat shuddered. The contents of the high-pressure air compressor reservoirs blasted into the central, fore, and aft ballast tanks. The pressurized air instantly replaced the water that had kept the U-boat submerged. Rushing through the pipelines, it produced a ghostly scream that sounded like a wounded pipe organ.

The sub began rising fast, nose high. Amber could see it on the video, slipping forward in relation to the yacht above them. She needed to stop the forward movement or they would surface on the other side of the *Ararat.* "Marty, planes up full."

"Planes up full."

The planes point where they want the sub to go—and up it went— a nine-hundred-ton steel rocket shooting to the surface.

The saw-toothed, anti-submarine net cutter on the prow of the U-boat caught the *Ararat*'s keel amidships and chewed deep into the yacht's fiberglass hull. The severed boat rose from the water on the nose of the sub like a doomed seal tossed upward by a great white shark.

Neither Petrosian nor Nazarian could support themselves as the deck abruptly shot upward beneath them. Their body weight crushed their ankles under the pressure and their knees slammed into the rising deck with such force that the teak flooring splintered when they hit. The impact broke both of Frik's femurs, Petrosian hit on his side, breaking his shoulder and left arm, and thrusting his splintered ulna through his shirt sleeve.

Its structural integrity compromised by the jagged teeth of the net cutter, *Ararat*'s hull split in mid-air with a deafening crack. The fiberglass fractured like an eggshell. The hull's broken sections twisted violently above the rising submarine, propelling the helpless Armenians across the gap between the halves, where they slammed into and shattered the closed mahogany panels of the companionway door.

As the U-boat began to stabilize, it rose and fell on the roiling water beneath it, and the two disconnected parts of *Ararat*'s hull pitched over. They caught on the sub's prow, spilling the engines, shattered cabinetry, and human contents.

The severed hull lay on the deck, its halves separated by the net cutter, caught on the sub's bow rails, and barely hanging on to either side.

As the air grew quiet, Chief Donikowski radioed command and reported he was crossing into Canada to rescue passengers from a private vessel. He did not elaborate.

Black-clad men, who had been hiding in *Ararat*'s cabin, began to escape in a panic from its shredded remnants. Some staggered and fell to the deck, some scrambled out of fear they might be caught up in the debris and pulled under. But none was going far. These were men from the desert and high mountains of Afghanistan, and not one knew how to swim. To save their own lives, they clung, wet and frightened, to the boarding net draped over the hull of the sub. Many of them were in shock, bleeding, and nursing broken bones. As a black Zodiac approached, they eagerly boarded or clung to its sides.

The SEALs dragged them aboard the inflatables, searched them for weapons, and zip-tied each terrorist's hands.

Colt flipped a pair of fenders over the rail and tied the Hatteras up alongside the sub.

Petrosian and Nazarian were found alive, but unconscious and bloody. They were loaded on the Zodiac while being administered first aid and hustled back to shore. Donikowski and three of the SEALs remained on the deck of the sub with Colt and Lacey.

Lacey headed toward the debris on the bow and called back to Colt and Donikowski. "I'm going to go see what we need to do to separate the sub from Petrosian's boat."

Colt nodded and keyed the talkie.

"We're clear guys, come on out."

Donikowski's jaw dropped as six teenagers emerged from the U-boat's forward hatch.

"Is this boat what I think it is?" Donikowski gestured toward the sub's deck, and when he did, he caught a look at Mish's paint job.

"*Doris?*"

Colt nodded and shrugged. "I didn't get a vote."

"You said 'off the books,' Gunny. But you meant off everybody's books, didn't you?"

Colt nodded slowly.

"And six teenagers crew this sub?"

Colt continued to nod and pointed at the approaching crew.

"That's them?"

"Roger that."

"You know what's a hoot, Gunny?"

"What's that?"

"They're civilians—kids—climbing out of a fully-functioning WWII submarine, on fucking Lake Erie, and DoD doesn't know a damn thing about it."

Colt turned to the Chief. "Makes you wonder what else they don't know."

"I can't imagine."

They turned and started walking toward the oncoming crew. "You know, Gunny, I've seen one of these before. U-701, a hundred-twenty feet down, twenty miles off Cape Hatteras. First U-boat we sank in World War Two. But this, this is pretty historic, too."

Donikowski noticed the pretty young girl with flowing black curls walking toward them, her hand held by a lanky young boy her age. She was wearing the white captain's hat Colt had given her.

"Amber, this is Chief Petty Officer Tom Donikowski. Tom, this is Amber Garcia, captain of this boat."

Donikowski smiled wide. "You drove this boat?"

"I did," Amber replied firmly.

"I'll be damned." The Chief reached out and shook her hand. "Well done, Captain. Gunny told me this would be my favorite mission ever and he was right."

Amber remained somber. Colt noted it, remembering how it takes some time to mentally adjust in the aftermath of combat. He deliberately moved the attention away from her.

Colt patted Charlie on the back and eased him toward the Chief. "And, Tom, this gentleman is Charlie LeClair. You're standing on his boat."

Donikowski shook Charlie's hand. "Seriously, your U-boat? I mean you *own* it?"

"Yep. Got it in writing."

"Where'd you get a U-boat?"

Charlie stared straight up, shrugged, and looked back at the SEAL. "You're not gonna believe this, but I found it in my basement."

The Chief looked at Colt, and again Colt nodded.

Donikowski just laughed. "I really want to hear this story, but right now, I need you and your entire crew to join us back on shore for our AAR—After-Action Review—it's a debriefing. Gunny, you and Lacey, too."

Just then, Spider walked up to the group with some news. "Blue Team is loading your parents onto a Zodiac. They're coming right over."

Amber breathed a sigh of relief. "How are they doing?"

Donikowski tapped his comms button. "Blue leader, how are the parents doing?"

He listened to the reply in his earpiece and then cleared his throat. "Miss, I probably shouldn't repeat what I just heard, but I *can* report that it sounds like they're all good—they're just a little worked up—but they're okay."

There was a bit of commotion as Lacey arrived, accompanied by Doubeck, Marty, and Stewart. The crew had not yet come down from the excitement they experienced moments earlier.

Colt shook Doubeck's hand. "Nice shootin', buddy. You owe me, you know."

Doubeck flexed his arms, clenched his fists, and shouted. "It was awesome! But Marty figured out the firing solution. He really deserves the credit. All I did was punch it in and throw the lever."

Amber poked Doubeck in the ribs. "You forgot to shut the outer door on the tube afterward."

"He leaves his fly down all the time, too," said Charlie.

Doubeck grinned and hung his head in mock embarrassment. "I just forgot. I was excited. I never blew anything up before"

Donikowski laughed and shook Doubeck's hand. "Hey, it never gets old."

Colt introduced everyone and then waved a hand to get their attention. "Everybody okay?"

The six looked at each other and back at Colt as if that was a strange question. "We're good," said Stewart.

"Oh, hey Stewart. By the way," said Colt. "Quick thinking. You probably prevented some serious damage and injury—a little risky—took some guts, but Petrosian never saw it coming."

"Thanks, Gunny. I figured seeing me would throw him off. We needed an excuse to dive, you know, so the sailboat's keel wouldn't trip over us."

"Can I ask, did anyone else get hurt?" said Mish.

"Yeah," said Donikowski. "Seven bloodied Taliban. Three, maybe more, have broken bones. The Armenians were still unconscious when they were

EVAC'd. They hit the deck pretty hard."

Mish looked relieved. "Well, I'm glad no one was killed."

"Rule number one, right, Gunny?" said Charlie.

"You got it, Charlie."

THE LAST U-BOAT

CLEANING UP

Ten frantic parents with open arms scrambled across the deck of the U-boat toward their children. In the melee, moms' faces streamed with tears, some screamed their child's name. Sweaters, hats, sandals, and scarves and been discarded or lost.

The overwrought women were oblivious to their torn clothing, and the rust stains and paint they acquired climbing onto the deck of the sub. The SEALs' efforts to help the parents board were largely ignored. The dads appeared dumbfounded as they tried to help their wives onto the sub without falling into the lake themselves.

Colt leaned toward Stewart. "I'm not getting good vibes." He grabbed Stewart's elbow, put an arm over his shoulder, and turned him away as the kids were getting their hugs. "Stewart, just so you know, I'm pretty sure those people are gonna come over here in a minute and give me hell. They might take some shots at you, too, if you're standing in the line of fire. So, you might want to keep your distance from me until they're done."

Stewart's eyes opened wide. "Heck, no, Gunny. You saved my life, I'm not gonna let you take any heat for doing the right thing."

"I really can't blame them if they come out swinging. They're moms and dads…and they just got a serious scare."

Stewart nodded, "Yeah, I get it."

The two turned back to witness the surreal scene. In the middle of Lake Erie, on the deck of a U-boat, weeping mothers wrapped their arms around their teenage children. Dads awkwardly tried to comfort their families while fighting their paternal instinct to punish their kids for causing such anxiety. All the while, men in wetsuits holding automatic weapons, wove in and around them, scanning the horizon while standing guard.

Colt saw Amber point in his direction. As she did, Fede Garcia left her side. He charged forward, his head lowered like a bull plowing through a crowded street in Pamplona.

Garcia needed only two seconds to reach Colt. He had his right arm cocked when the firm grip of two Navy SEALs froze him in time and space.

"Amber could have been killed, you maniac. You acted irresponsibly, with absolutely no regard for the safety of our children. Why did you not tell the authorities?"

"Tell them about what, sir?"

"About the two killers on that boat." Garcia pointed to the wreckage on the bow.

"I did, sir. That's why the Navy SEALS are here."

Hearing Fede's voice raise, the other parents approached. They supported Garcia's indignation by nodding, with gestures and comments to each other, but they didn't intervene.

When Garcia noticed the others gathered around, he composed himself and relaxed his arms. The SEALs felt his aggression fade so they released him. He took advantage of his freedom to gesture with his finger in Colt's face.

"These kids aren't in the military. What were you thinking?"

"These kids are sailors, Dr. Garcia. They trained to be sailors, and they used their own vessel to defend the United States."

Garcia sneered.

Colt continued. "Those men you saw taken away in the Zodiac were Taliban terrorists who invaded our country."

"Taliban?" Garcia became ashen.

"Yes. They came here for one purpose, to kill. Petrosian sold them a list of Afghan translators who had been given new lives and new identities in the US. The Taliban wanted to kill them because they helped us during the Afghan war."

Gracia took a deep breath. He had no idea of the larger drama behind the incident he had just witnessed. "Dr. Garcia, when I learned that you, the terrorists, and the sub were all going to be out here at the same time, I ordered the sub to stay away and I only called them when we absolutely needed them to stop the terrorists. We were right on the Canadian border and the SEALs could not cross into Canada. Your children were safe in that boat and their actions prevented any casualties on our side. They're heroes."

Fede squinted and clenched his jaw. Colt made his point, but Garcia wasn't going to let him go without venting all his anger and fear. "None of these is a reason for putting our children in harm's way."

"He did it to save my life," said Stewart.

The voice came from behind him. Garcia turned. "Who are you?"

"He's our friend," said Amber. "And it was my decision, not Colt's."

"My name is Stewart Swanson, Dr. Garcia. Gunny wanted to protect me because I was forced to drive the boat for the Armenians the night they committed murder. I was a witness and it was just a matter of time before they would decide to eliminate me."

"If there were murders, then driving their boat makes you an accomplice, not a witness." Fede turned back to Colt, "Is it considered noble now to harbor a fugitive?"

Colt relaxed his stance. "That's not the case. Stewart was never a fugitive. The authorities don't even know about the murders yet, as far as we know. If you really need proof that Stewart's telling the truth—remember that gunfire out on the water? That was Petrosian trying to kill him."

Amber put her hand on her father's back. "What happened today reminds me of the stories you've told me about your father fighting Fidel Castro and Che Guevara. How old was Abuelo Humberto when he chased the communists into the jungle?"

"He was sixteen. But that was much different."

"I'm seventeen," said Amber.

"You are a child. You are my child. You have a comfortable home. My father had nothing but a field of sugar cane that the communists wanted to take from him. He was fighting to keep his own house and his farm." Garcia punctuated his recollections with his fist. "He trained under *real* soldiers until he learned how to fight."

Colt's eyebrows shot upward.

"I'm a retired Marine Gunnery Sergeant, Dr. Garcia—a *real* Marine. I was a Senior Drill Instructor, and I've been deployed to some very nasty places. I can tell you, without hesitation, your daughter and her friends are among the bravest and most well-disciplined warriors I've ever served with."

Garcia turned to look at Amber and her friends standing together as a team. They looked very proud.

Colt wasn't going to let Garcia off the hook. "Yeah, they're young, you're right. Your father was young. I was, too. That's the way it's always been. Old men expect the young to do their fighting for them." Colt relaxed his shoulders and lowered the tone of his voice.

"It sounds to me, Doctor Garcia, like your family has a tradition of honor, patriotism, and loyalty. That's a good thing. Sometimes we forget all about those values when we get...comfortable. But if it's in your DNA, it never goes away."

Colt folded his arms across his chest. "Just don't tell me your daughter's not a trained warrior, because I know better. She drove a damned submarine in a battle against terrorists. Have any of you ever done anything even close to that?"

There was only silence in response. Colt nodded. "I didn't think so."

When he'd finished, Colt turned his eyes from the parents to the U-boat crew. Every one of them was smiling and they began to move as one. They put their arms around each other and congratulated each other, shouting with joy for having survived their ordeal.

The moms and dads watched silently, contemplating the brave acts of their children and the terrible risks they'd been willing to take to help a friend.

Tears welled up in his eyes as Fede Garcia looked at his daughter and considered the danger in what she had done. "Where on earth did you get a submarine?" he asked.

"It's not my submarine," she said.

"Then where did it come from?"

"It's a Nazi U-boat," said Doubeck.

"It's mine," said Charlie. "I found it."

Mike LeClair couldn't restrain himself. "This is the boat you found?"

"Yeah, Dad."

Mike pointed at the remnants of the Bayliner. "The one up there stuck on the submarine?"

"No, Dad. *Doris*. The U-boat."

The Chief brought his hand to his face to stifle a laugh. Colt saw it and turned his head away for the same reason.

"This is crazy." Fede Garcia turned to look at the rest of the crew and the assembled throng. "This can't be true," he said. No one answered, but every one of the kids nodded.

"It's all true," said Colt.

"You do understand my concern," said Garcia. "People were hurt. A boat was sunk and there's this story of a murder."

"It happened," said Amber.

Fede held his hand up. "But Amber, you weren't there."

"I *was* there." she insisted.

"What?" Dr. Garcia looked shocked.

"I was there less than an hour ago." Amber turned and spoke to the entire group. "On our way out this morning, Stewart said we were headed to the exact spot where the Armenians blew up a boat and killed everyone on board. Well, that boat is down there. We saw it on our video monitor and I recorded it with my phone, Dad. It's under us right now, on the bottom with the stern blown off."

Colt gave Stewart a pat on the back. It was evidence—not merely evidence of the crime—but also evidence that Stewart had friends willing to put their lives on the line for him.

Fede looked into his daughter's eyes. "Then it *did* happen?"

"Yes. It did," said Amber.

Garcia turned once again to Colt. "I suppose I should be glad they're alive. I think you were reckless. Mr. Colt. But, I do see you were in a difficult situation."

"I appreciate that, sir," said Colt. "You're right, we got caught in a tough spot. But your kids are extraordinary." Colt smiled. "You do realize they're going to be famous tomorrow."

Garcia grinned with obvious reluctance. "I imagine so." He reached out to Stewart and shook his hand. "And Stewart, if there's anything Ana and I can do for you, please let us know. You hang in there."

Donikowski stepped to the center of the group. "Everyone, please. Listen up. My name is Chief Petty Officer Tom Donikowski. I'm the SEAL team squad leader. Look folks, what happened today is a matter of national security." He turned as he talked to make eye contact with those gathered around. "Do not tell anyone *anything* until the news comes out. Don't confirm anything, no matter who asks, if it isn't already in the news. Even if it makes the news, you say, "No comment." The bad guys will be hungry for any kind of information they can get, so let's make sure they get nothing.

"My squad and I rely on secrecy to stay alive, so help us out. Some of what happened out here today will not be reported—ever. Please wait like twenty years to talk about it. Better yet, forget it all.

"Now, we want to interview all of you, your kids, too, in an after-action review."

Donikowski pointed at Amber. "Captain Garcia, what does your boat draw?"

Amber responded immediately. She knew her boat. "Twelve feet ordinarily, but our fuel tanks are full. I'd like sixteen."

Chief Donikowski made a note with his gloved finger on a rubber-encased electronic tablet. "Sixteen feet. Okay, then we're good. I need you and your crew to follow the Hatteras to the Coast Guard base at Presque Isle. That's where we'll be de-briefed…Oh, and stay on the surface, please." He grinned. "When you reach the Coast Guard, you'll be mooring right in the channel. It's dredged to twenty-five feet. We'll drape some fenders for you and we'll have a gangway ready. It's three hundred feet long so you can pretty much pick your spot. "

"Thank you," said Amber.

The Chief squinted. "You ever park this boat before?"

"Just once. It was very tricky."

"Hmm. Tell you what. I'll have a tug meet us a half-mile out and tow you in. Wouldn't want you to hit hard and sink in the channel."

Amber shook her head. "No, I wouldn't want that either."

"The westerlies will snug you right against the pier, so just have your helmsman keep you ten feet out and let the wind do the work." The SEAL removed the glove on his right hand. "I'll give you a few minutes to get organized and turn your boat around. I feel like I should salute you, but, if it's okay, I'd just like to shake your hand."

"Sure." Amber smiled and held out her hand.

"You're one hell of a sailor, Captain," said Donikowski.

"Sir?" Ana Garcia raised her hand. "Can we ride back on the submarine?"

The Chief thought about it for a second. "I got no problem with that, so long as it's okay with the captain..." Amber waved the group on as Donikowski continued,"...Have fun. And you." He pointed at Fede. "Captain Garcia number two. "You can follow us back, too. Since the other parents are riding on the sub, I'll send Spider, my comms specialist, along to help crew your sailboat. Does that work for you?"

"Yes, of course."

"We'll see what Spider thinks. He's been admiring your boat all afternoon." The Chief tapped his comms button. "Spider, you've been assigned to crew the SV *Nip and Tack* into port."

The comms remained silent, but a loud, "Hoorah!" rang from a distant Zodiac tied alongside the Hatteras.

Donikowski looked at Fede with a smile. "Yeah, he's good."

A loud scraping sound interrupted the conversation and rattled the deck as Lacey pulled the two halves of *Ararat* apart. He also had the help of an axe borrowed from the U-boat's fire station.

Once the hoses and cables stretching between the two halves of the yacht were severed, the debris submitted to gravity, falling to the water on opposite sides of the U-boat's nose. In less than thirty seconds, the shattered *Ararat* would rest forever on the sandy bottom of Lake Erie.

Lacey returned from his task brandishing the axe above his head. Shaking an axe in the air might help explain why people didn't notice he also carried a briefcase under his left arm—one he did not have with him on his way out to the boat. But Colt noticed, and from the opposite end of the sub, he gave his associate a big thumbs-up.

The next day, DHS arrived at Raccoon Bay Marina with two large box trucks to take everything out of the buildings and move it to a secure warehouse for investigation. Stewart accompanied Homeland Security Senior Special Agent Bryce Connelly to the marina to help his team find some specific items listed on their warrant.

"Stewart, what's in this office?" Connelly asked.

"Ah, it's all the business stuff. This was Oleg's office. The books, the files—like old invoices, bills. Petrosian wasn't a computer guy so the business is all on paper here somewhere."

"Okay. Along with the papers, we're seizing all his assets. There are engines in the shop, and boats on the dock that belong to customers. We don't want them. Where are those records?"

"All the dock leases are in the retail store across the hall. The parts and repairs are in the shop. I used to keep those records, so I can show you. And the paperwork for the boats Petrosian owned is in that file cabinet." Stewart pointed to a four-drawer wooden cabinet with an open file drawer.

"The titles are in that drawer?"

"Yes, sir," said Stewart. "That's where he keeps them."

Connelly squinted and turned toward Stewart. "He left this drawer open and unlocked?"

"He wasn't big on neatness," said Stewart.

Connelly turned back to the desk. "Yeah, I see that. Still, it's kinda dumb. Someone could grab a title and drive off in a new boat. Petrosian would have a hell of a time getting it back."

Stewart felt his face warming. "Pretty sure he had no idea what we did here. I think the boat business was just a front," he said.

"Very true," said Connelly. "We've been rolling up his network all week."

An agent slid a dolly under the cabinet and wheeled it out as Stewart and Connelly walked across the hall to the store.

Stewart looked around the room carefully. Colt's spy camera remained plugged in behind the cash register. "Oh, that's my phone charger," said Stewart. "Do you mind?"

Connelly looked at the charger on the wall and waved his hand. "No, go ahead. Just take it. Need any fish hooks, or a rod and reel? It's all just going to get trashed."

"Ah, no, I'm good," said Stewart.

Across town, Colt sat in his apartment watching and listening to the spy cam as Stewart ushered Special Agent Connelly through the store. When Stewart pulled the plug on the charger, Colt set the phone down and put his feet up on his coffee table. To his left lay a briefcase and a duffle bag. Both were open and filled with bundles of cash. A luggage tag on the duffle had Stewart's name on it in Colt's handwriting. On Colt's right was an open manila folder—the folder Lacey had handed him at the West Slip, the night Colt took the floating dock and half of Petrosian's money. Resting on the folder was an official-looking document bearing the seal of the Commonwealth of Pennsylvania. At the bottom, the ink was still drying on Colt's signature. It was the title to the Hatteras.

THE LAST U-BOAT

THE MAN
WITH
NO FACE

The wire services reported that two wanted criminals, Armenian nationals, had been apprehended attempting to flee to Canada by boat. Newscasters across the country stated that a restored German U-boat, on a shake-down cruise, deliberately struck the Armenians' boat. They claimed it happened after the sub picked up radio chatter from authorities in pursuit. There was no mention of terrorists, Taliban, or Navy SEALs.

The story spread across the globe and brought researchers and historians to Charlie's door. Charlie received bushels of mail from fans and military buffs week after week once the news got out.

One of those letters was the reason the crew found themselves near Halifax, Nova Scotia in late August. Their visit was in response to a fascinating letter from a ninety-six-year-old resident of St. Margaret's Bay Lodgings, a nursing home facility. The letter described in perfect detail the sub and the underground workshop, even referring to it as the Deep Room. The letter persuaded Charlie and his friends that Gunther Kraus, the man without a face from the VHS tape, had written it.

His invitation to visit was irresistible. Maybe he wanted to boast, or confess and bare his soul. Charlie and the crew would soon find out.

For Kraus, the meeting would write the final line, of the final chapter, of the event that took his face and reshaped his life.

A reception committee greeted the visitors, including the Lodgings Administrator, Alex MacDonald; the Director of Nursing, Hannah Braund, and the Director of Community Engagement, Brian Martin. They accompanied the Americans to a table beautifully set for them on the Lodgings terrace. The reception made the friends feel like celebrities.

The sky was filled with big puffy clouds that caused patches of sunlight to chase across the massive grounds in front of the terrace. The faint change of color in the leaves in the woodlands surrounding the residence reminded the crew that summer was nearly at an end.

The visitors were served a breakfast of tea, fruit, and pastries, after which their hosts excused themselves to give the group some privacy.

"I can't eat anything," said Charlie.

Colt nodded toward Doubeck. "Doubeck, how many danishes have you had?"

Doubeck shrugged.

"This place is pretty f'n bougie," said Mish.

Amber put her hand on Mish's knee. "I think we're all shook over this meeting."

Soon, Mr. MacDonald returned and spoke to the group. "Folks, Mr. Kraus is on his way. We'll come back to say goodbye before you leave."

"Thank you," said Charlie.

"Gunther, Mr. Kraus, is rather frail. I would just say, we know him well. I can assure you he's not a monster, although his appearance is quite difficult, to be sure. He is eager, almost desperate, to tell you his story. Hopefully, speaking with you may bring him some peace. So, for that, I'm certain he and those of us who know him are very grateful."

As MacDonald walked back to the building, an attendant in uniform appeared from around the corner, pushing a wheelchair holding the body of a slight person, well covered against the morning chill. A tuft of wispy gray hair, rising above a red and black wool tartan blanket, danced in the breeze.

"I'm scared, Gunny," said Mish.

Marty scratched his arm nervously. "Me, too," he said.

Colt turned his head toward the group so he could whisper and still be heard. "He's an old man, guys. He was younger than you when they abandoned the U-boat, you know."

The attendant smiled and greeted the group. "Good morning, everyone. My name is Olivia Baker and this gentleman is Gunther Kraus."

The group responded with a tentative, "Good morning."

Baker continued. "Mr. Kraus has asked me to tell you how grateful he is..."

Kraus interrupted. "Thank you, Olivia." His voice sounded stronger than one might have expected. His speech was quick and precise. He kept his head against the back of the chair and turned away to obscure the left side of his face. The face that had been devastated by the explosion that killed his brother.

He raised a frail, bony hand. "Which one of you is Charlie LeClair?"

"I am," said Charlie.

"Charlie. I've read every account of your adventure I could get my hands on. It's good to meet you."

"It's good to meet you, too," said Charlie. Immediately he felt conflicted about saying so, unable at that moment to rationalize having a conversation with a former Nazi.

"How's my Unterseeboot?" There was a smile in his tone.

"It's awesome, sir. It's an amazing boat. Amber is our captain. She's a sailor and she can tell you."

"Are you Amber?" Kraus looked at Mish.

A few feet away, Amber spoke up. "I'm Amber, Mr. Kraus."

Olivia swiveled the wheelchair to allow him to speak directly to Amber without having to turn his head and expose his scars.

"Hello, Amber. Please tell me, how does she handle?"

"Very smooth and responsive, Mr. Kraus. I think the reduced size from the original type 2 probably helped stabilize the boat."

"Yes, that's what they told us would happen! How marvelous to hear. Type 2 wanted to hang from the nose like a Christmas tree ornament. This is very good to hear...and who is Stewart?"

"I am, sir." Stewart rose slightly from his chair and sat again. Olivia turned the wheelchair toward Stewart.

"Mr. Swanson. Is it true that you were personally responsible for all the mechanical systems?"

"Yes, sir. But everything was so well lubricated and protected. Mostly, all I had to do was de-grease and clean the lines."

"What you did was remarkable. When we took that U-boat apart, not many miles from here, I saw all the mechanical systems. I was only a boy—younger than any of you are today. I wondered how we could ever possibly reassemble it in Pennsylvania. To me, the task was like trying to bring it to life. We were playing Doctor Frankenstein."

"I thought of it the same way," said Stewart.

"You did?" asked Kraus.

"Yes. I felt like it had living systems. Breathing, and muscles, and eyes, and circulation."

Kraus started a soft strained laughter, punctuated by a quiet, deep cough.

"You have been bitten by the bug, young man. The bug that makes you a mechanical genius, I suspect. But you are correct. I am so very glad you were able to launch the boat." Kraus paused and raised his hand to cover his face and began to sob.

Marty looked away as Charlie and Stewart stared at their hands, waiting for the moment to pass. Doubeck watched the old man's small body shake under the thin woolen blanket. Colt sat stiffly in his chair and studied each person's reaction.

Later, the group would conclude that this moment was likely the reason for the invitation. Gunther Kraus wept as he felt the weight of a lifetime of pain become just a little lighter. His tears were wrung from the emotional collision of his joy at the heroic story of the U-boat, and his personal loss. Add to that his mission's failure, his regrets, the shame he carried, his life-long exile, and the world's judgment rendered against the Nazi movement he and his family had embraced. It was a crushing weight he had carried for decades.

He wiped his cheek as he lowered his hand. His eyes caught Marty's.

"Mr. Silver?"

"Yes?" Marty replied.

"I know it was meant to bring war to America, but if my family could be forgiven our mistakes, and the world could simply marvel at our machine, that would be a legacy I would much prefer."

"We have a saying," said Marty.

"And what is that, Mr. Silver?"

"Never forget."

"But it does not say, 'never forgive,' does it?"

Marty leaned back in his chair, his head held high. "We're working on that."

Kraus closed his eyes, nodded his head, and took a deep breath. When he opened his eyes, he was smiling. "I'm sure you all have many questions. I would love to answer what I can. Olivia has already warned me, she will remove me without hesitation if she thinks I am under too much stress."

Labor Day in Northwest Pennsylvania can look a lot like the door has slammed shut on summer. But this day was beautiful. A man dressed in a summer weight navy blue suit tapped Colt on the shoulder, raising his voice to be heard over the McCullough High School concert band. "Gunnery Sergeant Colt?"

"Yes, sir."

"Chase Grissolm, Gunny. Semper Fi."

"Semper Fi...Oh, you're Congressman Grissolm."

"Yes, I am for at least two more years. And who's this lovely lady with you?"

"Congressman, I'd like you to meet my friend Doris Silver, from Cleveland."

"How do you do, Miss Silver."

"Congressman. It's a pleasure."

The congressman turned to Colt while still holding Doris's hand. "Listen, I followed up on our call. I've got some good news for your crew. Brought an Admiral with me to deliver it."

The conversation was interrupted by an announcement.

Ladies and Gentlemen, please take your seats, Pastor Gerard Donaldson of New Covenant Church will deliver the invocation.

The Labor Day festivities celebrated the discovery of the U-boat, the friends who recovered it and launched it, and its successful use against human traffickers—which is the way Oleg and Frik had ultimately been portrayed to the public.

Congressman Grissolm delivered a thoughtful and brief address about local issues that were under consideration in Congress. He then turned to the crew of the U-boat seated behind him. All six friends and Colt were there, the men in jackets and ties, the ladies in summer dresses. Each member of the crew wore their cover and pin.

"These young people here behind me, with the help of an heroic Marine Corps veteran, have accomplished many things in the past several months that even people twice their age could only dream of doing. To be fair, I should also include gray-haired Congressmen four times their age—like me.

"The US Navy is well aware of the skill, courage, intelligence, and resourcefulness required to put to sea in a submarine, especially one of this vintage. That is why I have asked Admiral Carter Chambers, Superintendent of the United States Naval Academy at Annapolis, to be here today."

The announcement of the Admiral's presence brought sustained applause.

"Thank you, Congressman. I am proud to be here to salute these citizen sailors. They've been criticized for taking risks, and I understand that. But I favor the view that they saw a monumental challenge and wanted to bring it to heel.

"President John Kennedy, a Navy man himself, once predicted that Americans would someday visit the moon and accomplish many other difficult things.

"Kennedy suggested it was inevitable we would do these things, and he described our motivation as quintessentially American. He said we'd take on the moon and other challenges:

> '...not because they are easy, but because they are hard, because that goal will serve to organize and measure the best of our energies and our skills, because that challenge is one we are willing to accept, one we are unwilling to postpone, and one which we intend to win.'

"These young sailors set out to do that thing, that hard thing Kennedy spoke of. And they knew, for certain, that everyone was going to tell them, using a thousand perfectly logical reasons, that it was a thing they couldn't *possibly* accomplish.

"And yet, here we are."

The admiral removed his glasses, closed his notes, and looked at those gathered in front of him. He turned and motioned for the group to stand, which they did as a roar of applause arose from the crowd. When they returned to their chairs, and as the cheers subsided, Admiral Chambers continued.

"With the right attitude, the intelligence, the skills, and the determination these young people demonstrated, you have what the United States Navy prizes most highly. That is why I am here today to announce that I am pleased to offer an appointment to attend the Naval Academy at Annapolis to each of these young men and women."

The crowd jumped to their feet as the admiral walked back to the crew and shook each of their hands. As he did, aides in white gloves followed and handed each person their appointment notice.

The presentation was executed in a manner worthy of such a high honor. When it was complete and the sound of applause diminished, the admiral returned to the microphone.

"Though they're called the Silent Service, you may be aware that the Navy has its own submariners who are provided some very fine boats that you folks paid for. Someday, perhaps, one of the people we're honoring today may actually serve on one of them. Time will tell.

"If they do, they will likely see a fellow sailor wearing a dolphin pin. The dolphin pin is the Navy's Submarine Warfare Insignia. It means the sailor who wears it has completed the submarine- qualification program and demonstrated proficiency in the knowledge and skills required to operate a sub.

"These sailors have demonstrated a very high degree of proficiency and, under my authority, I am awarding each of them the dolphin pin.

"I have commissioned these pins to be embedded in an acrylic display with an inscription on the base. I do hope, one day perhaps, one or more of you young heroes may receive another just like it that you will wear with pride on your Navy uniform. Well done."

The ceremony concluded with the band's rendition of "Anchors Aweigh." As the crowd made their way out, the parents of the honorees came forward from the audience to greet and congratulate their kids.

Charlie stood between Amber and Colt as Sharon LeClair rushed to her son's side. "Charlie, this is so exciting. We're so proud of you. Your dad's giving an interview right now to Channel 12.

"Oh, and there's this, as we were leaving the house, a DHL truck pulled up with this box. It's from Halifax." Sharon handed Charlie a package the size of a shoebox.

The crew overheard Sharon and they gathered around Charlie to watch him open the package. It contained a stack of notebooks and documents bundled in brown wrapping paper and secured with twine. On top was a note-card, a piece of St. Margaret's stationery. The note was from Brian Martin:

> *Dear Charlie,*
>
> *Mr. Kraus passed away Saturday evening. Shortly after you left, he asked that you receive his notes and keepsakes upon his death. He also insisted that we deliver the enclosed message. He had written a series of numbers on it that he believed would have some meaning to you.*

Charlie unfolded the paper. It had been torn from a legal pad and, as Mr. Martin's message had indicated, it was simply a series of numbers:

> *4654 8636 196 97*

Charlie passed the paper around.

"The first two sets have got to be phone numbers. We just need to figure out the area codes," said Colt.

"I hope it's a secret bank account in the Caymans," said Doubeck.

Marty reached out. "Can I see it?" Charlie handed him the paper and Marty shook his head. "I don't know. Could be anything." He looked at

Mish. "You're our puzzle solver. Got any ideas?"

Mish rolled her eyes like it should be obvious to everyone. "Yeah. It's a place."

"What? Mish, how can that be a place?" asked Doubeck

Mish gestured to Amber's purse. "Amber, you have that navigation app on your phone, don't you?"

"Yeah, I do," she said.

Amber reached into her bag, grabbed her phone, and opened the app. "Now what?"

Mish looked down at the paper as she spoke. "Search 46 degrees 54 minutes north latitude, 86 degrees 36 minutes west longitude."

Colt looked at the crew and grinned. "How does she do that?"

"She's a space alien," said Doubeck, drawing from Mish both the glare and the grin he had hoped to elicit.

"Ah, guys." Amber looked up from her phone. It's a location somewhere in Michigan." She continued pinching the screen to zoom in on the location.

"Why would Kraus send some random coordinates?" asked Stewart.

"They're not random. They're in Lake Superior." Amber confirmed the location and handed the phone around for the group to see. "Kraus wanted us to check this spot out. Why else would he give us coordinates?" she said.

"We can get to Lake Superior pretty easy through the locks on Lake Huron," Charlie added.

Amber shook her head. "Yeah, but we can't go here," she said tapping on her phone. "These coordinates point to the deepest spot in the Great Lakes. It's four times our crush depth. But that's where Kraus is telling us to go."

Charlie took the paper from Mish. "Then what are these numbers 196 and 97?"

Marty had been staring at the ground, puzzling over the numbers, but slowly his head began to lift. As he looked up, his eyes met those of his friends.

"Dudes, 196 point 97 is the atomic weight of gold."

ABOUT THE AUTHOR

Jack O'Brien retired a few years ago after spending more than fifty years in entertainment and advertising. His first book, *The Roundabout Way*, is a collection of short stories about fictional residents of the Villages, Florida. It remains a best-seller in The Villages' bookstores and is available on Amazon (KDP). Jack is also an artist. He was juried into membership in the Associated Artists of Pittsburgh as a stone and ceramic sculptor, and for his oil and acrylic painting.

Jack and his wife Pam, a published poet and retired professor emeritus of English from Pitt, moved to Florida in 2018 from Pittsburgh, Pennsylvania. They have three children and three grandchildren.

Made in the USA
Middletown, DE
06 May 2024

53925693R00235